Atonement Sky

Berkley titles by Nalini Singh

Psy-Changeling Series

SLAVE TO SENSATION
VISIONS OF HEAT
CARESSED BY ICE
MINE TO POSSESS
HOSTAGE TO PLEASURE
BRANDED BY FIRE
BLAZE OF MEMORY
BONDS OF JUSTICE
PLAY OF PASSION
KISS OF SNOW
TANGLE OF NEED
HEART OF OBSIDIAN
SHIELD OF WINTER
SHARDS OF HOPE
ALLEGIANCE OF HONOR

Psy-Changeling Trinity Series

SILVER SILENCE
OCEAN LIGHT
WOLF RAIN
ALPHA NIGHT
LAST GUARD
STORM ECHO
RESONANCE SURGE
PRIMAL MIRROR
ATONEMENT SKY

Guild Hunter Series

ANGELS' BLOOD
ARCHANGEL'S KISS
ARCHANGEL'S CONSORT
ARCHANGEL'S BLADE
ARCHANGEL'S STORM
ARCHANGEL'S LEGION
ARCHANGEL'S SHADOWS
ARCHANGEL'S ENIGMA
ARCHANGEL'S HEART
ARCHANGEL'S VIPER
ARCHANGEL'S PROPHECY
ARCHANGEL'S WAR
ARCHANGEL'S SUN
ARCHANGEL'S LIGHT
ARCHANGEL'S RESURRECTION
ARCHANGEL'S LINEAGE
ARCHANGEL'S ASCENSION

Thrillers

A MADNESS OF SUNSHINE
QUIET IN HER BONES
THERE SHOULD HAVE BEEN EIGHT

Anthologies

AN ENCHANTED SEASON
(with Maggie Shayne, Erin McCarthy, and Jean Johnson)

THE MAGICAL CHRISTMAS CAT
(with Lora Leigh, Erin McCarthy, and Linda Winstead Jones)

MUST LOVE HELLHOUNDS
(with Charlaine Harris, Ilona Andrews, and Meljean Brook)

BURNING UP
(with Angela Knight, Virginia Kantra, and Meljean Brook)

ANGELS OF DARKNESS
(with Ilona Andrews, Meljean Brook, and Sharon Shinn)

ANGELS' FLIGHT

WILD INVITATION

NIGHT SHIFT
(with Ilona Andrews, Lisa Shearin, and Milla Vane)

WILD EMBRACE

Specials

ANGELS' PAWN

ANGELS' DANCE

TEXTURE OF INTIMACY

DECLARATION OF COURTSHIP

WHISPER OF SIN

SECRETS AT MIDNIGHT

Atonement Sky

A PSY-CHANGELING TRINITY NOVEL

NALINI SINGH

BERKLEY
New York

BERKLEY
An imprint of Penguin Random House LLC
1745 Broadway, New York, NY 10019
penguinrandomhouse.com

Copyright © 2025 by Nalini Singh
Penguin Random House values and supports copyright. Copyright fuels creativity, encourages diverse voices, promotes free speech, and creates a vibrant culture. Thank you for buying an authorized edition of this book and for complying with copyright laws by not reproducing, scanning, or distributing any part of it in any form without permission. You are supporting writers and allowing Penguin Random House to continue to publish books for every reader. Please note that no part of this book may be used or reproduced in any manner for the purpose of training artificial intelligence technologies or systems.

BERKLEY and the BERKLEY & B colophon are registered trademarks of Penguin Random House LLC.

Library of Congress Cataloging-in-Publication Data

Names: Singh, Nalini, 1977- author.
Title: Atonement sky / Nalini Singh.
Description: New York: Berkley, 2025. | Series: Psy-changeling trinity series
Identifiers: LCCN 2024061295 (print) | LCCN 2024061296 (ebook) | ISBN 9780593819524 (hardcover) | ISBN 9780593819531 (ebook)
Subjects: LCGFT: Paranormal fiction. | Romance fiction. | Fantasy fiction. | Novels.
Classification: LCC PR9639.4.S566 A94 2025 (print) | LCC PR9639.4.S566 (ebook) | DDC 823/.92—dc23/eng/20250108
LC record available at https://lccn.loc.gov/2024061295
LC ebook record available at https://lccn.loc.gov/2024061296

Printed in the United States of America
1st Printing

The authorized representative in the EU for product safety and compliance is
Penguin Random House Ireland, Morrison Chambers, 32 Nassau Street,
Dublin D02 YH68, Ireland, https://eu-contact.penguin.ie.

Atonement Sky

Atonement

SILENCE HAS FALLEN.

The failing PsyNet draws struggling breath.

Holding on. Hanging on.

For a fragment in time that will be the last chance for Psy who stand with one foot in the past, their minds too altered by the conditioning demanded by Silence to embrace the present.

They aren't the Scarabs torn apart by violent psychic powers.

They aren't the rehabilitated with minds deliberately broken by the Council.

They aren't the ones who scream and sob because they're lost.

They are the ghosts in the Net, the impenetrable starless shadows that no longer weave in and out of the slipstreams of the vast psychic network, but instead stand in place in an effort to remain stable, remain present . . . for theirs is the task of atonement.

One final act of grace before there are no more grains in the hourglass of their lives.

Chapter 1

"Some of us didn't make it, Sophie. We've accepted that. Our final goal is to create a better world for the next generation of the children we once were."

"No, I won't let you do this."

"You have no choice—to be a good leader, you have to implement triage, focus your energy on the ones who are salvageable. Leave the rest of us to do what we do best. We've bathed in evil . . . there's no washing that off, so we might as well use it to lure monstrous prey."

—Heated discussion between Eleri Dias (J Corps) and Sophia Russo (director of the J Corps) (5 January 2084)

THE ROAD TO Raintree, Arizona, was composed of sprawling desert and rippling walls of red-orange rock. Eleri was no geologist, had no idea whether the rock was shale or limestone or something else altogether. All she saw were natural formations that looked as if they'd been created by an expert sculptor, each ripple and gradation of color put delicately in place.

Where the rocks fell away, the desert glinted, the only signs of life in any direction scraggly bushes of a sandy green hue and the majestic forms of saguaro cactus plants, their arms akimbo at ninety-degree angles.

The sky was a searing blue, the landscape as arid and dry as Eleri's heart and mind. It seemed fitting that it would all end here, in this place devoid of the lush greenery so prevalent in the place where she'd taken her first breath too many shadow memories ago.

LIAR!!

That echo was as vicious today as the day it had been born, his voice having haunted her through all the years in between. And the further she drove into Raintree, the higher the likelihood that she'd come face-to-face with him . . . with the one person to whom she could never atone. There was no way to bring back the dead, and he'd taken care of the justice at which she'd failed.

Eleri. That's pretty. My name is Adam.

Her fingers flexed on the steering wheel, the wall of numbness in her mind a gift against the past. How much worse would it be if she could truly experience it, instead of looking at it from beyond a vast gulf of nothingness?

She hadn't shared her latest PsyMed test results with Sophia. They would have distressed her, and she was already in a physically vulnerable state, her pregnancy now at seven and a half months.

Poor Sophie.

Trying so hard to save all of them when that was an impossibility. And a terrible irony, because it had been Sophia's refusal to give up on her fellow Js that had led to her forcible elevation to Director of the J Corps.

Sophia was Ruling Coalition member Nikita Duncan's senior aide, and had no time to head a group of damaged telepaths who had once been overseen by the J Corps Management Board. But when the Ruling Coalition wiped out that board—after Sophia brought its mismanagement of the Corps to the Coalition's attention—and asked all working Js in the world to get together to nominate their new leadership, they'd come back with a single name: Sophia "Sophie" Russo.

They'd dropped the mess of the J Corps into Sophia's lap and trusted her to build a better long-term structure for them. She could've said no, but of course she hadn't. Because Sophie wanted not just life for all of them, but a life filled with joy and hope.

"Sophia's as tough as fucking nails, except when it comes to Js."

It was Bram who'd said that in the conversation group of four he'd set up almost eighteen years ago: the Quatro Cartel. Bram's little joke because the biggest case in the news at the time—when the four of them had been between nine and ten—had involved a ruthless drug cartel that liked to remove organs from people who owed them money, for no reason except that it was horrific torture.

"Perhaps we should follow that cartel's example, Bram," Saffron had said two months ago in her whisper of a voice, her throat still healing from her altercation with a murderer on a rampage. "Remove organs one by one, make our targets suffer."

No one had told her that would take her into sociopath territory. Fact was, none of them had the patience for such games of torture, especially not Saffron, with her violent rages and extreme temper. Regardless, they agreed with her in principle—after what they'd seen in the minds they'd wandered, Eleri and the rest of the cartel of four had no doubts about evil and what it deserved.

Quatro had begun as a secret because they'd been children at a strict boarding school who'd wanted a private way to talk. It was Yúzé who'd taken Bram's initial idea and used his tech skills to move the chat into a secure online room—Eleri didn't understand how he'd done it, but then tech had always been Yúzé's specialty. As a J, he'd been pulled near exclusively into cases that involved high-tech elements of murder.

Quatro remained secret for a far darker reason. All four of them had begun to work as active Js at the same time, give or take a month or two. And all four of them had crossed a final dividing line within weeks of each other, whether by chance or because of the cases they'd been assigned over the years—Bram, Eleri, Saffron, and Yúzé ranged from 8.9 to 9.5 on the Gradient; they'd never been given any nonviolent cases after they completed their apprenticeships.

Theirs had been the realm of serial and spree murderers.

The four of them weren't going to make it on either the psychic or psychological level.

"No point hiding from it," Bram had written four months ago after Yúzé turned Sensitive, the last one of the Cartel to do so. "All four of us now have shields so thin that we pick up thoughts through even minor touch—staving off Exposure is going to take a mammoth effort, if it's even possible."

Exposure would mean the total loss of their shields, the psychic noise of the world crushing them until they screamed and tore at themselves in a futile effort to make it stop. No J ever voluntarily reached Exposure—the members of the Corps knew to choose their own exit route instead of being at the mercy of others after they'd lost their ability to function.

Eleri could imagine no worse death than being a mindless creature who could neither defend herself nor understand the screaming voices inside her head that would never, ever stop.

"This," Bram had added, "remains what it's always been—our online home, but it's also now a place to share data about our rates of disintegration. Whichever one of us falls last, your task will be to compile that data and put it into Sophia's hands, in the hope it'll assist her in saving more J lives. For now, it'll help the four of us set our affairs in order—including ensuring any delayed justice."

Delayed justice.

Bram had a way of couching murder by Js in language that sounded almost harmless, but they all knew what he'd meant. Because though none of them had reached thirty, with Eleri and Yúzé just past twenty-seven and Bram and Saffron twenty-eight, they were all senior Js who had completed their final assigned cases.

While they technically remained Js in the system, with all the official access to information, their badges yet valid, it was understood that what time they had was their own; the four of them planned to use that time to correct mistakes in that system for which they'd been culpable—or which they hadn't been able to stop.

As part of their pact to share everything they could to help each other plan their unavoidable descent into the abyss, Eleri had posted her PsyMed results an hour after she'd received them: Predicted status change from Sensitive to Exposed now at six months.

"Fuck, Eleri." Saffron was angry in a way Eleri simply couldn't become any longer, their brains having reacted in diametrically opposing ways to repeated reconditionings.

Where Saffron screamed her rage, Eleri drowned in nothingness.

"Six months?" Saffron had picked up and thrown the object nearest to her—a water glass that had shattered into bright shards of sound. "Fuck!"

Because Eleri was the first of them to be given the Exposure diagnosis, she'd added further context: I retain full cognitive and physical function. However, I can't sleep for more than three hours at a stretch, and memories from retrievals early in my career have begun to surface at increasing speed.

Eleri was the canary in the coal mine now, hers the descent the others would watch in order to prepare for their own. The part of her that understood she'd once felt emotion on a deep level was glad that she could offer this gift to the people who had been her friends since the day she'd walked into class as a six-year-old child who'd been told she'd never again be going home.

Later, that same information might help others born far after the end of her own childhood.

"If the PsyMed specialists and empaths know what to watch for," Bram had said when talking about compiling the information on their descent into Sensitivity, then Exposure, to pass on to Sophia, "they might actually be able to head it off at the pass."

It'd be their second contribution to saving the J Corps. Their first had been to ensure Sophie became their leader—between the four of them, their network was labyrinthine and they'd put all their power behind the woman who was now their director.

That Sophie had a direct link to the Ruling Coalition was important, but they'd have disregarded that if she hadn't also had their trust.

Sophie might work for Nikita Duncan, but she remained a J to her core, her determination to protect her fellow Js an elemental part of her nature.

A sense of movement in Eleri's peripheral vision.

Glancing out the window of her vehicle, she glimpsed a large bird wing lazily over the desert landscape, its upper feathers a deep gray with a bluish tone. On the underside were bands of white interspersed with black. Dark eyes, with feathers of a much darker hue under those eyes.

A peregrine falcon, an extraordinary aerial hunter with acute vision, and the majority type of falcon that made up the WindHaven clan. She'd researched them as much as she could before heading toward the town that had been linked to the predatory clan throughout known history—but the falcons were as reticent as most other changelings, and all she had was scraps.

This falcon kept easy pace with her as she passed the sign that marked the town boundary: WELCOME TO RAINTREE! WHERE THE CANYONS ARE VAST AND THE SKIES ENDLESS. The background image was of a lush forested area nestled against a towering rock face painted in the colors of sunset.

The changeling winged away at that point—and she knew it had been a changeling from the size. Changeling birds were much larger than their natural counterparts—though not as much as they should have been given their size in human form. She'd found endless online threads talking about the mass differential in certain changeling species—many had theories, but none answers.

LIAR! It was no mistake!

Strokes of green began to color the landscape as she drove deeper into Raintree and into the echoes of the past. This far out, she saw only the odd sign of habitation. From her research, the town had natural access to a tributary of the Colorado River that caused it to be somewhat of an oasis in this arid region. She saw that firsthand when she came around the corner . . . and into a sudden explosion of dark green.

Raintree didn't quite fit in this landscape.

It was too fertile, too abundant. As if it had been plucked out of the Pacific Northwest and dropped into this landscape of desert browns and rust reds, an intruder that had decided to settle in for the long haul.

Shaking off the sense of wrongness but making note of it because it might be a sign of mental degradation, she lowered her speed. This seemed like the kind of place where children might run across roads while neighbors gossiped on corners.

Turned out she'd been a little too early in her caution; she didn't see any sign of true civilization until at least five minutes later. The houses that began to pop up at that point were small and neat, with well-maintained front yards, some of which had a number of desert rocks in them.

Greenery crawled over the rock, life defying the desert Eleri had just traversed.

But the green was no challenge to the soaring rock faces striated with orange and yellow, red and pink, that rose on either side of the town. They rippled like water, the rough surface appearing smooth as glass from this distance.

Raintree, she realized, was based *inside* a canyon that leaned in to shadow the town from both sides; the sunlight that reached Raintree would mostly be on either end of the day rather than in the blistering middle. Add in its proximity to water, and no wonder the town had such an unexpected microclimate.

Almost at a standstill on the road now, she looked up to the looming canyon wall to the left of the town and frowned. Either she was having vision issues or someone was standing high up on the *side* of the rock face.

A rock climber on a ledge?

Her vision wasn't sharp enough to make out details from so far out, but then she saw a pair of wings sweep out over the person on the ledge and sucked in a breath.

Falcons.

She understood now. They were linked to Raintree, but it wasn't their home. That sat high above the town. She should've realized that; why would winged changelings want to live on the ground when they could live in a nest in the sky?

Liar! You fucking liar!

Her hands tightened on the steering wheel, the renewed roar of the memory a thunderous force . . . as if it had gained strength from the sight of the lone falcon who stood so high above Raintree, his confidence apparent in his stance even from this distance.

Eleri. That's pretty. My name is Adam.

Chapter 2

Winged changelings, especially the raptors, are interesting in the most fascinating way. While their clans follow a similar internal structure to those of earthbound predatory packs like the wolves and bears, they have a unique culture built on the freedom extended by their wings.

A clan will consider itself a clan even if its people are scattered in a hundred tiny pairs or groups across the country.

Yet, despite the fact that winged changelings travel far and wide, often alone, they are one of the most tight-knit of the changeling species. Harm one and you become the enemy of them all.

—From the 2037 archives of *Wild* magazine (now known as *Wild Woman* magazine: "Skin Privileges, Style & Primal Sophistication")

ADAM WATCHED THE black SUV with tinted windows drive into Raintree's small but active main street from his vantage point high above the town.

He didn't know why the vehicle had caught his attention. Raintree was no metropolis but neither was it a dead-end town. Not only did it house WindHaven's cutting-edge aeronautics facility and thus play host to the attendant business traffic, it was also home to a thriving arts scene that drew visitors from around the state and country. Its remote location meant Raintree would never be overrun, but the traffic in and out was steady.

Maybe it was the simple fact that it had been the only vehicle on the road at the time he stepped out onto the ledge and glanced down. He had the feeling the driver had been looking up, too—they'd pretty much stopped at one point.

An arm sliding around his waist, a head full of wild red-kissed mahogany curls tucking itself under his own arm when he lifted it. "Surveying your kingdom, oh great wing leader?" snarked his fifteen-year-old niece, Malia.

"As is my right as lord and master," he said dryly.

She giggled, her pixie face hidden from view by that glorious mass of hair she'd inherited from Adam's older sister, Saoirse. Both had a slight hint of red in their feathers in falcon form, too. As had Saoirse and Adam's mother, Taazbaa'.

A living line of history.

He dropped a kiss on Malia's hair. "Why haven't you left for school, Mali-bug?" All WindHaven fledglings went to the Raintree schools—like most winged clans, WindHaven was a relatively small group; it didn't make sense for them to have schools of their own.

They could have leveraged their long-held connections to other winged clans throughout the state to set up a joint school, but then the fledglings would have long commutes on the wing.

It also made sense for the kids to interact with the wider community. Especially in a clan such as WindHaven, where their home, which they simply called the Canyon, overlooked a settlement of humans—and the odd Psy who had decided to live in this quiet and striking landscape. It had been that way for centuries, humans and changelings living in relative harmony because the geography allowed it.

The humans stuck to the cool canyon floor, while the falcons claimed the space high above—but falcon territory was much wider. A mere few minutes of flight in one direction led to another canyon with a breathtaking blue-green pool, but turn their wings in another direction, and they'd soar over endless desert vistas.

"I won't be late," Malia said with cheerful self-assurance. "I've got a free period this morning and we're allowed to come in after as long as we have something to show for it. I finished a week's worth of physics homework already." She buffed her pink-painted nails against her sweater. "You're looking at the next aeronautical engineer in the family, Uncle Adam."

He grinned, his falcon as proud of her spirit as he was of her intelligence. "You're not planning to shift today, are you?"

"And lose my nail polish *and* my makeup?" She made a quintessentially teenage sound of disgust, her nose crinkling when she looked up at him. The morning sun brushed skin that wasn't the deep copper-toned brown of Adam's or Saoirse's, rather a paler hue that was a meld of her parents', but her eyes were pure Garrett: a pale tawny brown.

"Only drawback to being a changeling, honestly," she added. "I can't *wait* until I can afford that fancy DNA-encoded polish my friends in CloudNest *swear* doesn't come off during a shift." She sounded dubious. "Jessie, who's talking it up the most, her sister's like the CEO of the company making it, so I'm all eagle on it."

She narrowed her eyes, as if imitating the extreme visual acuity of their cousins in the sky. Peregrine eyesight was one of the keenest in the animal kingdom, their raptors able to keep prey in sight even when diving at phenomenal speeds from the sky, but the eagles blew past them when it came to the sheer distances they could see.

Peregrines had eagles beat on speed, though, a point falcons never failed to bring up anytime the eagles got too smug.

Adam's cheeks creased, while below, he saw the SUV—which had done a U-turn at the end of Main Street and headed back up the road as if leaving town—turn into a quiet street that led eventually to the small parking lot of the Raintree Inn. That inn was positioned at enough of a distance from Main Street that it was quiet and private—especially given that it sat nestled inside an oasis of greenery.

A figure in a black pantsuit got out of the now-parked vehicle, and his vision was sharp enough to make out that it was a woman. Going to the back of the car, she removed a small case, then headed toward the office area—at which point she disappeared from view. That part of the inn was overshadowed by cypress trees with large canopies of a green that held a bluish cast.

"Looks like Mrs. Park has a new guest. She'll be happy," Malia commented. "She was complaining how guest numbers were low while I was at the diner the other day."

"She was complaining guest numbers were low when *I* was your age," Adam pointed out. "Yet here she is, still the main gossip distribution system in Raintree."

His eyes kept being drawn to the inn even though there'd been nothing unusual about the guest—she'd looked like any other businessperson who'd stopped in for a day for a meeting. Could be at the WindHaven facility, or at one of the smaller operations in town that were in related industries.

Malia's laughter was big and wide, just like Saoirse's.

Just like her grandfather Cormac's had been. Adam's mother had once told Adam that she'd fallen in love with his father before she ever saw his face. "I heard that laugh over the booth wall and my heart went, wow, I want to be with a man who finds such joy in the world."

"Come on," Adam said, awash on a wave of love and memory. "I'll drive you to school so you don't have to hitchhike." That "hitchhiking" involved walking down the sole road in or out of the Canyon and making pleading faces at adult clanmates going about their lives until someone took pity on the student in question and let them jump in.

Otherwise, WindHaven had a normal school run on a regular schedule, where assigned clanmates drove in students who didn't feel like flying down that day. All the kids had a change of clothes in a private locker room near the school—WindHaven had built them that private area, because while changelings might shrug off nudity after a shift as a natural part of life, the majority of their schoolmates wouldn't.

And teenagers were teenagers: they wanted to be cool.

"Eeee!" Malia threw her arms around him. "Thanks, Uncle Adam! You're the best! Even if the girlies are going to flutter their eyelashes at you. *So rude!* I'm like, he's my uncle, stop looking, and they're like, but he's mega hot and only twenty-eight so totally not ancient."

Shoulders shaking at her shudder, he nudged her back from the opening in the rock that acted as an exit from the intricate maze inside the Canyon. It housed mostly meeting rooms or other communal areas like kitchens, as the majority of Adam's people preferred to nest either up on the plateau or in aeries on the edges of the canyon wall, where they could fly in or out at will.

The internal area had, however, been built with winged creatures in mind—the tunnels were wide and high, both so falcons could fly in or out above the heads of clanmates in human form, and so no one felt claustrophobic if their work meant they had to spend more time in a room inside.

They'd also upgraded the lighting to artificial sunlight and moonlight as soon as the tech became available, turning their internal nest from basic and functional to warm and inviting. The carvings that lined the walls further created that warmth and sense of family, for each one memorialized a falcon beloved.

The carving of his parents was near where his grandparents had nested.

A young clanmate winged by at that point, being sure to swipe a talon at Malia's curls as he headed for the exit. Instead of yelping, she swiped up with her nails, as if attempting to pluck the errant juvenile's feathers.

Adam knew he should really discipline the two, but he'd been the annoying little brother once, and he understood their interaction. It made his falcon chuckle deep within. "Does Tahir have a free period, too?"

"No, he's late. Even flying." A smug smile. "Detention for him. Oh, soooo sad."

He grinned. "Go grab your stuff for school. I'll meet you at the garage." The clan parked most vehicles in a cool space inside, protecting them from the dust and grit of the arid climate as much as they could.

Their lands were breathtaking, but not always friendly.

Adam couldn't imagine living anywhere else.

He turned left while Malia ran off to the right, and saw Amir walking toward him. The man with eyes of cool blue and smooth white skin that barely tanned, his hair a dark brown feathered with strands of ash, was dressed for the day in jeans and a short-sleeved black shirt and carried a mug of coffee in hand.

"Is that Tahir's feather on your shoulder?" Adam's brother-in-law—and senior wing commander—drawled with an amused smile. "I warned him he'd be late, but he told me to 'stop hovering, Daaaad—it's so kestrel.' Guess who'll be explaining himself to his extremely *not*-amused mother today. Though I suppose at least my youngest progeny's insults are well-informed."

Adam picked off the feather with a grin. "Wouldn't want to be your boy." Quite aside from being the lead engineer on WindHaven's jet-shield projects, Saoirse was a senior maternal in the pack hierarchy and the terror of all misbehaving juveniles. "Chirp already at work?" Adam's sister had a tendency to rise at four a.m. bright-eyed and chirpy—hence Chirp.

Amir's smile was slow and full of the secrets between mates. "I flew her in while the fledglings were asleep."

And no doubt got up to all kinds of things Adam didn't need to know about. He might be wing leader, but he was also Saoirse's younger brother by a good six years. "I'm driving Mali down."

"I'll walk my girl to the garage. See you in a few." Amir bumped fists with him.

Adam had only gone a few feet when he saw another clanmate with a mug of coffee in hand, but this one was barefoot and in a bathrobe, with her thick black hair held up by some sort of giant claw clip. He could just glimpse a lock of the white streak she'd had since she was a kid.

"Seriously?" Adam looked the tall wing-second up and down.

Dahlia just grunted before gulping down her coffee as if it was the nectar of the gods. "Hot date last night," she said after the ritual gulping. "Damn tiger wore me out."

"There aren't any tigers anywhere near us." Adam, as the most dominant being in the region, would have been alerted—for the other changeling's own safety. Their kind didn't fuck around when it came to territorial boundaries.

"Not an actual tiger, but man definitely could growl." Dahlia shrugged off the memory the next second, her skin as vibrant and healthy as if she hadn't been carousing all night. "Oh well, he was just passing through. One night is all we'll ever have."

Adam didn't comment; he was used to his wing-second's chaotic sex life over the past year. Never relationships, only ever hookups. They didn't talk about the whys of it—because Adam had been there when Dahlia's fiancé left her at the altar. Asshole had *texted* her later that day, saying that tall, voluptuous, and ruthlessly loyal Dahlia was "too domineering" and that he'd realized he needed a "more feminine wife, a woman who knows how to treat her man."

Adam would've ripped off the fucker's nonexistent balls and stuffed them in his mouth if Dahlia hadn't told him to leave it, that she'd be humiliated if her wing leader went after a man for not wanting her. "This is my mess, Adam. I'll clean it up."

Worst of it was that she'd been in love with the dickhead. Enough to agree to his request of a full-on wedding, complete with a formal white gown, when she'd never been comfortable in dresses. In the aftermath, Adam had watched her rip the bottom of the fucking gown off with her talons. She hadn't cried a single tear while doing it, and all the while, Adam had known her heart was breaking.

He—all of WindHaven—had been ready to wrap their wings around her, let her vent and rage, but Dahlia had chosen to stride out to the limo that had been meant to take her and her new husband to their exclusive "wedding night" hotel. Yet another thing the asshole had wanted—Dahlia, Adam knew, would've far preferred a quiet desert bungalow.

"I need to be alone," she'd said to Adam when he'd got in her way. "I can't stand *anyone's* sympathy—please keep the clan away from me."

It had gone against his every instinct to do as she asked, to let this wounded member of his clan fly on her own, but Dahlia so rarely asked for anything—and that day, he'd heard the tremor of tears in her voice and known this proud falcon would hate breaking down in front of him. So he'd given her the gift of space and time despite himself.

Dahlia had returned to the Canyon twenty-four hours later, dry-eyed and back to her no-nonsense self. Except she'd never been the same. It infuriated Adam that a man who'd never deserved her had damaged their fiery, dangerous Dahlia so much that she didn't trust her own heart any longer.

"You should've come—my tiger arrived with a firecracker of a fellow trucker," she added today, as a passing clanmate grabbed her empty mug and thrust a full one in her hand.

Dahlia serenaded the clanmate with thanks as he walked away.

Adam folded his arms. "Now you're training people to shove coffee in your face in the mornings?" he said, not worried that it was because Pascal was concerned about Dahlia being functional at the scheduled meeting of the day-shift team.

Dahlia would be ready.

"Won't happen again," she'd promised Adam the morning after she got blackout drunk at the local bar three weeks after her aborted wedding.

"I know," he'd said, able to see the shame in her eyes and wishing he could beat her useless ex to a pulp without crossing the boundary she'd laid down; Dahlia had always been one of the toughest and most confident of them all.

Adam hated that she was still hurting, her breezy surface no barrier to a wing leader's ability to see through to his people's hearts, but there was only so far anyone could go with their tough Dahlia; she'd retreat if pushed on the subject.

"Hah, it's a gift of thanks," Dahlia protested after a gulp of the fresh coffee. "My tiger's smoke show of a friend? Guess who she went home with?" A wriggle of the eyebrows. "I made the introductions." Another gulp. "Seriously, Adam, you should come out with us sometime."

"I have and lived to tell the tale. Never again."

While Dahlia dropped it, Adam could see the wing-second was worried about Adam's current monk-like existence. All changelings needed tactile contact to remain stable; the more dominant the changeling, the more important the need.

Without touch, they turned aggressive, dangerous.

Affection was enough to fill that need in their young, but the older they got, the more the sexual side of their nature kicked in—but if a changeling didn't want to go on the prowl, intimate skin privileges could be found within the clan. However, with WindHaven small in numbers compared to the larger packs across the border in California, Adam didn't play within its walls.

He'd had a human lover in Raintree until eight months ago, when she'd moved to Brazil for work. Older than him by seven years, she was a widow who'd lost her husband too young and had no desire for anything beyond a warm and trusting friendship, which had suited Adam fine.

The truth was that he'd never been as carefree as many of his clanmates when it came to intimate skin privileges. He wanted what his parents had had. That wing-to-wing, side-by-side, endless-laughter, and forever-love kind of deal. A true mating of the heart and soul.

He'd never been interested in the casual, and Dahlia knew that. Only his best friend and second-in-command Jacques knew the rest of it, the painful reason behind Adam's inability to commit to anyone, how his world had shattered in every way possible ten years ago.

The fact that Dahlia had brought up the subject at all . . . fuck.

Leaving her to continue on her way to breakfast, he changed course to swing by the infirmary. Naia looked up from where she was going over patient charts, all big dark eyes and dark hair against skin the shade of rich cream, her lips lush and her body a dramatic landscape of curves.

"Am I causing problems in the clan?" he asked bluntly. "Aggression, I mean."

Naia was WindHaven's healer. She didn't ask him to expound on the subject. "No, but I'd say you were on the edge of it. I was planning to talk to you about it this week." Rising from her desk, she walked over. "You'll need to figure something out before you cross that line."

Jaw tight, Adam was still chewing over her words when he walked into the otherwise silent garage. He'd just maneuvered a vehicle out of its bay when Malia came jogging in with Amir prowling beside her. She had her bookbag slung over her shoulder and an organizer clutched to her chest, her hair down but pulled back on one side with a glittery comb.

The rest of her was a cascade of color.

Tight jeans of vivid blue, a sunset-hued T-shirt over which she'd thrown a textured vest on which were sewn patches from all the places she'd traveled with her family, and long dangling earrings that she'd made herself of tiny shed feathers interwoven with turquoise beads.

She was a bright spark, their Mali.

"Ready?"

"Yep." She turned to kiss Amir on the cheek, having to stand on tiptoe because she'd inherited Saoirse's height rather than her father's. "Bye, Dad. Your favorite child loves you!"

Amir chuckled as he shut the passenger door behind her, then leaned his arms on the window to talk to Adam. "You coming to the meeting this morning?"

"No. Pascal can give me the rundown when I'm back—got something to take care of."

He drove out seconds later, his mind on the visitor who'd drawn his attention, the thought a niggling thorn in his mind. Adam wasn't one to ignore his instincts. He'd check her out after he dropped Malia off at school.

Chapter 3

On the two counts of first-degree murder, we, the jury, find the defendant not guilty.

—Judgment in *State v. Draycott* (11 November 2073)

PRIOR TO WALKING into the inn's small front office, Eleri had pulled on the fine black gloves that she wore in all situations where she might come into contact with another sentient being. She could've chosen gloves in a shade closer to that of her pale brown skin tone, but that would defeat their secondary purpose: to act as a visual warning to others not to make contact.

The office was unattended.

After pressing the bell on the counter and hearing it ring within, she waited a good five minutes.

She pressed the bell again at that point, finally heard the sound of rushing footsteps. A small human woman with a round face devoid of wrinkles, her cheeks red and her silver hair cut in a neat bob, appeared from the door behind the counter. "Oh, you must be Eleri Dias! You're here early just like you said!"

The woman beamed. "Where are my manners? I'm Mi-ja Park, named after both my grandmothers, wouldn't you know it? Apparently they'd get jealous otherwise, so I got Mi from one and Ja from the other and, well, Park was my husband's name, Ju-won Park, God rest his soul."

Eleri had long ago learned the socially acceptable things to say when dealing with non-Psy, the words rote by now. "Thank you for the welcome. Is the room ready or should I go into town to wait?" In actuality, she'd just head out to park in a private spot where she could review her files.

"Oh, no need for that." The innkeeper waved a hand. "I've got it all set up for you. Come along, dear."

The outside air was balmy, no hint here of winter's cold breath, though they were a week into January.

Eleri's diminutive host insisted on showing her to her room, chattering all the while. "Have you got a bit of Korean in you, too? The cheekbones say you might."

"It's possible." Eleri's genetic makeup was a mélange more complex than Mi-ja could imagine; she'd been born into a family who'd run calculation after calculation on the best genetic matches for extreme Psy ability.

They'd succeeded in that Eleri was 9.2 on the Gradient. Too bad she'd come out a J and not a prized pure telepath to carry on the family legacy as comms specialists. They'd have accepted a telekinetic, too, of course, even a high-level M. But a J with only the most minor F ability? Far too pedestrian in terms of the status Eleri could deliver to the family unit.

Housing and feeding her until she was old enough to be shipped permanently to boarding school had been—to their mind—more than could be expected of them. The cold truth of it was that they were right; under the regime of the Council, unwanted children like Eleri had suffered an unfortunate number of convenient accidents.

"I see a bit of Scandinavia in you, too," Mi-ja continued with a musing look. "Such lovely greenish hazel eyes. But then you have that beautiful brown skin." She hurried on. "This here's your personal parking spot, right in front of your room."

She opened the door and stepped into the room before handing Eleri the old-fashioned key. "Call me if you have any problem at all, or just come to the office. My son, Dae, does all the maintenance, so I can have him over here in a jiffy and he'll sort it all out."

"Thank you." Eleri fought her natural inclination to rush the older woman out the door; she needed data, and the same instinct that had brought her to this town now told her that Mi-ja Park would be an excellent source to cultivate.

"I'm here as part of a cold-case investigation run out of Nevada," she said, because cold cases from other jurisdictions made for good cover stories.

No one could prove or disprove anything if she stayed vague.

Mi-ja's eyes lit up. "Oh, anything I can help with?"

"To be honest, the link to Raintree is tangential at best but needs to be checked out to close the file. The primary participants are all deceased, and the DA wants it off his desk."

"Oh." Mi-ja made a face. "Just paperwork, then? Nothing exciting?"

Eleri nodded. "Exactly so. But Raintree strikes me as a great place to which to relocate. I'm wondering how other Psy like it. Do you have many in town?" Because her target was Psy—the victims' brains had borne every hallmark of a vicious telepathic attack.

No changeling or human could've done that, not even with the most advanced weapons on the planet. The task force had also, thanks to the lines of communication fostered by the Trinity Accord, managed to rule out anyone affiliated with the Forgotten—the descendants of Psy who had dropped out of the Net at the onset of Silence.

While the Forgotten weren't about to entrust information about their people to just anyone, they had an innate empathy that meant they'd been willing to talk off-the-record with the task force in an effort to help catch the killer. Which was why Eleri knew that the Forgotten had been intensively tracking their descendants over the past few years.

"There are zero indications of anyone connected to our people in that region," the liaison had said, "but even if we're wrong on that point, you're talking about someone with enough psychic power to need to be in a neural network. I can confirm that we have no one in our network in that area."

Someone could be traveling in and out, but that didn't make sense; the entirety of the crimes spoke to a killer with intimate familiarity of the region.

That left only one option: Vivian, Kriti, and Sarah had been murdered by one of Eleri's own kind.

Mi-ja clapped her hands—delicate, the skin fine with blue veins beneath—in renewed excitement. "Oh, how wonderful! I told Dae that now the Psy don't have that strange Silent thing anymore, they'll travel for leisure. So many more potential visitors!"

She leaned in a little closer. "My view," she said, tone conspiratorial, "is that Raintree's exhausted the market in the state and nearby areas—the tourism would be so much stronger if the falcons did an air show, but they just say no whenever the town council asks."

Eleri couldn't imagine the boy she'd met putting on a show for anyone, but she nodded along with the innkeeper. "So there aren't any Psy here already?" That'd derail her entire theory of this being the Sandman's base of operations.

"Oh no, I never meant that!" Mi-ja corrected at once. "There's Ralph out by the far canyon wall—I think the man is half-crazy, but he's not the only one like that around here. Got a few full-crazy old human coots, too."

Then, as Eleri listened, the innkeeper ran through a number of other Psy who called Raintree home—including two young teachers who'd landed jobs at the local high school around the time of the first murder, and several more who worked in a facility at the other end of town that made high-tech components for flying craft.

"Owned by the falcons," the innkeeper was saying. "Biggest employer in town, and they don't discriminate on who they hire as long as you have the skills. Been around, oh, twenty years at least."

Despite Mi-ja's belief in the falcons' hiring practices, Eleri had a feeling that if she dug deeper, she'd find firewalls built into the system to ensure no proprietary information ever leaked to the Psy—which meant no Psy with high-level access inside the facility.

Its success over a long period confirmed the latter for her—because prior to the fall of Silence and the Council, the Psy had had a bad habit of not just stealing the work of others, but believing it their right due to their status as the "superior" race.

Whether that deep-rooted sense of superiority would change after the fall of Silence was an open question—but the current dangerous instability in the PsyNet would seem to make any such delusions moot.

Their "superior" race was in danger of total extinction.

Eleri should have been concerned about the fall of the psychic network she needed for survival, but that would've required a depth of feeling of which she was no longer capable. All she had left in her was the drive to finish this last task, a droplet of penance in an unfillable bowl.

"Do the falcons build aircraft?"

"Oh no, not here. Though I think Adam's people do own part of a company way out in . . . I can't remember where. They . . ."

The rest of the other woman's words faded in the static inside Eleri's brain.

My name is Adam.

She'd known WindHaven called this place home, had guessed the boy she'd met a decade ago . . . not a boy now, not anymore, might be in residence, but the confirmation still hit like a punch to the gut, the reverberation strong enough to seep through the wall of numbness inside her mind.

Then she realized what Mi-ja had implied. "Adam's people? He's the alpha?" Eleri had access to multiple databases, could have long ago searched for his name, but she'd never been able to make herself take that step.

It would've simply been further acid dripping into an already open wound.

"Wing leader," Mi-ja corrected. "Yes, took over from Aria when she passed." Her face fell. "She was a good friend to me, his grandmother. Used to complain I talked like a myna bird." A shaky smile. "But she never minded, said she liked how I always managed to draw out even the shyest person."

A flicker in Eleri's mind, a clear memory of a fierce woman with snow-white hair and a steel-straight spine wearing multiple turquoise and silver bracelets. Her arms had been thin but strong as she took an angry and grief-stricken young man into her embrace, his long silky hair falling down her back as he buried his face against her neck.

Eleri had been too far away to hear what she'd said, but Adam had stopped his attempts to get at Reagan and Eleri, his rage banked.

". . . over by the school."

Eleri emerged back into the conversation to realize Mi-ja had moved on to another topic altogether, but she didn't interrupt until it became clear the other woman wasn't going to return to talk about the Psy in town.

Eleri nudged her back to the topic with a couple of subtle questions.

At the end of it, she realized Raintree had far more Psy residents than she'd guessed. Per Mi-ja, the Dewdrop Diner was the best place to meet at least a few of them.

"Sally—she's the owner and chief cook—well, she went ahead and made up a whole Psy-friendly menu. She's like me, getting ready to welcome a lot more Psy visitors. Psy menu's real light on any kind of flavorings. You should try it."

"Thank you," Eleri said. "It sounds like the ideal place to get a meal." In truth, she ate like a machine these days—just enough calories to keep her going, keep her strong enough to do her self-imposed work.

Nutrition bars made up her entire meal plan. Unlike many of her brethren, she hadn't chosen to bury herself in the sensation of taste after the fall of Silence. There was no point, when her brain's ability to process sensation was profoundly damaged. Cinnamon or nutmeg, salt or sugar, it all tasted the same.

Eleri had tried each at Saffron's insistence.

Mi-ja opened her mouth as if to carry on, then glanced suddenly out the open door.

Eleri had caught the movement as well—a small red car had just stopped by the office.

"Oh! That's Mary, here for our morning catch-up." The innkeeper bustled out, saying, "Remember, I'm just a call away!" as she hurried off the small porch area surrounded by flowers and down toward the office, all the while waving to catch her friend's attention.

After shutting her door, Eleri opened up the small case she'd brought inside and consciously pushed aside any and every thought to do with the falcon she'd met only once and never forgotten. That confrontation would come; whether she'd survive it was another matter, to be left to the future.

For now, she had a monster to hunt.

She got to work upgrading the room's security. Accustomed as she was to working on the road, and to motel rooms with flimsy locks, this was second nature. The inn proved to be much more solidly built than most of her temporary residences; it wouldn't surprise her if it was over a hundred years old.

No one would be able to break down that heavy door, but as for the rest...

She placed her own removable locks on every window as well as the door. Linked to her integrated comms device—the best on the market because Eleri never spent her wages on anything but necessities and had plenty of funds—the locks would alert her to any attempted entry.

She also placed multiple all-but-invisible sensors on the walls that sent out beams of light imperceptible to the naked eye and that would, once she set the system to live operation, tell her if a teleporter had 'ported inside, or if someone else had managed to gain entry via a route she'd either missed or not considered.

It had been Reagan who'd taught her to accept that she couldn't foresee everything and to prepare for the impossible. "Once," he'd told her, "I had a psychopath who didn't want me on the case book the room below mine and literally *cut* his way in to create his own trapdoor.

"Only reason he didn't succeed in surprising me with his murderous little hatchet when I got in is that another guest called management about the use of power tools that early in the morning—despite his liking for implements, said psychopath wasn't the sharpest tool in the shed."

Her throat moved as she swallowed, the emotions tangled up with Reagan's memory so deeply embedded in her psyche that not even her increasing descent into nothingness could erase them.

Even today, so many years after she'd held his dying body in her arms, her eyes locked with his scared and lost ones, pain stabbed through her insides—born of the anguish of knowing they'd never finish the fight they'd been having for over four years at that point, ever since she'd realized what he'd done in that courtroom filled with broken dreams and bloody rage.

"I hope you never lose the piece of you that's innocent enough to believe that good should always win," Reagan had said when she confronted him, an exhaustion in his features that had dug hollows into his cheeks and turned his skin ashen. "Sometimes, Eleri, evil wins."

He'd been in his early thirties when he'd taken her on as his trainee, and only forty when he died. The only man who'd come even close to holding the role of father in her life had died not even a third of the way into the projected average life span of their time.

Except, of course, it wasn't the average life span for Js, was it?

She snapped the tight band on her wrist when she felt the memories begin to take hold, unravel one by one. So many nights she and Reagan had sat across from each other as he taught her how to scan a memory into her own mind, then how to project that "impression" to others. So many days she'd sat beside him in the courtroom as he waited to go up into the witness box.

The sting of the elastic band was just enough to snap her out of the loop. It wasn't the pain—she'd experienced far more pain in her life. It was the fact that she'd been doing the same thing for years, ever since she took her first involuntary step on the path to becoming a Sensitive. A little dissonance loop she'd built for herself outside the laws and rules of Silence.

Most of the time, the memories that threatened to drown her were those of the monsters, but every so often, it was her own memory of Reagan as he'd been at the very end.

Blood, so much blood, his throat gurgling and hand clutching at her as he gasped for breath.

Allowing Reagan to be sucked into the black hole of the past with the snap of the band, Eleri considered her next steps. With the room secure, she could leave her clothing and other items here—other than the mobile comm, which was always on her wrist, she had nothing worth stealing. But she could as easily unload her overnight bag after she'd taken a first pass at the diner.

Decision made, she left the room, engaged her security system, then crossed over to her vehicle. Once inside, she thought about peeling off her gloves but decided against it. Much as she craved time without that physical shield on her hands, the diner wasn't far per the search she'd just run. She'd only have to put them back on again, and no doubt people would be watching her as soon as she pulled up.

Small towns loved to watch outsiders.

The cypress trees that lined the drive to the inn threw dappled shadows across her vehicle as she drove out, and without thought, she lowered her window to listen to the silence.

Adam.

He'd caused this crack in the wall between her and the world today, a fracture that might yet take her under.

She snapped the rubber band again . . . and rolled up the window.

Turning left out of the drive, she found herself looking down the deserted road shadowed by trees to a vehicle parked up ahead. A man in jeans and a short-sleeve white shirt leaned against it. His skin glowed in the sunlight, his silky hair dark and just long enough to flow around his face, and his body far more muscled than it had been ten years ago.

He'd been younger then, his body lankier and not quite finished.

Her pulse accelerated though she'd long ago stopped being nervous with anyone. Js were too often in the minds of the dregs of civilization for their Silence to stay in any way perfect, so the nervousness itself hadn't disqualified her from her job. Reagan had just taught her to think past it.

Then it had dulled and dulled again, each reconditioning stealing a little more of her soul—if she'd ever had one to begin with. Until at last, she felt nothing at all when she sat across from the most vicious criminals the world had ever seen and waded into the fetid swamp of their minds and memories.

But today, her tongue dried up, her pulse kicked, and she found herself driving slower and slower as she neared the man who had once, long ago, made her wonder if she could have another life, an existence devoid of murder and violence and a relentless march of screams.

Chapter 4

I would argue that Justice Psy hold the highest position of trust of any of the Psy designations or subdesignations that might be called in as expert witnesses.

Js put themselves into dangerous situations day after day when they walk into prisons and other facilities to read the minds of those who have committed crimes beyond the pale. Later, they share those memory impressions with the court and authorized observers.

We see what they see.

With J-Psy, there are no gray areas.

—Editorial in the *Boston Law Quarterly* (Spring 2067)

ADAM HAD PARKED before he got to the inn, his intention to shift and fly over to see what he could glean about the stranger who'd pulled him toward her though they were separated by air and sky. Then he'd heard the quiet purr of a vehicle and guessed it to be hers—no other guests at the inn right now.

So he'd got out and waited, just a local who'd paused to take in some air.

The rugged all-terrain SUV turned out of the inn's drive with the clear intent to pick up speed, but Adam didn't flinch. He could get out of the way without losing a feather if it came to that. But the driver began to slow some distance out and brought the tough vehicle to a stop three feet from him. The windows were tinted but the windscreen clear.

Her gaze was unreadable as she looked at him . . . and his rage a hurricane.

Her.

His talons thrust at the tips of his fingers, the raptor inside him ready to rip her to shreds. She'd lost the softness, a sharp thinness to her face that made her look far older than he knew her to be, but it was definitely her. The pretty J with eyes like the desert after the rains who'd made him smile in sheer joy only an hour before she stood unmoving and silent next to the man who had stolen justice from Adam and his family for an unforgivable and premeditated crime.

He could still remember each and every second of the experience that had forever altered him, destroying in minutes a life he'd only just discovered. Justice Psy were called that because they were telepaths who could reach into the minds of Psy and humans, pull out memories to do with a specific incident or crime, then broadcast those memories out to humans and Psy.

Changelings were excluded because of their powerful natural shields. Too hard to get anything in or out without smashing their minds to pieces. But that hadn't been a disadvantage in that courtroom where an arrogant Psy landholder was meant to be held to account for the murder of Adam's parents.

His paternal grandmother was human, as was Jenesse, his mother's closest friend and a woman who'd been an aunt in all but blood to Saoirse and Adam. The two women had allowed the broadcast to reach their minds, watching the supposed "memory" from start to finish even as the court's designated J-Psy interpreter spoke the memory aloud for the rest of them.

J-Psy were trusted because they were meant to be unable to change the memories they retrieved. They *had* to be trusted—once they went in and took a memory, it could never again be retrieved by another J.

That day Adam learned that the whole "Js can't lie" thing was a pile of fucking bullshit. The J who'd stood beside the woman in the vehicle had altered the perpetrator's memories.

And a double murderer had walked free.

He didn't even realize he'd moved until he found himself staring straight through the windscreen at the woman on the other side, the hard metal of the car brushing his thighs as the wild creature in him rose to the surface in a blaze of rage . . . and things unspoken too long contained.

MEMORIES and nightmares aside, nothing much affected Eleri these days, the blurred glass between her and the world an all but impenetrable shield. That was why she'd told Sophie she would keep on doing this job of hunting serial murderers as long as she lived—because she could. She was in no danger of being broken or damaged in ways that might alter her life.

All of that had been the pure truth . . . until now.

His hair was a dark brown with reddish glints that reached his nape; it was cut in silky waves that were currently tumbled, as if he'd run his hand through it. It had been much longer the first time they'd met, the waves pulled out of it by the weight of its length.

He'd worn it open, a sleek rain down the back of his perfectly pressed suit.

His stance that day had been far from aggressive—he'd likely learned to affect languid relaxation to put others at ease. Because even then, Adam Garrett had been a tall boy who gave the impression of power and strength.

He'd grown into a big man who moved with a predator's grace.

His neutral stance against his vehicle had altered the same instant that her heart began to race, her breath catching as her hands clenched on the steering wheel. Then she'd brought the SUV to a stop, and he'd moved with a slow and deadly intent that told her she was unlikely to make it out of this alive.

Instead of reacting to back off, drive away, she froze . . . as time began to unravel at furious speed, shoving her back into the very first courtroom in which she'd stood in an official capacity, no longer Reagan's trainee but his intern. She should've remembered that day for that reason, looked back on it with what happiness she could feel through her numbed psyche, considered it a positive touchstone.

But as Reagan had once said, "Should-have-beens are the lament of those who failed."

The courtroom had been one of the old ones, with dark wood paneling and the judge up in a high position behind a heavy bracket of wood, the jury to the right behind another barrier created of wood.

Her job had been to stand there, be all but invisible, to learn from her superior and not say a word. There wasn't much she could do, in any case. Only one J could go into a mind at a time. She'd been with Reagan to learn how to behave in court, how to act in front of a judge and jury and the lawyers. Allowed into the courtroom by permission of the judge, who had, prior to the start of the proceedings, taken the time to welcome her to the world of Justice.

Js, considered neutral by their very nature, were expert witnesses in good standing with the court system. Expensive and not so numerous that they could be used for all cases, or even most cases. But for a rare few special exceptions due to people with connections pulling strings, Js were only ever brought in on the worst cases, the ones to do with violence and terrible destruction.

Bombers, murderers, serial offenders against the person, child kidnappers . . . a parade of depravity.

This one had been a murder case. Two changeling falcons shot out of the sky by a Psy who had never denied that he'd done it; his defense was that the sun had been in his eyes and he'd believed the birds a pair of natural raptors who'd been preying on his stock of genetically modified farm animals.

Not many Psy owned farms, but Wayne Draycott had made a living from modifying animals to create more resilient strains free of diseases.

He'd been more than willing to pay the fine for attempting to kill what he'd thought were natural falcons—creatures not on the list of species that could be hunted by farmers to protect stock—but he'd maintained that it was an honest mistake that he'd shot changelings instead of natural birds.

Eleri'd had no prior knowledge of whether that was true or not; she wasn't the one who'd gone into his memories. But she'd known something was very, *very* wrong the second her mentor began to broadcast the memory from where they both stood behind the bulletproof glass of the witness box.

Reagan had shared memories with her many times over the years as part of her training. He'd begun with the less depraved ones, his aim only to teach her the technicalities of how to make the projection to a limited group. Because while Js had a facility for it, it still required knowledge of methodology alongside practice to do it well.

He'd amped up the darkness of what he showed her when she was a few months out from seventeen, readying her for the vile assault on her senses that would be her first walk through the mind of a violent criminal. In truth, nothing could've prepared her, but Reagan had done his best. All the senior Js did their best—the vast majority of them weren't like some of the other specialists, who treated their juniors with cruelty and coldness.

The J Corps were compatriots who walked the same hell. Js understood that in the end, all they had was each other. Their loyalty to one another was absolute and the purest thing in their lives.

"Should a Councilor stand in this room and tell me to shoot you," Reagan had said once, "I'd put the weapon to my own head. What would be the point in living if I destroy the one thing that makes me feel good about myself?"

Eleri, young though she'd been, had already understood what he meant, understood that to be a J was to be part of a family that had its own unique system of survival and protection. It was why Eleri had quietly helped eliminate an assassination threat against Sophie from a group of Psy who thought she had too much influence on Nikita Duncan, and why Bram had formed the Quatro Cartel when they were children.

Because Js were all other Js had.

So she'd been in no way ready for her response to Reagan's memory capture that day in the courtroom. It hadn't even been that violent, not in comparison to the scenes of mutilation and torture he'd shared with her just the previous week in an effort to build up her tolerance.

She'd thrown up then, her stomach revolting against the ugliness in her mind.

But that day, in the courtroom, her response hadn't come from horror and disgust at the memories. It had been born of another reason altogether. She'd barely heard the court interpreter speaking the memory aloud, her heart was thumping so hard, her face ablaze.

He's out in the field, heading toward a corralled batch of lambs. He has his testing kit in hand, and his long-range rifle on his back. "I don't care about the fines for killing species on the protected list," he's saying, the glossy black of a phone transmitter curved over his ear. "I'm sick of the birds taking my animals or just leaving them mauled."

Shadows overhead, the sweep of wings. The sun in his eyes, blinding him. He shoots without being able to see, the scream of a falcon piercing the air even as the second arrows down toward him.

He shoots a second time, is hit by the bird as it falls on top of him.

It claws him even as it takes him down, and only then does he drop the weapon, sit up in panic. "It's too big—this bird is too big. I shot a changeling! I didn't know! What have I done?"

Seventeen-year-old Eleri had jerked back into her own mind and senses in a whiplash of panic. She'd known she couldn't interrupt Reagan while he was broadcasting, but she could feel the *wrongness* of it, the sense of a memory twisted through a fun-house mirror until it was distorted and *not* right.

Reagan, she'd telepathed urgently. *Reagan, something's wrong. The memory feels—*

Be quiet unless you want to end up on a slab, had come the clipped mental command, the man she trusted most in the world staring straight ahead at the judge without expression.

But the memory is wrong! She'd been taught all her life that Js never lied, that they were the truth sayers, the final arbiters in a courtroom.

It was the fulcrum of her being.

The merest glance at her after Reagan finished the broadcast. *If you can sense it, then you can do it.* A kind of exhaustion in his telepathic voice. *Never, ever reveal that, Eleri. I did, and now here we stand.*

She'd heard a commotion behind her even as she struggled to comprehend this thing that threatened to splinter her entire sense of reality.

She wasn't supposed to turn, wasn't supposed to make any kind of contact with the families of the victims, but she hadn't been able to help herself. Heart yet racing, she'd shifted on her heel and met the pale tawny brown eyes of the eighteen-year-old boy named Adam who'd smiled at her in a way that had made her world tilt sideways.

That Adam was gone.

This one had dark, dark eyes ringed by a feral yellow and was being held back by two older men as he screamed, "Liar! You fucking liar!"

His grief was palpable, his rage a heat she could almost sense against her skin . . . and the truth of his words absolute.

Reagan had *lied*.

Eleri hadn't known Js could lie, hadn't known they could *change* memories. Not until that day in a courtroom in chaos as bailiffs rushed to control a changeling whose talons had thrust out of his skin as his eyes morphed into those of a falcon.

That same changeling stood in front of her SUV on this lonely road.

And the rage that pulsed off him . . . it was potent, more mature than that of the boy he'd been, a thing that had grown stronger with time.

Back when she'd still understood hope, she'd hoped this day would never come, that she could make it to the end of her life without losing the final shreds of the dream she'd never been meant to have, the whispers of a future that could never be hers. But it had come, of course it had.

The price always had to be paid.

Turning off the car, she opened the door and stepped out, ready to face the reckoning that had been written in the blood-soaked bodies of Adam Garrett's murdered parents.

Chapter 5

To the winds we scatter the ashes of Taazbaa' and Cormac, clanmates and parents of two cherished fledglings who mourn their loss and celebrate their love.

She was the child of my womb, the oh-so-wanted daughter who held my mate's hand as she learned to walk, the generous and sweet friend who brought light into the lives of her clanmates, the mother who played with Saoirse and Adam with the mischievousness of a child—and the woman who loved her mate with all her dancer's spirit.

He was the man who loved her and their fledglings so well that we could do nothing but love him, too, the falcon from a distant green land who made everyone in the clan laugh with his humor, the son who filled his parents with pride each and every day—and the father who was an oak, solid and strong, for Saoirse and Adam as they grew.

Fly now, beloveds, your wings entwined for all eternity. Your fledglings, your families, and your clan will ever remember your laughing spirits, the memory of you etched onto our bones and into the walls of our home.

—The last eulogy for Taazbaa' and Cormac Garrett, spoken by Aria, wing leader of WindHaven, prior to their committal to the skies (3 May 2073)

THE PAST TEN years had sheared her to the bone, Adam thought. There'd been a softness to her face in the courtroom, not a real plumpness—the Psy hadn't permitted their children to buck the mandated values of perfection back then. Those who'd broken Silence since had shared that under the protocol, children were put on a regimen of nutrients designed to give them the exact right amount of fuel for their bodies.

No candy slipped to them by a favorite aunt or uncle.

No hot chocolates on a cold night.

No treats to celebrate a birthday.

So no, she hadn't been plump. She'd just had that hint of childish softness to her cheeks and her chin that even a Silent regime couldn't erase. Her dark brown—almost black—hair, however, had been tightly scraped back into a braid, not a strand out of place. No makeup on her face, the pale brown of her skin smooth and without flaw.

He had no idea of her ethnic background, her features such that she could've as easily slipped into a South American family portrait as she could an Iranian or Indian one. Word was the Psy mixed and matched genes for strong psychic abilities, so she was likely a combination of multiple lines that were themselves equally complex.

That didn't mean she had a bland, forgettable face. No. Never that. Her face was arresting, had haunted him for ten years. Lush lips that looked too soft against the sharp cheekbones, hollow cheeks, and clean jawline. Eyes of a light hazel tinted with brown in one light, green in another, so direct it was striking—and then, when you looked deeper, *there*, the merest glimmer of a yellowish gold in the iris.

Look long enough and you'd convince yourself she wasn't Psy at all but a changeling of unknown origin.

But Adam didn't really care about any of that.

He was fighting a rage such as he hadn't felt since the day his parents' murder had been ruled an accident. Their murderer had paid a *fine*. A fucking *fine*. And the smug bastard had believed he'd gotten away with it.

If Adam's clan had left it to the Psy, he would have.

Now one of the killer's accomplices walked toward him in a black suit that was a little worn at the edges paired with a white shirt that she'd buttoned up to the neck, and scuffed black shoes that were closer to trail boots than dress shoes.

Thin, she was thin. Not fragile or weak, however. This was the thin of someone who ate just enough and possibly forgot to eat at all when concentrating on other matters. There was muscle on her, a kind of fluidity to her walk that told him whatever her eating habits, she put time into maintaining her strength.

She'd been softer back then, less akin to a puma ready for the hunt.

He drew in a breath and, though the changeling falcon sense of smell was closer to that of humans than other wild predators, caught a scent that had no threads of metal to it, as happened to those Psy who were so far in their Silence that they were never going to get back out. But her face was expressionless, those distinctive eyes so flat as to be disturbingly lifeless.

When she came to a stop two feet from him, their height difference was enough that she had to tip her head slightly back to meet his gaze, but she did so without flinching. "You were right," she said in a tone that held nothing but her voice. No emotion, no fragment of personality. "Reagan lied that day in the courtroom."

Whatever Adam had been expecting her to say, it wasn't that.

His falcon cocked its head, its talons still pricking the tips of his fingers, but no longer shoving. "Bit late to speak up." It came out shrapnel wrapped in icy calm; he was no longer the barely eighteen-year-old boy still naive enough to be shocked at the cruelty people could dole out with such ease.

His rage had had time to settle, become a thing of unbending steel.

"Yes," she said.

Adam flexed his hands at his sides, then curled his fingers back in. "You think it's that easy? That you just admit liability and it all goes away? I forgive you?"

"No."

He stared at her, as did his falcon, both parts of his nature weighing up this Psy who'd looked over at him in that courtroom with a shocked gaze that had made him believe she'd stop what was going on, make it right.

But she'd said nothing.

He could no longer fully recall the face of the J who'd actually lied, but her, he remembered. Would *always* remember.

His muscles grew painfully tight.

"You know he's dead?" he drawled, watching to see her reaction with a falcon's focus. "My parents' murderer."

"Yes. Wayne Draycott vanished without a trace two years, six months, and four days after he walked out of the courtroom. I kept track."

He asked the question without ever using his voice.

"Changelings don't forgive such crimes; I learned that during one of my very first cases." A direct gaze with nothing behind it that he could read. "Psy might believe we can cover up crimes, avoid justice, but changelings don't accept the authority of the courts when it comes to crimes against their people—you'll cooperate for the sake of appearances, and if things are open and fair, you'll accept the verdict. But this trial wasn't fair."

The falcon resettled its wings inside Adam, its eyes emerging through Adam's humanity as the wildness in him fought to get out, claim vengeance. The falcon's vision was far sharper than Adam's human sight—it could see the very pores on Eleri Dias's skin, catch even the most minute flutter of expression . . . but there was nothing to catch, nothing to see.

The woman might as well be made of stone.

"You don't seem concerned about standing in front of a changeling you seem convinced executed a Psy," he said, well aware his voice wasn't wholly human any longer.

"Execution is the changeling punishment for premeditated murder. You may have let it go had he been sentenced to the Psy equivalent of psychic and physical imprisonment for life. But he had influential friends, so he walked out of the courtroom a free man—and the second he did so, he signed his death warrant."

Adam couldn't understand this woman. She was definitely *not* the same girl who'd almost walked into him in the hallway outside the courtroom and upended everything he thought he knew about the world, and about himself. That girl had been a whole person, no matter if she was Silent, her personality vibrant in her every word.

Oh, I'm so sorry. I should've been looking up instead of at my organizer.

In contrast, the woman in front of him appeared devoid of personality; she gave off *no* cues by which he might judge her.

All he had were her words, and his finely honed ability to see through bullshit.

"What the fuck are you doing here?" he snarled, his chest tight with the hugeness of all the things he could never ever feel for her. "If you wanted to die, there are less painful ways to go about it." He waited for excuses, perhaps for an attempt at an impossible penance. He'd heard some Psy were out there trying to make up for their crimes.

There could be no making up for what she'd done, what she'd *failed* to do. Her. The one person in the entire world on whom he should've been able to rely. The one person who'd kicked his boyish heart so badly that he still wore the bruises.

She'd *hurt* him so much that he'd tried to turn cold and unfeeling in an effort to protect himself. It had been Saoirse who'd snapped him out of it. "I've already lost Mom and Dad," she'd said, unexpected tears in her eyes—his sister was one tough cookie who'd been running on anger since the day of the murders. "I can't lose my bighearted, annoying, loving bear of a little brother, too."

Chirp and Bear. What a delightful combination of fledglings we've made, Cormac.

Not only made, my dear heart, but managed to raise to near-adulthood with only minor calamities and three broken bones between them.

No, Dad, all three broken bones were Adam's. I'm far too graceful to go flying into canyon walls. Bear, on the other hand...

A cascade of memories upon memories of the family they'd once been, the loving parents whose honor this J had helped desecrate that day in the courtroom.

"There's a serial killer in this region" was her cold response to his question about what she was doing in his territory.

"The Sandman." Adam hated the media for glorifying the pathetic waste of space by giving him the pithy sobriquet. "I know."

"I think he's based in Raintree."

Adam stared at her. "Did you pull that out of your ass or do you have actual proof?" He was being aggressive far beyond anything those who knew him would ever expect, but she was lucky he hadn't given in to his falcon's urge to shred her the instant he saw her.

The wild creature that was his other self could forgive many people many things, but never her. Not *her*.

"You knew at once, didn't you?" he said before she could answer. "I saw it on your face."

She didn't startle at the apparent non sequitur. "Yes," she said again, with no attempt to downplay her involvement in a terrible miscarriage of justice. "I knew Reagan was lying the instant he began to speak."

"Why shouldn't I kill you here and now?" He focused on the haze of red across his vision, because rage he could handle. The problem was what lay below, the vulnerability so huge that he'd had to wall it off from his conscious mind all these years so he could remain the brother his sister knew and loved, so he could be a strong and affectionate and generous wing leader.

So he could be *Adam* and not a broken shadow of himself.

"I could rip you to pieces, throw those parts in the desert. No one would ever know what happened to you." It was a vicious threat, and he'd made it because he wanted to incite a response—any response.

The emotion inside him was a serrated and massive pressure defined by two moments that had forever altered his future. One in that hallway that had lit up his bleak world . . . the other in the courtroom that had destroyed it.

"If you kill me now," she said, with not even a flicker of an eyelash to show that she might be affected by either his words or her own, "you'll be putting multiple innocent young women in danger."

Adam made a sound deep in his throat that not many people ever heard from a changeling falcon and survived. At the same time, he heard the clunking engine of a familiar car starting up. Mary had finished her daily morning chat with Mi-ja and would now make her ponderous way to Main Street and the local grocer to pick up what she needed to make that day's lunch and dinner.

"We can't have this conversation here," he said, not sure how he was even managing to sound so rational when she'd smashed into his life all over again. "Go to the end of Main Street, turn left, then take the first right to the very end. I'll be there."

He got in his car without waiting for a response.

When he checked in his rearview mirror, she was still standing on the road, staring after him. His chest shuddered, his falcon wanting out, wanting the freedom of the skies . . . wanting her.

ELERI knew it would be an intensely stupid idea to get in her vehicle and follow a man who'd made it clear that he was a breath away from tearing her head from her neck. She also knew it'd be even worse to do so without alerting anyone else as to her whereabouts. She'd made a commitment to Sophia, to the Quatro Cartel, to the victims of the Sandman.

But her debt to Adam Garrett was a huge thing that predated all else.

If he wanted blood, so be it.

Turning on her heel as his car disappeared around the corner, she walked to her own and got in. A small red vehicle was just crawling out of the inn's drive as Eleri took the first corner. A ripple shimmered over and around her mind at the same instant.

Minor incident on the PsyNet.

It was easy to identify, given the events of the past year. The psychic network on which the vast majority of Psy on the planet depended for their survival had stabilized after the incident two months past, when a mind none of them could see had tangled the entire network in a spider-web that acted as a fine glue.

That glue, however, wasn't foolproof—because it waited for consent before attaching minds into the web, which left a number of unbalanced individuals as free radicals in the system.

It also had a use-by date.

The majority of the population didn't know the latter; they were relieved at the apparent solution and had begun to make plans for the future again. Unfortunately for the J Corps, they didn't have the option of that happy delusion; something in their brains meant they could see the gradual decline in the Net's inherent power.

Since most working Js had been through at least one reconditioning, however, they hadn't been sure they weren't just imagining things and had kept their observations to themselves for a considerable period. It wasn't as if there were a way to measure psychic output on the PsyNet, yet Js were convinced the output was inching closer to flatline with every passing day, albeit at a slower pace than before.

It was Sophia who'd found the answer. "We're not imagining it," she'd said. "Nikita confirmed it for me. The fix is temporary and the loss of PsyNet integrity expected. Our reports have helped put a timeline on that disintegration."

She'd rubbed a protective hand over her belly, fine lines around her mouth. "We can't allow the information to get out—it would cause widespread panic and further speed up the loss of integrity."

The J Corps had kept its silence.

They—each and every one, Sophie included—were viscerally aware of the young Js who stood a chance of survival in this new world. A world where Js weren't pieces of meat to be used up and thrown away. But to thrive, that new world needed the PsyNet to not only exist, but be healthy.

Eleri wasn't sure the latter was possible, but no J was going to do anything that might screw up even the small bit of hope currently flowing through the psychic highways of the Net.

Raintree's Main Street was active with people coming in and out of the various business premises, what traffic there was keeping to a slow speed because pedestrians kept crossing without looking—but all raised a hand in thanks to the vehicles that stopped for them. A few drivers gave a honk in return that was received with a smile, and some even pulled over to chat.

She found herself wondering if Adam Garrett had such friendly interactions with the locals. She couldn't see it given their own exchange—but then, he had a reason to be unfriendly with her. He'd been a different person during their very first meeting; his eyes had warmed from within as his lips curved, his body angled in a way that had felt oddly protective despite the fact that they'd been standing opposite each other.

Logic told her that she was lucky to have survived this latest encounter—and that same logic said that she was driving to her own death.

So be it.

All her private files on the Sandman were backed up to the Quatro Cartel's private storage system. If she died with her last task incomplete, Bram, Saffron, and Yúzé knew to push that data to her colleagues on the Sandman Task Force.

She turned left at the end of Main Street as instructed, then took the first right some way down. The houses disappeared within a few short minutes, the greenery falling away in the next few, as she left Raintree's microclimate behind to emerge into an arid landscape of browns and reds canopied by a searing blue sky.

But the desert vistas on either side of the narrow road came to an abrupt halt against a sweeping rise of rock and stone ten minutes later. Adam's car was nowhere in sight. The only signs of life were the cacti that stood sentinel in the desert behind her, not a single pair of wings in the sky, not even an insect's breath stirring beneath the winter sun.

Chapter 6

Be careful—especially now that you're working on your own. It's clear that your target's been watching you even before you became aware of his crimes.

—Message from Bram Priest to Eleri Dias (6 January 2084)

GETTING OUT, ELERI walked to the apparently impenetrable barrier... and saw that the road continued between the rock walls. The shadows there dropped the temperature in a precipitous dive, a reminder that the desert wasn't always hot, that once discarded by their murderer, the victims of the Sandman spent night after night blanketed in nothing but the cold air.

And she knew she'd ask Adam Garrett to stay her execution until after she'd finished this, brought the killer to justice. She'd never spoken any promises aloud to the dead, but she'd made them all the same, each and every time she found one of his victims. Because it was always Eleri who found the abused and violated remains.

The Sandman made sure of that.

The space narrowed as she drove on, the desert being eaten away by stone and rock, the road progressively less well maintained, until she found herself on a gravel track that led into a much more constricted canyon than the one that housed the town of Raintree.

Despite every instinct she had telling her to turn back, she didn't. Those instincts couldn't scream anymore. Nor did her heart race or her palms become sweaty. The involuntary reactions had stopped one by one after her fourth . . . or perhaps it had been her fifth reconditioning, the wall between her and who she'd once been so opaque that Eleri could no longer see through it.

Five minutes of driving over rugged terrain brought her to a small flat area—and Adam's dust-coated vehicle. When she exited her own, she saw that he'd walked down a cascade of jagged rock to stand next to a waterway that reflected the red and orange of the rocks all around them.

The shadows thrown by the canyon walls created an artificial twilight on this side of the waterway, while the sunlight on the other side glittered off minerals embedded in the stone.

Truths and lies.

Shadows and shine.

Eleri and Adam.

She walked down to join him.

"This is Blood Canyon," he told her, with a nod to the water that, from this angle, rippled a dark red. "I thought it appropriate. Locals—including most of my clan—avoid it due to superstition passed on from generation to generation, so we won't be interrupted."

Eleri drew in a deep breath of the crisp, clear air and asked a question she hadn't known she was going to ask until she spoke. "What's it like, living in so much space, no one pushing down on you from every side?" That was what it felt like in her mind if she ever slipped in maintaining her telepathic shields, as if she was one breath away from being crushed by an avalanche of other people's dreams and thoughts, nightmares and horrors.

His facial muscles tight, Adam set his booted feet apart as he faced her. "You don't get to ask the questions here. Tell me why you think Raintree might be home base for a serial killer."

Perhaps she wouldn't have to ask him to let her finish this task after all. While she didn't know how changeling packs and clans functioned except on the most basic level, she did understand that the people at the very top of the hierarchy were highly protective of those who looked to them for leadership.

Of course Adam Garrett would want to excise the Sandman out of the place his clan called home.

"It's easier if I show you." Eleri gathered up a few nearby bits of rock and stone, put them in a pile, then cleared a section of the sandy ground.

The dust and grit clung to her gloves, tiny flecks that highlighted her inability to protect her own mind.

"This is Raintree." She put a gray rock in the center. "This is where the body of Vivian Chang—his first confirmed victim—was discovered." A small black stone to mark the place where Eleri had brushed sand off the body of the cellist whose hands would never again create music soaring and haunting.

"This is where the body of Kriti Kumar, his second confirmed victim, was found." Another petite young woman with dark eyes and hair. That was all Kriti had been to the killer. He hadn't known or cared that she dressed up as a fairy for her much younger siblings' birthday parties, or that she was the bubbly, vibrant center around which her friends spun.

As he hadn't cared about Vivian's spoiled pet dogs who'd refused to eat for days after she vanished, their eyes trained on the door as they waited for her to return. It was Vivian's father who'd told Eleri that, his own face hollowed out.

"Why are you handling this instead of Enforcement?" Adam asked, even as he hunkered down beside her.

"I work with them," she said. "Specialist attached to the serial crimes unit, and presently specifically to the Sandman Task Force."

"Full-time?" A question with an edge. "I figured you'd be needed in the court system."

"I'm a worn-out J." Just a simple fact. "No longer any good for the basic work of the Corps, but it turns out many of us old Js are excellent at hunting serial killers."

When Adam tapped the side of his head, she shook her own. "No, nothing psychic. It's due to our years of experience walking in depraved minds. We're each profilers in specific subsets of criminals, depending on which crimes we worked on most during our tenure."

Eleri had never compared their workloads, but one thing she knew: all senior Js had scars. Losing her ability to react and respond, to *feel*, was nothing in comparison to the price demanded of the others. Saffron eaten up by her fury until she overloaded in seizures, Yúzé so calm and precise and insane in ways that would show up on no PsyMed test, Bram with a brain that couldn't shut down to sleep without heavy chemical inducement that left him locked in night terrors.

"There are a lot of serial killers on the loose at the current time," she added because this was a brutal truth that should be widely disseminated, should be exposed to the light. "The Psy Council protected a large number because the killers were useful to them in some capacity. At least half that group managed to slither away in the aftermath of the Council's fall without anyone being the wiser of their proclivities."

She could feel Adam staring at the side of her face, the intensity of his attention a near-scald that should've made her afraid . . . only she'd lost the ability to feel fear first of all, her mind burning out on the overload of it as she walked in minds so horrific that she wished she could go back in time and end their genetic lines where they began.

"This is where I discovered the body of the third victim, Sarah Wells."

"You, personally?"

Eleri gave a curt nod. "I had a tip-off."

ADAM'S gut tensed as he stared at the primitive map she'd laid out in front of him. Unless she was fucking with him—and no reason for her to do that, not when she had to know that as the head of WindHaven, he'd have access to the kind of people who could verify her claims—she was right.

Raintree sat at the direct center of the body dumps, the sun with all its horrific satellites. "Chance you've missed abductions that don't fit into your pattern?"

"Low." A firm answer, no hesitation.

"What aren't you telling me?"

Rising, she said, "The answer's in my vehicle."

Adam followed her without a word, and because he was behind her, he caught the slight sway of her body. It was instinct to reach out—but he stopped himself with conscious force.

He couldn't touch her.

Not her.

"Careful."

"I'm fine." A response that was neither defensive nor explicatory.

It just . . . was.

Going around to the back of her SUV while he was still scowling at her beyond-robotic affect, she opened the trunk, then lifted out the trunk liner to prop it up against the side of the car. Below, where in most vehicles would be tools for the car or an emergency battery, were three locked cases.

Including one that he knew must hold a weapon.

Eleri reached for the one next to it.

After pulling it out, she placed it atop the one that held the weapon, then unlocked it using an iris print combined with a numerical code. He wasn't sure what he was expecting when she lifted the black metal lid, but it wasn't a thin pile of what looked to be paper letters that had been removed from their envelopes. Said envelopes lay neatly bound in a stack below.

Pulling out the letter at the bottom, Eleri handed it to Adam.

The handwriting was fluid and stylish, the words altogether sickening.

My dearest Eleri,

You don't mind if I call you that, do you? I feel like we know each other so well . . . though I suppose you won't even remember our meeting. In fairness, it wasn't a real meeting. I wanted it to be, but they're so strict in the places you most often go, aren't they? Courts, jails . . . and, well, where else do you go?

As far as I can figure out, you don't have a home.

I've seen you though, lots of times, and I've tried to imagine what it would be like to have your mind inside mine. I'm shuddering now as I imagine the pleasure of it, of having you invade me like I invade my chosen ones. But to experience your psychic touch, I'd have to give up my freedom and I'm having so much fun out here.

Which brings me to this. I've decided that if I can't get close to you any other way, then I'll have to do something bad and clever enough that they'll pull you out of retirement to deal with me.

Oh yes, I know you've retired from Justice. Saw the gloves—dead giveaway, no pun intended. Js who start wearing the gloves don't tend to be around much longer afterward, but maybe that'll change with this new Ruling Coalition?

I'm not taking the risk.

Consider this the first step of my courtship and our relationship.

Below the final line were what appeared to be GPS coordinates.

And right at the bottom was the closing salutation: *Yours in admiration* followed by *xx*.

Adam fought the urge to haul her close, spread his wings over her, even as his decade-old rage burned ever hotter. He wasn't a man given to holding grudges or withholding affection—his sister had nicknamed him Bear for a reason—but Eleri Dias's betrayal was a barbed thorn in his heart that wouldn't let him forget.

He focused only on the here and now and the possible threat to his clan. "The coordinates?"

"Led to Vivian's body. She'd turned seventeen two weeks prior. Kriti, the oldest victim, was still only a bare nineteen, Sarah six months younger."

Eleri pulled out another letter. "After that initial letter, he began writing to me *before* each abduction, then after. He's never given me exact coordinates for the bodies again, says there'll be no 'thrill' in it for me if he makes it too easy—but he gives me *just* enough that I and my colleagues can figure it out."

"Playing a game with you?" Adam said. "So you'll run yourself ragged trying to stop the abductions?"

"No. He's been careful not to say anything in those pre-abduction letters that could lead me to him or to his future victim." Though Eleri's face was motionless in the shadow of the canyon, Adam wondered if she really was as unmoved as she appeared.

He hadn't missed the fact that she'd named each victim. Then again, perhaps it was easy for her because she didn't feel.

No guilt. No grief. No anger for lives stolen.

As Adam unfolded the second letter, Eleri put away the first. "They're not originals, just copies that I've handled until they look like it. The originals are in a forensic lab and have been analyzed both on the level of physical evidence and in terms of what the words might mean."

"Still a big jump from fantasy to acting it out," Adam said.

"The first kill wasn't clean. From the state of her body, we believe Vivian almost escaped." Eleri looked out at the water that, from here, was no river of blood but a glittering golden thread in the landscape.

"Animals are often the first target," she added. "That may have been his practice ground."

Neck rigid with tension, Adam didn't interrupt.

"This particular pattern of abduction and murder, with the victims kept for what appears to be exactly seventy-two hours before he kills them with a massive telepathic surge that burns out their brains? That began with Vivian Chang.

"There are no other like crimes in any database to which we have access—and that includes the database set up by the Ruling Coalition in which they enter any and all data to do with psychopaths who may have been allowed to commit their crimes by the Council."

"Who's the we? Your Enforcement task force?"

"Yes. I also work with a network of Js who share information as we work our personal cases."

"What does the task force think of your theory?"

A long pause before she said, "That I'm seeing ghosts because I've become too personally invested. They believe the important locations are the *abduction* and captivity sites, and that the body dumps are opportunistic—it would tie with the theory that he's an individual with a transient job. Sales. Trucking. Road engineer.

"To date, we've only found one place where he held a victim—that was with Vivian Chang. She was kept captive in a warehouse meant to store road construction items; that's how we found it. The roading crew turned up three weeks after she vanished and found her ID onsite, along with specks of blood."

Adam narrowed his eyes, seeing where her colleagues were going—especially given that particular site. "What happens if you take the location of the abductions and that warehouse into account?"

"It triangulates to a totally different area." Eleri put away the second letter. "Nowhere near Raintree."

"I'm assuming your colleagues aren't idiots, so why are they focused on the abduction sites and not where the bodies were found?" He watched her, wondering if she'd lie, try to spin things her way.

Instead, she said, "Because the abductions appear to be opportunistic—as if he was just passing by on one of his normal routes when he spotted them. Vivian was walking home from a late band practice, Kriti's car broke down on a highway, and Sarah went to a party with new friends. No one remembers when she left or with who—but we know she was at the party, and that she never made it home."

Eleri put the trunk liner back on. "The bodies, on the other hand . . . they're posed in a way that takes considerable time. He *builds* open-sided shelters for them on the spot, then decorates the shelters like his fantasy of a woman's bedroom. Silk hangings, vases of flowers, candles. That takes time, takes materials, takes tools—and the bodies aren't decomposed enough when I find them."

Her tone, Adam realized, hadn't altered through the entire grim recitation. There was nothing in her eyes, either. As if he was speaking to an automaton.

His senses spiked in a rejection that wasn't born of rage but of something else altogether, something that he'd succeeded in burying for ten long years.

Oh, you've cut your knuckles. Let me get a bandage from the first aid—
No, stay, it will heal up real quick. Changeling skin is tough.
Eleri. I'm Eleri.
Eleri. That's pretty. My name is Adam.

Chapter 7

The Psy race considers humankind prey, our minds theirs to violate at will. Humans will never achieve our true potential as long as we have to conceal our light in order to escape drawing Psy attention.

—Bowen Knight, security chief of the Human Alliance (circa February 2077)

SHOVING ASIDE THE echoes of a past that had destroyed the boy he'd been, Adam considered her words. "You think he builds the shelters ahead of time, then goes trawling for victims."

Eleri turned those beautiful mutable eyes on him. "Yes, so they have to be in places he can reach on a regular basis—like after work. Sixty minutes in a high-speed vehicle to the furthest shelter, ninety if in a lower-spec car, three-hour maximum round-trip total.

"Add in a couple of hours of construction on the shelter and—if he finishes work at five or six—he'd still be in bed by eleven, midnight at the latest. I also don't think the abductions were opportunistic; he's just taken care to make them appear that way—I believe he goes out of his home range on purpose, to stop anyone tracing him back to Raintree."

Adam agreed with her thought process, while being aware that he was only getting one side of the story. "What would your colleagues say if I asked them?"

"That he must prefabricate the shelters so he can put them up within an hour, and that he's as opportunistic in the captivity sites as he is in his abductions. Several members believe he might even keep the victims in his truck or other similar vehicle."

Adam held that gaze, his falcon in his eyes—both parts of him trying to see through to the truth of her. "And yet you think you're right. Why?"

"Instinct," was the toneless response. "The same thing that means I can track serial killers across the PsyNet by their psychic signatures."

A disbelieving lift of his eyebrow, his gaze not human in any fashion as he watched her. Adam Garrett was a raptor designed to rend his prey to pieces, and he remained, Eleri thought, a breath away from doing the same to her.

"If you can track murderers on your Net, why all this?" He waved at her car, the evidence she carried.

"First, I need to pick up the scent. The PsyNet is a vast place." What Eleri didn't say was that for a J like her, a Sensitive on the verge of Exposure, the PsyNet was also a place she tried to avoid as much as possible.

Its psychic fabric teemed with millions upon millions of memories that had slipped free of people's shields and now floated around in disembodied pieces. Those fragments didn't affect undamaged Js, but Eleri could no longer claim that status; she risked the memories burrowing their way into her and setting up home atop the vicious memories of far sicker strangers.

"Funny," Bram had said the last time the four of them had gotten together, "you'd think we'd want those random memories to settle in, dampen the ones from our work."

Only, of course, it didn't work that way. The fragments had razored edges that drew psychic blood, and when one embedded itself, it stirred older, darker memories to the surface, like a stone thrown into a still pond.

So no, memory shards weren't a good thing.

The only time Eleri stepped foot in the psychic network anymore was when she was sure enough of the identity of a killer that she could stalk him on the psychic level. She'd led Enforcement to three so far by that method, and for two others . . . well, some people didn't need any kind of a second chance to do what they'd done, and Js were experts at stealth assassinations.

Her mind opened the box of her own memories, time scrolling backward.

"Are you shocked I executed Prisoner 45TN?" Reagan, sitting across from her two years after the court case that had ripped the veil from her eyes.

He'd had a faded smile on his face that night. "It's a madness in Js," he'd told her. "It's why the wardens and guards are meant to watch us closely when we're in jails or other places with such prisoners. Something breaks in us and we no longer have control when it comes to ending deviant minds."

Eleri had known her mentor too well by then to fall for that. "You were in control. You chose it."

"Yes. Because 45TN's crimes involved children. That's the one thing I'm incapable of forgiving even to the extent of permitting the justice system to deal with them."

Eleri had adopted the same line in the sand . . . and added a number more. And she'd bettered her mentor by becoming expert at inducing death in a way that left no trace of any external involvement.

She had every intention of using those skills on the Sandman. "I'm certain he's here," she said when Adam Garrett didn't respond. "All I need is the time to track him down. After that, you're free to do with me what you will."

The falcon who had once looked at her out of a smiling young man's face today stared at her with the grim visage of a wing leader. His talons weren't out as they'd been in that courtroom, but she knew this man was far more dangerous than the boy she'd first met . . . the one who'd made her wonder for a blip in time whether her destiny wasn't set in stone after all.

"Go," he said at last. "Start your search. I'll find you after I've checked on your information."

Eleri nodded.

But he said, "Wait," when she would've got in the car. "What are the chances he'll strike in Raintree?"

"Low. If he does, he risks compromising his bolt-hole." She hesitated, then shared the rest. "Unless he suffers a catastrophic psychic break, which he shows no signs of doing, I don't think I'll find him because he makes a mistake here—I'll find him because he made mistakes at the other sites that give me clues as to who he is. I just don't know what those mistakes are yet."

JACQUES snarled when Adam told his best friend and most senior wing-second about the visitor in town. "She the liar?" he asked, because Jacques and Adam had been friends since the day they met, and now that Adam's grandmother was gone, Jacques was the only person in the world who knew this story. Or at least most of it.

Adam had never actually told Aria—but she'd been his wing leader as well as his grandmother. She'd known the instant she'd looked at his face in the hallway outside the courtroom. "Ah, Bear," she'd murmured when she caught his gaze on the J-Psy trainee who had, at that point, been standing with her senior outside the courtroom. "What trouble are you getting into now?"

Despite the lightness of the question, her tone had been uneasy... concerned. Because Aria had already understood what it had taken Eleri's betrayal for Adam to comprehend: Psy could not be trusted.

Not even Psy who made their changeling hearts sing.

"She was the junior on the case," Adam said to Jacques today, because what she'd done was bad enough; there was no point in blaming her for something she *hadn't* done. "Around the same age as us."

Jacques's brown eyes didn't soften, the mahogany of his skin stretched taut over thick muscle. "We knew right and wrong at that age."

"Yes, we did." Adam was fully aware that his anger at Eleri was irrational—because he'd always been *more* angry at her than at the now-dead senior J who'd made the actual scan and done the witness broadcast.

He'd expected her to be better. And she'd let him down at a point in his life when he'd been the most wounded, the most vulnerable. The same Eleri who'd offered to tend his cuts with a sweet and unexpected empathy had thrust a stiletto straight into his stupidly soft and unshielded heart.

That she was Psy and could never truly grasp the injury she'd inflicted? Neither man nor falcon cared. Because he'd seen how she'd looked at him the day they'd met, witnessed the glimmer of realization in the hazel that altered color as quickly as Eleri altered loyalties.

Some part of her had *known*.

"You want me to run her out of town?" Jacques walked with him to the edge of the Canyon plateau, the hot desert winds making their wings stir against the inside of their skin as their falcons readied themselves for flight.

"Fuck you," Adam said without altering his tone. "I can run anyone I want out of town."

A wicked grin that came out rarely among strangers but was deeply familiar to Jacques's friends. "I dunno, man. You've always been weird about her."

The other man ran his hand over the dark hair he kept cut close to his skull, the edges shaved with the same precision he showed in his work for the clan. "You raged about her after you got home, and it was only later that I realized she hadn't been the actual J on the case."

Adam shrugged and gave his best friend a partial answer, not able to share the rest even with him. "Maybe it was because she was close to our age. Not as cold or as hard as the older Js—I expected better from her. Expected her to care."

Jacques's smile faded. "That was ten years ago. She still like that?"

"No." Adam couldn't get over the sheer flatness of her emotional response, the complete *lack* of personality. It was a stark contrast to the girl whose pupils had gone huge with shock at a connection that had hit them both without warning . . . and yet she'd stayed, offered him a bandage . . . and looked back to meet his gaze when she was called over by her superior.

What had happened to Eleri Dias in the years in between?

Jacques blew out a breath. "So, why's she here?"

When Adam told him, Jacques frowned. "Her theory makes sense, but we only have her word for it. You going to touch base with your Enforcement friends to verify?"

"Yeah. I'm not about to take her allegations on trust." Once, she could've told him the sky was green and the earth blue, and he'd no doubt have followed along like an infatuated puppy. Adam didn't know how to put limits on his love—he was all in with his family, his friends, his clan.

But Eleri had put paid to that possibility between them with a single act of complicit silence.

"Let's debrief after I get back." Lifting his arms, Jacques stripped off his T-shirt to reveal a chiseled chest brushed with curled dark hair. Over his shoulder draped part of a tattoo that Adam knew covered the left half of his back.

He'd been there when Jacques designed that tat—and when the final DNA-encoded ink was needled into his cells. Adam was no scientist, didn't know how the ink held through the shift, but that it did was unquestioned.

He knew not just because of Jacques, but because of the tattoo he carried on his own left front pectoral, a memory of grief etched in flesh that had, over time, become a reminder of love.

Two falcons side by side, their wings forever stretched in flight.

Adam would never forgive his parents' murder, but he was no longer blinded by it until that was all he remembered of them.

Or he hadn't been.

Until *her*.

"Seriously?" Adam managed to keep his voice light even as his spine threatened to lock, his talons to release. "I do not want to see your pasty butt."

"My butt is a delicious chocolate brown, per any number of admiring lady friends, thank you very much."

As they laughed together with the ease of old friends who'd shifted together many a time, Jacques stripped to the skin and threw his clothes over a nearby rock before shifting into his falcon form.

Like Adam, he was a peregrine, but his feathers tended toward a more intense gray coloration with less of a blue undertone. As for the tattoo, it didn't vanish but was scattered across one wing in a spray of black that gave him a distinct appearance. Ink wasn't always that visible in both forms, but Jacques had a lot of it; the one that had caught Adam's eye today was far from his only one.

After fussing with and settling his wings a couple of times—a pure Jacques trait—WindHaven's second-in-command dropped off the edge of the plateau, his wings opening out in a smooth glide, a falcon at home in the skies.

Adam watched his best friend soar across Raintree.

Shaking off his own need to fly, to just get this energy out, he grabbed the other man's clothes and dropped them in one of the closed bins they had out here for that purpose. The bins were sunk into the earth, with only the lids visible. Once he'd placed the clothes inside, he entered Jacques's name on the digital label so his friend could find his clothes on his return.

No one stopped him on his way back from the plateau, and he deliberately avoided venturing into the section on the right that held a cluster of residences up against the cliff edge.

Today wasn't a day to stop by for a chat with clanmates.

Instead, he entered the internal part of the Canyon, then made his way to his office, where he input the comm code that would connect him to a human friend in Enforcement. The investigative service had a bad rap because it had been controlled and manipulated by Psy for a long time—

not just politically, but through interference with the minds of the humans who made up a large percentage of Enforcement ranks. Unlike changelings, humans had no natural protective shield.

That didn't mean there weren't good people in there, people who wanted justice and worked toward it. Adam's contact had survived unmolested because he'd made certain he didn't get promoted beyond the first rank of detective.

As a result, he was often the "junior" on important cases, even though his experience meant he knew far more than his supervising officers. Since he also didn't care for credit, his senior officers let him do pretty much what he wanted as long as he got the work done.

Today, when the other man answered, it was to showcase a face with countless prison-style tattoos and a large and thick black beard against truly pasty skin. "Undercover?" Adam asked the man four years his senior with whom he'd once played hockey in college. "Or a really bad drunk that left you with permanent reminders?"

Damon's grin was huge, revealing a newly chipped tooth. "You'll have to stay in suspense until the next favor you ask me."

"According to my records, I'm in favor credits." Truth was, the two of them had long ago stopped keeping track.

"My mama always told me to watch out for smooth-talking birds. So, what's happening?"

"You know anything about the Sandman?" Adam gave him the basic facts—including why he was asking the question.

Damon scratched at his upper jaw through the mass of the beard. "I've been on a big drug case the entire time since that kicked off, but a couple of my buddies just got pulled into the task force, so they'll know more.

"I have heard about your J, though. She's got a reputation—a good one. No personality but also no bullshit, and she *always* finds the bastards once she's on the hunt." He scratched the other side of his jaw. "Fucking beard's driving me insane. Anyway, give me a few hours and I'll see what I can scare up."

"Thanks, man," Adam said. "Don't drop your guard on the home stretch."

"No chance. Got a hot date waiting."

"Say hi to Mira for me." Adam had no idea how Damon's relationship with his sweetheart of a wife remained so strong with how often the other man had to disappear into underground worlds, but the two had been married for seven years and counting, so they'd gotten something right.

Just like Adam's parents, he thought as the other man shot him a lazy salute before signing off. Even though Taazbaa' and Cormac Garrett had never felt the pull of the mating bond, they'd been a forever pair, their breaths entwined. Adam had grown up in the warm shadow of that love, their wings spread over him until he'd begun to display a need for independence.

Then they'd taken him flying, taught him the ways of the Diné and of his father's Irish ancestors . . . and set him free. That was the falcon creed. They didn't cage their young or keep them to tightly contained areas—such would be torture to a winged being. Rather, they set boundaries meant to ensure a child's safety, taught their fledglings how to protect themselves in the air, and took them flying often with the family and clan unit when younger.

"Remember, Adam." His father's hand ruffling his hair. "Stay above the safety line. You don't want some idiot kid from school shooting up with a gun, real or meant for sport, and clipping you."

"You've only told me three billion times, Dad."

"You got off easy, then," his sister had interjected in her droll way. "I was at four billion by the time I got to fly solo."

His father's deep laughter, intermingled with his mother's kiss on the cheek, followed by a from-behind hug for a giggling Saoirse. "Just wait until you have a fledgling," she'd threatened her nineteen-year-old daughter, her laugh bringing out the dimple in her right cheek. "I'll be sitting right there with a glass of wine watching you lose your mind as your baby bird flies the nest."

Many years after the sky ceremonies that had set their parents' spirits free, when Adam was in his mid-twenties, Saoirse had told him something that she could only share with an adult little brother, and not the young teen he'd been during the events themselves. They'd been seated at a bonfire on the plateau, and Amir had taken both Malia and Tahir over to roast marshmallows, his arms around the children as he crouched down to their height.

"I was scared when I got pregnant at twenty," Saoirse had murmured, her eyes on her mate and children silhouetted against the firelight. "I mean, it was with my mate, but I was so young. But now, I think it was a gift. Mom and Dad got to meet both my fledglings, and they stood with us the entire way, until we figured out what we were doing."

She'd taken his hand, tears thick in her voice as she said, "I know I'm not Mom or Dad, Bear, but when it's your time, I'll be there for you like they were for me. Amir and I will teach you and your mate all the things Mom and Dad taught us for our fledglings."

Able to feel the weight of her guilt that she'd had the chance to experience something he never would, he'd hugged her close. "Don't be a silly goose, Chirp." A kiss pressed to her curls. "I loved seeing them with Tahir and Malia, loved teasing them as they went from strict parents to grandparents who loved to spoil the babies."

He'd been there when Taazbaa' watched Malia learn to fly, a doting grandmother who'd plied her granddaughter with tiny food treats after each fall and cuddled her until Malia was ready to try again.

None of them had ever imagined that she wouldn't be there by the time her adored "baby Mali" was ready to fly solo . . . or that Cormac wouldn't be around to take Adam for his first adult drink as he'd promised. "You'll be having a Guinness, my lad, else your Irish ancestors will roll in their graves!"

How could either he or Saoirse foresee the nightmare to come, their mom and dad the ones who'd find themselves shot out of the sky?

Chapter 8

The serial perpetrator known as the Sandman is a highly organized killer who (at this point in time) appears to be further refining his skills with every abduction and murder.

The only hint of disorganization (and it is a significant one) is in the timing of his kills—the first two were four months apart, but the third only seven weeks after the second. Should this trend continue, he could strike again in less than a month.

—Working profile on the Sandman, prepared for the joint California-Arizona Sandman Task Force (10 December 2083)

JACQUES HAD INTENDED to fly with no particular destination in mind, but Adam's comments about a possible killer in their territory had him turning east; he wanted to check out something he'd spotted the previous day in the desert. In a hurry to make a meeting with his wing at the time, he'd noted it with the intention of sending a couple of junior soldiers out to check what it was and clear it up if necessary.

From his fleeting glance, it had appeared to be either a dumped vehicle or parts of one. The folks around this area were good about not polluting the landscape, but there remained the occasional idiot who thought to take the cheaper route, never mind what might leach into the soil and from there into the water supply.

But the spot he'd noted would also make an excellent place to *stash* a vehicle, Jacques had realized after he took flight. All but invisible from the air, it was directly off a dirt track that was pretty much unused, but that did eventually lead to a major highway. The specific area wasn't quite a canyon, more a depression in the landscape with a few scraggly trees around, and *there*, an overhang below which a large object glinted metallic under the sun.

After ensuring there was no movement below, he came down to land on the immediate top of the overhang, where he sat and listened for any hint of another presence.

Nothing.

Satisfied, he flew down to land in front of the overhang before peering into the shallow cave beneath with his falcon's piercing vision.

This, thought the human part of his mind, was no dumped vehicle.

While hardly the newest model or in the best outward condition, it was obvious to him that the vehicle was in working order. Similar to the kind of rugged four-wheel drives the clan used to go up and down the Canyon, the tires were high, with an excellent grip, the body one that could handle the harsh desert environment.

Shifting in a cascade of light that was pure pain and brutal ecstasy, he rose from his crouch to look inside the vehicle through the windows, but made sure not to touch anything. If it *was* being used for criminal purposes, the last thing he wanted to do was wipe off or contaminate the evidence.

Though the likelihood was that it was wholly unconnected to murder—could just be a local who liked off-roading in the desert. If that were the case, however, there'd be no reason to leave it out here, exposed to the elements—the overhang was enough to shield it from overhead sight, but not from the desert winds and heat.

Unless, of course, it wasn't registered or had issues that meant it wasn't roadworthy, but the owner considered it plenty good enough to drive around the desert—and had a strong dislike of any kind of authority. Jacques could appreciate that. He didn't exactly like any authority aside from his wing leader's. Many of the humans in Raintree felt the same way.

There was a reason they lived in a town without a mayor.

He spotted nothing much inside except for a crumpled-up wrapper from what might've been an energy bar, and a bottle of water, but that was enough to tell him the vehicle was in current use.

No dust on the dashboard, either.

As for the back, the windows were tinted to such an extent that he couldn't see anything through them. It didn't matter. He had enough to run the car, find out to whom it belonged.

He shifted back into falcon form.

As always, his vision became even sharper, his heartbeat faster, his sense of himself expanding and contracting at the same time. He was now closer to the ground than in his human form, but the span of his presence was wider, his wings bigger than his arms. He took off with the raptor part of him at the forefront of his consciousness, his aim to head directly back to the Canyon.

Despite his focus on his destination, however, he never lost sight of his surroundings—he'd been a scout for the clan in his younger years, had excellent peripheral senses and reflexes—so he saw the shiny car parked on the side of the road a bare five-minute drive from the hidden vehicle. Spotted, too, the person next to it.

That person lifted their arm in a wave, and Jacques dipped his wing in reply. When the individual waved him urgently closer, he went lower. He had no reason not to . . . and no reason to expect that the next thing the person raised would be a weapon. He was fast, he was trained, and he was strong. He managed to turn enough that the first shot from the laser weapon barely singed his wing.

But he was also a creature of the air who'd been lured too close to the ground. The second shot pierced his torso while he was still climbing—even as he released a warning cry to his clan. Agony exploded through his body, but some part of him was thinking through the pain, and that part attempted to shift.

He'd break a few bones if he fell from this height, but he wouldn't die—and the thin blade of laser weaponry would injure far less integral organs in his human body than in his falcon self.

The third bolt of icy fire caught him mid-shift.

He fell hard enough to send a storm of dust into the air, felt his heart stutter . . . and heard the cries of falcons responding from a distance.

The car on the road started up.

The coward who'd shot him, the imposter in the skin of one trusted, was running away. Too late. Jacques had seen them.

Jacques would . . .

The thought slipped out of his grasp even as he attempted to hold on to it, the taste of wet iron filling his mouth.

The last thing he saw was red spreading on the ground in front of him.

Chapter 9

The perpetrator is careful not to leave any traces, on the victims or otherwise. DNA, prints, other physical evidence findings have all so far been negative. The only lead we have is the method of murder: it requires telepathic ability.

—Sandman Task Force briefing (2 October 2083)

ADAM'S ENTIRE BODY jolted, his blood bond with Jacques shrieking with the kind of pain that could only mean a mortal wound.

"Jacques!" He was running almost before he'd processed the primal surge, was still in stride as he cleared the lip of the exit into the Canyon, and shifted while in his clothes. They disintegrated away, so much fine dust under the force of the act that turned a changeling into their other self.

Clanmates who'd been near him when he sensed Jacques fall flew out behind him.

His falcon called out, got no reply from his best friend—but caught the faint ripple of panicked cries across the skies. His clanmates stayed silent so those distant cries could be heard. And those falcons, the ones closer to Jacques, were relaying back that this was the worst of the worst.

Jacques, big and moody and loyal to the bone, was down.

Adam knew he didn't have to worry about contacting Naia—he'd felt WindHaven's healer take to the air right after him, and one of her team would already be racing down the Canyon road in a vehicle fully equipped to function as an ambulance.

Naia would've grabbed a locator beacon from the plateau after she shifted; it'd allow the person on the ground to track her location even if they lost sight of her or of Adam. He didn't wait for her—his blood bond with Jacques might mean Adam could hold him to the world long enough for Naia to help him.

His wings ached with the speed of his flight, but he still caught a glimpse of a lone figure in black looking up at him from the parking lot of the only diner in Raintree, her hand held up to shade her eyes as she watched him and others streak across the sky.

Then he'd left her and the town behind, was out in the desert.

The blood bond wasn't a perfect homing beacon, couldn't lead him directly to injured clanmates, but it could give him a direction—and in this case, that was all he needed. Because others, who'd been closer when Jacques went down had heard his cry for help, found him; two of the clan circled above the location, giving Adam aerial notice that he'd arrived at the right place.

A third stood guard beside Jacques's mangled body.

Adam landed hard in his falcon form before shifting into his human one, while the clanmate who'd stood sentinel lifted off to help guard the area. Old memories threatened to crowd his mind, a cold wind. He hadn't witnessed his parents' murder, but he'd seen the pictures taken by the cops after breaking into his grandmother's files, and those images had haunted him every time he closed his eyes for years.

Funnily enough, his own plummet from the sky after being shot in DarkRiver territory had barely made an impact on his psyche. Likely because his shooters—deluded though they'd been—had been fighting a kind of war. They'd been on the wrong side of it, but they hadn't known that. Their actions hadn't been done with any sense of malice toward him; he'd just been collateral damage.

His parents' murder, in contrast, had been all about malice.

Adam shut down the unraveling past with a single grim command. Because his parents were gone; the best friend who'd run whooping through the Canyon with him after they escaped the crèche might yet make it.

"Fuck, Jacques," he said as he took in the other man's body.

One arm was a crumpled and broken wing, the other a human arm with the palm flat on the ground. Part of his body was feathered, while his right leg had been truncated at midthigh but wasn't bleeding. Not torn off. Just not there.

One side of his face was falcon, the other human.

Like all changelings, Adam had heard horror stories of changelings frozen mid-shift, but he'd never seen anything like this. It didn't matter. Nothing mattered but the gaping holes in Jacques's body. The edges bore the telltale burns of high-impact lasers, and when Adam turned his friend over with care, he saw that the main injury went from one side of Jacques's body to the other in a sideways angle.

Adam sucked in a sharp breath.

Had whoever shot Jacques hit his heart?

He couldn't tell, not with the carnage, but the blood bond hadn't snapped, so Jacques was holding on. Adam did the only thing he could and, taking his best friend's hand, poured the clan's energy into the other man, giving him the raw fuel to cling to life. "I've got you, J."

Naia landed next to him with none of her usual grace and dropped the locator beacon to the side before she shifted. Though she was as calm and competent as always while she worked to heal Jacques, he could feel the depth of her pain. Healers were tough and stubborn enough to keep on going until they literally dropped where they stood, but they also had the softest hearts in the clan.

"Something's wrong," she said while their clanmates continued to keep watch in the air.

"Talk to me."

"The physical injuries are bad enough, but I think the worst blow caught him mid-shift." Naia's fingers were gentle on Jacques's twisted body, the heat of her healing energy a pulse Adam could feel through the blood bond.

"We've discussed this among the healer network"—her tone was absent, tight, her focus on Jacques—"and while there have been cases over the years of a changeling being hurt mid-shift, the results have either been fatal at once, or a misforming that was immediately rectified by another shift. I've never heard of a case where a changeling ended up locked in a partial shift."

Sweat beaded along Adam's spine and it had nothing to do with the climate. "His brain," he said, "did it shift either way?" Either falcon or human and Jacques might come out of it okay—as long as he had a functioning brain that Adam or Naia could reach, they could nudge him to complete the shift one way or the other.

But Naia pressed her lips together and shook her head. "I can't reach him with my healer senses, can't tell if he's there at all." A look at him out of eyes gone falcon, the deep brown ringed by yellow. "Adam, he's breathing but I can't tell if he's *in there*."

Adam had prepared for anything—a broken back, a pierced heart, collapsed lungs, even worse injuries—but he'd never even allowed himself to consider that Jacques's brain, that intelligent, surly, and unique organ, might be permanently damaged.

"Wake the hell up, you asshole," he gritted out as he lifted Jacques into his arms after Naia gave him the go-ahead.

The other man didn't weigh anywhere near what he should have; the shift did weird things to mass, with their human bodies far heavier than their falcon forms. Jacques's lightness when he was at least seventy-five percent human right now was another indication that things had gone wrong on the cellular level.

The emergency medical vehicle screeched to a halt near them just then. Dust coated its olive green paint job, the ambulance a converted and extended four-wheel drive that could deal with their environment, especially the more challenging unpaved roads.

Adam carried his badly wounded—dying—friend to it, placed him gently inside. Naia climbed in afterward, and Adam shut the door.

As the vehicle raced off, he ordered those who remained to search the area. "All indications are that he was shot while at low altitude—he wouldn't have gone that low without reason." Jacques far preferred to stay high, ride the air currents. "We need to find out what attracted his attention."

"I've got it, Adam," Dahlia said, grim-eyed and nothing at all like the hungover woman he'd run into that morning. "You take care of Jacques."

Adam shifted on her statement and was soon shadowing the ambulance. As wing leader, he could direct energy to both Naia and Jacques, the clan filling him up with unending generosity.

Together they would fight for their fallen.

ELERI had known something was up the instant she saw the cadre of falcons flying in a single direction, the force of their intent clear. Her eyes had been drawn to one particular falcon—he had the distinctive coloring of a peregrine, but he was bigger and faster than the other peregrines on his tail.

She was certain that was Adam Garrett.

Instinct again, but she'd long given up pretending that that wasn't one of her driving forces.

She'd also noticed one other falcon, but only because it hadn't been a peregrine. Someone in Adam's clan was a gyrfalcon, the biggest species of falcon. But even that powerful bird couldn't keep up with Adam.

The subject of the falcons' flight was the topic of conversation between the two officers present in the Enforcement station when she finally managed to find it open. She'd come by prior to her visit to the local diner, only to find it deserted.

"Sorry about that," Detective Rex Beaufort said after she'd introduced herself and told him why she was in town. "We have an admin but she's out sick." Older, with lines feathering the corners of his eyes, his cheekbones high and flat and his skin holding coppery tones akin to Adam's, he added, "Look, I won't think to tell you your job, but Raintree and a serial killer? I can't see it."

His younger colleague, Jocasta Whitten—a petite Black woman with her thinly braided hair worn in a bun—nodded. "Biggest excitement we usually have is when one of the kids manages to steal Donny's prized muscle car and take it for a joyride."

The phone on the desk rang right then and she went to grab it. Eleri heard her say, "Deputy Whitten, Raintree station."

"You don't mind if I investigate, however?" Eleri clarified, because having the cooperation of the local authorities was always helpful.

"Can't see any problems with it, but you'll have to talk to the chief when he gets back—he's out of—" Beaufort broke off as Deputy Whitten's voice became clipped and urgent.

"Where? Shit. We're on our way." Hanging up, she looked over, her pupils huge against the brown of her irises. "Someone shot down Jacques. Injuries might be fatal. Falcons have him, are out at the site."

Beaufort's face turned grim. "A kid acting stupid with their parent's gun?"

"High-powered laser. Not a toy. And multiple hits."

"Shooter's as good as dead if Adam finds them." A sharp look at Eleri.

"I work with Enforcement," she said. "I understand confidentiality. Is there anything I can do to assist? I'm used to dealing with complex scenes." And she owed Adam, would always owe him.

A speaking glance between the two cops before the older one said, "Follow us to the site. Whitten can run your credentials on the way."

Two minutes later, as Eleri drove out behind the officers who were obviously shell-shocked at the violence despite their attempt to act professional, she considered the odds of this being unconnected to her presence in Raintree. It seemed an unusual coincidence that a falcon would be intentionally shot down right after she'd arrived in town on the trail of a murderer.

No. She internally frowned. It didn't make sense.

Prior to her conversation with Beaufort and Whitten, only Adam had known the reason for her presence. Everyone else she'd spoken to was under the impression that she was working a decades-old cold case.

Even if the killer had seen and recognized her in the short time that she'd been in Raintree, it was no reason for him to panic. The personality type that found amusement in sending her those letters would be exhilarated at the chance to play games with her in person.

And shooting wasn't the Sandman's style.

His style was terror doled out over days, the final murder a fatal and deeply personal assault to the brain. Guns were too long-distance a weapon for a man who found pleasure in locking eyes with his victim as he pulverized her brain.

Chapter 10

Today, I watched Adam go hug Saoirse because she was sad over a fight with her friend. He gave her his favorite cookie and just stayed tucked against her until she started to feel better.

He's so like Cormac. Or as you called him when I first brought him home—my wild Irish boy. Huge hearts both of them, no boundaries in how they love.

—Letter from Taazbaa' Garrett to Aria (27 March 2064)

NAIA WORKED ON Jacques through the afternoon and deep into the night, but while she managed to stabilize his body, it left Jacques hooked up to multiple machines.

"I've got faint signs of brain activity," she said when Adam forced her to stop, her exhaustion so great that to allow her to go on would have been a dereliction of his duty as wing leader.

"I can't see it." Adam had enough familiarity with the machines to be able to read them on a basic level, and right now, the brain scan was a deadly blank.

"Here." Naia zoomed in to the most rudimentary of the graphical readings, and yes, there they were—tiny spikes and blips.

Adam's gut had been a knot since the instant they'd found Jacques;

now it twisted with harsh physical pain. He didn't say anything to Naia, however. It was obvious that she needed this minuscule bit of hope . . . even if he knew it wasn't anything on which she could base that hope.

That reading? It could be nothing but the final agonal pulses of a dying brain.

Adam had no idea what being trapped mid-shift while badly wounded did to a brain, but he knew it couldn't be good. Adam couldn't even *feel* Jacques through the blood bond any longer, though the bond hadn't completely severed.

The awareness had begun to fade seconds after he landed beside Jacques, as if his best friend had started to let go once under his wing leader's watch—only Jacques wasn't the kind to *let* go. He was a stubborn fucker. So it hadn't been a choice. If Jacques could've hung on, he would have.

Adam said none of that to Naia, didn't even allow a hint of his fear to seep through as he nudged her to the small room in the infirmary that she'd set up with a bed. There was no point in fighting to take her to her actual suite—Naia wouldn't go, not with Jacques in such a critical state.

"Kavi is here to watch over him," he reminded her when she hesitated on the way out of the patient room. "Amir is going to keep her company—remember, he also has paramedic training, so he can help her if she needs it."

Naia didn't move.

"We both need to sleep," he added, then threw in a dose of guilt to force her hand. "I can't rest until you do."

That did it. He made sure she didn't stop again, not even to give her nurse further instructions. Not only was Kavita Roshan highly experienced—she'd been Naia's right hand for years—she was currently in the second year of a study plan that meant she had begun to take over a number of the more routine procedures from Naia.

Kavi helped Adam by slipping out of sight when she saw them emerge from Jacques's room, while Amir stayed in sight. "Kavi and I will make sure he's never alone," the wing commander promised. "Sleep so you can help him when you wake."

Bleary-eyed, her body trembling, Naia just nodded and was soon lying in the bed. She was asleep by the time Adam covered her with a blanket, but deep lines marked her forehead, her hands were clenched tight under her head, and the normally rich cream hue of her skin held a grayish pallor.

Sitting down on the edge of the bed, he stroked her hair and leaned down to press a kiss to her cheek. "Rest. Your clan watches over Jacques. We need you whole and healthy." He kept up the gentle strokes, using skin privileges to reach the most primal core of her, the part that was of the falcon within and that accepted its wing leader's word as law.

Natural falcons didn't act the same way, were often solitary flyers, but changelings weren't the same as their wild brethren. As with feline changelings, their human halves changed the equation, made them crave community.

Healers were the most community-minded of them all, the softest, and apt to wear themselves down to the bone to care for their clanmates. That was why wing leaders were so hyper-protective of their healers—Adam included. As far as he was concerned, Naia had no self-protective instincts at all.

Amir was waiting outside when Adam left Naia—after she finally fell into a sleep deep enough to be restful. "Kavi is with Jacques," his brother-in-law said. "No other patients in the infirmary right now, so he has our full attention. If Kavi has to deal with anything, I'll step in. We won't leave him alone." An attempt at a smile. "He might wake up out of plain irritation—you know how he scowls when we drag him to social events."

Neither one of them laughed, the idea of Jacques's scowl being missing from future parties one neither of them could face. "Wake me if anything happens."

A quick nod. "But you have to rest—you can't be so worn-out that you crash if Naia needs to draw more energy from you."

Adam nodded; Amir was right. The energy transfer would suffer a catastrophic glitch if Adam's body just couldn't take it anymore. It was what his grandmother had feared most as she began to age—and why she'd urged Adam to take on the mantle long before her death.

He'd refused that, because no one wanted Aria as anything but the leader of WindHaven, but he *had* agreed that Naia—already Wind-Haven's healer at the time—would monitor her blood bond with Aria to ensure no possibility of a delay in an emergency.

"That's our deal, kiddo." His grandmother's thin but strong fingers against his jaw. "If the bond begins to flicker, you step into position as wing leader."

Truth was that Aria should've still been alive. Yes, she'd given birth to Adam's mother at forty-five, but she'd still only been a hundred at her death. Most changelings of her generation were healthy and strong for another two, even three decades.

"Losing her daughter and the son-in-law she adored wounded her to the core," his mother's best friend, Jenesse, had said to Adam after the clan scattered Aria's ashes to the winds. "Her heart was broken, as was your grandfather's. They kept going because she knew her duty as wing leader—and he would never abandon her to that duty alone."

Adam's grandfather, Luis, had been a man as patient and calm as Aria was a storm force. He'd loved her with a quiet devotion to his last breath—and he'd stood by her through all the seasons of life, as he'd stood by Adam and Saoirse . . . until his heart just couldn't take it anymore. He'd gone to sleep one day and never woken.

"But duty alone wouldn't have kept either Aria or Luis here so many years," Jenesse had added. "That was you and Saoirse and those babies of Saoirse's. I think if Luis hadn't passed away, Aria would have fought on, but losing him? It was too much, Adam. Even for that powerful, generous heart that sheltered WindHaven for so very long."

Adam had known that, his bond with his grandmother one that wouldn't permit her to go without giving him warning, but hearing Jenesse speak the words had fractured his heart all the same.

The night after his grandmother's funeral, Jacques had sat with Adam for hours on a remote plateau while the stars glittered above. As those stars faded into the coming dawn, he'd clapped Adam on the shoulder, and said, "For life, Adam. The two of us. To the end."

The memory of Jacques's deep voice meshed with that of his mother.

Just wait until you have a fledgling. I'll be sitting right there with a glass of wine watching you lose your mind as your baby bird flies the nest.

Adam had lost too many people. He couldn't bear to lose his best friend, too.

ELERI couldn't sleep.

Her sleepless nights had begun to increase over the past weeks, though she wasn't as bad as Bram and could still snatch a couple of hours here and there without medicinal assistance.

Today, she got up, showered, and dressed, though it was only four in the morning. No point in pretending she might fall back asleep—she wouldn't, not given the message that had been waiting for her when she returned from the site of the falcon shooting.

Eleri, you received another letter from the Sandman. Sent to the task force HQ as usual. We're processing it now, but I'm attaching a scan for you. —Tim

Senior detective Tim Xiao had worked with her many times over the years, their relationship built on mutual respect, but she knew that even he thought she was going off the rails with her obsession with Raintree.

He'd said so to her face.

It had, she knew, been an attempt to help. Tim didn't want her to tank her career. But Tim, for all his experience, was human and had no comprehension of what happened to Js, why they tended to "retire" so early and vanish off the face of the planet.

Eleri didn't intend to educate him.

He was a good cop, would've been a good friend to her if she'd had the capacity for friendship any longer. There was no point in bringing him into her hell—better he think she'd just "lost the plot," as he'd put it, than that he realize this was the last throw of the dice for her.

Eleri had no need to protect a future career.

Once dressed, she made herself a glass of nutrients because her personal comm device had a flashing alarm that told her she'd missed two doses. It tasted like nothing, and she had no reaction to that, either.

At times, a distant part of her brain tried to scream, to tell her that she should be angry about her utter lack of response to the world. But that part was so deeply muffled by the wall of numbness induced by multiple reconditionings that she was barely even aware of it.

"I envy you sometimes," Saffron had said once. "That you've disassociated to that degree. The rage that burns in me . . . I'll go insane before I ever hit Exposure."

She'd shaken her head almost immediately afterward, the intense red of her hair a shock of color against the gray winter's day. "I'm sorry. I shouldn't have said that. It must be terrible for you, to see our people experiencing life without emotional chains only to be unable to participate in it."

Eleri hadn't had the words to tell Saffron that she hadn't been offended by the other J's words. It *was* easier to live this life if she couldn't feel the pain of grief at all she'd lost before she'd even had it.

My name is Adam.

Prior to the numbness, their encounter had haunted her. Not only what had happened in the courtroom, but what had taken place in the hallway earlier that morning. The boy she'd met, the open smile he'd given her, the way her entire being had resonated with him on a psychic frequency of which she'd never previously been aware . . . the dreams she'd dared nurture for a heartbeat in time.

Those dreams were gone, buried with her ability to feel.

Nutrients finished, she sat down in a chair that she'd moved so it faced the hotel door and pulled up the latest letter on her secured organizer. It had been sent seven days prior to her arrival in Raintree, an actual physical letter like all the others, the prepaid envelope dropped into a postbox across the border in California.

They'd all been like that, the letters routed to the task force office from different cities and towns in California. Though such postboxes were no longer as popular as they'd once been, they weren't rare, either, used as they were mostly for dropping off prepaid packages.

Due to centralization when the volume of physical mail dropped below a certain threshold half a century earlier, there was no way to track a letter back to the actual box in which it had been posted, not after it ended up in the sorting center for that region, but Eleri and the task force had tried nonetheless. And failed.

A resident of Raintree could reach the closest California postbox within ninety minutes. Push it an hour further, and their choices expanded many times over. There was no way to put all of them under surveillance, but Eleri had paid out of pocket to place subtle computronic surveillance on the three closest boxes.

She'd already gone over all the footage from the relevant time, with a wide window on either side, and come up with no one with a link to Raintree. The Sandman must've driven deeper into the state to send the letter.

She looked down, began to read.

My dearest Eleri,

It's been too long since we conversed—and I do think of it as a conversation. After all, you always respond to my letters. This time, however, no response is required. I haven't chosen a new sleeping beauty yet; I just missed you, wanted to drop you a note.

I thought I'd tell you about my work. The media is full of that profiler bleating on about how I'm a drifter who picks up odd jobs. I'd have strangled him by now if I was you. He has annoying piggy eyes and I can just imagine how they'd bulge out of his head as I squeezed and squeezed.

I'm no drifter. I have a home, family who love me, even have neighbors who invite me over for drinks. I'm good at my job, considered an asset by my team. Just like you, Eleri. We have that in common—we both work hard, though I admit I put more energy into my passion. As you put your energy into me.

We'll talk again soon. I hope one day, face-to-face.

With love,
The Sandman

Eleri moved on to study the "first glance" notes of their profiler on this letter and found she agreed with them for the most part. The task force profiler was a Psy woman of seventy who never appeared in the media, the one with "annoying piggy eyes" a talking-head academic whom Tim had already reached out to warn.

"He's angry at what he sees as being denigrated," the task force profiler had written, "but that doesn't mean he isn't Psy. He's clearly always been a maladaptive personality, so none of the norms of our race can be expected to apply. And the method of the Sandman murders makes the point moot regardless.

"As for his claims about his work and general life, none of that can be taken at face value. He is an excellent liar given that he's escaped detection this long. My previous profile of a male in his twenties or early thirties who has a stable job that allows him at least some flexibility, and no wife or children, still applies. He could not move as freely otherwise.

"However, it appears his obsession with Specialist Eleri Dias has grown in intensity. I strongly suggest a protective detail for her."

Tim hadn't even bothered to raise the latter option—they'd had this discussion and he wasn't technically her superior, couldn't order her to work under protection. Sophia wouldn't step in on that point, either; she might argue against Eleri's desire to spend her time in the shadow of evil, but she understood Eleri's need for freedom as only another J could.

Leaving the organizer on the desk, Eleri got up and walked out the front door to stand in the middle of the parking lot. The world was silent and cold, the moon a luminous globe high above . . . and she could just glimpse the edge of the Canyon from this position. No wings flew out of it, no lights glowed in the small section she could see.

What would my life be like now if I'd spoken up that day in the courtroom?

Chapter 11

Mating is a complex subject on which changelings are reticent to speak with outsiders, more so in the aftermath of the catastrophic violence in the recent past. And even those willing to speak on the subject a minor amount will shut down when asked about rumors of mates who ended up on opposite sides of the battle lines during the wars.

—*The Traveler's Guide to Changelings* (1st edition, 1836)

FOUR HOURS AFTER convincing Naia to go to bed, Adam woke from a dreamless sleep of his own. He'd forced himself into it—he couldn't feed their healer energy if he was out of it himself. And being wing leader didn't allow for such niceties as emotional exhaustion. Adam functioned because he *had* to function.

Since Amir hadn't woken him, it meant nothing had changed.

Wanting to rage at the world, he got ready for the day though it was still pitch-dark outside, then went to track down one of his senior people who was awake. Someone would be, not only because that was how a clan functioned, with the watch never down, but also because they'd work around the clock until they found the person who'd dared hurt one of their own.

He ran into Saoirse a minute later.

She took one look at him and enfolded him in her arms, the springy curls of her hair a familiar brush against his cheek. And though he was the most powerful person in the clan, for a moment, he allowed himself to be nothing but Saoirse's little brother, whom she'd bossed around and protected in equal measure throughout his childhood. Her hold was warm and strong like their mother's, the scent of her a thing of comfort.

"You off to work?" he asked when they drew apart, having noted that she'd already showered and dressed for the day.

"No, I'm going to the kitchen to grab coffee and snacks for Amir and Kavi." Worry in the familiar tawny brown of her eyes. "I'll stay put and get our fledglings to school—I have a feeling they'll want to fly or drive down with Mom today. They love Jacques."

"Yeah." Jacques was a champion at putting on a grim face, but the fact that the kids followed him around just the same told the true story of his nature. Adam had seen his gruff friend sit down in a tiny chair across from a five-year-old Malia after Adam's niece invited them both for teatime with her plushies.

Now he tugged on one of his sister's curls, the act one he'd done since he'd been that little brother who wanted to annoy his much older and cooler big sister. "How about you, Chirp?" With Jacques and Adam having been friends since crèche days, she treated him as another little brother.

A hard swallow. "Telling myself he's stubborn and will make it out of pure contrariness."

It was Adam's turn to hold her, press a kiss to her curls as he'd done to Malia only yesterday . . . and a lifetime ago. Before they parted, his big sister said, "You want me to get you coffee and snacks, too, Bear?"

Jacques would've grinned at that sisterly offer—then demanded his own snacks. "No, I think I'll grab something after I get an update on the situation."

"I saw Dahlia in her office."

"Thanks."

"You take care, little brother, or I'll go big sis on your ass and make you sit down for a proper meal."

He found Dahlia where Saoirse had last spotted her—she was pacing the space, which had a direct exit to the Canyon—while she stared at a large wall screen on which he saw a report from local Enforcement, along with information on everything their own people had found.

Dressed in khaki pants and an olive green tee that she'd tucked into them, she'd scraped her hair off her face into a tight ponytail. Multiple cups of half-drunk coffee sat on her desk.

"DeeDee," he said, the nickname a young Jacques had given her when they'd learned her last name was Dehlavi rolling off his tongue before he could think better of it.

She flinched.

"Shit. Sorry."

Dahlia waved it off. "No, it's fine. I'd do anything to hear him call me DeeDee while turning down yet another invitation to a party." A rough inhale. "You want a recap?"

"Yeah. What've we got?"

"Not fucking much," Dahlia spit out. "Signs a vehicle was parked toward the end of the nearest road, but the tire impressions were smudged and, from what we could tell, could fit half the vehicles in the region anyway. Enforcement forensics took a print, will run it, but I don't hold out any hope—Beaufort also pointed out that it hasn't rained for a while; print could've been there for days."

"Not much cause to be on that road. It dead-ends in the desert."

Dahlia nodded. "Yeah, I'm with you—prints have to be the shooter's." Folding her arms, she turned her attention back to the screen as Adam came around to stand beside her. "I *can* confirm the shooter didn't leave Raintree. We overflew the area in every direction for miles as soon as Jacques was away and only saw three people heading out of town.

"One was Jerry, on his usual delivery route—no time in there to fit in a detour, and the other a young Psy couple heading off to the airport.

I had a quiet word with their neighbors—the two were definitely at home at the time of the shooting. On the off chance that the fucker had just hunkered down until we lost interest, I've kept up the sweeps, and we're making note of every vehicle that's heading out."

"What's this?" He tapped an image of a vehicle that looked like the kind of old runaround a local might keep for desert excursions.

"I think this is what got Jacques hurt." Dahlia's expression was grim; she and Jacques weren't close, not like Adam and the other man, but they were clan through and through, would go to the wire for each other.

"We located it not far on the wing from where Jacques went down," she continued. "Unregistered for the past two years—Beaufort already tracked down the previous owner, and he's a hundred-year-old currently enjoying retired life in Fiji. Was excited to get a call from Enforcement and very happy to talk.

"Says he sold the car at a vehicle market and that the buyer was a 'nice young man' who promised to take care of all the paperwork. The buyer did exactly that in the sense that the previous owner is no longer responsible for it, but he never registered it under his own name. Deal was done in cash."

"Any description on the buyer?"

Lips pursed tight, Dahlia shook her head. "Owner sold it because he was having vision problems. Fixed now, but at the time, he could 'barely see beyond his own foot'—and per Beaufort, that's a direct quote."

Adam liked the detective, but he'd have felt better if Chief Cross had been handling the investigation. The older man had come into the position while Aria was wing leader, so Adam had known him for two decades, while Beaufort had only moved to Raintree two years prior, after accepting the open position on the small force.

"That's not a coincidence—the buyer going for a seller with vision issues," Adam murmured. "Someone planned this out." And the fact that he'd done it two years ago? *Fuck.*

An image of Eleri flashed to the forefront of his mind, her changeable gaze emotionless as she talked to him about a serial killer who might be using Raintree as a base.

Dahlia folded her arms across her chest. "A drug thing? Everyone knows we don't put up with that shit, but there's always some idiot who wants to try."

"Could be, but there's another possibility." He told her about Eleri's theory, having always intended to bring her into the loop. If Jacques hadn't been shot, the three of them would've had a meeting last night to touch base—Adam only had two wing-seconds, a small number in comparison to the seconds who reported to the SnowDancer alpha across the border, but SnowDancer was massive in size when compared to WindHaven.

The reason the wolves as well as the leopards had allied with them had nothing to do with the size of their clan, and everything to do with their cleverness at having held their territory for centuries, including through the Territorial Wars, melded with how far Adam's people flew, their range vast.

WindHaven was not only one of the oldest clans in the entire country, it had a seamless record of transition from one wing leader to another, with no battles for succession. It wasn't about blood, either, his and Aria's relationship an anomaly; it was a thing of pride to support the clan rather than chance tearing it apart, a fierce loyalty born of their very size.

The sum of it all had put them on equal footing when it came to initial negotiations.

As for him, Dahlia, and Jacques, the three of them worked as a streamlined unit with support from their senior wing commanders. Naia was welcome to sit in on any and all meetings, her rank in the clan akin to Dahlia and Jacques's.

Now his sole remaining wing-second just stared at him, her dark eyes huge against the cream-toned skin she'd inherited from her Iranian mother—who'd also passed on that white streak in her hair. Dahlia's Diné father had been known to joke that his mate had cloned herself to create their fledgling, but he'd given Dahlia her height and physical strength.

"Seriously?" she said at last. "Well, shit."

"Make sure Enforcement orders a full sweep on that vehicle. If he's left anything of himself in there, I want it."

"I already got Beaufort to put in that order," Dahlia said. "Stayed with the vehicle until the forensic crew came, did the site sweep, then loaded up the vehicle. Spoke to the head forensic technician myself—she's solid."

Adam thrust a hand through his hair. "Sorry, D. I should've known you would."

"We're all on edge." She leaned slightly into him, about as far as this new, prickly Dahlia would go toward asking for affection from her wing leader.

He wrapped his arms around her, her height so close to his own that he could press his cheek to hers. "He's tough."

"Bastards always are." Her voice was thick. "You know he found me even after I told everyone to leave me alone the night of my non-wedding? I'd have broken down if it was you, just collapsed into you and sobbed like a fledgling, and I'd have hated that."

"I get it." He stroked her back, understanding her to the core—because he'd cried in Aria's arms even when he'd been able to stand strong against all others. But she'd been older, and his grandmother, the emotional balance between them far different from his relationship with his ferociously independent wing-second. "I'm glad he tracked you down, that you weren't alone that night."

"Because it was Jacques, I got pissed. I yelled at him to fuck the hell off—and he just egged me on with that smirk he gets when he's trying to be irritating. Like he knew I needed to rage at a target tough enough to take me on.

"After I was exhausted from fighting with him, he got me drunk. Tequila shots followed by disgusting rum chasers, all while I was in my newly shortened wedding gown."

"Jacques never told me about that," Adam said.

Which was just like his friend—he pretended not to care, did kind things, and never spoke about it. "Did you want to be drunk?"

"Hell yes," she muttered. "Don't know how he found me in that no-name dive bar, though. Accused him of having a tracker on me—asshole told me he just followed the trail of sparkles from my wedding gown." A sniff against Adam's ear. "He's such a shit and I don't want him to be hurt, Adam."

"I know, D." His own voice was pure grit, his eyes hot.

The two of them just stood there, holding each other for several minutes before they separated. "You should get some rest now that I'm up," he told her. "We'll have to trade off for the duration while Jacques is down, pull in Amir and Maraea to cover some of the duties."

Dahlia nodded, stubborn but not illogical. "What are you going to do?"

"Tap my contacts in Raintree, see if they've heard anything. I think the shooting was done in panic, so there's a chance he made a mistake." No rational person would've called a vengeance-bound WindHaven down on their heads.

Falcons did not let go. The man who'd murdered Taazbaa' and Cormac Garrett had learned that on a cold fall day when he'd been driving along a lonely highway far from falcon territory, and far, he'd believed, from any kind of justice.

He'd been wrong.

His bones now lay scattered across the bottom of the ocean, the shattered pieces of him carried there on the wing by a clan of falcons who had never, ever forgotten. And a son who had vowed vengeance the day the justice system—and the woman who should've been his everything—let him down.

Today, he didn't wait till dawn to make his calls. The people to whom he needed to talk were more comfortable in the dark hours. Leaving Dahlia to finish up before she got some shut-eye, he returned to his room and stood in the maw of the exit into the Canyon to touch base with his contacts.

The first two on his list didn't have the best reputations. One was a drunk, the other barely talked to anyone, but when push came to shove, they fell on the side of good. Each had a reason for being how they were, personal pain they handled without involving others. One happened to be ex-Enforcement from Chicago, the other a fucking actual spook from a major international organization who'd burned out.

They watched and noticed things without anyone ever seeing them.

The world outside was still dark by the time he finished talking to them—both had already heard about Jacques but had nothing to report as yet. Knowing they'd message him if they picked up anything, he looked down at the town. It remained draped in darkness but for the odd light—like the one from the bakery, where Geraldine and her wife of multiple decades would already be hard at work.

A single light burned at the Enforcement station, too. Probably one of the two deputies: Jocasta Whitten or John Hendricks. The JJs, the two called themselves, both young enough that the shine hadn't rubbed off yet.

Adam's eyes went back to the inn, to the wing where he knew Eleri had been assigned a room, but the tree canopy blocked his view of that spot, and right now, despite his compulsion to speak to her—a compulsion that he fucking *hated*—her knowledge was background, not fresh.

He made another call.

"Sally," he said when a woman with a throaty voice answered the phone after a few rings.

"Adam, I heard," said the proprietor of the Dewdrop Diner—and a woman who was always awake at this early hour because that was when her first customers began to drift in. The long-haul truckers about to start their journeys, the business types heading out of town, folks who'd been out partying a little too late and desperately needed food. "How is he?"

"Not good," Adam said, because Sally was a friend of the clan from way back when she'd gone to school with Adam's mother. "Have you heard anything?"

"I figure you already know about the stranger—the J?"

"Yeah."

"Not that she seemed suspicious. She said she's looking into a cold case when I asked, and I saw her with Beaufort and Whitten yesterday coming back from the site of Jacques's shooting, so I figure she's legit."

Adam frowned; he should've realized Eleri would find a way to look at the scene. She might be shit at justice, but as Damon had confirmed, she was damn good at working with cops to hunt killers. "Nothing else?"

"Nothing on who might've done it, but John Hendricks was just in here to grab a coffee and mentioned the chief flew in late last night, cut his trip short as soon as he heard about Jacques. Drove home from the airport straightaway."

That drive was a good two hours, so the chief would've arrived in Raintree after Adam crashed. "Thanks, Sally."

"No need for that," she said gruffly. "I'll call you if I pick up anything else."

Adam glanced at the time after Sally hung up and figured that despite his late night, Chief Cross would be up and at work. The man was a good cop, one who'd be angry at what had taken place in his town.

Adam decided to go see him, but first he looked in on the infirmary.

"She's still sleeping," Amir told him when he asked about Naia. "And Jacques . . . no change. Kavi is in there with him taking readings." Shadows lined his eyes. "I've held off all visitors. Saoirse also put out the word."

"Good." Jacques wouldn't want to be seen this way.

But that wasn't what had Adam's gut in knots.

"If I get injured and there's no hope," Jacques had said one night as they sat at the local bar nursing beers, "I don't want a parade of visitors and I especially don't want to be kept artificially alive. Pull the plug, scatter me into the mountain sky."

"What brought this on?" Adam had asked.

"Just got word from my kid sister about the passing of someone I got to be friends with when we'd fly to visit my father's clan. His family couldn't let go, kept him alive for fucking months. Rick would've hated that. So you promise me, Adam. If I'm that badly messed up, you make sure I get to fly."

Adam's chest grew tight. *I'll keep my promise, Jacques. Just let me exhaust all possible options first.*

"I'm going to see Chief Cross, and Dahlia's catching some sleep."

"I'll hold the fort." Amir indicated the small table against the wall. "Saoirse brought us enough food to feed an army." A wealth of love in his tone. "She told me you two spoke."

Adam nodded. "Hand things over to Pascal as soon as he's up. I'll need you to take a late shift again. None of us can afford to wear ourselves out."

"Will do. You recall Maraea and Edward?"

"Right before I fell asleep—they'll land sometime around midday." Amir and Pascal's fellow wing commander and her nurse husband had been visiting family in another clan. Their return would shore up their ranks on both the security and medical fronts.

"You driving down?"

"No, I need to fly." His falcon was hurting, needed the balm of the sky, and the clan had a clothing stockpile not too far from the chief's place, so it wouldn't be an issue to fly down instead of driving.

He was on the wing a minute later, his takeoff smooth in the morning quiet. He held back the falcon's need to voice its angry pain until he was high above the desert, where the sound wouldn't scare or wake his people. Only once he'd flown off the first bite of anguish did he head to the unassuming two-story home that had been the chief's residence as long as Adam had known him.

The lights of an emergency vehicle flickered on the street below.

An ambulance about to turn into the chief's drive.

Chapter 12

Telepathy is a catchall designation that—technically—contains the entire Psy race, for all Psy have to have at least Gradient 1 telepathy to jack into the PsyNet. In practical terms, however, it's only those above 3 on the Gradient who are considered true telepaths—but that is just the beginning. Telepathy is a designation with a multitude of subdesignations.

—From the section titled "Telepathy (Tp)" in *Overview of Gradient Levels* (24th edition) by Professor J. Paul Emory and K. V. Dutta, assigned textbook for PsyMed Foundation Courses 1 & 2

ADAM LANDED ABOUT five hundred meters away from the chief's home, near the clothing cache, got dressed at lightning speed, then ran the rest of the way . . . to emerge into a blaze of emergency lights. The ambulance he'd seen from the air stood in the drive, its back doors thrown wide open.

Though its lights continued to strobe, the siren was off.

A paramedic jumped out of the back—a former local who'd shifted to be closer to the main hospital. "Adam." He jolted. "Shit, where'd you come from?"

Adam ignored the question. "What happened?"

"Massive heart attack," the stocky Black man said as he headed back inside with a stretcher. "We just stabilized him for transport."

No one stopped Adam when he followed the other man inside, and the chief's wife sobbed in what looked like relief when she saw him. The usually perfectly dressed woman's hair was a rain of silver-black around her, her face devoid of the red lipstick that was her trademark. "Adam, oh God, Adam," she said from where she crouched bedside the chief.

"My Barry, he just fell." She shifted from English to Diné Bizaad, the rhythms of her speech the same as his mother and grandmother's, for the Diné, like all of the world's peoples, ran the gamut from human to Psy to changeling.

Rafina Cross was human but had spent many a dinner up at the Canyon.

"You know how he is in the mornings, loves to get up with his cup of coffee when the world is quiet. Like your sister—he still uses that 'early bird' mug she gave him." A trembling lower lip. "Remember how they both laughed when I told them they were taking greeting the sun and letting its spirit suffuse them too far?"

Having come down beside her, Adam cradled her suddenly fragile-seeming frame to his side. "How did he fall, Rafina?"

"We didn't get in till one, but still he was up at four thirty. He usually wakes me at about five thirty with a cup of coffee and a kiss, and when I woke it was six already and he hadn't been . . . I don't know how long he was lying here!" Her sobs were heartbreaking, her hands fluttering into the air as the paramedics moved her husband onto the stretcher.

The older man was pale, his lips holding a bluish tinge and his sturdy body limp.

Adam had run into him right before he left for his "thirtieth honeymoon," as he'd put it, and the seventy-five-year-old man had looked as fit as ever. Add in the fact that it had happened now . . . the pile of coincidences was getting far too big, but Adam didn't know how anyone could incite a heart attack in a healthy man.

There was also the question of why anyone would want to attack the chief—if he'd known something about Jacques's shooting, he'd have already called Adam . . . except it had been extremely early in the day when he went down, and the chief knew enough about changeling healing to know that Adam would've been assisting Naia for hours.

It was possible he'd waited to speak to Adam.

It was also possible this was just bad luck and bad timing. The chief had, after all, returned home only hours ago. The chances of him having discovered anything probative were close to nil.

Whatever the answer, Adam let it go for now and helped Rafina out to the ambulance, so she could ride to the nearest hospital—fifty highspeed minutes away—with her grievously ill husband. Naia often stepped in to assist with Raintree emergencies, but with her exhausted and the chief having suffered a major incident, that wasn't an option.

Naia couldn't reach humans with her healing abilities.

He wasn't surprised to see a squad car parked on the road when he emerged from the house—whoever was on duty would've alerted the others as soon as they got word of the emergency request.

All three—Beaufort, Whitten, and Hendricks—were hovering near the ambulance but didn't interfere or ask questions as the paramedics loaded the chief inside. Adam then all but lifted Rafina into the ambulance. "I'll call Laurel," he told her because he knew she'd start to worry about that as soon as she could think straight again. "Make sure she knows where you'll both be."

Laurel was the Crosses' only daughter and lived about an hour out of Raintree—close to the hospital where her father was being taken. Married with two kids, she'd gone to school the same time as Saoirse, been friends with Adam's sister. They still kept in touch in the distant way of old high school friends.

Rafina Cross squeezed his hand. "She's pregnant." A shaky tremor in her voice. "Tell her husband instead, then he can . . ."

"Got it. You just worry about the chief." Stepping back, Adam shut the doors, then watched the ambulance move out of the drive and down the quiet suburban street. The siren didn't streak into the air until about a minute later, when they would've turned onto a main thoroughfare and picked up speed.

Adam had joined the cops by then, to be asked by them if he knew anything further. "Heart attack—no more details yet," he said. "I arrived as the paramedics did."

"How did they beat us here?" Hendricks asked, the twenty-six-year-old's uniform as snug as always on his muscular frame; the handsome deputy's favorite off-work activity was lifting weights, a hobby he shared with a couple of Adam's clanmates.

Today, however, his normally crisp uniform bore the wrinkles of a long night. "Usually," Hendricks added, "we're the first responders in Raintree."

"They were already nearby," Beaufort said; while he was in full uniform, too, his was much fresher, his silver-tinged black hair neatly combed.

Adam guessed he'd come back on shift halfway through Hendricks's, doing much the same as Adam: juggling people so no one was left alone too long and everyone had a chance to rest. Not a concern in sleepy Raintree most of the time, but this wasn't a usual situation by any measure.

"Mildred called about chest pains and she looked pretty bad when I swung by to see her," Beaufort said, "so I tagged the paramedics. Turned out to be gas, but by my reckoning, they would've been barely on the way out when the call came about the chief."

Whitten—in street clothes, her braids in a messy bun—whistled. "Our resident hypochondriac might've saved the chief's life." She shook her head. "I'll have to stop moaning every time I have to respond to a call from her."

"Damn, the chief's lucky it wasn't me that took that call," Hendricks admitted with a long face, his dark eyes awash in worry. "I'm so over Mildred I would've probably just told her to take antacids and ended up killing the chief."

Whitten patted his arm in silent sympathy.

"Did any of you know the chief had heart problems?" Adam asked, also well aware of Mildred Abernathy's long list of imagined health complaints; according to his grandmother, Mildred had been dying of one illness or another since they were in kindergarten together.

How Aria would've grinned at this turn of events.

Beaufort and Whitten shook their heads, but Hendricks shoved a hand through the dark brown of his curls and frowned. "He was complaining about feeling off when he called to say he was headed home, but he said he probably just ate something wrong."

"I wish I'd had the chance to talk to him," Beaufort said.

"I asked," Hendricks told his superior officer, no longer the macho young male who was a favorite with the women in town, but a young deputy afraid he'd done something wrong. "But he said to let you sleep and he'd call you once he was awake and you could give him a full debrief."

"Talking of which . . ." Beaufort reached into his squad car and retrieved an organizer that he passed on to Adam. "Here's the interim report from the forensics people. They worked late to process at least some of the materials."

"Thanks."

"The chief always said to share things with you when it concerned WindHaven, and I know you've got an excellent team after what I saw at the site." The experienced detective put his hands on his hips, his gray eyes narrowed. "The J, you met her?"

Adam was in no mood to think about Eleri, much less discuss her; he just said a clipped "Yes" as he scanned the forensic report.

"She's got a good eye, was the one who first located the tire tracks."

Passing back the organizer—the interim report held nothing that could help them hunt down the person who'd shot Jacques—he said, "You'll update us as you get more data?"

"Yes, I know it's what the chief would want."

"I appreciate that, Rex." Adam shook hands with the other man.

"I can clean up the chief's place if anything got messed up during his heart attack," Hendricks offered hesitantly as the group went to part ways. "I'll make it nice like Mrs. Cross always keeps it. I know when my granddad had a stroke and fell, he hit a shelf and everything fell out. The mess made my grandma cry because it was a reminder, you know?"

Adam found himself speaking without thinking about it. "Rafina Cross is also pretty territorial about how she likes things arranged. I wouldn't touch anything, just lock up the house. From what I saw, there isn't much of a mess regardless."

Beaufort chuckled and it was weak. "Yeah, she's real particular. I think Adam's right—we leave it as it is, and turn up to ask if she needs help once she's back."

That decided, Adam watched Beaufort lock up the house. Whitten left at the same time to shower and change in readiness for her day shift, while Hendricks headed back to the station to write up his reports before he clocked out.

"You know you can always call us if you need help dealing with anything?" Adam said to the detective when they were alone. "We consider Raintree part of our home, want to keep it safe." He'd always before dealt with Chief Cross—and the older man had long ago had these conversations with Adam's grandmother.

To his surprise, Beaufort scowled, his skin pulled tight over his bones. "I have no idea what the fuck is going on, Adam, but this smells to me. The chief going down right after the attack on Jacques? Nothing ever happens in Raintree. Now this? I'm not buying coincidence."

"Yeah, I don't like it, either. You have the authority to ask the hospital to run full tox panels?" Adam asked.

"Poison?" A dark look. "I'll make some calls—I should be able to get it done. Chief's got a lot of friends all over the region."

Leaving the other man to it, Adam began to jog back to the clothing cache—but halfway there, he could no longer fight the compulsion that was acid inside him. He'd thought he'd cut it out of him, burned it to ash, but it lived, a primal need that would not take no for an answer—and his heart was aching today, was hurt.

It wanted to see *her*, wanted to find comfort in her when the woman who'd come to Raintree clearly had no awareness of what that even meant.

Dawn was a pink light on the horizon by the time he reached the inn, but it was still early—though he wasn't surprised to spot Dae Park's black work truck leaving the inn as Adam began to walk down the driveway.

The burly twenty-six-year-old saw him but didn't stop. That was par for the course with Mi-ja's only son; he seemed to have maintained his surly teenage phase right into his twenties. Sally over at the diner had been known to joke that the reason Dae lived with his mother was because no other woman would put up with his moodiness.

Adam frowned, his mind on a serial killer who seemed to be driven by the sick desire to punish pretty young women. Shifting on his heel, he watched Dae's truck turn onto the road. A robust vehicle suitable for the harsh desert environment outside of Raintree's microclimate, it also had a covered flatbed that the other man used to carry tools for his handyman work—but that was also big enough to transport a body.

"So are a whole bunch of other cars in town," Adam muttered to himself as the truck disappeared down the road. "And Dae's no telepath who can pulverize brains from the inside out." Still, he made a mental note to dig into the other man, see if there was even a remote possibility that he could be doing dark things of which no one was aware.

Eleri might be convinced it was one killer, but serial killers had been known to take partners. A human/telepath partnership made sense, especially if the telepath was physically weak, while the human was strong. Dae definitely had the muscle to lift bodies and the skill to build the kind of structures under which the Sandman left his victims.

Disturbed by the idea, he made it across the all-but-empty parking lot—only Mi-ja's and Eleri's vehicles in sight—without attracting

Mi-ja's attention. She was probably still pottering about her kitchen cleaning up after Dae's breakfast. Everyone knew she got up to make him breakfast—because Mi-ja proudly shared that piece of information with anyone who'd listen.

"Well, I mean, he doesn't have a wife, does he?" she'd say. "And I can't let my boy survive on toast!"

Adam had no idea what Dae thought of her hovering because they'd never had any kind of conversation about it—or any kind of real conversation at all. Dae had been two years below him in school, a stark divide at that age, and Dae never seemed to hang out at the bar or diner or anywhere else where Adam might've had a chance to talk to him as an adult.

However, unlike a number of the humans in town, he didn't find it strange that mother and adult son cohabited. Changeling clans and packs were all about cohabitation. To the vast majority of changelings, regardless of species, being on their own was a painful loneliness.

That falcons flew long distances alone was an entirely different situation—they always knew that when they chose to turn back, ride the winds home, they'd be welcomed into the warm embrace of clan.

The only reason Adam had noted the arrangement as anything odd was Dae's surliness and—to outside eyes—complete isolation from all relationships aside from the one with his mother. Adam's clan cohabitated, yes, but fostering emotional independence in their fledglings was a core tenet.

"We're here," they'd say. "We'll help you. But you must learn to fly. Come with me, little bird. Let me show you the sky."

That included teaching their young how to build social bonds outside of the clan. Most human families did the same, but Dae . . . Mi-ja's son was known to turn up on time to fix plumbing and electricity problems, and his repairs stood the test of time. He was never short of business as a result, but per his customers, he ignored any overtures of friendship, even something so small as an offer of a cold drink on a hot day.

Might be the man just hated small-town life but was stuck here because he didn't want to leave his mother alone. He'd gone to college a few hours away and could have an entire social group no one knew about. Adam had spotted his truck heading out of town for a few days on more than one occasion.

Well, shit.

Ice in his gut as he reached Eleri's room. No light glowed beyond the windows, but he could hear movement through the door.

His heart kicked, his skin hot.

He hated this. He hated *her*.

The door opened even as he fought the driving urges of his body and told himself to turn back, get away from her. Whatever they could've once been, that chance lay dead and buried with the murderer she'd helped set free.

"Adam." Her gaze was alert, her body clad in slim black suit pants and a crisp white shirt that she'd tucked into the pants. "I saw you."

He followed her glance to see a tiny camera eye above the door. That definitely wasn't standard issue at the inn. "You were awake."

"I don't sleep much." The deep purple bruises under her eyes bore harsh witness to her words . . . but he hadn't spotted them yesterday.

"And use makeup to hide the effects."

"People focus on the wrong things otherwise." She looked straight at him, the eye contact unaggressive because her gaze was so flat.

It enraged him, the distance of her, the *lack* in her. He wanted to shake her, tell her to stop being a ghost. He couldn't fight with a ghost, couldn't let his anger burn through a ghost. He needed a living, breathing woman who'd feel his pain, his grief, his fury at her.

"Your clanmate?" When Adam just shook his head, she added, "We only discovered two major pieces of information at the site."

"The tire marks and the vehicle, yeah. I heard." Leaning up against the outside wall, he tried not to draw in her scent and did so all the same.

It was as faded and flat as her expression.

"The chief of Raintree Enforcement just suffered a severe heart attack," he said, even as the raptor inside him flared its wings in agitation. "He's the most experienced officer in the area, probably knows everyone in town *and* any relevant history."

Eleri's hand tightened on the doorjamb. "I don't believe in coincidences."

Adam found himself hyper-focused on that betraying hand devoid of the thin black barrier she'd worn yesterday. The urge to touch her, see if she was real or a two-dimensional illusion, was so strong that his entire body pounded with it.

Chapter 13

Our ancestors made the decision to embrace Silence after a ten-year debate. It was no quick decision, no desperate grab at any offered solution. It was, they came to believe, the *only* viable solution.

What I find problematic is that no one in those ten years of debate brought up the possibility of such a regime fostering psychopathy in the populace. To be clear, I believe it *must* have been raised as a concern—nothing else makes sense in the context of such a huge and wide-ranging discussion.

Yet no official records of such concerns survive. Which leads me to the conclusion that those records were wiped by Councils past. Our history is a patchwork quilt with countless missing pieces.

—Excerpted from draft of upcoming *PsyNet Beacon* editorial (pending review for accuracy)

IT TOOK EVERYTHING Adam had to fight the roar of need, to not attempt to initiate skin privileges with this woman who had always, *always* called to his wild changeling soul. "Can a Psy cause a heart attack in an otherwise healthy person?" he asked, his tone rough.

"Yes, but it's not an ability so much as a side effect in most cases. It's said that Tk-Cells can do so by exerting physical pressure on the organ, but that subdesignation is so rare that it might as well be a myth.

Telepaths can do so accidentally when pushing at a mind in order to nudge their target into doing something—the strain can lead to myocardial infarction.

"But in most cases of attempted telepathic interference, it's a stroke that leads to death, not heart issues. Actually creating a heart attack that passes all the medical tests? Very, *very* difficult and not something I'd expect from the kind of Psy who live in this town. It'd require Arrow-level training."

Adam knew about the Arrows due to the Trinity Accord, of which WindHaven was a member. They were the Psy race's most deadly soldiers, black ops pushed to the nth degree. "Yeah, we definitely don't have an undercover Arrow in town, I can promise you that."

Adam knew exactly who lived in Raintree, and had run background checks on all the Psy who'd moved in after the fall of Silence. "As for passing medical scrutiny—we'll have to wait on the chief's medical reports. On the off chance I'm wrong about the Psy in Raintree, you pick up anything problematic?"

Eleri shook her head, her cheekbones too sharp against her skin. "No alarm bells so far. They seem to be people who didn't like their lives and took the chance offered by the fall of Silence to build a new one. Most were more scared of me than otherwise until I mentioned my cover story."

"They thought you were what, an operative sent to haul them back?" Adam guessed.

"The scars of the past will take a long time to fade." She stared off into the parking lot with that calm statement that offered no insight into what she thought about the decision her Psy ancestors had made to condition emotion out of their young.

A decision that had, from what Adam had learned, begun in a desperate attempt to keep those children safe—but ended up with psychopaths at the top of their hierarchy.

"The assault on your clanmate," Eleri said, "the chief's heart attack . . . I was the first domino."

"Maybe. Timing doesn't quite fit for me—you'd barely spoken to anyone when Jacques was shot." It would've been easy to blame her, but if it was related to the Sandman case, then the serial murderer had always been hiding in Raintree. All Eleri had done was bring the problem into the light.

"I'm recognizable to the Sandman," Eleri said. "His letters indicate he stalked me for years before the first letter. I wouldn't have had to talk to him—it could be as simple as him glimpsing me when I first drove down Main Street."

Adam's entire body was a knot of muscle. "Jacques would stand in front of a hundred guns if it would help expose a murderer of innocents. I do, however, think, Sandman or another bastard, the shooting was a mistake, an act of impulse—impetus as yet unknown. We need to use that mistake to pin him down."

Eleri continued to stare out at the dawn, but her next words weren't to do with blame, her brain clearly having shifted track with Adam's words. "There's a chance he's decompensating—some serial killers are stable for a long time, while others disintegrate into chaos with unexpected rapidity. The pathologist on the case has reported signs of increasing violence on the brains of our victims, as if he's losing control rather than refining his skill. I've seen that kind of rapid decline before."

Even as Adam wondered what it had done to the girl he'd met to walk into minds vicious and twisted day after day, what it had stolen from her, how it had altered her, Eleri continued to speak.

"The assault on your clanmate could," she said, "as easily be a thing of proximity and chance. Let's say it's our killer, and he *is* aware I'm in town. I think he'd be excited, hyped, not scared. The letters show that he wants my attention in a way that's disturbing."

Adam's talons pricked at the inside of his skin. "Yet you work alone."

"He won't murder me. Not yet. I'm his audience." Eleri still didn't look at him, her gaze fathomless as she stared past him. "Let's say seeing me arouses him on the emotional level, leading him to want to go sit in his vehicle, relive his crimes."

"Only Jacques beat him to the site, and took flight right as the killer parked and got out," Adam said, seeing where she was going. "It had to be someone Jacques knew, could identify." Which meant it was also someone Adam would know, perhaps even a person he called a friend.

"It wouldn't have mattered if the killer had kept a cool head, pretended he was out for a drive and spotted Jacques so stopped," Eleri said. "But he couldn't take the risk, especially not when his mind was full of what he'd done, the excitement of his crimes."

Her eyes met his again, the hazel more green today and devoid of any hint of personality. "It can't be about the car alone. Anyone who's spent even a day in Raintree would know your people would react with speed to the assault on Jacques—the car was forfeit the instant the shooter took aim."

"Not if Jacques died before calling for help." Adam would've been left to search the desert for his fallen clanmate, the blood bond severed. "The shooter—possibly your killer—made a mistake, yes, but we can't be sure *which* mistake."

"You're right." She released the doorjamb and flexed her hand . . . then stared, as if suddenly aware of her exposed skin.

"Why the gloves?" Adam asked at that moment. "None of the Psy in town wear them, but I've seen a few others over the years."

ELERI considered whether to lie or otherwise obfuscate, because to tell him the truth would be to make herself vulnerable. But he already hated her for a lie; she wouldn't add to that. Not because she expected him to feel any differently about her and not because any part of her was still that young girl who'd run into him in the hallway outside the courtroom, but because she'd made a promise to herself to never again betray Adam Garrett.

She didn't know why it mattered so much when they'd interacted only once, spoken only once.

But it did.

It always had.

Always would.

"Working as a J," she began, "eventually wears away the shielding that means Psy don't pick up thoughts through touch." It was a natural barrier, that shielding, because babies, who'd had no training in creating shields, didn't scream from an influx of thoughts while being cradled by their nurses. "I'm a Sensitive on the far end of the spectrum. I could die if I touch the wrong person with my bare hands."

Adam's pupils expanded, the unusual pale brown of his eyes gaining a fine edge of intense yellow. "What about if a person touched you on another exposed section of skin, like your face?"

"Same result," she said, "but it'd take longer. For whatever reason, the hands seem to be the strongest conduit—perhaps because we're wired to use them to connect with people? I can't explain. No one's ever studied it." Because no one cared; Js lived, did their work, then they died.

The end.

A flush across the top of Adam's cheekbones. "So if this serial killer assaults you and manages to touch your bare skin, he could kill you?"

A small fragment of her wanted to believe it mattered to him if she lived or died. She'd been wrong after all . . . the girl she'd once been wasn't wholly dead. "I think if I'm that close to him, then my death is already on the table." A simple fact. "That's why I need to hunt him down, rather than the opposite."

Adam shifted to put himself in her line of sight, bracing his arms above the doorjamb; his muscular biceps were rigid against the soft gray of his T-shirt, his wide shoulders taut. "Putting yourself in the line of fire isn't an act of penance that'll wipe out the past."

The blow got through the wall of numbness enough to reverberate throughout her psyche. "No," she said, shockingly aware of the heat and power of him in this fleeting instant when the wall had fractured, "but it might save a number of futures."

What, she thought in the wake of the psychic shock wave, would she feel if she touched Adam Garrett without gloves? "It's a fair enough trade."

Their eyes locked, held, that unspoken thing a living, breathing creature between them.

A muscle ticced in Adam's jaw, and for an instant she thought he'd break the impasse, speak about the topic they were both willfully avoiding—and she couldn't bear to face it, even in her numbness—but then Mi-ja's voice rang out across the parking lot. "Yoo-hoo! Adam! I heard about Jacques! Such a terrible thing."

Adam moved to look at Mi-ja—who continued to talk on the subject as she made her way to them. "Do you have any idea who could've done it? It had to be an out-of-towner, surely? I mean, why would one of *us* attack Jacques?"

Eleri watched Adam's expression shift to one of quiet patience. "We don't know much right now," he told the older woman. "What I do know is that you have your finger on the pulse of the town. If you hear anything, you'll tell me?"

"Oh, of course!" Her small face scrunched up into a scowl. "I'd like to string up whoever it was that hurt him. That boy was always nice to my Dae when other kids used to bully him. Jacques put a stop to it straightaway."

Adam frowned. "I forgot about that. They were in the same manufacturing class that one semester, weren't they? The one that took students across grades?"

"Yes, and how they got on—Dae would tell me all the stories of their adventures." Her smile was shaky. "He's so shy that he's always had trouble making friends—it made me happy that he'd linked up with Jacques. I think the two of them still have a beer together sometimes."

"They meet up lately?"

"No, Dae's been so busy with work." Her lips turned down. "Were you thinking Jacques might've mentioned something? Well, if he had, Dae would've told me last night, when we first got word of the shooting."

"You'll ask him to pass on anything he hears, too?"

"I'll message him straightaway." She took her phone out of her pocket as she spoke. "He wanted to eat breakfast at the diner today." A roll of her eyes. "Says my waffles are terrible, but doesn't he scarf them up when I make them?" Message sent and phone back in her pocket, she threw up her hands. "Kids!" Then she turned and headed back to her office. "Toodle-oo! Have a businessman coming in today—have to get his room sorted."

Adam spoke after the other woman was out of earshot. "Watch Dae. I don't know what he's up to, but he gives me a bad feeling. I know for certain that he and Jacques weren't friends at school. Maybe he just made up a story to placate his mother when she worried about him making friends, but the fact he's kept up the lie this long worries me."

Eleri nodded. "Hero worship turned deadly when Jacques didn't act as he needed him to act?" It wouldn't be the first case of love turned destructive that Eleri had seen in her career; one of the first cases she'd studied during her training had involved a man who'd stabbed his lover—another man—to death in a frenzy of jealousy after discovering intimate photos of a third man on his comm.

"It's possible. I'm going to put a watch on him." Adam locked those strange, wild eyes on her again, the yellow inhuman and beautiful. "You can't rely on Mi-ja to protect you if anything goes wrong with Dae—she'd do anything for her son, even bury a body."

Eleri had long ago stopped being shocked by what people would do for those they considered their own. She'd lied with her silence for Reagan, hadn't she?

Where's the honor and justice in that?

Words she'd thrown at Reagan when she'd finally realized the duplicity that was part and parcel of being a J under the reign of the Council.

He'd given her a pensive look. "You're a strong one, Eleri, to still have the will to ask such questions. Most of us forget them by the time we get to where you are in your training. It's easier to forget, easier to just walk on without looking too carefully into the shadows."

"Is that what you did?"

"I'm here, aren't I?" had been his answer.

Today, she just said, "I understand."

Adam's only response was, "Don't forget your gloves," before he turned and headed back down the stairs.

Eleri didn't know why she'd stepped outside after he vanished from sight until several minutes later, when a large falcon winged overhead. It circled over her once before heading to the Canyon. To a place she'd never go, never experience, his home as far out of her reach as the sky that was in his every breath.

Her heart, that long-ossified organ, ached at that.

"Now," she told herself, "it's time for you to do the only thing you're good at—and that might be useful."

Don't forget your gloves.

It meant nothing. He just didn't want her disabled should the attack on his clanmate be related to her serial killer case. It was a sensible precaution.

And still, she tucked it away with all her hoarded memories of him.

Do you work at the court?

Not really. I'm an intern—I get paid a small stipend but my job is to learn, here and during our lectures. Are you a student, too?

Yes. Business with a minor in—don't laugh—ancient epics like Beowulf. *My mom . . . she loved old stories.*

Eleri hadn't known anything about *Beowulf* then, but she'd read the epic poem obsessively over the months that followed. Searching futilely for a way back to the boy whose eyes had gone so sad when he'd mentioned his mother, but who'd also looked at Eleri in a way that said she was special, that she made him happy.

Until she'd shattered his heart, destroyed his trust . . . and any hope of a future in the warmth of those beautiful wild eyes.

Chapter 14

Full board, including any vacation periods and weekends. Medical power of attorney has been assigned to the school. Invoice for year one has been paid in full. Future invoices will be paid in full on January 1st of each year until the child turns eighteen.

The family does not wish for any contact regarding the child except for the invoices—any disciplinary and medical matters are to be handled by the school.

—Note in intake file of Eleri Dias (age 6) at the Maxwelton Boarding School (21 November 2062)

DAE PARK WASN'T in the diner when Eleri walked in to take a seat at the counter. "I was hoping to run into Dae," she said to the proprietor, Sally, a tall woman with sharp eyes and striking bone structure under skin of glowing ebony.

"He tell his ma he was having breakfast here again?" Sally chuckled, her voice husky. "Honey, he's a healthy young male trapped in a house with his mother—I ain't never seen him for breakfast. I haven't figured out who his lady friend is, but he's surely got one. Good on him, I say—man finally broke out of his shell."

Eleri dropped the subject, but she added this lie to the one Dae had told about Jacques and found him inching higher on the scale of suspects—at least when it came to the shooting. His humanity still placed him as an outlier on the Sandman suspect list unless she wanted to revise her opinion that it was a single killer rather than a pair.

"Thank you," she said as Sally put her plate in front of her—it was the "Psy special," a bland arrangement of bread spread with nutrient paste, along with a hot cup of an herbal tea with no discernible taste that Eleri could fathom.

"You mind if I ask you a question?" Sally said after returning from topping up a heavily bearded man's coffee. "I always wondered if the memories you took as a J haunted you."

"We have eidetic memories," Eleri told the other woman. "But only for the memories we take from others in the course of our duties. We cannot forget."

Sally sucked in a short, hard breath. "Why would your parents allow you to go into that kind of work? I would *never* let my daughter do something like that—I don't care if she's full grown and in charge of herself!"

Eleri thought about her own mother, a slender 7.9 telepath she barely remembered who'd had no idea what to do with the daughter who'd been born with an ability that could bring no advantage to the family. Maria Dias had blamed herself for not fully researching Eleri's paternal line for "discrepancies" before their fertilization agreement and had ignored the child except for ensuring her physical needs were met.

Eleri had far preferred her life in boarding school, especially after she met Bram, then Saffron and Yúzé. A small family. Her real family, the memories they'd created between them potent enough that she remembered her emotions toward them even behind the wall of nothingness.

Once, she had been able to love them.

"Most Js before the fall of Silence were funneled into the job," she told Sally, leaving out the political reasons for it—for the vast majority of Js, the control of the Council never came into play, but it was nonetheless the reason the Council wanted Js in the system.

So they could alter cases at will.

LIAR!

The wall had regrown, thick and all but impenetrable, and so she could speak past the brutal echo of Adam's accusation. "Js now have a choice." They could learn to use their abilities in less damaging ways, could even have careers that had nothing to do with their skills at memory retrieval and broadcast.

Two people hugged outside the window of the diner, young women who were smiling at each other in welcome. It was an experience Eleri would never have. The contact could kill or disable her at her current level of Sensitivity.

A flicker in her mind, eyes that were no longer fully human looking into hers as Adam told her not to forget her gloves.

Changelings had natural shields.

People with natural shields were no threat to Sensitives.

Shaking off the thought that was apropos of nothing, because physical contact with Adam wasn't within the realm of possibility, she ate a bite of her toast while Sally went to chat to the bearded patron. Their conversation, however, lingered with her.

What choice, she thought, would she have made had she had a *true* choice?

Her brain had trouble even comprehending the question. Fact was, she'd never had any inkling of a choice, having been put into specialized training the moment she passed her Silence tests, and at this point couldn't even imagine what she'd do if she wasn't a J. This was what she was good at, and what she was good at could make the world a safer place.

Putting yourself in the line of fire isn't an act of penance that'll wipe out the past.

Her fingers tightened on the cup of tea just as the Enforcement deputy she'd met yesterday—Jocasta Whitten—entered with a male colleague in a rumpled uniform. He was about Adam's height, had tumbled dark curls and sculpted musculature that was obvious under his tailored uniform.

Cheeks creasing in a tired smile, he said, "Hey, Sally. Breakfast for me and Jo. Our usual."

"I thought you'd be off shift by now, Hendricks," Sally said as she turned to call in the order to her cook.

"Decided to wait so I could eat with Jo," the deputy named Hendricks answered, his curious gaze cutting to Eleri.

Whitten, meanwhile, wandered over to her. "Hey, you want to join us at a booth? We can catch each other up and I can introduce you to Hendricks."

"Sure."

Once they were seated and introductions made, the two deputies shared what they knew about the chief. "No news from the hospital yet," Whitten said right as Sally slid their plates onto the table.

After which, the conversation shifted to the shooting.

"I think it looks panicked," the female deputy said. "At least three shots from a high-powered laser rifle. Overkill and messy with it."

"I mean, I dunno," Hendricks mumbled from around his eggs before taking a gulp of coffee from a refillable silver flask that Sally had topped up with a smile. "The falcons are tough. Way I figure it, the shooter was making sure he got the job done. Not panic, more like not wanting to take the risk of Jacques surviving."

Eleri could see both points of view, because Hendricks was right—the shooter had to have known that should Jacques survive and talk, their life would be forfeit. Adam and his clan would come after them like arrows unleashed.

"Is it rude to ask about the gloves?" Hendricks's voice broke into her thoughts.

"It's just to stop accidental contact," Eleri said, not in the mood to offer further details.

"Huh. I heard online that it was for Psy who can sense stuff through touch."

"I'm no psychometric."

"Must be weird to be one," Whitten said as Hendricks shrugged and got back to buttering a thick slice of toast. "Like imagine touching the tire tracks at the scene of the shooting and getting snapshots of the shooter. No idea if that's how it works, but maybe Enforcement should think about recruiting psychometrics. They can go around zapping crime scenes and just telling us what happened."

Eleri had met a few Ps-Psy through her work, and it didn't quite work like that, but she let it go because the two deputies seemed fascinated by the idea.

"What would be the fun in our work if they could just give us the answers?" Hendricks made a face after swallowing his bite of toast. "No actual investigating. Nah, I say leave the psychometric people to do whatever they're doing now."

He tapped the side of his head. "Now, telepathy, that I could get onboard with. It'd be straight-up ice being able to talk to another cop without the criminals ever figuring it out. Imagine how you could use it to stymie them in an interrogation."

Whitten snorted. "Calm down, John. You work in Raintree. We interrogate teenagers and drunks, hardly criminal masterminds."

Instead of being offended, Hendricks grinned. "Just you watch. I'm going to pass my detective exams and get myself a shiny new badge in a big-city station."

"You know I'll be there with bells on to celebrate the day. So will your falcon gym buddies."

Hendricks's smile faded. "Jacques is a good guy," he said. "I don't know him real well, but I've run into him a few times when he dropped by to use a few of the machines they don't have up in the Canyon.

"And WindHaven's helped us out with a ton of searches," he added, to Whitten's solemn nod, "finding people who got lost in the desert. We don't need to hunt down jet-choppers or search planes because the falcons have our back and act as air support."

Eleri thought of seeing those wings in flight, of the ease with which Adam rode the air currents, and wondered what it was like to be so free. "That's a stroke of luck in this remote region."

"Yeah, but even they can't help us with this." Whitten pushed her waffles around her plate, having only taken a few bites. "No one knows anything."

"What about other crimes in town?" Eleri was certain the Sandman hadn't hunted on his home ground, but compulsions were strange things and could've driven him to other criminal acts. "Anything else disturbing?"

"Last 'big' crime"—Hendricks hooked his fingers in air quotes—"was when Dexter Camp's little group of budding criminals took the high school principal's SUV for a joyride and left it stuck in the desert."

Whitten rolled her eyes. "The kids were never in danger of getting away with it. They'd blabbed to their other mates before they were even back in town—and we were waiting for them."

"Nothing else?"

"Nothing beyond drunkenness and the odd break-in." Whitten drank a bit of orange juice. "Whoever's breaking in doesn't even take anything except for stupid stuff—like one time, it was clear they'd spent time in the kitchen cutting up and eating big chunks of leftover birthday cake; they exited by the back door just as the couple who lived there returned—couple heard the door close."

Hendricks grinned. "My favorite was the one where the owners came home and their puppy was sleeping surrounded by toys they'd put up in a box for later in the day. The burglar had spent time playing with the pup, tired it out, then had a *shower*. Homeowners say the bathroom was full of steam when they got back."

"It's bored kids." Whitten added more syrup to her waffles. "We've done fingerprints for all the break-ins, but no luck so far. Some group of kids probably has a bet going on about how long they can keep it up."

Eleri wasn't so sure it was anything that petty. Her antennae had quivered to attention at the first mention of a burglary that wasn't a burglary . . . and of an intruder who timed his crimes to *just* miss the people whose home he'd violated. That was an escalation that could turn deadly, because she was sure this person or pair—unlikely a group as the deputies believed—had begun with entries that hadn't been detected, before moving on to more risky actions.

Stage three would be an intrusion while the people inside were present but asleep. Then would come the intrusions while the residents were awake. And worst-case scenario would be a full home invasion, with the residents terrorized and murdered.

"Since we have no new data on Jacques," Eleri said, "and I haven't picked up anything in Raintree on my case, I can have a look at the files to do with the break-ins, see if I notice anything."

"We'll have to ask Beaufort," Whitten said. "Only he or the chief can authorize that."

Eleri nodded, leaving it at that. It didn't really matter; she had ways to get the files without authorization. Because it turned out that a woman who hunted serial killers with great success had a hell of a lot of contacts who owed her favors.

She glanced at the gloved hand she had on the table.

Not long left for her to collect on the favors. Might as well cash in one now.

Don't forget your gloves.

She polished the memory of their morning interaction, made sure it was in high definition before she stored it carefully away. Because while her memories were only eidetic when it came to the traces she took, she'd never forgotten a single detail of her interactions with him.

Never wanted to forget.

IT was three hours later when she returned to the inn. She'd spent the time working her imaginary cold case while making contact with the

Psy residents of the town. Still no red flags, but the Sandman had been flying under the radar *because* he was good at hiding his true face. She planned to dig into each and every person to whom she'd spoken.

Having already used her mobile comm to check her security system, she pushed open the door . . . and felt her boot press down on something that crackled softly. Lifting her foot at once, she looked down to see what looked to be printouts of online articles. She crouched down so she was close enough to read the headlines without having to touch the paper.

The Sandman Strikes Again!

Missing woman identified as Kriti Kumar, an engineering student from ASU.

Breaking News: Body discovered!

Vivian Chang's Parents on Why They Still Have Hope

Rumors of a Serial Killer in Arizona!

They were all like that, every single printout that she could see. Someone had gone to great lengths to find articles on the Sandman going back all the way to the beginning. That interview with Vivian's parents, for one, had been right back at the start, when she'd been a missing person.

But that wasn't what held her attention: it was the printout in the center of the haphazard mass—of an article that included a black-and-white image of the location where Eleri had discovered Sarah Wells's body.

She was standing next to Tim, the two of them in conversation.

The person who'd slipped the printouts under her door had drawn a smiley face next to Eleri's image.

Chapter 15

This is a common misconception—and understandable, given the relatively recent "return" of Designation E to the PsyNet—but no, empaths do not all function much the same.

The E designation carries multiple subdesignations, some of which we may not discover for years, or even longer. We have almost no historical resources to mine, for the Councils of Silence took great care to wipe empaths from the world.

—*PsyNet Beacon:* Response to reader question by Jaya Laila Storm (medical empath and Social Interaction columnist) (7 June 2083)

AS THE FIRST empath to wake to her nature in this generation, Sascha had known that she wasn't the right E for the job the instant the Wind-Haven healer contacted her. Jacques needed a specialist E, one with the ability to reach a comatose mind.

"I'll find you the best person," she'd promised Naia, then immediately got to work.

Her first choice, Jaya, proved to be in a mandated recovery period after almost burning herself out, but the other woman recommended another E—a young male named Hanz.

When Sascha met the empath at the nearest airport to falcon territory, having been led to him by her two-and-a-half-year-old daughter—who was holding a print of the ID photo Jaya had sent them—the youth turned out to have a German accent that went perfectly with his name, skin a darker hue of brown than her own, floppy dark hair, and hazel eyes that looked unseeing out at the world.

Sensors ringed his fingers.

She assumed he'd lost his vision in an accident as a teenager, for the Psy hadn't been forgiving of any kind of obvious physical difference when Hanz would've been born.

"Hi, Hanz! We're here!" Naya piped up and touched her fingers very, very lightly to the back of one of his hands before withdrawing.

Sascha's daughter knew not to touch Psy without permission, but she seemed to have made a rapid calculation in that terrifyingly smart little brain that Hanz might need a physical reference to her presence. He didn't, of course; he could have sensed them with his empathic ability.

"*Hallo*, 'we,'" Hanz said before Sascha could introduce herself, his lips curved in a smile and his head directed unerringly down at Naya's diminutive height. "That's quite an unusual name, *ja*?"

Naya laughed, a huge and delighted thing. Sascha had moments when she worried her daughter—half-changeling, half-Psy—would feel constrained by living outside the sprawling vastness of the PsyNet, but then she'd hear Naya laugh and it'd all melt away.

It helped that her own mother, who never sugarcoated anything, had bluntly said, "The child is hitting all her psychic markers ahead of schedule. The DarkRiver network is, quite frankly, far stronger and safer for her right now than any corner of the PsyNet."

"No, I'm Naya!" her daughter clarified. "This is Mama."

"Otherwise known as Sascha." Sascha smiled. "Thank you for flying out on such short notice." DarkRiver had attempted to arrange a teleport, but everyone in the Net was running on fumes, and the only 'porter outside the Net they knew had just flamed out doing an emergency medical teleport for a SnowDancer juvenile who'd been badly injured in the mountains.

The juvenile would be okay, but Judd was out for the count.

Sascha and Naya themselves had flown in on a jet-chopper piloted by their escort, DarkRiver sentinel Dorian Christensen; they'd landed just ahead of Hanz's commercial flight.

"It is an honor to meet you." Hanz inclined his head, his face aglow. "Without you, we would all yet be locked in amber."

Sascha had come to terms with her status as the first E to embrace who she was, but she didn't know quite how to process the adoration of young Es like Hanz. "I think it was just time," she said. "One of us would've broken through—if not me, then Ivy or Memory or Jaya . . . so many of us were on the precipice."

Naya tugged at her hand.

When she glanced down, her baby pointed to where Dorian stood a short distance away—from where he could watch everything and everyone. While the pack had picked up no indications of any active threats against either one of them, Sascha was the mate of the DarkRiver alpha . . . and the daughter of Nikita Duncan. Which made her a valuable target, and her and Lucas's precious cub an even bigger one.

But Naya was on this trip because she loved seeing her falcon friends and adored that she shared a name with Naia, the falcon healer, even if the spelling wasn't identical. She called the healer "big Naia" and herself "little Naya."

It didn't seem to occur to her that she could use her given name of Nadiya—likely because the only person who ever used it was her Psy grandmother. Who Naya got along with far better than Sascha could've once imagined; Nikita as a grandmother wasn't the same woman who'd raised Sascha.

As for any risk—the one thing Sascha would never do was stop her child from living in order to keep her safe. Nikita's choices had been different; to save her child, she'd had to lock up Sascha's mind and conceal the truth of her very nature, but that didn't mean that choice hadn't left deep scars.

Now the baby Sascha was raising in freedom had pointed out that Dorian was nudging a thumb over his shoulder. "I'm sorry to rush you, Hanz," she said. "But we only have a short-term spot on the landing pad. If you could follow us."

"I can hold your hand!" Naya volunteered, smart but young enough that she didn't understand Hanz didn't need the assist.

"Oh, my cublet, you're very kind to offer that," Sascha said, "but see the sensors on Hanz's fingers? They're connected to his brain, so he can see the world around him."

Her daughter's face lit up. "Whiskers! Like me!"

Hanz's smile was as bright as Naya's. "Yes, I suppose they do act like whiskers, just like your leopard's."

"I a panther," Naya piped up. "Like Papa."

"I think your panther must be strong and smart." Hanz held out his right hand, leaving his left free for navigation. "How about we walk each other?"

A happy Naya tucked her hand into his, and the three of them made their way to the sentinel with hair of a brilliant white blond and surfer blue eyes who was one of the most dangerous people in DarkRiver.

The resulting flight was much shorter than their trip to the airport, and Naya was as glued to the window as she'd been on their first flight. Sascha and Lucas's cub had already asked Dorian if he could teach her to fly the big machine—giving her mother palpitations. Raising a fearless panther cub was going to turn her gray by the time Naya was eighteen, of that she was certain, but Sascha planned to white-knuckle her way through.

Never would she permit her own fears to stifle her baby's primal heart.

"Dori, Dori!" that wild cub said now. "The big X!"

"Good spotting," Dorian responded without taking his attention off the flight controls. "Now, sit back while I take us down."

That landing—directly on the marked spot on the Canyon plateau—was as soft as a feather. Adam was waiting for them, ready to lead Sascha and Hanz inside. "Hello, little Naya," he said, crouching down to close his arms around Naya when she ran over for a hug.

"Big Naia?"

"She's busy right now, but you can say hi to her later." He glanced over his shoulder. "Someone else has been waiting all day for you."

Naya made a happy sound at seeing her small friend but didn't run off; she might be a panther, but she was also a DarkRiver cub raised with the boundaries a strong changeling child needed to feel safe—and to grow into a trustworthy and disciplined member of the pack. "Mama, I go play with Jina?"

"I've got her," Dorian said when Sascha glanced at him.

To trust the sentinel with this living piece of her heart wasn't even a question. "Yes, go play. And mind your manners if you go to Jina's house."

Leaving her daughter to play, safe in the knowledge that she'd be watched over in this landscape that wasn't theirs and held dangers Naya might not understand, she followed Adam inside the Canyon, Hanz at her side.

The youth paused outside the infirmary. "I need baselines," he said. "I've never had reason to interact with or read falcon changelings before. I don't have any idea of your emotional normal."

When Adam glanced at Sascha, she gave a nod.

He extended his hand. "Please go ahead."

Hanz frowned after he made contact. "I held your daughter's hand," he said, his head angled toward Sascha. "I made no attempt to read her, of course, but her surface self felt primal in a way I've never experienced. However, you, Adam, are closer to the husband of my trainer, Jaya. Wildness contained."

Jaya's husband was an Arrow, a lethal soldier. And so, Sascha thought, was Adam. Alphas—and wing leaders—tended to be that way. She should know.

"Adult versus child," Adam said as "big Naia" came to join them, his voice gruff. "Jacques is my right hand. He should feel similar to me."

After Hanz nodded and broke contact, he said, "Jaya said she called you. She did explain that I might not be able to get through? Changeling shields are formidable."

It was Naia who answered, her fingers touching Sascha's in a silent hello. "Yes. She also said the shield might be more permeable due to the serious nature of his injuries, but that there were no guarantees."

"Just do your best," Adam said, his tone the encouraging one of an alpha to a young packmate.

He reminded Sascha of Lucas in many ways. Both of them leaders with huge hearts. As Naia reminded her of Tamsyn, another healer who'd give her blood itself if it would help her packmates.

"Thank you for coming," Adam said to Sascha in a low tone as Naia led Hanz to Jacques's room. "We have no way to monitor the E, see what he might be doing to Jacques."

"I understand." The Es had a strict code of ethics, but to expect a changeling pack to blindly trust a being from a race that had so often been their enemy was to ask the impossible.

"I spoke to him on the flight from the airport, and he's relieved to have me shadow him in a telepathic sense. He wants the oversight, is scared he'll screw something up."

"Kid's young." A frown between Adam's eyebrows. "You sure this won't hurt him?"

There it was, that protective heart. "There aren't many Es with Jaya's—and Hanz's—specialty, so he's been pulled into active service earlier than might be optimal, but Jaya told me he's passed every single test to check his psychological and psychic readiness, and that to hold him back would be detrimental to his development. He also knows he can walk away at any point."

"Good. Last thing Jacques would want is to scar an E."

A sucked-in gulp of air, distressed telepathic contact. *Sascha, he's so hurt. My sensors are picking up amputations and other variations they can't process.*

Leaving Adam's side at once, Sascha went straight to Hanz's. And though Naia had described the extent of Jacques's injuries, Sascha's own stomach twisted at the sight. The last time she'd seen the falcon male, he'd been scowling down at her cub, saying no to playing a game of swords and dragons, but in the way of a man who knew he was going to do it but had to make a show of resisting first.

Right then, she'd known that her cub would be as safe with Jacques as she was with Dorian. If her heart hurt at seeing him so wounded, how much worse must it be for his clan?

Do you want me to telepath you a visual? she asked Hanz, forcing herself to keep her tone calm because if she wavered, the younger E might crumple. *Will your receptors be able to process it?*

No, I was born blind. I have no visual parameters beyond how I perceive the world with my sensors. Please describe him to me.

Hiding her surprise at his revelation of his congenital blindness—and hoping the story behind it was of a loving family that refused to buckle to societal and Council pressure—she spoke aloud to keep the others in the loop. "Hanz needs a description of Jacques's physical state. His sensors are having trouble processing it. I'll—"

"No," Adam interrupted. "I'll do it." Then, as Naia's face trembled before she schooled it into professional calm, he gave a crisp, clear description of the man Sascha knew was his closest friend. "We don't know about the internal semi-shift beyond what we can scan. His brain . . . that's why you're here, Hanz."

Hanz's throat moved as he swallowed. "Thank you. I'm sorry for causing you pain."

Adam shook his head and touched Hanz on the shoulder, a changeling who understood when another being needed physical contact to feel safe. "It's fine. You ask for whatever you need."

"Sascha?" Hanz held out his hand.

Taking it, she said, "Ready?"

A nod, but inside her mind came a scared question. *What if he's trapped in there?*

If he is and we can find him, that means he can come back once he heals, can finish the shift either way. She didn't actually know that, and neither did any healers Naia had contacted, but it was their best hope. *It would mean he's just stuck, not gone.*

Hanz's eyes met hers, the sightless orbs swimming with distress and determination both. *You'll watch? I don't want to make a mistake, make him worse.*

You won't. Jaya wouldn't have sent you if she didn't trust you could handle it. Sascha squeezed his hand before requesting a telepathic connection through his shields that would permit her to shadow him.

Hanz opened on his end at once, and she could immediately see everything he was doing as he did it. While she'd worked with Jaya on previous occasions, it was once again a revelation to see how their E abilities worked when compared to her own.

She saw Hanz take an initial broad emotional read of the room before he filtered out the "noise" and began to drill down through the layers of what appeared to his mind to be a heavy black blanket that stifled Jacques's. It was obvious that he was being methodical in not skipping a single step as he built not a bridge but a tunnel.

I can get in, he said on a psychic exhale. *It's as if his natural shield suffered a quake. It's here but in pieces with large gaps in between.*

He was caught mid-shift, Sascha replied, *perhaps right as the shield was resetting from one form to the next.* Because when changelings shifted, they did so on every level.

Hanz didn't reply, his attention on his work.

I'm trying to find him, the E said to Sascha. *When people are lost in their minds, or when they've retreated to a protected bit of the brain, we have to drill. It sounds harsh, but it's not, I promise.*

I know. Jaya showed me once.

She's so good at it, can do multiple tunnels at once, but I can only do one at a time.

Trust yourself, Hanz. Jaya does.

A long and deep breath before Hanz settled in, having already indicated he preferred to work standing up.

He went through three nutrient drinks and an equal number of hours of work before collapsing in the chair Adam had earlier dragged over for him—before the falcon wing leader had to leave to take a meeting that was urgent for the clan's bottom line.

The heads of clans and packs didn't have the luxury of giving in to their emotions, and their sentinels and seconds were cut from the same cloth. Sascha knew Jacques would've been the first person to remind Adam of his responsibilities had he shown any signs of forgetting. That was a sentinel's—or second's—job.

"I can't find him," Hanz said aloud to Sascha and Naia, his lower lip trembling and one of his hands clutching Sascha's.

Naia, her face dark with grief, nonetheless put a reassuring hand on Hanz's shoulder, while Sascha blanketed him in emotions warm and comforting.

Tears rolled down the young E's face. "I want to try again," he said through the roar of his own visceral emotions. "I don't want to give up."

Sascha's heart was heavy, and though she agreed with Hanz that he should try again after a couple of hours of rest to rebuild his strength, she was conscious that success was unlikely. And much as she didn't want to say that, she had to—Jacques's clan deserved to have all available information.

"I saw every bit of what he did," she told Adam and Naia after Hanz fell asleep. "He didn't cut any corners, went over each area of Jacques's mind multiple times."

Face pinched, Naia folded her arms but let Adam haul her against him, his chin on her hair. "So he's gone?"

"That's the problem." Sascha rubbed her hands down her own arms, her thin black sweater no proof against the cold inside her. "And it's why Hanz wants to try again—there's something there, but he couldn't get to it, and he told me he's never seen anything even similar."

"That indistinct brain wave reading." Naia's head lifted, hope a soft melody in her tone.

Sascha nodded, but, much as she wanted to nurture that hope, said, "Hanz said it's so faint an impression that he doesn't believe even Jaya would be able to reach it—if it *can* be reached. It doesn't feel . . . whole."

Adam pinned her with a raptor's angry gaze, but she knew the anger had nothing to do with her. "And you? You're more experienced. What do you think?"

"This isn't my field, but I agree with him that it's too faint. As for the wholeness, I have far more experience with changeling minds on the emotional level, and Jacques's doesn't feel right." She pressed a fist to her heart, as if that would stop the pain. "Not wild enough. Not human enough, either."

"Stuck," Adam said, his tone curt.

"Stuck," she agreed, giving shape to the horrific nightmare that was Jacques's reality. She could only hope that he felt none of it. Because if he *was* in there and conscious on any level . . .

Her gut twisted.

Chapter 16

"So is Jacques playing dumb or has he really not figured it out yet?"

"You ever known Jacques to play those kinds of games? Man is oblivious."

"Wow. You could drop a hint, do the best-friend wingman thing—pun intended."

"Oh no, I don't think either one of them would appreciate that. Trust me, it's going to hit him over the head with the force of a boulder one day soon enough."

"I'm going to make sure I'm stocked up on popcorn."

—Conversation between Dahlia Dehlavi and Adam Garrett (circa September 2083)

ADAM KNEW THE answer he was going to get even before Sascha, Hanz, and Naia walked out of Jacques's room after Hanz's second attempt. Hanz was crying, his young face marked by exhaustion. Naia held his hand and murmured words of comfort, while Sascha had her arm around the male.

She shook her head gently at Adam, her cardinal eyes devoid of starlight.

Fuck!

The scream was internal, and echoed by the falcon who was his other half. But out loud he said, "Thank you for trying," and—going on instinct—cradled the boy against his chest.

The E held on to him, apologizing.

"There's nothing to apologize for," Adam reassured him, viscerally aware of the kid's youth, his falcon spreading its wings over the boy. "You did all you could, and for that, you will always be a friend to WindHaven."

After Sascha led Hanz out to the bedroom the clan had made up for him, Adam turned to Naia. She'd held it together till then, been strong for the boy, but now his dedicated, empathic healer, to whom the entire clan were pieces of her heart, collapsed into his arms.

Adam couldn't cry, his tears locked deep within, but an hour later, after everyone else was lost to sleep and Kavi was in her office, he sat exhausted and restless beside Jacques's bed and told his best friend off for being a fucking asshole and leaving them all when they needed him so much.

Even then, the tears wouldn't come, his anger too huge a rock in his chest.

"You're meant to be by my side for decades. Meant to be the hard head who knocks sense into me if I lose it. You're not meant to fucking die, Jacques."

Even with all hope gone, he didn't want to take the final step. But quite aside from his promise to Jacques, that was part of what being wing leader meant—he had to stand in front of all the hits, take the hardest blows. As he wished he could've taken the blows that had smashed his best friend out of the sky.

"I reached out across the entire healer network again," Naia had told him before she let sleep suck her under, her grief an open wound. "Just in case."

"No results," Adam guessed, because if anyone had come up with a solution, Naia wouldn't be in this state.

"No." She'd kept her head on his chest, his one of the few she could lean on in the clan—it wasn't about love, but about people looking to her for their cue on how to react to the unfolding tragedy.

The minute Naia cracked, so would the rest of them.

Even Malia, so determinedly cheerful when she dropped off memory cubes for Jacques with his favorite music and her chatty updates on the clan, would crack with a finality that couldn't be repaired.

"Sascha pulled every string she could for us to get Hanz," he told Jacques now.

Thanks to your grandmother's willingness to embrace change.

Words his best friend would've said if he could. He'd always been one of Aria's biggest fans.

"I can see which way the wind is blowing, Adam," his grandmother had said to him when he was yet the most junior of her wing-seconds. "We can't fly alone anymore, relying on nothing but flight path agreements."

A cupping of his face with her aged hands. "You're going to take us into the future, my boy. And it's time I talked to you about what that means."

Adam had long known he'd lead WindHaven after his grandmother—it wasn't about nepotism or getting elected. Changeling clans didn't work that way. It came down to an inner hum of power that spoke to every other member of the clan. Adam's had exploded to the surface that day in the courtroom when he'd almost managed to break the hold of two powerful adult wing-seconds.

It was that same part of him that allowed a teleport to the Canyon forty-five minutes after he'd returned to sit with Jacques. Sascha, the right side of her face marked with the lines of her short rest, was the one who'd tracked him down to Jacques's room to request he permit the teleporter and his passenger—another E.

"They'll have to come in on the plateau," Adam said, without explaining why. "The X is still up there for a visual reference."

Adam led the couple into the infirmary less than three minutes later.

"I don't know how Jaya managed to convince Abbot to teleport her," she told Adam as the E in question attempted to reach Jacques, while an Arrow with blue eyes reminiscent of the sea watched over her. "She's running on fumes, and he knows it."

Jaya Storm's exhaustion was clear in the droop of her shoulders and the heaviness in her face, but Adam also saw a look of determination that he recognized from his own healer. "Nothing could've stopped her, and her mate knows it." That the two were mated was clear to his changeling senses. "Better he comes with her so he can keep an eye on her."

"She's stubborn," Sascha agreed. "She was the first E to realize that some of us are born with the ability to get through to people locked inside their minds—whether in comas, or due to accidents that take away their ability to communicate in any other fashion."

Now, as Adam watched, Jaya swayed beside the bed. Her mate was with her in a heartbeat, grabbing hold of her. Jaya turned to Adam with eyes gone obsidian, no whites, no irises, and managed to gasp out, "I couldn't reach him."

Adam's neck stiffened, his chest a giant bruise.

Abbot swung her into his arms at that instant, paused, then shot Adam a look that said he'd just tried to teleport out . . . and failed. But he kept his silence as Adam led him quickly back outside, leaving Sascha to wait with Jacques. The Arrow met his gaze out on the darkness of the plateau, his mate already unconscious, and said, "Empaths take a vow of confidentiality when it comes to any action related to a patient. As her escort, I'm bound by the same vow."

Adam appreciated the clear verbal assurance that neither of the pair would be sharing what they'd learned here this night. "Understood."

"There's no one else?" he asked Sascha after the couple had left and he'd returned to the infirmary.

Not a single star in Sascha's eyes. "No, I'm so sorry, Adam."

Adam knew they'd been lucky to get Hanz, much less Jaya. He'd kept up with what was going on in the PsyNet, had even blood-bonded Psy children into the clan when it appeared their PsyNet was about to collapse with catastrophic effect. Those children were now part of his heart, even though their pulses were distant and muffled because they'd never been fully integrated into the clan, their link to the PsyNet the far stronger bond.

"I was hoping for a miracle." Naia's statement was a husky murmur when he told her what had happened only a bare fifty minutes later, the night yet heavy around them. He'd known she wouldn't sleep much, not just because she was a healer, but because this was Jacques.

"That faint line on the brain wave pattern." She stroked her hand over Jacques's tight curls, the shadows under her eyes a dark mauve. "I thought they'd find him in there, just lost."

"Yeah." It was all Adam could get out.

Naia, so gentle of heart but with a steel core when it came to the well-being of her clan, came to take his hand, her own warm and soft. "He wouldn't want this." A crack in her voice even as she fought for Jacques's right to leave them for skies eternal. "But you'll have to make the call." Gentle voice, her other hand closing around his upper arm in silent comfort. "His parents are in no state to decide."

Jacques's parents had been in flight in a distant part of the state when he was shot and had arrived home just in time to see him before Hanz went in to attempt contact. His mother's tears had been silent and constant; his father's rage a thing Adam well understood. His sister had arrived a couple of hours after them; younger than Jacques, still a student at a university on the other side of the country, she was barely holding it together. Jacques was her big brother, the one who'd been known to fly all the way across the country just to visit with her over breakfast or lunch.

She'd spent an hour sobbing in Adam's arms.

"I would never ask his family to make the decision. It's a wing leader's job." Because they weren't human, were changeling. "How long before we have no choice?"

"I can keep him alive on machines forever," was Naia's quiet response. "There remains that faint brain pattern . . . and we have the tech to keep his body going."

"No." If the mind and heart and soul that made Jacques a hard-assed protector, a loving son and brother, and a blood-loyal friend were gone, then Adam had to let his body go, too. Jacques had spent more time in the air than any of them. If some small part of him was alive in there, he'd *hate* to be tied to this bed.

"The clan needs to say good-bye, but he wouldn't want to be seen like this." Adam broke contact with Naia, squeezed his hands open and shut.

"We can say good-bye to his spirit," Naia said, "without ever exposing his body." A single tear rolled down her cheek, to be quickly followed by others. "I'm going to miss you, my friend." Leaning down, she pressed a kiss to his cheek. "I wonder if you ever knew how much I adore you, you bad-tempered, beautiful man."

Adam had known, had been waiting for Jacques to figure it out. Now time had run out for his best friend and for the woman who thought he hung the moon.

The last clan funeral had been Aria's.

That good-bye had hurt, but it had been part of the natural way of things, Aria having lived a life long enough by her standards.

"Too long, Adam," she'd said to him one night, as the two of them sat under the desert moon, their backs to the Canyon wall. "I've outlived a daughter, outlived the man that daughter loved, outlived the mate I loved with all my being."

Then she'd turned to him, stroked her hand over his hair.

"But I also got to watch two strong and wild grandchildren, then great-grandchildren being born, got to hold each of them on the days of their births. And I got to bear a child, love her, and love the man who helped me make her. It's been a good life in the grand scheme of things."

A breath. "And I've upheld my vows as wing leader. When I go, I will leave WindHaven in good hands. I can hear the desert singing to me, Adam." She'd sighed. "My father's father used to say that our clan lands were blessed with the quietest places, that we were renowned for it until many came here to bathe in the silence, but I've always heard the song. Now it calls me home."

He'd wanted to ask her to stay a little longer, but the tiredness in her voice had been an ache. So he'd put his arm around his grandmother and for the first and only time in their relationship, he'd held her as if he was the wing leader, she the member of his clan who needed his strength.

And, swallowing back his tears at the thought of her presence missing from his life, he'd told her that if she wanted to fly, he'd hold her clan safe for her. "I promise, Shimásání."

Two days later, Aria, beloved of her family and of her clan, ever to be remembered in their songs, had slipped away to fly wing tip to wing tip with Adam's grandfather, their skies distant from this world.

Jacques's death would be nothing akin to Aria's. They'd mourned her, but they'd also been able to celebrate her. Those who'd known her as a youth—themselves graybeards—had told raucous tales of the young woman she'd been, and of her courtship of Adam's far quieter and more submissive grandfather.

"She might as well have been a bear as far as he was concerned!" one old friend had said with a slap to his knee. "Poor man didn't know whether to run or surrender."

With Jacques, there would be no celebration, only pain and a horrible sense of unfairness. He was Adam's age, their birthdays exactly three weeks apart, had been in the prime of his life.

Adam walked back to Jacques after Naia was called away to deal with a minor injury. His best friend lay motionless underneath the domed lid of the medical bed that was keeping his body alive, only his face exposed to the air.

And that face . . .

Adam's gut twisted. No, this wasn't Jacques, and Adam couldn't put off the final call any longer. He'd give Jacques's family time to say their farewells in the day to come, and then . . . then he'd let Jacques go.

That thought was heavy in his gut as he left the infirmary, and he was glad not to run into anyone else as he made his way to his office. This far from dawn, the clan slept. Shutting the door to his office regardless, he picked up a pen he never used but couldn't throw out, then pulled up the documents Jacques had left in the clan's keeping in the event of his death.

He knew it was a way to delay the conversation he needed to have with Jacques's mom and dad and sister, but on this day when he knew he'd lose his friend, he gave himself that grace. He had to come to terms with it first before he went to them, so he could be strong while they fell apart.

He pulled up the first document—a letter to him.

Well, shit, Adam, if you're reading this, I'm fucking dead.

A laugh tore out of him even as his eyes burned.

Unable to bear it, he shut down the document and, thrusting the pen back down on his desk, strode out through the quiet hallways, to exit out into the canyon on the wings of a falcon. He didn't even know where he was flying to through the cool darkness until he swept over the inn and saw her vehicle parked in front of her room.

Chapter 17

A breath

Fingers that do not touch

An uncrossable divide

Some stories . . .

. . . are unfinished

—"Story Fragment" by Adina Mercant, poet (b. 1832, d. 1901)

ADAM LANDED AT the clothing cache nearest the inn.

It took him only a minute to pull on a pair of jeans and a black tee. Then he was jogging barefoot through the trees with the familiarity of a man who'd been a boy on this same soil, knew it inside out. The darkness embraced him in a way that brought comfort, muffling the anguish to come on the dawn.

When he emerged behind the inn, it was to see Eleri's lights on at an hour when the rest of the world slept.

I don't sleep much.

She opened the door before he could knock once again, and the fact that she was wearing her suit pants and a white shirt with the sleeves rolled up, her hair sleeked back into a neat bun, told him she either hadn't gone to bed at all—or had woken after a couple of hours and decided to ready herself for the day.

"What's happened?" Her eyes searched him with a quickness he could almost read as concern. "Jacques?"

She went as if to pull him inside, only to hesitate right before her bare fingers made contact with his arm. The air hung, the moment frozen.

Dropping her hand, she stepped back. "Come inside."

He entered.

He could lie, tell himself he didn't know why he'd come to her, but he knew. He'd *always* known.

Striding in, he pushed the door shut behind him with extreme care only because otherwise he would've slammed it and woken the other guest—who Mi-ja had put three rooms over, if the guest's shiny sedan was parked in the correct spot.

"Did you feel *anything*?" he found himself asking this woman who'd haunted him for ten years. Only it wasn't an ask, rather a demand stripped of all niceties. "That first time. In the—"

"—hallway," she completed, her eyes locked to his in the hushed silence of a world swathed in darkness. "You were leaning up against a wall away from the rest of your clan, your tie askew and your knuckles raw."

"I'd just punched one of the courthouse's stone columns." His throat was lined with grit, his words serrated. "And I haven't worn a tie since that day." He'd done it to honor his parents, and to ensure their party would be taken seriously in the courtroom—he'd still believed in justice then.

"I didn't know who you were," Eleri said, her own voice different in a way he couldn't quite pinpoint—it wasn't that she was suddenly awash in emotion. She was just . . . less flat by a fraction. "But I could tell you were changeling, so I thought you must have some connection to the case, because as far as I knew, it was the only changeling-related case on the docket that day."

"You offered me a bandage." He'd been struck dumb by the sight of her as she turned the corner, a slim young woman in a crisp black pantsuit paired with a white shirt buttoned up to the neck, her hair in a neat braid.

"You stared at me for a long time before you said for me to stay, that it would 'heal up real quick. Changeling skin is tough.'"

His heart punched against his rib cage at her exact recitation of his long-ago words. "I heard Js have eidetic memories."

"Only for the memories we read. Our own . . . we lose them over time, so much flotsam in the sea of other people's echoes."

"But you remember that day, that moment."

"That day defined my existence," she said, her voice quiet now, and still with no depth, as if he spoke to a shadow. "In more ways than one."

He went to grasp her upper arms, shake her, but halted. "What happens if I touch you?" He expected her to say he had no right to touch her. Or if not that, to tell him that he'd kill her by overloading her.

He would believe her, would *have* to believe her. Because the idea of actually doing her harm? *Fuck, no.*

But Eleri said, "I don't know. Changelings have natural shields. Sophie's husband has a natural shield."

Adam frowned. "I met a J with dark hair, purplish blue eyes once. Her name was Sophia." It had been in a home that sat partially on DarkRiver lands, partially on SnowDancer. The woman he'd met had been a visitor whose stay had overlapped his by only a few minutes; she'd been leaving the home of DarkRiver sentinel Mercy, who was mated to a SnowDancer lieutenant.

A number of packmates from both packs had been floating around at the time, the couple having hosted a casual afternoon gathering of friends. DarkRiver and SnowDancer's alliance had gone far beyond agreements and territorial lines to a thing of blood in the children Mercy and her mate had created.

Triplets who were cherished by both packs.

Winged clans tended not to bond that way to other clans for the simple reason that their ways were not those of the predatory changelings who claimed the ground, but seeing how the wolves laughed with the leopards while ribbing them mercilessly—and vice versa—had made Adam consider if winged clans could learn from their example.

After all, a falcon was as deadly a predator as a wolf.

That day, as Mercy walked her guest out, she'd stopped by Adam. "Adam, this is Sophia."

"Hi, Sophia." Having spotted the black gloves on Mercy's guest's hands, Adam hadn't offered her a handshake—he hadn't known what the gloves meant at the time, but it didn't take a genius to work out that it was a subtle message not to touch.

"Adam's a falcon," Mercy had told Sophia with a grin. "I know it's driving you crazy."

Sophia's eyes had crinkled at the corners. "It was. You . . . feel different," she'd said to Adam. "The way you walk, your presence, it's hard to put my finger on it. I apologize if I was being unintentionally nosy."

Adam had waved off the apology, smiled. "We play the same game with Psy—telepath, telekinetic, something else? It's as hard to tell for us as it is for you to figure out our animals."

"Sophia's a former J," Mercy had shared even as she leaned down to scoop up a baby who was doing a race-crawl toward a large platter of chips on a low table. "Nope, nope, nope," she'd said to the baby in a voice both firm and full of love. "You do not want to pull those down on your head. No, not even if you're adorable."

Laughing, the baby had smacked her with a wet kiss before said baby was stolen away by a passing young packmate who threw the delighted child over his muscular shoulder as he headed outside.

"These days," Mercy had said without missing a beat, "Sophia keeps Nikita Duncan in line." While Adam was still digesting the latter, Mercy had pointed out the window at a lean, dark-haired male. "That's her husband, Max, out by the car with Clay. Next time, you'll have to coordinate your visits so I can do a proper introduction."

"Max," Adam said on the heels of the memory. "Her husband's name was Max."

Eleri nodded. "Yes, that's Sophie." She didn't break eye contact. "Max is human, but he has a natural shield."

"I saw them touch." It had been after Sophia walked over to join Max. "She looked happy, not under stress."

Locking his gaze to Eleri's in a silent question, he telegraphed his intention to touch her by raising his hand. When she didn't move, he very, *very* lightly placed his hand against her clothed upper arm. She didn't react. So he exerted more pressure.

A reaction now, a motionlessness. But—"There's no overload." She was the one to raise her bare hand, reach for him.

He flinched.

She halted.

"It could kill you if you're wrong," he ground out, because no matter what he'd said to her that first day, no matter his anger and raw sense of betrayal, Adam would *never, ever hurt her.*

"Fleeting contact when I'm prepared won't cause harm." She moved her fingers slowly toward his bare forearm.

A butterfly brush of his rigid skin.

An exhale. "Nothing." She tried again, this time holding the contact for a second. "Nothing but you." A whisper. "I sense a turbulent wildness on the edge of my perception, an awareness of a great winged creature . . . but there's no pain, no sense of overload. I don't feel your memories."

It hit him then. "How long since you've touched another person?"

She still had her fingers on his forearm, was staring at the connection, didn't seem to hear him.

"Eleri." He shook her a little, just a little, with that one hand he had on her upper arm.

"I found Reagan," she whispered, her hand dropping away. "I held his body as he died. He mistimed it, was still alive in the physical sense. I was able to hold him so he didn't die alone. Maybe he knew."

Another wave of rage, primal with the falcon's fury. His hands tightened on her biceps and only then did he realize he was gripping her with both hands now. "I can't hear that name. Don't say it around me."

The falcon clawed at him, wanting out, wanting to strike at a foe long dead. "The only reason that fucker didn't die at my hands is because it would've brought the Council's attention to the clan." He'd still have gone after him if his grandmother hadn't managed to calm him down.

"Our vengeance will be against the one who took their lives," she'd said, her face grim. "The one who helped in the injustice is our unknowing ally—he set the murderer free for us to find."

He'd held on to that logic because it had been the only thing keeping him sane.

Eleri's eyes were black now, but they were nothing like Sascha's. The empath's darkness had held grief, the black soft with shadows. Eleri's were an endless nothingness. "He was my mentor; more than that, he was the only paternal figure of any kind I ever had."

Adam wanted to thrust her away from him, but he couldn't. That was the problem. "I *hate you*," he said, and it was a harsh, grating whisper that hid a heart torn and bleeding. "For showing me what could've been only to tear it away so viciously."

He squeezed her biceps, his talons curling around her but not cutting through. Never cutting through. "Did you know?" She wasn't changeling, their ways not hers.

"I thought you were the most beautiful being I had seen in all my life," she said in that flat tone that held none of the wonder in her words. "I didn't know someone that beautiful could exist."

Her fingers rising, brushing his jaw. "I felt a compulsion to go to you, to give you something, anything. But you wouldn't even take a bandage from me." She pressed her hand over his heart. "I felt another, even deeper compulsion to take your hand and just run, *hide* both of us. I didn't even know you and I wanted desperately to *keep you*. I thought I was going mad."

Her words scraped away the scars to reveal the throbbing wound she'd inflicted on his heart that day. "You did give me something," he found himself saying.

"No. I'd remember. I remember everything about that interaction."

So did he. Down to the way her lashes had come down over her eyes, and how her pulse had jumped in her throat. "When the bailiff called your name, and you walked away to head to the courtroom, you dropped a pen."

He'd caught it before it hit the floor, which attracted her attention, and put it in his pocket. A symbol of good luck, he'd thought then, because surely the fact that he'd met her on this benighted day meant everything. Maybe even that his parents were there, giving him one final gift.

He'd met his *mate* at only eighteen.

He'd heard of such sudden meetings but mostly in entertainment shows. All the mated couples he knew had grown toward each other over time until the mating bond kicked in. Or like his grandparents; they'd been part of the same clan or friendly groups of clans, their paths crisscrossing since childhood.

Mating at first sight was a romantic myth, he'd thought when making fun of Saoirse's romance novels like the arrogant kid brother he'd been. Then it had hit him like a roundhouse punch, both sides of his nature in perfect harmony.

There she is. My mate. Mine.

Later, after the horror of that courtroom, he'd laughed at himself through a haze of angry tears. And he'd seen the same pen he'd so carefully tucked away as a scalpel thrust into his heart. "I kept it all this time as a reminder to never seek you out, that whatever might've been between us died that day."

He was still holding her, their bodies too close, their breaths intermingling as she tipped her head back to meet his gaze. "I'm sorry. I know there's no forgiveness, and it's selfish of me even to speak the words, but I can no more stop them than I could stop myself from talking to you that day. I'm sorry, Adam."

A shine on the right side of her face, a single tear rolling down her cheek.

He took one hand off her, caught the tear with his fingertip, his heart thudding to a different beat now. "You're crying." A part of him that would never forget her, even as it couldn't forgive her, wanted to hope.

She looked at the teardrop balanced on his fingertip as if she was looking at something unrelated to herself. "You reach a part of me beyond the numbness. So deep that even I can't feel it. All I see is a wall of gray."

She touched her finger to the teardrop, took the finger to her mouth as if to taste her own pain.

He gripped her jaw. "I *can't* forgive you." The betrayal was too huge, the anguish too enormous. "I needed you to choose me that day! I needed you to fight for us!" That it had been an irrational expectation didn't matter, not between them. Not when it was her.

"I know." Her hand on his heart again, and he had the sense she was listening to his heartbeat. "There can never be anything that will balance those scales."

He wanted to shake her all over again. "How can you be like this?" he asked in a snarl before finally releasing her and striding away, the falcon inside him beating its wings.

"Js feel too much," she said. "That's why the Council kept reconditioning us. Reconditioning me. Making me perfect over and over again, until there's not much of my original personality left . . . and nothing but a gray wall in its place."

It wasn't, he realized, an excuse. She'd never once tried to obfuscate things from him since the moment they met again.

The true horror of what she was saying seeped into him drop by cold drop.

Chapter 18

Further to our previous discussions on the lack of satisfactory Silence in a percentage of our younger adults, I would like to present to you an option my team has termed "reconditioning."

It is a less rigorous process than Councilor Adelaja's brilliant suggestion of "rehabilitation" but could be utilized for more minor cases of deviation from the protocol.

—Councilor Vey Gunasekara to fellow members of the Psy Council (circa 2013)

"WHAT DO YOU mean not much of your original personality left?" he demanded.

"Have you heard of rehabilitation?" She continued before he could answer. "It wipes out the person, leaves a shell behind. Reconditioning, on the other hand, just sands away the edges, smooths over any cracks, erases any hint of a breach in Silence . . . or it did, before the fall of the protocol."

She shook her head. "With Js, there are always breaches. You saw that when you met me—I felt and felt deeply. Js walk in the minds of the worst of the worst—there's no protocol that can hold strong against such a barrage from *inside* our shields."

Adam knew his eyes had gone falcon long ago. Now he forced his talons back in before he began to use them on the room. "How many times?"

She stared into nothingness for a moment. "Seven, I think. Though it could be more. I stopped keeping track as much after the fourth time—I didn't feel I had many edges left by then. There wasn't much to protect or to mourn."

"Sophia's older than you. She's not like you," he said, wanting her to tell him this could be reversed—because the two of them? They weren't fucking done. "I met her, saw her smile and laugh."

"I think Sophie's cleverer than I am, hid her edges better," Eleri said. "But she also told me she had an experience in childhood that altered her in profound ways, anchoring her to the PsyNet. Perhaps that helped her retain more pieces of herself."

Adam could hear neither admiration nor grief nor hope in Eleri's voice. It was as if she was a statue frozen in time. "Can you reverse it?" he asked even when he knew there was no point.

What hope could there be for a mating born in betrayal and coated with heartbroken anger?

Eleri shook her head. "It's why reconditioning wasn't used more generally. It works but it eventually destroys the mind and the personality. With working Js, that's not a bad trade-off, since before Silence, we just went insane anyway after a certain period."

Adam's face was hot, his falcon wanting to tear out of his skin. They'd taken everything from that sweet, pretty girl who'd wanted to give him a bandage. Even her ability to be angry at what they'd done to her. And in so doing . . . they'd taken everything from him. Because only now, standing here in this room where Eleri told him there could be no hope, did he realize he'd never quite given up on her.

Some desperate part of him had hoped that she would find her way to him . . . and find a way to make up for what she'd done.

He'd been waiting for her all this time.

Adam suddenly couldn't think about that any longer, the weight of it too huge. Shifting on his heel, he paced mindlessly to the table where she'd obviously been working. His eye fell on a number of printouts sealed inside what appeared to be clear evidence envelopes. "What are these? You keeping a scrapbook about the Sandman?"

A pause that went on long enough that the hairs on his nape stirred. He turned, looked at her. "Eleri?"

"They were slipped under my door." She strode over to group them together, then put them into a folder. "I'll be handing them over to the task force—"

He gripped her chin, fear a surge in his blood. "He knows you're here."

"It might not be him." She didn't move. "It could be anyone who recognized me."

"Don't bullshit me."

"If anything," she said, "it's good news. Now I don't suspect I'm on the right track. I know it."

Even as ice crawled up his spine, she pulled out of his hold to store the evidence in the case she'd shown him, the one that held the letters. She locked it as he watched. "I can't let them out of my sight until they're en route, but I don't expect the forensic team to find anything. He's too smart to have left prints. Someone authorized to transport them should arrive in Raintree before lunch."

Shifting on her heel before he could snap at her for her utter lack of response to the danger she was in, she said, "How is Jacques?" and the pinpoint accuracy of her question was a bullet through the heart.

Because a mate would act that way, would just know what was wrong with him.

"I have to let him go." The words came out grating, broken. "No one can reach him, and his brain readings are so faint as to not exist."

"I'm sorry. I've lost friends. Each loss takes a piece of you." Unadorned, flat, and piercing in their bluntness, her words helped in ways he'd never expected.

She was a woman he'd told himself to hate over and over again, and yet it felt as if they'd never stopped their conversation in the hallway. She was still offering him bandages, this time for his soul.

And on this morning, dark and cold and crushing, he was too hurt and lost to push her away. He collapsed onto the sofa, his hands in his hair as he stared down at the old-fashioned carpet. "We were crèchemates. We grew up together." Adam could still see the wild and brash eighteen-year-old Jacques had been. "He's been part of every important moment of my entire life."

A thousand memories overflowed his mind. "He was right there beside me on our first solo flights as fledglings, and he was there the day my grandmother told me my parents had been murdered. The same man celebrated wildly with me when I was made a wing-second two months before his own promotion."

Happiness or grief, Jacques had stood beside Adam for all of it. "He was meant to grow into a disreputable old man with me. I was meant to babysit his fledglings so he could go on date-night flights with his mate—he always wanted a huge brood. He promised me that he'd be there to the very end."

Eleri's legs in front of him, her body so close he could've grabbed her, pressed his face to her stomach as he allowed his emotions to roar through him. If she'd been his mate, he wouldn't have hesitated, would've let her comfort him, love him, make this terrible thing somehow bearable.

Hands fisted, he dropped them to his thighs and looked up.

"There's no hope at all?" She tucked a strand of hair behind her ear, her bones far too visible beneath her skin for all her obvious strength.

Following the movement because watching her when she was close was a compulsion, he suddenly jerked to his feet, his heart thundering. "*How* sensitive are your hands with an unshielded being?"

"On the extreme end. If I deteriorate any further, the gloves won't work." Eleri looked at his face, then down at her hands. "You want me to see if I can pick up anything from your injured clanmate?"

Again, she followed his thoughts so quickly, as if she'd known him a lifetime. "Can you?" he asked past the torment of knowing what they could've been.

"Js read memories," Eleri said, but her brain was connecting the dots Adam already had. "But we *are* telepaths, and Sensitivity ramps up that ability to deadly levels. So yes, it's possible I could sense something, but if he's unconscious, it's an E you need. They—"

"Two empaths who specialize in comatose patients have already attempted to reach him—they can't."

His pain was writ large in the grooves carved into his face, his emotions open to the world.

Adam Garrett would never hide who he was and who he loved.

A part of her, perhaps the same part that could still cry even if she couldn't feel the sorrow that engendered the tear, wondered what it would be like to mean that much to her beautiful boy grown into a powerful man.

I have missed you all my life without ever knowing you.

Words she could never speak aloud. Words she'd barely dared to think in the depths of Silence. Words she would take with her to her grave.

"If the empaths haven't been able to reach him . . ." She didn't want to say it, didn't want to tell him the blunt truth. Because even numbed by repeated reconditionings, she never again wanted to hurt Adam Garrett. "Why do you think I might succeed where they haven't?"

"Jacques is caught between his two selves. His mind isn't like any the Es would've encountered before, his brain pathways neither falcon nor human." Adam paced the room. "Since your sensitivity is instinctive, you might react to him on a primal level."

He paused, turned to hold her gaze with that of a falcon, the ring of yellow vivid in the low light inside the room. "I need to know if my friend is in there. I have to be sure before I let him go."

Eleri nodded. "I'm willing to make the attempt." The truth was that she'd have given Adam anything he wanted. The imprint he'd left on her was far beyond anything she understood, and it predated the repeated reconditionings and the piece-by-piece fragmentation of her personality—and that imprint said that she was his in any way he'd permit.

But then Adam's expression turned dark. "What's the risk to you?" he asked, striding back to stand toe-to-toe with her, the silk of his hair tumbled around his face. "Could it cause an overload?"

"The risk is negligible, given what you said about the Es. I've heard the ones who work with coma patients can sense even the most subtle emotional response." Not that it would've stopped her regardless. Because despite everything, she was still that girl who wanted to give Adam something.

Adam didn't move, his eyes once more on her hands. "What happens if Jacques rises to consciousness without warning and you get the full blast of his emotions?"

"That's so unlikely as to not matter," she said with as much care as she could, but knew it came out robotic. "If there was a chance of that, the Es wouldn't have given up. He's down too deep to rise to the surface at speed."

Adam still didn't head for the door, didn't tell her to follow. "How will I know if you're overloaded so I can break the connection? Will that protect you?"

"If it's fast enough, the damage will be minor. Are any of the Es still at the Canyon?"

"Both, but the young one has done enough, has no more to give, and I won't ask it of him. Sascha's there and ready to help."

Sascha.

He had to mean Sascha Duncan, a woman who had done what Eleri couldn't and defected out of the Net to create an entirely new existence for herself inside a changeling pack.

Eleri said, "She should be able to feel my distress—I won't be able to control it, not if Jacques's thoughts breach my mind."

Stepping back, she said, "I'll get my gloves. We should do it now while your clan sleeps. Less chance of contact with me."

That day in the hallway, Adam had dreamed of introducing her to his grandmother, showing her off to Jacques. "My mate," he'd have said with a huge grin. "My *mate*."

The joy of it had been enough to overcome the pain of that day—because he'd known his parents would've been delighted for him, too. Shocked no doubt, because she was Psy, and back then, no Psy had mated a changeling for so long that they'd forgotten it had ever been any different. But happy all the same . . . and full of advice about the importance of going slow, of giving Eleri room to become used to the idea.

"You're both so young," he could imagine his mother saying, a soft smile curving her generous lips, her skin a glowing copper-toned brown she'd passed on to both him and Saoirse. "You have your whole lives ahead of you. Play together, learn one another, become friends before you become mates."

He would've done exactly as she'd advised, would've given Eleri all of himself and all the time she needed. Because in the end, she would've been his—they'd both felt the promise in the air that day, not just him.

Today, too many years between then and now, he waited for her to reemerge from the small nook that held the bed, then said, "We can take your vehicle. I flew."

Eleri stilled for a moment. "I can't quite conceptualize a shift," she said at last. "I've seen falcons flying overhead, and I know from their size that they're changelings, but my brain snags when attempting to explain the conversion."

Adam's falcon, so close to his skin, wanted to show her then and there. He barely controlled the urge. "I'll have to drive. You'll never get up to the Canyon in the dark."

"I'll program you in," she said, and once they were at the car—evidence stowed and locked inside the trunk—she proceeded to do exactly that.

Getting in, he waited only until she was secured before moving the vehicle out without turning on the headlights until they were well down the drive. "Any dealings with Dae since we spoke?"

"He knocked on the door last night asking me if I'd had any issues with the lights, as the businessperson who stayed in the room the night before my arrival complained about that. But he didn't make any attempt to stay or talk his way inside when I said no."

Adam frowned. "How late?"

"After dark but just. Mi-ja was in the administration building—I could see the lights." She pulled out a miniature organizer from her pocket, tapped at it, and small clear screens flipped out on all four corners to seamlessly create a much larger visual field.

Adam whistled. "Expensive tech."

"Js are well compensated due to the short terms we're able to work during our lives," Eleri said, her eyes on her screen.

Adam's hands squeezed the steering wheel. "Why," he said, asking the question he'd avoided since the day she'd walked back into his life, "are there no old Js?" It was a fact of which he'd become consciously aware two years after he'd met her—because he hadn't been able to stop reading news articles about J-Psy despite himself.

Eleri didn't reply, her silence a heavy weight in the air.

"Tell me," he demanded, stripped down to the bone from what she'd already shared about her reconditioning and what it meant.

No flinch from his passenger, but she looked up from her organizer. "The only old Js are the ones who managed to stop active work at an early age and stay under the radar.

"Active Js tend to self-terminate more often than any other Psy specialty. Sensitivity can lead to Exposure. Gloves, shields, nothing works at that point. We become a living and wide-open psychic nerve. We prefer to exit the world prior to that—because we can't once Exposed. We're no longer functional."

Adam's talons thrust out of his fingers, his falcon's feathers a shadow under the skin. "Why aren't you angry? Why aren't you furious at the injustice of having given your life to a system that just throws you away?"

Her apathy enraged him.

Eleri's response was to change the subject. "I had a friend in Enforcement check if Dae had a record."

Adam wasn't one to let things go, but this wasn't just about the two of them—because that conversation, they *would* be having. "He didn't last time the clan ran a check."

"Two hits while he was still a juvenile, both for breaking and entering. Wiped from his adult record, but my contact has ways to see below the wipe."

Adam thought past his instinctive reaction to Dae. "Lot of the human kids in Raintree do petty shit like that, though I wouldn't have guessed Dae to be one of them." The falcon fledglings knew not to even think about it, because the clan's punishment would be far worse than anything Enforcement meted out.

WindHaven kids also had the whole sky to burn off their energy, could travel long distances on a whim if they wanted to go to a club or meet up with distant friends. And they were changeling, they didn't hanker for big-city living beyond taking flights over new regions. Flying to a private grotto to go swimming and just hang out was "peak vacation," per his niece.

"Agreed," Eleri said now. "It's not anything probative." Closing up her organizer, she slid it away into a pocket of her suit coat. "Do you know about the recent spate of strange break-ins?"

"Yeah. Deputies blamed it on 'punk kids' and so did the chief back at the beginning, but he was starting to change his mind."

"The escalation. Near-contact."

Adam nodded. "Last we talked, he was considering calling in a favor, getting a profile done. He also told people to lock their doors, but place like Raintree? No one really worries."

He turned onto the road up to the Canyon. "As for Dae, we've put a tracker on his van." Adam had asked Pascal to handle it, the senior wing commander one of the clan's best at computronics.

"Good." Eleri's voice was calm. "If nothing else, it'll eliminate him from our list. The chance my serial is non-Psy is minuscule, but Dae could be developing into another kind of predator."

Silence again, the unspoken words between them daggers in the dark.

You were meant to be the one person I could trust without question all my life. You betrayed me.

The angry denunciation of the youth he'd been.

The man he'd grown into knew it wasn't that simple, that Eleri had had other masters to please . . . and still, he couldn't forgive her. Had it been any other day, any other event . . . maybe. But for her to choose not to speak when it was about justice for the cold-blooded murder of his parents?

Adam's entire being rejected the idea of forgiveness.

Chapter 19

We failed to enter WindHaven's home base. We don't know why, but we tried multiple times. There is something very strange about that canyon.

—Fragment of handwritten text discovered after a fire gutted the library of Clan IceHorizon (circa 1763)

"ANGER," ELERI SAID into the quiet heavy with all the words she could never speak. "It's an emotion with which I had more than a passing acquaintance in my younger years." She could still remember the fury that had unfurled in her after her first major memory reads and recalls.

"No amount of scrubbing could remove the filth that clung to me after I walked through the minds of people who are warped in ways most of the world will never understand." She'd stood in the shower attempting to get clean until her skin was raw and thick with welts. "I couldn't sleep with the rage inside me. I paced all night, ended up so wired that my mind buzzed with a thousand angry bees."

Adam shot her a glance before returning his eyes to the dark road into the Canyon. "It led to your first reconditioning?" His entire frame was a lesson in anger silent and deadly.

"No, it led to my first execution," she said, and was aware of his head jerking toward her before he looked back to the road. "It's an unspoken rule in the system that Js are never to be left alone with certain types of criminals. We . . . break. No amount of reconditioning can fix that tendency."

She spoke on because this time in the dark might be all they'd ever have and she wanted him to remember her . . . because he might.

Reagan was gone.

Saffron, Yúzé, and Bram would follow her into the abyss all too soon.

Her family of record had long erased her from their minds.

Adam Garrett was the only one who might one day *want* to remember her . . . and she wanted him to know her. Not who she'd been in that long-ago hallway, but who she'd become over the years in between. Even if what she was about to say might repulse him.

"During my time, we had to undergo mandatory and intensive counseling sessions with specialist M-Psy—it was an attempt to program us not to kill." The M-Psy hadn't been empaths, of course, and thus had stood no chance against the steel-trap minds of Js who had long ago learned to pretend to be Silent when theirs was a designation that could never be perfect under the protocol.

"We might even have been the only designation under Silence to receive counseling as part of our training. To their credit, the Ms linked to the J Corps did their best. They were as traumatized as their Js in the end—losing client after client to suicide turns out to have a catastrophic effect on all the healing fields." M-Psy linked to Js had higher rates of suicide and madness than any other.

"The Council kept trying nonetheless because Js were important to their hold on power. They were willing to sacrifice a few Ms in the pursuit of that power." It wasn't, after all, one of the rare designations.

"If you're talking about the kind of criminals I think you are," Adam said, his voice no longer wholly human, "then I won't be crying any tears over their executions."

"It's considered vigilante justice." Eleri didn't disagree with that take; she also didn't believe all vigilante justice was bad. "I got very good at releasing my anger by entering certain minds and turning them off." There was no other way to explain the mechanism of what she did.

"Others cause the targets to mutilate themselves, or to suffer nightmares, but I like to go into their minds without warning—so the targets know they're not in control mere seconds before they collapse of 'natural causes.'"

Eleri had never questioned her actions. She'd walked in those minds, knew *exactly* the horrors they'd committed. "The problem with my anger was that it kept growing. Until there were three deaths in my vicinity within the space of three days.

"Multiple senior Js pulled me aside and warned me I was at risk of total rehabilitation unless I reined it in—the authorities turned a blind eye to this 'minor problem' with active Js, but they had their limits."

She could still remember Reagan telling her that if she got herself rehabilitated, she'd leave the world with one less very effective soldier against evil. "Our version of final justice is a temporary release," he'd pointed out. "You have more than a decade of active service left in you—so many more monsters yet to stop—but you won't get the chance if you don't get a grip."

He'd been wrong about how many years she had left, but right otherwise.

"I didn't want to rein it in," Eleri said. "I was a being of rage by then. But Reagan had saved me in so many ways—first by telling me never to let my ability to bend memories come to the attention of the authorities, and second, by covering up some of my executions by calling in favors he'd collected over a lifetime. He asked me to make it out."

Eleri's spine felt as stiff as a rod of steel. "To do that, I had to put my rage in a place where I could control it." It had caused her physical pain at the start, this version of Silence she'd chosen for herself. "I might not have managed to hold on to it, but two months after I began to try, Reagan chose death . . . and it was the last promise he asked of me."

The forces inside Adam churned in a turbulent storm. To him,

Reagan had made a choice that turned him into a villain. But to Eleri, the same villain had been a hero. A hero who had probably saved her life. As for what she'd done, who better to play judge, jury, and executioner than the woman who had walked in the minds of her targets?

The changeling in him found nothing wrong with justified kills.

But part of the storm was his need for her to *feel*. "So that's it?" he said. "Your anger is just gone?"

"No." Nothing in her tone. "It lives far below the surface of my conscious mind—like a great beast beneath a frozen ocean, a shadow lurking. I'd be at high risk of a catastrophic loss of control if it ever broke through."

Adam wasn't done with this, but it would have to wait—he'd almost arrived at the entrance to the underground garage inside the Canyon. The entrance sat a small distance below the plateau, ensuring late-night comings and goings wouldn't disturb those who lived up top.

It was then that he realized how much he wanted to tell Eleri about his people, how much he wanted to have every conversation under the sun with her. It wasn't love; it was the primal pull of the mating bond—meant to be born of love or to turn into love.

The latter pathway didn't exist for them.

We become a living and wide-open psychic nerve. We prefer to exit the world prior to that...

His inner fury darkened, grew ever more animalistic, until Adam wondered who he'd be by the time this was all over.

The SUV's headlights flashed against the subtle road marker designed for falcon eyes. "We're here."

"That looks like a solid wall of stone."

"It's meant to." A quick turn and he was driving into the garage, which was lit up only the softest amount—enough for safety and visibility to their clan, but not enough to permit any light to leak out to outside watchers or those who might think to invade their inner core under the shadow of darkness.

Of course, any such invaders would be at a serious disadvantage, since WindHaven always had patrols in the air above the heart of their home—the place where their young could always feel safe. The memories of the Territorial Wars had never left his people, for while they'd survived as a clan, they'd been devastated in the aftermath.

No one, the survivors had vowed together, would take any of them unawares again. That wary distrust included the Psy who had made him a promise that he believed, but whom he couldn't trust. And though his heart twisted on that acceptance, he didn't fight it.

A wing leader's loyalty was first to his people.

"Aren't you worried I'll take telepathic images of your clan's home location for a teleport lock?" Eleri asked, as if reading his mind.

He could've told her that something in the composition of the Canyon disrupted teleport locks. His clan had discovered that accidentally during the Territorial Wars of the eighteenth century. One of the clans they'd been battling had included a family of teleporters—and they'd been using that advantage to the nth degree.

Except they couldn't get into the Canyon, no matter how many different image locks they managed to acquire. It was a decade postwar, after the two clans were united by a mating, that their once-enemy had shared that strange fact. Adam, conscious that information from the past could become distorted over time, had asked Judd Lauren from the SnowDancer wolves to test the Canyon's impermeability to teleporters.

"Never felt anything like it," the intrigued teleporter had said afterward, staring up at the Canyon from Raintree. "The best way I can describe it is mineral static. Like the stone somehow catches psychic energy and twists it. You ever had it tested?"

"Far as our scientists can tell, it's the same as any other rock around here. Our geologists and others continue to do research on it. My sister's even gotten in on the act, and she's an aeronautical engineer."

"Well, hit me up if you need another test," Judd had said. "This stuff could be the best anti-Tk material ever known. Take a whole massive threat out of the equation. Lot of people—Psy included—would pay money for that." A frown. "I wonder if Kaleb or Vasic could 'port through it."

While Adam knew Judd trusted both men, they were effective strangers to WindHaven, so that question would remain unanswered for the time being. Judd wouldn't unilaterally mention it to them, either, the trust between SnowDancer and WindHaven as strong as the rocks that made up the Canyon.

But Adam didn't tell Eleri that.

Instead, he spoke in a space jagged and broken and private that belonged to them alone. "You betrayed me once. You've promised never to do it again." It didn't come out a threat—it was deeper and harder than that, a challenge from his falcon heart.

"Yes," she said, undaunted and unemotional as he brought the vehicle to a stop. "I don't make promises I don't intend to keep."

Adam felt as if he kept on smashing his head against a stone wall when it came to her, but he couldn't stop doing it even knowing this could have no happy ending. "How many promises have you made?"

He expected silence, but she said, "Not many." A pause before she added, "As a young J, I promised a mother that I would ensure justice for the death of her child. I failed. I executed the man who'd hurt the child, but he died with no blemish on his record."

She took a breath, her hand on the door release. "But the first promise I made as a J was to myself—to always serve justice. I failed."

Beyond his betrayed rage, Adam had always understood that the young J she'd been, the young J who'd changed his life and world in a heartbeat, had had no control over the events in that courtroom. Others had pulled the strings, ensured that a cold-blooded murderer roamed free. Yet she'd made no justifications or excuses no matter how harsh his denunciation, taken the whole burden on herself . . . and he found himself disagreeing with her choice.

"You weren't the one in control," he gritted out. "Even I get that."

"I chose life—for me, for Reagan—over integrity." She pushed open the door. "I sold my honor."

I chose life . . .

Adam got out of the vehicle himself, his heart thundering as her words settled deep inside the hurt of the boy he'd once been. That boy had been so angry that he'd never once considered what he was asking of her when he looked to her in that courtroom, never once realized what she risked if she spoke.

It fractured the entire foundation of his rage.

I SOLD *my honor.*

Eleri deliberately moved that cold truth to the corner of her mind where it always lived. To do otherwise would be to become useless, unable to attempt what Adam had asked of her.

This place, so new and unknown, it helped. "I always thought you'd live in an open area."

"Anyone who lives inside the Canyon has a room that opens out into the sky. Only places like our infirmary and offices are internal."

Something tugged at her . . . a dulled sense of wonder? How extraordinary, that that tiny speck of her had survived, but she was glad of it. "What about your human clanmates?" she said. "Aren't they scared to live in places so high and open to the sky?"

"We make adjustments as needed. Some non-winged clanmates—human and changeling—prefer the plateau. Others like the view from the Canyon, just want a safety barrier that ameliorates the risk. No different from living in a high-rise."

"Yes," Eleri said aloud, but to her mind it was very different. This place with its walls of roughly polished stone had a resonant wildness. She wanted to talk to Adam about that, wanted to know just a little more about his world, steal just a fragment more time.

He stopped in front of an open door. "Here's the infirmary."

All such places, Eleri thought as she stepped inside, had the same tense quiet to them—though this one was missing the scent of antiseptics . . . or perhaps she just couldn't smell them.

Many changelings, after all, had a far stronger sense of smell than Psy or humans. It made sense to her that they'd come up with a formulation that didn't assault their senses. Far different, too, to have an infirmary inside your clan's home than to suffer it for a short time in a hospital.

"You should be sleeping," Adam murmured to the tall and curvy woman who met them at the main door. His voice was rough, the hand he touched to the woman's hollowed-out cheek gentle.

The woman turned her face into his touch, a curl of ebony escaping the clip on the back of her head. "I can't bear to leave him."

A long-numbed part of Eleri stirred, ached, and she understood enough of herself to understand that it was yearning. Once, to survive, she'd have slammed the door shut on the emotion, then told herself she'd never felt anything in the first place . . . but that time was done, the hourglass of her remaining lifetime bare flecks of sand.

Even should Adam forgive her for the unforgivable, her brain had been stripped of all but the merest film of protection. Reconditioning couldn't be reversed; the lost layers couldn't be replaced. There was no walking backward on that dark road littered with the violent and depraved memories of serial killers.

So she let herself feel this one thing that wasn't about pain or guilt, but about a promise of something that might've once been between a young woman who hadn't yet been scarred by evil and a young man who hadn't understood how deep betrayal could cut.

But then the yearning twisted, turned, and became a stabbing that threatened to disable her, and that she couldn't allow, not on this one day when she had made a promise to Adam.

Who turned right then to look at her. "You still okay to attempt to read Jacques?"

She gave a short nod.

But the beautiful woman with black hair and creamy skin hesitated.

"I know a little about the gloves," she said to Eleri. "Information is being shared post-Silence among M-Psy, healers, doctors. Since we might come up against gloved Psy who need help."

"Eleri told me she could handle it since Jacques is in a coma." Adam's fingers gripping Eleri's jaw, the contact already so familiar that the yearning threatened to overwhelm her with thoughts of a future where such touch was commonplace. "You lie?"

"No," Eleri said even as the healer told Adam to break contact in a sharp tone, her body moving as if she'd force the break. As if she had the right to do so.

Changeling hierarchy, Eleri thought, was far more complex than she'd realized.

"It's all right," Eleri said to her. "Changelings have natural shields."

The healer halted, looked between the two of them with a frown.

"To my knowledge," Eleri said to Adam, "the risk is exactly as I told you. The only thing I didn't articulate is that I don't believe he's in there any longer." She softened her voice as much as she could and knew it wasn't enough. "The Es are the specialists. If they couldn't find him . . ."

Adam didn't release her and she didn't pull away. "I know it's worse than a long shot."

It was as if he, too, was attempting to live a lifetime in a moment. The yearning inside her grew so intense that it was a visceral physical pain. "I should do it now," she said, because this was all she had left to give her beautiful boy. "While your clan house is quiet."

"The Canyon," Adam said roughly, the heat of his body a caress against the coldness of her. "We call the entirety of our home the Canyon."

"The Canyon." She hugged the knowledge close as Adam released her at last.

It was time for her to break his heart one more time.

Chapter 20

Eleri, I should be arriving in approximately three hours.

—Message from Bram Priest to Eleri Dias (now)

THE HEALER, WHO Adam introduced as Naia, continued to appear worried, but she didn't stop Eleri from entering the patient room, her eyes dark and huge. Hopeful despite herself, Eleri thought, clinging to this last shred of a chance.

I am so sorry.

She didn't know what she'd been expecting when she walked inside, but it wasn't the twisted half-falcon, half-human body that lay beneath the curving plas of the high-spec monitoring bed that wouldn't have been out of place in an intensive-care unit. He was covered by a sheet below it, but the amputations and malformations were obvious, his face bearing stark evidence of a shift gone catastrophically wrong.

Not halting in her path to the bed because the wall of numbness inside her buried her initial violent shock, she went to stand beside it. "Could you give me an update on his status?" she asked Naia, who'd gone to the foot of the bed. "Especially as it pertains to his brain."

Adam stood in silence beside her as the healer read off the latest numbers from the screen at the end of the bed. The sum total of it all was that Jacques was reading as close to brain-dead as possible except for that one strange pattern that no one could explain. It could, Eleri realized, simply be an error caused by the incomplete shift, his brain readings so askew the computronic system couldn't make sense of them.

Adam and Naia no doubt understood that, too. But they had to be sure they weren't killing their friend and clanmate when they shut down the machines. They had to *know* beyond any doubt that the neural reading wasn't because Jacques was trapped inside, with no way out.

Eleri wanted to give them an answer. "I'm ready."

Naia took a deep breath. "I'm lowering the protective plas."

The clear barrier slipped back into the sides of the bed, leaving Jacques accessible for tactile contact.

Eleri stripped off her gloves, but Adam gripped her forearm when she would've put her hand on the part of Jacques's hand that bore human skin.

Sensing her eyes going pure black on a surge that was her reaction to Adam's proximity, she said, "I won't harm him." She glanced past Naia. "Where is Sascha Duncan? She can mak—"

"Are you *sure* this is safe for you?" Adam interrupted her to demand, and his response spoke to that tiny fragment of her that could feel yearning.

"Yes, I'm sure." She wondered what it would be like to touch him as he'd touched Naia, attempt to offer comfort in the physical changeling way. She could never do that, but she could try with her words. "I'm sorry."

A cardinal-eyed woman dressed in black sweatpants and a black T-shirt, her hair in a loose braid that had begun to unravel and the honey brown of her skin dull with tiredness, perhaps sorrow, rushed into the room. "Naia," Sascha Duncan said. "I got your message. What's happened?"

Even as Naia explained, Adam's fingers tightened on Eleri's forearm, as if to pull her away.

"Let me." A quiet request to allow her to attempt this absolution even if it was destined to fail. He would hate her even more after it was done, but at least he would be at peace with making the call to let Jacques go. She could take that with her to the end. One good thing she'd done for the boy who'd smiled at her.

His jaw worked before he released her.

"Don't shadow me," she said to Sascha, the E who had started an unstoppable avalanche of change. "Even if I can effectively lower my shields, which is doubtful given the progression of my Sensitivity"—her brain fighting desperately to protect her—"I can't protect you from the memories inside me." They floated everywhere now, ugly splinters of evil.

"I can monitor Jacques instead," Sascha said, but when Eleri went to touch Jacques's partially twisted and taloned hand, the empath frowned. "Maybe try another area. Not one where the two sides of his nature are entwined. It might make a difference."

Eleri saw no reason not to follow her advice. "If it's permitted, I'll use the side of his neck. It's visible and appears to have remained fully human." A glance at Naia.

"No falcon structures beneath," Naia confirmed.

"Do it," Adam said, closing his own hand over Jacques's mangled one for a second. "We're coming for you, Jacques. Fly toward us."

Eleri waited until he'd released his friend's hand before placing her fingertips against Jacques's skin. It was warm, his body alive, his pulse slow and steady. But inside him was . . . silence.

Not the kind in which she'd been raised, but the kind that was a void. No wind, no sound, no motion. A quiet so pristine that it was a glass pond deeper than the one she'd experienced with an elderly human once—the woman had been a monk who'd practiced meditation for five decades, and who'd held out her hand in an invitation to touch when a young Eleri looked at her with curiosity.

"I have no shield, child," she'd said after Eleri gasped at the peace of her mind, "because I need no shield. I am one with time and the universe."

Jacques was no monk who lived in a forest. Yet this pristine silence . . . it was too profound, too oddly *thick*. "Is he like you?" she asked Adam. "Wild energy under the skin? Or is he a calmer personality?"

Adam snorted. "Jacques is about as wild as they come."

Naia's smile was bittersweet. "It's why he and Adam are so close. They're as wild as each other."

"Did he meditate?"

Naia broke into shocked laughter. "Jacques? I'd like to see anyone get him to do that." Her tone was rich with affection. "No, he's not the meditating kind."

Eleri walked into the thick silence again; into the void that wasn't empty, wasn't dead, but wasn't quite alive, either.

A paradox.

Was her Psy brain unable to sense him because he was in limbo?

Breaking contact with the injured falcon, she reached her other hand instinctively toward Adam, and for a second, her heart just stopped.

A primal warmth against her, a sense of a huge and wild creature enclosing her in its massive wings.

Protecting, not assaulting.

She could have stood there all day, all night, all year, to the last drops of her existence, but this wasn't about her. Keeping hold of Adam with one hand, she reinitiated contact with Jacques with her other, acting on the same instincts that made her such a ruthless hunter.

The pond rippled.

The wild creature that was Adam went motionless.

A shout so distant it was a dull echo through stone, music as heard through her reconditioned brain.

She gripped Adam's hand harder while pressing her palm against Jacques's neck.

The shout was louder . . . though "loud" was a misnomer, because it remained quieter than the brush of a butterfly's wing. But against her nonexistent psychic skin, it was very much an active *sound*. She was suddenly aware of Adam's urgent voice, wanted to tell him to be quiet so she could focus.

The ripples spread.

She attempted to use the faint motion to shove her psychic hand through the glassy surface.

She pierced it . . . but only the merest inch. And what she touched on the other side, it felt wrong, off. The semi-shift *had* affected Jacques's brain, neither part of him strong enough to be sentient in any true form.

A hard pull from Adam, his hand gripping the one she had on Jacques and physically hauling it off the other man's skin. "You're bleeding." It was a snarl as he released one hand to grab tissues held out by Sascha while Naia ran to grab a scanner.

He pressed the wad to her nose. "You told me this wasn't dangerous." An accusation.

"He's in there," she managed to get out, then took over holding the tissues. "I don't know why I'm bleeding." She turned to let Naia scan her. "I was just *listening* really hard."

Adam's jaw was a granite line, his hand still tight on hers—and his eyes pure falcon. "*Eleri.*"

"I'm sure," she said, hearing the question in the crack in his voice. "But I don't know how to get him out. He's in two pieces and neither piece is . . . complete enough to take action."

"*Fuck*," Adam said at the same time that Naia's expression dropped.

But the healer said, "No damage beyond a few burst blood vessels," to Eleri before swallowing hard. "Nothing you did had any effect?"

Eleri went to reply, sucked in a breath.

The spreading ripples. Invisible droplets falling onto the pristine surface.

"Wait, wait." She pulled away her hand with force, forfeiting the precious contact with Adam. "Don't touch me until I say so."

She put her hand back on Jacques. Nothing. Silence. Glass. "Now."

Adam's fingers sliding through hers.

The pond rippled, that faint shout spearing through.

"It's you," she whispered. "He's reacting to you." And though she wanted this to be her gift to Adam, she knew she wasn't the expert in guiding lost minds to the surface, far less a mind cracked in two.

She looked at Sascha. "Try your empathy again, but this time while in contact with Adam. I'll retain the contact, too."

Giving an immediate nod, Sascha held out a hand across Jacques's body, and Adam took it. Then the empath placed her fingers against Jacques's neck on the opposite side from Eleri. Her intake of breath was audible . . . right before those eyes of darkest obsidian filled with multi-hued light.

Eleri had heard that empathic eyes could do that, but she'd never thought to see it in person.

"Come on, Jacques." Adam's rough voice, his big body all but vibrating as it pushed half against Eleri . . . until she felt held against his wide chest.

Sascha broke contact with Jacques. "I can sense him, but he didn't react to any stimuli." She looked at Eleri, who'd also lifted her hand from Jacques's neck. "What did you feel?"

"A reaction every time Adam was in contact with me, a distant shout."

Sascha frowned. "Can we try again? Perhaps he's just tired after the first attempts."

Nodding, Eleri touched Jacques as Sascha did the same. And heard his shout; if anything, it seemed stronger, more resonant. "I hear him," she said to Sascha.

"I can't. But . . . you're not reading him with your high-level psychic senses. You're using the most instinctual part of you, a part that's never supposed to be revealed or used because it's too close to your vulnerable psychic core."

What a strange irony, that the thing that was killing her might save a life.

"What do I do?" she asked the empath. "I don't know how to pull him out."

Adam made a rough sound in his throat next to her. "You're bleeding again."

"Don't stop me," she ordered before he could pull her away. "It's like a thread that gets stronger the longer we maintain contact."

"Which will be useless if you collapse." Adam hauled her away. "Sit fucking down."

The next thing she knew, she had a chair behind her and was crumpling into it, her vision blurred. "Oh." She was bleeding badly enough from the eyes that it had impacted her vision. "I don't feel anything," she protested. "No pain."

"Be quiet," Adam snapped, while dabbing at the corners of her eyes with unexpected gentleness. "You don't just bleed out of your fucking *eyes* because everything is all right."

Naia ran the scanner over her again, deep grooves around either side of her mouth. "I'm seeing too many broken or damaged blood vessels for my liking, but no neural damage."

"There isn't any," Eleri said, and, when no one would listen to her, grabbed Adam's wrist, the bone and muscle of him her anchor. "*Please.* He's trapped. I need to pull him out. I can't leave him in there."

Chapter 21

5 a.m. Eleri, what's with the silent treatment? I know you're awake. You're always awake at the ass crack of dawn.

6 a.m. If I don't get a reply soon, I'm calling the Bates Motel you checked into. Oh sorry, the Raintree Inn. (Are you sure the innkeeper is actually alive and her son doesn't have her preserved in the basement?)

7 a.m. Bram says he's going to see you today. I told him to make you call me before I go all lunatic redhead on you.

—Saffron Bianca to Eleri Dias (today)

IT WAS THE most emotion Adam had seen from Eleri since she'd come to Raintree, and even then, it was a muted thing that told a story of destruction he refused to accept. But that she was fighting through it to help Jacques, it meant something.

"Naia scans you the entire time," he said. "Jacques won't thank me if we kill you getting him out." His best friend was a protector, and he'd expect Adam to make sure no one hurt themselves in an effort to save him.

"Fine."

When Adam wove his fingers through Eleri's again, he was struck by how fine her bones were when he'd gotten used to seeing her as tough and unflinching. "You start bleeding too much and I'm hauling you out." No room for negotiation. "As for the other thing"—the guilt that drove her, the need for absolution—"forget it."

He hadn't thought he'd ever get to that point, but seeing her bleeding out and still trying to help Jacques? It shattered the wall of anger that had kept him sane since the day he'd met her . . . only to realize that was it, the only relationship they'd ever have. It had been easier to be angry with her than to grieve her loss on top of his grief over his parents.

Eleri didn't ask him what he meant. She just said, "I can't."

The quiet words destroyed him.

Then she turned and put her hand on Jacques once more.

The next hour was one of the most excruciating Adam had ever endured. His best friend was locked in his body, while the woman who had haunted him for ten years kept bleeding but *would not* allow him to pull her away.

"Each time you break the connection," she said the first time he attempted it, "I have to start again."

It took everything he had to let her see this through.

Eleri was crying tears of a red so dark that Naia was clearly about to tell him to intervene when he felt it—a tug on his blood bond with Jacques.

Too light, too weak, Eleri's tears increasing in volume.

"Her vitals are dropping." Naia's voice was healer-firm. "We have to stop her."

"No," Eleri whispered, her voice coming as if from a vast distance.

He gritted his teeth and allowed her to have another minute, even as the scent of iron suffused the room. The tug on the blood bond grew stronger in tandem with the thickening scent of Eleri's blood.

Making a deep sound in his throat, he put every ounce of the power of Clan WindHaven in his voice as he said, "Jacques, you need to get the fuck out here *now*."

His friend shifted into a million particles of light in front of them.

Eleri jerked her hand away with a startled sound, and he held her trembling body against him, one hand on the back of her head, his gut tight, and anguish a knot in his chest as he waited to see if his best friend would come back to them.

The light coalesced . . . and there was Jacques in his full human form.

No amputated limbs.

No arm that was a wing.

No fingers turned into talons.

Naia rushed to the other man's side, reattaching all the medical lines that had become detached due to his shift. A few embedded elements had disintegrated in the shift, but changeling medical tech was designed for such eventualities and Naia was able to quickly swap out the damaged parts.

"He's with us." Sascha's smile was warm with relief as she helped Naia by wrapping a monitoring cuff around Jacques's biceps. "I can feel him."

"So can I." Naia's voice was thick, but she moved at speed to give Jacques everything he needed. "I'll do a full body scan to check parts of him haven't semi-shifted in ways we can't see, but my healing abilities say we have him in one piece—and one form."

Adam had no time to celebrate.

Eleri's body went limp in his arms, blood trickling out of her ears and the corners of her eyes. And his fucking heart, it twisted in agony. "Naia," he said, tone rough.

Naia's head jerked up, her excitement wiped out by worry. "Pulse, respiration?"

"Slow but steady. Shallow." He grabbed the scanner she threw over and read the results back to her after he ran it over Eleri.

"She'll be okay"—relief in Naia's tone—"but needs a transfusion. Put her in the next room—I'll grab the supplies and get the blood into her."

Sascha spoke as he scooped Eleri's too-light body into his arms. "I sensed a massive psychic burst toward the end. I'm fairly certain she's flamed out and, given her condition, will probably sleep for a good chunk of time."

Cradling Eleri close, he carried her to the spare patient room and laid her down on the bed. Even unconscious, her face held its strict lines, as if she'd learned to never lower her guard, not even in rest.

His Eleri had never found safe harbor.

The first thing he did was wipe the blood off her. *He'd* driven her to this with his unending fury at her, even knowing that she'd never been in charge. She sought penance because she carried a guilt that had never been her weight to bear . . . and she did it for the same reason he'd been so angry with her all this time.

Eleri might not be changeling, but she'd felt the same thing he had. She might not have understood what it was . . . but it hadn't mattered. It had altered her. As it had forever altered him.

"I'm sorry," he said roughly as he removed her shoes so she'd be more comfortable. "I was a complete asshole. You know why, don't you?" His breath hitched in his chest as he spoke the truth for the first time. "It wasn't just grief at the loss of my parents. It was grief at losing you."

Trauma upon trauma at the worst point of his existence. "I can forgive the kid I was—he was messed up, angry, and grieving before he ever met you. But the way I've been since you walked back into my life? I hope you kick the hell out of me in return. I'm pretty sure Jacques will do it for you once you tell him what a shit I've been to you."

He wanted his best friend and his mate to meet, to like each other, to gang up against him when he was an ass. He wanted to introduce Eleri to his sister, to Amir and Malia and Tahir. He wanted to tell her all about his parents and grandparents. And he wanted her embedded in his clan, surrounded by people who'd die for her and whose loyalty she never, ever had to question.

"No matter what happens from this point on"—he cradled her face—"I'm yours. And I will fight for you. For us. *I* will be your safe harbor as I should've always been."

Because he wasn't fucking ready to just accept that his mate's death had been preordained by the psychic butchers who'd gone in and eviscerated the heart and soul of the girl who'd wanted to bandage his hurts so many years ago.

His falcon released a battle cry.

Chapter 22

Break-in at the Daniel home. Nothing appears missing, except for a fresh quart of milk that the intruder emptied and left on the kitchen table. Mrs. Daniel thinks he also helped himself to cookies from her jar. (She showed me the crumbs around the jar.)

Mr. Daniel thinks it's "punk-ass teenagers" doing it as a dare. Likelihood of that being true is very high.

I did a walkaround regardless. No broken latches or locks, and the Daniels say they leave their door unlocked more often than not, so the intruder must've just walked in.

—Report logged by Deputy Jocasta Whitten, Raintree Enforcement
(12 December 2083)

THE INTRUDER SAT in the sleeping family's home as the first brush of dawn kissed the sky outside, calmly drinking a cup of coffee he'd made using their fancy coffeemaker. They'd start waking in the next fifteen minutes. First mom and dad, then the adorable two point five kids.

He'd looked in on the point five. Cute kid. A few months old it looked like, but he was no good at judging the age of babies, so who knew? But it had been awake and kicking its legs in the crib when he'd glanced into the nursery. He'd have had to make a run for it if the kid had started bawling—he didn't hurt babies; he wasn't a psychopath. But the baby had just gurgled baby nonsense at him.

Adorable.

Smiling back at the little chubster, he'd started up the mobile of sea creatures above the kid's bed, after making sure the sound was off. The baby had grinned and stared up with big blue eyes.

The intruder had padded away from the nursery and down the stairs as quietly as he'd gone up. He was hungry, but there was no time to make a good breakfast. The coffee, however, was excellent—rich but not bitter.

It calmed his racing mind, allowed him to think. He'd been running on too little sleep of late, burning the candle at both ends, as that old-bat neighbor of his liked to say; she was always watching, that one. Tiny pinprick eyes in that wrinkled-up prune face. She was lucky he'd shaken off the urge to strangle her and just taken to drugging her nightly milk toddy while she was upstairs changing into her nightgown.

No point drawing attention to himself by having a murdered neighbor. Old bat would drop dead soon enough anyway. But he *was* making mistakes in other ways. If he hadn't been, then Eleri Dias wouldn't be at the inn, wouldn't be poking around town. Even these break-ins on home soil were careless.

He'd started them in an effort to stave off the whispers in his head.

After all, he was no ordinary serial killer driven by impulse. He had a *plan*, had a timeline. Yes, he hadn't expected the J who was his playmate in this game to track down his home ground so quickly, but she was here now.

No point avoiding it.

Better if he used it, ramped up the game.

The whispers were eager now, his entire body humming.

He tapped a gloved finger against the bone china of his coffee cup.

She'd spent a bit of time with Adam Garrett. The falcon leader had visited her at the inn. Most people probably wouldn't have noticed, but he wasn't most people. He'd made it a point to notice.

Hmm...

Finishing up his coffee, he went to the sink and thoroughly washed the cup. As he did so, he considered the twenty-year-old girl in the bed upstairs. College student home for a short vacation. Petite frame. Irritating voice. Smart. He could make it to her room as soundlessly as he had the nursery.

But then he'd have to rush, waste the opportunity.

"Another time," he promised the whispers and put his clean but wet coffee cup on the kitchen table.

There, all done. He was a conscientious guest.

He closed the back door silently behind him.

Wouldn't want to scare his unknowing hosts.

Chapter 23

Eleri, I'm two minutes away. Answer Saffy in the interim—she's blowing up my phone. I think she's in one of her manic phases.

—Bram Priest to Eleri Dias (now)

ELERI'S PHONE BUZZED on the bedside table two hours after Naia had stabilized her. Frowning, Adam remembered what she'd said about the printouts being collected today and picked up the phone.

It proved fully secured, not allowing him to answer the call.

Putting it back down, he used his own phone to ring the inn. Mi-ja, phone always in her pocket, answered at once. "The Raintree Inn!" she chirped.

"Mi-ja, it's Adam. Is there someone at Eleri's door?"

"Why, yes! How did you know?" Her voice becoming breathless as she no doubt quick-walked over. "Dae just mentioned the new car to me. I was going over to say hello."

A minute later and Adam was talking to a deep-voiced man who confirmed he was there to see Eleri. Wanting to check out the other man's credentials, Adam told him to wait, that he'd be down soon.

The man's response was, "Why can't I reach Eleri on the PsyNet?" and it wasn't a professional query, for all its coldness.

Adam's eyes narrowed. "We'll talk when I arrive." Hanging up, he made sure Eleri was resting peacefully before he looked in on Jacques.

His friend remained in a coma.

"That's for the best," a much more ebullient Naia had said after she was satisfied both her patients were stable. "He has a number of major injuries that didn't begin to heal until he fully shifted. It'll go much faster if he's motionless."

"Chance he'll remain comatose?" Because they weren't out of the woods yet.

"Unknown, but since Sascha can sense him with her empathy, it means the specialist Es can nudge him awake if he doesn't come through on his own." Naia had exhaled. "I have a feeling Jacques will choose his own time."

As for Eleri, Sascha had warned him not to permit any Psy he didn't trust near her until her shields regenerated.

"PsyNet?" Adam had asked.

"That shield is holding—I asked Sophia to check. Figured she'd be able to find Eleri in the Net. She also told me that a lot of Js have Net shields like Eleri's—they're pretty much independent, they're so deeply embedded into their psyches. A protection against accidental exposure during Silence that's become second nature."

Adam thought of that girl with the innocent hazel eyes who'd felt things that had put her in danger. Now, in the bright morning sunshine, he left her in the care of his clan and drove her vehicle not down to the inn, but to a quiet lay-by a short distance away, where he'd told the courier to meet him.

The last thing they needed was Mi-ja's avid attention.

The black SUV that waited for him was identical to Eleri's, but it was a man of about Adam's height who stood outside it. Built wide across the shoulders, he wore a dark gray suit with a white shirt, and his prematurely gray hair was buzzed close to his skull, his skin paler than was common in this area, his eyes an icy blue.

He held out his ID the instant Adam walked over.

"Bram Priest," he said. "J Corps. Where is Eleri?"

Adam wasn't the kind of wing leader who went about posturing and preening, but that didn't mean he didn't have a massive level of dominance. If the J was attempting to intimidate him, he'd chosen the wrong target. "I need to verify your ID before I tell you anything," he said, and messaged an image of the ID as well as Bram's face to Damon, who he'd alerted ahead of time.

The response came after a tense twenty seconds: Senior J attached to the Sandman Task Force as a consultant on an ad hoc basis. Also, the computer cross-references automatically and your guy shows up on the files of three other Js, including that of the J you asked about before—Eleri Dias. The four of them seem to be each other's next of kin.

Adam's falcon looked at the man in a whole new light.

After thanking Damon, he put away his phone. "Eleri flamed out after doing an emergency psychic assist. She's being looked after by my clan's healer, and by a cardinal empath."

"You expect me to take your words at face value?" was the grim response.

"I can't take you into the heart of my clan." Adam kept his tone nonaggressive; if this man had acted as family to Eleri, then Adam fucking *owed* him. Bram Priest had been there for Eleri when she needed someone. "But you can contact Sophia Russo for confirmation that she's in good hands."

An unblinking gaze. "If you've done anything to harm her, I'll make sure the consequences are deadly." No anger, no threatening tone. A simple statement.

Adam liked him the better for it. "You can speak to her the instant she wakes up." He jerked a thumb over his shoulder. "She locked up the evidence in the trunk. Not sure if it'll maintain chain of evidence, but no one but Eleri can open that case."

"Pinpointing the Sandman is what matters."

The serial killer, Adam understood at once, would never see the inside of a courtroom should the Js involved believe he would slither free. In that, they were very changeling in their thinking.

After the J had retrieved the case, Adam said, "You're Eleri's family. Clan."

The man took time putting away the case. When he did speak, he said, "The J Corps looks after its own." He met Adam's gaze again. "I'll crush your brain from the inside out if she has so much as a bruise on her."

This man, Adam thought, wasn't numb like Eleri, but rather the opposite. "Come to dinner once she's better. Bring the other two." No flicker in Bram's expression at Adam's awareness of there being four of them in the family. "I want to meet her family . . . and I want her to meet mine."

Bram's expression shifted at last, some unknown emotion cracking the glacial cold of his eyes. "You don't know her."

"I know all about the reconditionings." Adam folded his arms. "I also know that Psy have defected out of the PsyNet and survived with changeling clans. Far as I'm aware, no J has attempted it. You know any different?"

For the first time, Bram seemed to actually look at him and see him as anything other than a threat. "No," he said at last. "To my knowledge, the defectors from the PsyNet haven't been like us. None were Sensitives."

"And there were no active empaths until Sascha Duncan dropped out of the Net." Adam was just getting started on this fight. "Someone has to be the first."

"I think you truly believe you can fight this," Bram said, an exhaustion on his face that was so deep, Adam couldn't understand how he'd hidden it until now. "But the damage they did to us? It's permanent. Our brains will never return to what they once were."

The other man shook his head. "But, despite that, I'm glad Eleri has someone who's willing to fight for her." He held out his gloved hand. "If you can, give her good days, days devoid of evil."

Adam shook the other man's hand. "Oh, I will. But not because I'm about to lose her—because it's going to be the start of a long and happy life." Adam had the bit between his teeth, and he wasn't letting go.

Bram gave him a long look. "I can't decide if you're delusional or not. But . . . I wish you luck, Adam Garrett. I'll keep Saffron and Yúzé—the other two—from breaking down your door, but you should expect calls to the private line you gave me. We'll want updates."

"You'll have them."

Adam watched Bram leave in silence, the trees stirring around him as the sound of the vehicle quieted into emptiness. And he knew he would fight for Eleri again and again and again. As he should've fought for her after he'd found her. Because he hadn't, because he'd been so *angry* at her, she'd been hurt over and over and over again.

The reconditionings? A life surrounded by evil?

His fucking fault.

He had abandoned his mate.

His eyes burned, his hands white-knuckled fists as he threw back his head and screamed.

Chapter 24

Flameout should be avoided unless there are exigent circumstances where your resulting psychic vulnerability will not be more dangerous than the alternate option. The general timeline of recovery runs from twenty-four to thirty-six hours, but may stretch into days in severe instances.

—Part of the mandatory Foundational Psychic Mechanics course taught in the final year of elementary Psy education

ELERI CAME AWAKE to the sounds of quiet movement and the sense of a fog in her head that felt different from her usual numbness. When she went to scan her surroundings using her telepathic senses, her brain ached as if bruised.

Flameout.

She'd experienced it before, but never to this extent—until she was no longer a being of the Psy. She didn't even know what it meant for her safety against others of her kind.

It was a good thing she was in a changeling den.

Warm, strong fingers around her own, a rough-skinned hand squeezing hers. "I know you're awake."

She lifted her lashes, afraid it was a dream, that Adam's voice, the *way* he sounded, were just things she wanted and not things she could ever have—because that yearning . . . she could still feel it. But there he was, his hair tumbled over his forehead and his upper body clad in a short-sleeved shirt rather than the tee she'd seen him in before her flameout.

"Twenty-six hours," he said, as if he'd read her mind, the falcon looking back at her out of his eyes. "Perfect timing for breakfast."

She'd slept away an entire day. That was bad. Flameouts didn't ordinarily cause unconsciousness for that long, but she remembered the feeling of strain in her head before she went down, the blood on her fingers when she'd touched them to the liquid by her ears.

When she made as if to rise, Adam put his hand under her back to help her up. That was when she realized she wasn't wearing her suit, but pajamas of a blue material soft against her skin.

Her hand clenched on the edge of the sheet.

"Naia refused to leave you in the suit." Adam's gaze held hers even as the heat and strength of him wrapped around her, his size even more apparent to her this close. "She's the one who took care of that."

Her muscles relaxed. She could accept the healer's touch but would've never accepted Adam's, not like this, not now, not when a lifetime and one terrible choice stood between them. "Jacques?" Her voice came out dry, cracked.

Adam passed her a glass of water. "Far more responsive to Naia, and readings show a healthy brain."

"Good." She drank half the glass. "That's good."

"You think you can get up?" Taking the glass from her, he put it on the bedside table.

"Yes. I'm fine on the physical level, just out of juice on the psychic." And well past the twenty-four-hour mark when she should've already begun to recover. Whatever had taken place, whatever she'd done, it had wiped her out, the effect likely exacerbated by her extreme Sensitivity.

As she swung her legs around, Adam stood watch as if ready to catch her. "There's no one nearby who will hurt you. Hanz—the young

E you didn't meet—has already left, and Sascha will be heading off within the hour and is happy to keep her distance unless you want to see her. We're not calling in any other Es until Jacques stabilizes further. You're safe."

Safe.

Eleri had never felt safe, not truly. As a young child, she'd known she was unwanted, an error who needed to be handled. Bram, Saffy, and Yúzé had made boarding school better, but they'd all been under constant watch there for the signs of serious instability that affected a minor percentage of young Js.

The four of them had been powerless children together.

Later, for a few fleeting years, she'd thought Reagan might be safe, that she could trust him with all the pieces of her. Then he'd lied in that courtroom and she'd understood that Reagan had his secrets, that all he showed her was the surface gloss.

She wasn't sure she even understood the concept of being safe.

But today, as she got off the bed and saw Adam tense as if to catch her should she fall, she got a glimmer. "I'm stable," she said, even as part of her wanted to pretend she wasn't, a sensation as deep as the yearning . . . and nowhere near deep enough. Because a flameout couldn't fix what multiple reconditionings had taken from her.

"And I would like to say good-bye to Sascha. I think . . . she tried to help me at the end." It had felt like a warm embrace that gave her body and mind just enough respite that she could haul Jacques out of the glass pond.

"I'll ask her to come by." Adam brushed a strand of hair off her face with a tenderness that she wished she could feel as far more than the merest brush. "We have to talk. It's time."

Eleri swallowed hard, and it was a numbed echo of a scream that she was swallowing back. Because there was nothing left of her now that this time had come at last. "Yes," was all she said aloud, because she couldn't give it up, even if it was a faded copy of what once might've been.

Adam dropped his hand, and it felt as if he did so with reluctance. "Shower's through there," he said, pointing to the door. "Anything you need, just yell out. I'll be outside your room. We're going to breakfast afterward, because first you need to eat.

"In lieu of breaking in, I asked Mi-ja to let me into your room so I could get your luggage—she's no doubt told the entire town you're in the Canyon by now, probably with embellishment." An amused smile. "Clan also laundered and pressed your suit if you prefer that over what you have in your luggage. Take as long as you want in the shower—I'm not going anywhere."

The final words felt like a promise.

Eleri just nodded, but when the water fell over her face only minutes later, she wondered if this was what it felt like to cry. She couldn't, hadn't been able to for a long, long time, so long that she'd forgotten. But today, she had things tight and hard and hot in her chest, and the water was raining down her face, and in this place full of changelings with natural shields, she didn't have to worry about being a Sensitive.

Life was . . . beautiful . . . and more painful than death.

ADAM'S mate looked as cold and as remote as always when she stepped out of her room dressed in black suit pants into which she'd tucked a white shirt buttoned at the neck and wrists. She'd scraped her hair into a tight knot at the base of her neck, her facial bones sharp and her expression flat.

But Adam saw through the wall now, and to the woman within, the one who'd been willing to lay her life on the line to help a stranger. No one truly cold of heart would've spent even a moment considering that.

"I would like to see Jacques," were the first words out of her mouth.

Nodding, he led her into his friend's room, and when she walked to stand beside the bed, she didn't touch Jacques even though her hands were ungloved. "I wouldn't sense anything even if his shields remain fragmented," she said at his questioning look. "My psychic senses flatlined, will stay that way until my mind heals. I have no frame of reference for comparison in terms of a timeline for that healing."

He took her hand because they were past the angry distance, the attempts to ignore who they were meant to be to each other. And she'd given him permission to take skin privileges—he wasn't about to stop using that permission until she took it back.

She hesitated, her gaze flicking to his before she curled her fingers around his.

"You feel okay?" he murmured. "Losing your psychic senses, it must hurt."

"I feel . . . unmoored." She flexed her free hand flat, stared at it. "As if I've lost a limb or an organ of which I was never conscious, but now realize I need to breathe."

"It's only temporary," he reminded her. "An overused muscle that needs to rest."

Eleri's nod was quiet.

"Adam?" Edward poked his head into the room, having taken over from Kavi for the day shift. "Sascha's here."

Thanking the nurse for the heads-up, Adam walked out with Eleri to find the cardinal E waiting in the hallway, her cub at her side, both of them dressed for the journey home—in the case of Naya, that included a tiny backpack in which Adam had once seen her stow a bedraggled stuffed wolf.

"Hello, little Naya." Releasing Eleri's hand, Adam crouched down to hug this child wild of heart who would always be welcome in Wind-Haven. She smelled of soft, sweet shampoo and candy.

"Bye, Adam," she said with her tiny arms around his neck. "We go home. I miss Papa."

Smiling, Adam kissed her on the cheek before rising to his feet with her in his arms. "I have a feeling he misses you, too." Lucas Hunter was a man who loved his mate and child and didn't care who knew it—it was exactly how Adam intended to be with his own mate and fledglings, how he'd always been built to be.

... there's not much of my original personality left ... and nothing but a gray wall in its place ...

No, he would not accept that, he vowed again, as Eleri and Sascha said their good-byes next to him. He heard Eleri ask what Sascha had done at the end, and Sascha reply, but didn't hear the words through the roar of determination in his mind.

Then little Naya piped up after her mother stopped speaking. "Hi!" The greeting was directed at Eleri, before she glanced at Sascha. "Mama, I practice?"

Sascha's returning smile was patient, loving. "Remember, we talked about asking for permission from the other person? Like skin privileges?"

"Oh yeah." Turning back to face Eleri, Naya took a deep breath and said, "I telepath you, please? I practice."

Eleri's expression remained all but impossible to read, it was so devoid of any cues, but Adam had the sense that she was startled at finding herself facing a changeling child with telepathic abilities. But she replied quickly enough. "I would be pleased to telepath with you, but my telepathy isn't currently working."

A sudden alertness to Sascha's posture that told Adam he'd missed something—Sascha, he realized, would've never instructed her little girl to ask for permission if she'd believed Eleri to still be in flameout. She'd have told her child that Eleri couldn't telepath to her at present.

"Oh?" little Naya said at that instant. "You got a big ouch?" She touched her head to indicate the location of the "ouch." "Mama had big ouch before."

Her language skills—not just comprehension, but the clarity with which she spoke—continued to impress Adam. He had the feeling it had to do with the telepathy, her mind in casual contact with Sascha's throughout the day. It made him wonder about the vocal development of Psy children in general.

Beside him, Eleri nodded slowly at this childish explanation of flameout. "Yes. A big ouch. Perhaps we can telepath when we next meet."

The cub was agreeable, but Sascha frowned. "Eleri, do you need an M-Psy to look you over? We have a clanmate who's completely trustworthy."

"No." Eleri shook her head. "It's the Sensitivity. It means my mind was already strained before the flameout. It's intensified the effect."

"Yes, that makes sense." Shoulders easing, Sascha took Naya's hand when Adam put the little girl down. "But please reach out if you do decide you want a consult—especially if the flameout lasts beyond the forty-eight-hour mark."

"If she doesn't, I will," Adam said with a scowl, but kept it at that until after Dorian joined Sascha and Naya and the three of them headed off to the jet-chopper on the plateau.

"You should've told me you're badly wounded," he growled at Eleri, as if he was a leopard like Dorian and not a creature of the sky.

"The sensation is as expected," Eleri said. "A sense of emptiness where my Psy abilities should be—it's just the recovery that's impacted by my Sensitivity. I'm less able to rebound as fast." Eyes downcast, she turned her bare hands up, then down as if fascinated by their ungloved state.

The naked vulnerability of her in that moment speared through his worry, making him want only to wrap her up in his wings and in his affection, atone for all the years when she'd been alone in the dark, without her mate by her side. He'd fucked up and bad, the grief of the youth he'd been no excuse for how he hadn't returned for her once he was an adult—but he planned to spend his entire life making it up to her.

Shifting close, he cupped her face in his hands. "What do you need, Eleri?" A raw question. "Tell me and I'll give it to you. I'm your mate. I'll go capture the moon for you if you want."

Her fingers settled against his left wrist, the touch cooler than his own body temperature. "Today, why don't we act . . . as if we just met in that hallway? As if the years and the choices of the past don't stand between us."

It was a kick to the gut. "Come on, then, pretty girl with the big eyes," he said, shoving aside all other plans, including his intention to talk to her about their relationship, a mating too long suspended in amber.

The harder conversations could wait until Eleri healed.

Today, he'd give his mate what she'd asked for, be the boy she'd wanted to tend to that long-ago day. "Let me show you my lair . . . and seduce you into the kiss I wanted to steal the first time I saw you."

Chapter 25

Dear Aunt Rita,
  This is a weird question. I apologize in advance. But I really don't know anyone else I can ask.
  So . . . I have a falcon changeling friend. We've known each other since way back, after we ended up on the same soccer team at school. Only, um, she's done something very strange: she flew over me the other day—I knew it was her from the markings—and dropped a hunk of meat in my arms.
  It was wrapped up in butcher's paper, and had the seal of a local shop, so I thought she'd dropped her groceries and waited for her to come back. But she didn't, just sent me a message saying: *Did you like it? I got you the prime cut.*
  Then yesterday, she hovered over me with a package until I opened my arms out of desperation . . . and caught a roasted leg of lamb sealed up in tinfoil, complete with rosemary sprigs. It was still warm from the oven.
  Does my friend need help? Like, should I call a psychiatrist? Please help.
  ~Soccer Fiend

Dear Soccer Fiend,
  This seems to be the edition of the column with food-related queries. I have to say, however, of all the queries I've answered over the years, yours is the first one that has made me cackle so hard I couldn't see through the tears.
  I do apologize for my response. It's just that I thought I'd heard of every food-related shenanigan there was . . . but no, the raptors always take it to the next level. I suppose bears would do the same if they could fly—literally food bomb the targets of their ardor.

You are beloved, my dear Fiend. However, if you don't reciprocate your friend's affections, this could get awkward. If that is the case, then the next time you receive a delivery, you should go immediately to their nesting place and gently hand it back to them saying thank you, but that you don't need it.

If you do reciprocate . . . well, invite her to share in the feast.

~Aunt Rita

—From the February 2073 issue of *Wild Woman* magazine: "Skin Privileges, Style & Primal Sophistication"

THEY WERE ONLY ten seconds away from the infirmary when Malia ran around the corner. "Is Jacques awake?" Her eyes shone, her curls pushed back from her face by a glittery headband. "Mom and Dad both said he's doing much better."

"No, he's not awake yet." Adam didn't lie to his fledglings, and Malia was mature enough for the complete truth, so he added, "But his brain activity is solid—his body just needs more time to heal."

Making a high-pitched sound, his niece jumped into his arms, all energy and happiness. He had to release Eleri's hand to catch her. Laughing, he squeezed her tight. "Where are your manners, little bird?" He tapped her on the nose after he put her down. "Say hi to the reason Jacques is doing better. This is Eleri."

Malia all but bounced on her toes but knew better than to touch Eleri without permission. "Are you an E?" That she'd figured out Eleri wasn't changeling or human wasn't a surprise—Eleri's expression, the way she held herself, it was all Psy.

All *her*.

"No, I'm a J."

"Oh." Saoirse and Amir's eldest fledgling frowned before shrugging with teenage insouciance. "Do you hug?"

When Eleri shook her head, Malia released a large exhale. "I *highly* recommend it. It's the best. And Uncle Adam's a gazillion-star expert!" She squeezed him again. "Can I go see Jacques?"

"Not just yet." He pulled on a single curl with affectionate care. Blackbird tendencies or not, he'd grown up with a sister who had the same curls—he knew better than to mess them up when so much time had clearly gone into separating them out with perfection.

"Ask Naia for permission in a few more days," he added, "and she'll make the call." Jacques wouldn't mind being surrounded by clan when he was on the road to recovery—it was the idea of being cried over by people who had to watch him die that he'd hated.

"I definitely will!" His niece beamed at Eleri. "Thanks, Eleri!"

Then she was gone, a whirlwind of a child with a falcon's soaring heart.

Eleri was quiet as she watched after her. "How does it work, you being her uncle and her wing leader?"

"Context." Adam shrugged. "In daily life, I'm Malia's uncle, but when it comes to matters of the clan and of discipline, I'm her wing leader. It's instinctive, that understanding—her falcon understands it so deep that confusion is impossible."

A nod, but Eleri's attention was still on where Malia had vanished. "I wonder now that Silence has fallen, if our children will grow up this wild and free . . . this confident in their right to exist exactly as they are."

"Why the hell wouldn't they?" Adam demanded, having caught the hesitation in her tone.

"Our minds make us different from humans and changelings in ways subtle but profound. Control, control is everything."

Adam raised a hand, sliced out his talons. "Try again."

Her hand lifted, her fingers brushing his talons in a caress that made his falcon spread its wings inside him, the raptor wanting to show itself to her.

"I'm not sure it's the same. Because there's an inherent wildness in this, too." She touched his talons again. "But telepathy like mine? There's a pressure to it from the very beginning, an *inward* threat—

because if a changeling doesn't learn to handle their strength, they might hurt others. If *we* don't learn to shield, we will be the ones hurt. Our control is self-protective in a way that teaches us to be wary from childhood."

"We can argue about that over breakfast." When he took her hand again, she wove her fingers through his, but her expression was . . . melancholy?

"It isn't too late," he said roughly. "We're young. A lot of people don't even meet until after their third or fourth decade."

The look she sent him was unreadable. "You have to understand, Adam." A soft plea. "I lost countless pieces of myself in the intervening years. There's no coming back from this, no future road. Even if I manage to stave off Exposure by a hitherto unknown method, I'm never again going to be who I once was."

"You're enough. You've always been enough."

Her eyes shimmered, then went black. "I really am hungry." A quiet diversion.

Falcons were patient hunters, so he'd be patient, and he'd wait until she was ready to listen, ready to trust. "Then let's feed you."

It was late enough by then that only a few clanmates sat in the main kitchen and dining area—which had a massive opening out to the canyon through which fell sunshine bright and warm. On rainy days, it was the wet that came through, and anyone who didn't want to get it on them just sat further inside.

Today, three clanmates in falcon form sat at the edge, soaking up the sun.

Eleri caught her breath at the sight. "This is a place built for beings with wings," she said, as if working through her own thoughts. "From the height of the ceilings to the width of the corridors, to these winged roads in and out."

There were other, more secret exits and entrances, too, literally tunnels drilled into the Canyon through which a full-grown falcon could travel in flight a significant distance before emerging through exits concealed by careful placement of rocks. Created in the lead-up to the Territorial Wars by a wing leader who'd seen trouble fomenting, they meant no falcon would ever be trapped inside the Canyon, even should their enemy hover jet-choppers all around their living area.

He was excited to see his mate's reaction to the incredible skill of the clan's ancestors. This morning, however, he wanted to look after her. Like bears, falcons liked to feed their mates during the mating dance. Wild falcons had a habit of dropping dead prey in front of the one they wished to court.

Changelings were a touch more sophisticated—most of the time.

In committed pairs, preening was a profound part of how they showed affection and intimacy; if she let him, Adam could spend an hour just combing Eleri's hair or massaging oil into every inch of her skin until she was drowsy and half-asleep and all tended.

But even had food held no meaning for him beyond nourishment, he'd have wanted to give it to her, because it was a small thing that brought great joy. It was clear from her thin but strong build that she ate only to fuel her bones and muscles and brain. She didn't grab a handful of strawberries to snack on because they were sweet and juicy, or sink her teeth into a sandwich overfilled to the brim with her favorite fillings.

What had been done to her, the damage to her brain? Adam couldn't turn back the clock on that, but he could show her small joys bit by tempting bit. He began by leading her to where today's kitchen team had laid out the food and let her choose what she wanted. She stuck to relatively bland items, though she did also accept the bowl of fresh-cut fruit salad he scooped up for her.

Small bites of sweetness, crisp and colorful.

While she finished making up her plate, he went into the kitchen, to return with a packet of nutrients she could mix into water or juice; the clan stocked it for Psy friends like Sascha and Judd. "I know you need it after that psychic burn," he said.

"Yes, nothing else works as well."

Once he'd grabbed some food, too, he took them over to where Dahlia sat alone at a table that caught the edge of the sunshine. The second had shot them an avidly curious gaze when they walked in, but not intruded—not because she was a falcon, but because she was Dahlia.

Adam's clanmates could be as nosy as a flock of geese at times.

"You're raptors!" he'd been known to yell while trying not to laugh. "Have some decorum!"

Now, he slipped in beside Dahlia so that Eleri could have the seat across from him that permitted a view out of the opening into the natural splendor of the canyon. Much as he wanted to hoard Eleri to himself, he wanted more to bring her into his clan, make her part of its living, beating heart.

"Dahlia, this is Eleri. Eleri, Dahlia is my wing-second alongside Jacques."

Dahlia's smile was big and open, a thing that had gone missing for too long after her failed wedding. She'd found it again—but it remained far too rare. Adam hated knowing that his generous, courageous clanmate was hurting, but being unable to fix it for her.

"I hear you're the magician who broke Jacques out of semi-shift jail." Dahlia lifted her glass of iced tea in a toast. "I'd kiss you if I could."

Eleri stirred the nutrients into a glass of water, her voice ice when she replied. "Don't. Js are taught to break arms and other body parts as part of our training."

Dahlia's laugh was a huge thing, her eyes ringed by falcon yellow. "Oh, I *like* you. Especially since you have the best poker face I've ever seen—I can't tell if you're dead serious or if you're messing with me."

Adam had the instinctive sense that it was the latter. Eleri acting as the girl she'd once been? The girl who'd had within her the ability to feel the entire rainbow of emotions, from amusement to anguish. That girl might've joked this way with a young Dahlia—and Dahlia, being as tough and blunt as she was, would've appreciated such a friend.

"I," Eleri replied as he sat back and let the two women talk, "once read the memory of a poker player who murdered her partner after said partner colluded with external forces to throw a Las Vegas match for money. Unfortunately for the partner, he underestimated her passion for the game."

Dahlia poked her fork into a piece of honeydew melon but didn't bring it to her lips. "Fair enough. I can't stand cheats, either. How'd she do it?"

"Poisoned his whiskey. Nothing easy, either—a drug that took three days to kill him, all the while making him so sick that he couldn't get out of bed. She, meanwhile, kept on playing throughout. She was what the media termed a 'knockout blonde.'"

Dahlia whistled. "I think she fits the definition of 'tough broad' like in those vintage movies Jacques likes to watch. Can I ask what it was like? Being in her mind?"

Adam stiffened, his protective urges rising to the surface. He knew he should keep his mouth shut—his grandmother would rise from the ashes and slap him upside the head any moment now, but he couldn't stop himself. Not when Eleri's face had been a mask of blood so recently.

Then Eleri shot him a look as he went to part his lips. And he wanted to grin. Yes, she was his mate all right; they might not have bonded yet, but she'd known exactly what shit he was about to pull and had called him out on it without saying a word. He shut up . . . and imagined a lifetime of such piercing knowing between them.

Fuck, he couldn't wait to live life with her by his side.

There's no coming back from this, no future road.

Adam's falcon released its talons inside him. He'd meant what he'd said; he wanted her exactly as she was, exactly as the years had shaped her to be, not some image of perfection—and he planned to make her see that, understand that.

Mates were for always, through every season of life.

"Not all Js like to talk about the minds in which we've walked," Eleri told Dahlia. "But I don't mind answering about the poker player—her mind was pristine, a house with not a single item out of place.

"She didn't have obsessive thoughts about murdering and torturing people, would've never committed murder if not for her addiction to the game. Even the torturous murder of her former partner was, to her, a fair punishment. She didn't revel in it. To her, it simply had to be done."

Dahlia narrowed her eyes as she chewed, swallowed. "That'd be me," she said at last. "If I were to murder my hypothetical cheating partner. Gotta be done. Nothing personal."

"No, you have too much passion in you," Eleri responded. "You'd go into a frenzy. No premeditation."

Only Adam saw the wistfulness in her gaze, heard it in the voice that seemed to give away nothing. Far from judging her, Eleri envied Dahlia for her ability to feel with such violent depth.

"Well," Dahlia said after a pause to drink her iced tea, "I did track down my ex and sat there on his balcony at midnight deciding whether or not I wanted to rip off his balls with my talons, so yeah, it's possible you're right."

"Use a knife. Talons would make it obvious it was you."

Dahlia almost snorted the tea out of her nose.

Grinning, Adam slapped her on the back.

When his second recovered, she said, "You and me, Eleri. We're going to be best friends." She glanced at Adam, then at Eleri again, but whatever suspicions she had, she didn't voice them.

Instead, having finished her meal, she got to her feet. "Time for me to take a short flight to wind down, then rest up for an afternoon shift. We'll talk about the exact knife later." A wink aimed at Eleri.

After they were alone, Adam touched his mate's booted foot with his own. "You like her, don't you?"

Eleri was overwhelmed in ways she'd never experienced. By this place full of sunlight and warmth. By the man whose legs now bracketed hers, and whose big body sat in a relaxed sprawl that did nothing to hide his deadly core. By the falcons who sunned themselves only feet from her.

By this glimpse at a life she could've had.

"Yes," she managed to say through the emotional deluge strong enough to penetrate the gray wall. "She reminds me of a friend of mine. He can be hot-tempered, too, but he'll never let you down, always have your back."

"Bram Priest?"

Chapter 26

Bayani: Ran the sample through my fancy new gadget and got exactly nothing. That'll teach me to shop late at night and fall for Internet ads about mobile geological survey devices with cutting-edge "diamond laser" tech.

Saoirse: Don't worry. I tried to see if it'd hold against the shield disrupter we use to test the capacity of our aeronautical shields. I now have a lot of sand in the machine.

Bayani: Why are we like this?

Saoirse: We're scientists.

—Messages in the *Why Is the Canyon Weird* investigation group (circa fall 2082)

ELERI STARED AT Adam. "How do you know Bram?"

"He came to grab your evidence—and threatened me with grievous bodily harm if I'd done anything to you," Adam drawled with a grin. "You should give him a quick call so he doesn't come after me."

She'd all but forgotten that she'd asked Bram to act as courier; she appreciated her task force colleagues, but her relationship with Bram went far beyond trust. She'd wanted to see him, talk through her theories with him, just be in his presence, even if she could no longer feel what she once had when she was around him and the others.

The memory of emotion was enough.

"Bram's . . . protective of us," she said. "There are four of us—me, Bram, Saffron, and Yúzé. All Sensitives. All survivors of multiple reconditionings."

Adam's smile faded, his shoulders tight. "He's not like you."

"The damage doesn't express in an identical way in each individual. Yúzé says it's because the brain is so complex and that reconditioning, despite the Council's claims to the contrary, was a blunt hammer that cut and bruised different parts with each unique pass."

A tic in Adam's jaw, his body so tense that she thought he would snap. But when he spoke, it wasn't with anger. "They're your family."

"Yes." She would put her life on the line for any of the Cartel, the emotional resonance so strong after all these years that she didn't need to feel it today to accept it. "I'll make the call now. Bram won't stop worrying until I do." She accessed her phone. "Oh, I have a hundred messages from Saffy. I'll reply to her, too."

"Not Yúzé?"

"He'll be with Saffron. They began to live together when . . ." She paused, her loyalty to the Quatro Cartel coming up against her need to share herself, share this precious and broken little family, with Adam.

"Saffy and Yúzé need each other," she said at last. "It's safer for them to live together." So they could monitor one another, so Yúzé could ensure Saffron didn't harm herself in her rages, and Saffron could keep an eye on Yúzé when he began to spiral in his quiet, dangerous way.

It worked because the two had chosen the arrangement of their own free will.

Eleri and Bram worried most about Yúzé even though Saffron was the more volatile. Yúzé's pain didn't show; he just had a tendency to quietly investigate those who did evil without being noticed or seen, then he murdered them while sipping a cup of coffee in a café or walking past his target in the street.

Not so different from what Eleri or Bram or Saffron had done, but Yúzé couldn't stop drawing memories once he started. He'd once convinced himself he was a molester of the innocent after he'd siphoned another—viciously evil—man's entire memory, and he would've slit his own throat if Saffron hadn't literally knocked him unconscious with a kick to the head. She'd been sobbing in the aftermath when she called Eleri, but she'd saved Yúzé's life.

Now all Yúzé's search history went automatically to the Quatro Cartel's private chat, and he'd promised them he wouldn't hunt on the PsyNet. But Yúzé couldn't always control his impulses, no matter how hard he tried, so Saffron and he had a debrief every night where he never lied to her, that a promise he'd made after he came to after the near-deadly incident to find Saffron inconsolable because she'd had to hurt him.

Saffy, in turn, was more stable because she fought to be stable for Yúzé.

Across from her, Adam nodded. "I get it. Many a falcon flies better, stronger, with a friend by his side. We all fall sometimes."

Eleri's entire self seemed to sigh. He did get it. Understood that at times, broken columns needed each other to prop them up.

After finishing the nutrients, she got up to make the call.

Adam didn't attempt to stop her when she walked over to the place where the falcons sunned. Glancing at her, they inched to the right, as if giving her a spot on the ledge. Something bloomed inside her chest, and she looked back at Adam, wondering if he had any idea of the gift he was giving her this day.

But he was looking the other way, answering a question from another clanmate, a slight grin on his face. She traced the line from his shoulder, up his neck, to his jaw, and found herself thinking about what it might feel like to touch that powerful body, feel those tendons and muscles under her fingertips.

A wave of air, a flutter of sound, wings unfurling.

She turned back just in time to see the falcons taking off. At first, she thought they'd disappeared because of her... but then she saw four others swoop in from the right, then watched as her three fell into formation with them, not a feather out of place.

A fighting unit, she realized. The group of lazily sunning creatures had all been soldiers trained to defend the clan.

A sense of wonder struggled to break through the wall of numbness inside her. Failed.

Sensitivity level at maximum. Exposure imminent unless all psychic abilities kept at a permanent flatline.

She'd thought she'd accepted that diagnosis and its impossible "cure," but today, she realized she'd been numb to the possibility of any other life when she'd done so. Numb to the world in which she could live if she only had the chance.

Instead, she was locked in a state of permanent dull equilibrium, unable even to experience the wonder of this moment where she stood on the lip of a cliff watching a wing of falcons begin to practice maneuvers.

Inputting Bram's code, she lifted the phone to her ear. "I'm alive," she said in greeting. "Any results from the evidence Adam passed on?"

"No fingerprints or DNA," came the expected answer. "How are you, Eleri?"

"Not good," she admitted to this member of the Cartel who was the force that had brought them and kept them together.

Then, for the first time, she spoke the truth she'd hidden in her heart since she was seventeen and a beautiful boy had smiled at her. "I want more than this life, Bram."

"Adam Garrett seems pretty determined to figure out a solution to your Sensitivity," Bram said, but unspoken was that they'd been through the entire gamut of possibilities and come up blank. Because the Cartel wasn't fatalistic by design—they'd fought for her, as she'd fought for them. Without success.

"Saffron, Yúzé?" she asked.

"Yúzé managed to talk her down from her manic state after I assured them both you were safe, and he's focused on her for the time being, so stable enough."

"You?"

A short pause. "Going in for a meds change today."

Translation: he hadn't slept last night, and possibly the night prior. "How long since your last switch-up?"

"Two months."

At this rate, he'd run out of all possible drug interventions within the year. And then what? How would Bram sleep? "Have you spoken to an empath?" she asked, thinking of Sascha Duncan and the other Es who'd assisted Jacques.

"It's a neurological issue, El," Bram reminded her. "Not psychological or emotional. The part of my brain that regulates sleep no longer functions as it should."

She knew that, but she couldn't help grasping for hope through the wall of reconditioning. "Tell me what the medics say," she said. "You... matter to me, Bram." She'd never told him that, never verbalized it, and it seemed very important she do so now. "You're my family, my brother."

Bram's answer was quiet. "He's good for you, that falcon. Take the time, El."

She would, she thought as she hung up the call. At least today. She could justify stepping away from the hunt for the killer while her brain was at flatline, so vulnerable that she couldn't fight him off if he assaulted her. And there was no reason for him to escalate to another kidnapping so soon after his last one.

But first, she'd reply to Saffy—who loved messages far more than calls: I'm in a falcon aerie, watching a wing fly in front of me against a backdrop of reds and oranges and desert gold. I flamed out after a psychic event, but I'm healing. I'm also surrounded by changelings with natural shields—it's the best place I could've found to heal.

The response came back at lightning speed: I would think you were delusional if Bram hadn't told us you were with the falcons. Is it really like that?

Eleri took a photo, careful not to reveal anything that wouldn't be visible to someone on the ground looking up. Falcons in the air, against the wild blue sky.

Saffron's response was about ten exclamation marks followed by more curious questions, all of which Eleri answered, because she knew that Saffy just wanted to talk to her. If Bram was the glue that held them together, Saffron was the little sister who'd always brought light and color into their lives. It didn't matter that, in biological terms, Eleri was younger than her by a year—Saffy had always been softer, sweeter, younger in the heart.

Left alone to bloom, Eleri had always thought their Saffy would have become an artist, a designer of clothes vibrant and eye-catching. At seven, she used to sketch pretty dresses and fancy hats. Until the teachers and trainers had crushed the color out of her, taught her to live in a world of shadow memories.

When they signed off today, it was with a promise to chat again the next day.

The sound of wings coming closer as she slipped away her phone, the tenor different from when the falcons had taken off. Faster, more rushed. She saw why when the flyer winged into view . . . it was the smallest falcon she'd ever seen, its feathers still slightly white and fluffy in patches.

A child.

Beating its wings with far more force and less finesse than its elders, it dove into the opening . . . to land on Eleri's arm, which she'd outstretched without thinking about it. The child's chest heaved as it settled its feathers, its tiny heartbeat rapid. Its talons gripped Eleri's forearm tight but without breaking through her shirt.

A larger falcon landed on the ledge moments later, and she had the certainty that this was one of the child's parents. Giving their fledgling freedom while hovering protectively close.

The adult falcon shot her a penetrating glance before settling its wings and remaining in place where it had landed.

She knew why, could feel Adam's heat against her back. "This fledgling is heavier than they look," she murmured, unable to believe what was happening to her, what she was doing, what she was experiencing. Even dulled as it was by the reconditioning, it was more beautiful than anything she'd ever before done or felt.

Adam reached around to scratch the top of the child's head.

Closing their eyes, the child leaned their head further into the contact. Adam chuckled. "He's a rocket, this one. Races around the Canyon like it's a track. Probably outpace me soon."

The child spread its feathers, and even though Eleri knew little about falcon ways, she knew the fledgling was proud at the praise. The pull she'd felt toward Adam from the day they met was a thing visceral, but this, seeing him with his clan, how his people lit up near him, how this child trusted him, it altered the primal into an emotion far more conscious: Adam was a good wing leader, a good *man*.

Eleri wanted to know this man in every way.

"Here." Moving to her free side, he held out his hand, on which were small tidbits of food. "It's his favorite."

The falcon made tiny sounds that Eleri thought must be excitement. Managing to curl her arm slightly to better take the baby falcon's weight, she picked up a piece of what seemed to be a pastry from Adam's palm and held it to the fledgling's beak. He took it from her fingers with more politeness than she'd expected, given the excited way he was fluttering his wings and moving his talons on her arm.

Adam lifted his forearm. "Hop over, little wind racer." A glance at Eleri as the child obeyed. "Your arm would fall off otherwise. He likes to perch. Now you can feed him for longer."

Eleri did just that—after first shaking out her own arm. Adam was right; it took more strength than it seemed to hold up even a small changeling falcon. The little raptor accepted every small morsel with happiness and, when Eleri held up the final pieces in her palm, didn't peck but picked it up with care not to hurt her.

"He's very gentle." She dared touch him as Adam had, the sheer softness of his downy feathers feeling an impossibility.

"He's a smart, kind, boy, our little Ollie."

When the child opened his beak in a yawn, Adam curled his arm to his chest where the fledgling nuzzled into him, and Adam used his free hand to cradle him close. His hand covered the tiny child's back, a protective shield as he made sounds in his throat that had the fledgling making little sounds in return that were clearly of happiness.

Eleri, her shoulder aching, determined to start exercising those muscles much more regularly so she— But no, she wouldn't have many more chances to offer a fledgling a perch. "How old is he?" she asked, pushing aside the future to come for the beauty of today.

"Four," Adam murmured. "Only four and tired from his morning flight with his mom." The larger falcon turned and walked over—just as a man of medium height with dark hair and brown skin, his eyes rounded and cheekbones flat, entered the dining area and made a smiling beeline to them.

"I've got him, sweetheart." His glance at the adult falcon held the kind of affection and comfort that wasn't born in a single day or a week, but over many months, even years.

This, she knew without being told, was the child's father.

Adam handed over the fledgling, who mumbled sleepily as he nestled against his father's chest. "Morning, Bayani. Ollie's getting stronger."

"Tell me about it," the man grumbled, but it was clear his heart wasn't in it, his hand tender on his son's back. "No one ever told me that mating with a hot falcon I saw in a bar one night would mean having a kid who thinks it's the height of hilarity to fly to a ceiling perch when he's in trouble with his papa."

Adam's shoulders shook even as the child's mother opened her beak in what seemed to be a falconish laugh.

Raising a hand, Adam slapped the other man on the shoulder. "If he gets too cheeky, call me." A grin. "That's what a wing leader is for—and it's not just because you're human. I had to put the fear of Adam into Simsim the other day after she decided she was big enough to fly to Raintree on her own."

"I'd have had a heart attack. Sweet mercy. Ollie listens if I tell him to stick with me, so I can take the ceiling taunts." A deep crease in his cheek. "One day, he fell asleep up there. I climbed up, fetched him down, and tucked him in, and he was amazed to wake up in bed."

"This is Eleri," Adam said. "Bayani Bautista, geologist and professor. And that's Harper Jay"—a nod at the falcon—"our head accountant, without whom our finances would be in shambles."

"We heard you helped Jacques," Bayani said with a warm smile, while his mate made a low, almost cooing sound. "Thank you and welcome to our home. If you'd like a geological tour, hit me up." A grin. "I've bored everyone else already."

The couple left soon afterward, with the falcon flying out the exit and her mate walking into the Canyon with their son, the two having agreed to meet up at their plateau home. "Do you have a lot of human clanmates?"

"About fifteen percent of our population. No Psy clanmates, though." Human eyes ringed by falcon yellow locked on hers. "Not yet."

Eleri's past receded in a rush, the future a blank.

Here, this moment in time when everything was possible, was her forever. Except . . . Adam was brushing his fingertip over her cheekbone and all she could feel was a dull sense of need that wasn't even a ghost of her breathless wonder from that day outside the courtroom.

Inside her was a scream locked in black fog, silenced by her own mind.

Chapter 27

Reagan Marke: DOA. Self-inflicted bullet wound to the left temple.

—Note on medical file (31 July 2078)

ELERI DIDN'T GIVE up the day, even knowing that what she experienced today would be a pale shadow of what could've been. She finished breakfast with Adam, then walked with him as he took her hand and told her he wanted to show her a place called the Green Grotto.

"It's not as stunning as the red one further out," he said after they'd exited the Canyon through a narrow opening that soon led to a downward-sloping path. "But because of that, it's not as popular, and more private."

"Do you remember the first time you came to this grotto?" she asked, wanting more memories to add to her hoard, more pieces of him to secrete away inside her.

His expression altered, lips no longer curved up and skin tight over his cheekbones. "With my parents when I was too young to understand time. It was one of my favorite splashing places."

Eleri's blood froze; this was the one area where she could not tread, could never seek to go.

Adam saw Eleri's expression go motionless and shook his head. "It was never your fault." Squeezing her hand, he tugged her close enough that he could cup one side of her face.

"My anger at you for what happened in the courtroom was irrational," he reiterated. "The rage of a tempestuous and heartbroken youth." So young and hurt that he'd taken it out on the one person he was meant to protect. "We'd barely spoken, had no commitment to each other, but I expected you to be loyal."

"We did have a commitment," Eleri said flatly. "From the instant we met. I didn't know what to call it, but I knew it existed. You were mine and I was yours, and I *knew* that."

His entire heart swelled, twisted. "So did I," he said. "And I still left you—to be hurt over and over, to be fucking *reconditioned*. I will live with that reality every single minute of my life."

She stared up at him. "Adam, no, there was no way you could've got me out. If you'd tried, the Council would've annihilated your entire clan just to send a message." WindHaven was far smaller and less powerful than DarkRiver, and Eleri had no Councilor mother.

It didn't matter if Nikita Duncan had or hadn't protected Sascha; the optics of going after such a high-profile cardinal just wouldn't have looked good. Js, on the other hand . . . Js were disposable—and ironically valuable enough for the Council to want them in its iron fist.

"I didn't even fucking try, my wild bird with eyes like the rain and the desert all at once." He pressed his fingers to her lips. "Don't waste your breath on telling me otherwise."

Agitation below the glacial ice. "You're wrong," she said, unflinching. "Just like Reagan was wrong. His actions went against all the vows we take as Js. But he was as close as I ever had to a father—and Adam? I need to talk about him."

Adam struggled with his rising rage against the man . . . which was now intermingled with endless gratitude. Because the same man who had attempted to steal justice from his parents had also saved Adam's mate. "Okay," he said, the word jagged in his throat.

"I found out that if Reagan didn't do what he did that day," Eleri told him, "he would've been dead by the end of the day... and I couldn't hate him for choosing to survive." Again, a single, betraying tear that escaped the vicious mauling of her mind. "I needed him."

The two emotions inside Adam collided in a turbulent storm. "I don't think I can ever forgive him... but I can accept what he was to you and that he was a good man who made a terrible choice."

He took a rough breath. "Talk about him as much as you want, Eleri. I didn't understand what I was asking when I told you never to mention him." He could damn well fight his instinctive anger if it would help his mate come to terms with her own grief and pain at the loss of the man who had saved her in so many ways, who had protected her when Adam hadn't even realized the danger.

"I don't think Reagan ever forgave himself, either." The Canyon rustled around them in a soft wind. "And he made sure I would never, ever be put in the same position. Because I can do what he can. I can bend memories."

As Adam's chest compressed and compressed in a punishing tightness, he waited for her to reveal what horrors she'd covered up with that gift. But no matter what, he wasn't letting her go.

Not again. Never again.

Whatever happened, whatever she'd done or the mistakes he'd made, they'd figure it out hand in hand.

"Reagan realized it during the WindHaven case, when I was able to sense *his* bending of the memory." Eleri's tone was hollow. "He told me never to reveal my ability to anyone else. With that, he gave me the only freedom he could in a world under Silence, under the Council."

Once again, Adam thought, the man he had vowed to hate had saved his mate. To say that his emotions toward Reagan Marke were complicated was a vast oversimplification.

"Your parents' murderer had influential friends," Eleri continued, as if now that she'd begun to speak, she couldn't stop. "Js aren't ordered to bend memories for anyone but the powerful. Reagan didn't know who those friends were, but the orders came from people he couldn't disobey and live."

"Wealth and family," Adam gritted out. "We dug deep, found links to two Councilors, both of whom are now dead but were in power at the time."

"Did you ever find out why he did it?" she asked, her hand pressed over his heart in a way that already felt familiar. "We never knew. Reagan didn't see that in the memory."

"A reason formed of evil and avarice." Adam told her all of it.

How the Psy had wanted a piece of land his parents owned; like many winged changelings, they'd invested in a small plot where they could rest up on long flights and that would give them an anchor point in another region. It had required the permission of the changelings who otherwise controlled that region when it came to their kind, but most changelings were accepting of lone or pairs of winged changelings who wanted to have a temporary home.

His parents had loved their little cabin on the plains and had often flown there to spend a week or two at random times. Adam had grown up going there with them—first in a vehicle because Adam couldn't fly that far even if Saoirse could, then later as a fledgling who'd had to take many rest breaks.

Each and every trip had been an adventure, his father showing him his favorite landing spots, his mother digging up a high-energy treat from her seemingly endless supply of caches across the route, and Saoirse teaching him sky games.

"Asshole thought he'd be able to annex that land after their deaths by legal maneuvers he'd set in play," Adam added. "He was so arrogant that he didn't do even the most basic research into changeling ownership structures, had no idea that all that belonged to my parents also belonged to our clan. It's the changeling way."

They *could* own things on their own; there was no rule against it. But most changelings were community-minded by nature and made certain that should anything go wrong, the clan would be able to assume control over their assets. In turn, a good clan, a clan that looked after its people, never took advantage of that faith.

WindHaven had held the property in trust for Saoirse and Adam. "Fucker discovered he couldn't outmaneuver an entire pissed-off clan with more than a few lawyers in it." Angry pain that was talons raking his insides. "He killed my parents for nothing."

It was Eleri's turn to hold him, her thin arms tight and strong as she let him bury his face against the side of her head and just breathe. "My grandmother executed him," he told her, his voice a rasp. "I fought for the right but she told me I was too young to be stained by blood, that this was her task as both my wing leader and my mother's mother."

Adam hadn't been able to fight Aria's right, not when she said it like that. "But she allowed me to bear witness, allowed me to watch her end him." She hadn't been frail then, Aria, but she hadn't gone alone—that would've been stupid, and his grandmother had never been stupid.

Her seconds had stood with her and Adam. Saoirse hadn't come, his sister's maternal heart not built for violence. But she'd waited for him on the plateau and embraced him with fierce love when he returned home. "You did the right thing, Bear," she'd said, holding his face in her hands. "He thought to prey on our family. He paid the price."

Saoirse's approval had mattered. He'd idolized her as a little boy, and still valued her opinions now that he was wing leader. His big sister had always been whip-smart—and had a generous heart, but one that did not forgive trespasses against those she loved.

Maternals might abhor violence, but should the Canyon be invaded, Saoirse and others of her ilk would shoot out the eyes of any invaders without flinching in order to help the fledglings escape. Not wanting violence and being ready to use it as a necessary weapon were two wholly different things.

"Will you tell me more about your family?" Eleri's question was hesitant.

"Yes," he said, stepping back so he could look at her face. "I want you to know them. I especially want you to meet my sister—she's going to love you." He pushed back a strand of hair that had become stuck to her skin where she'd cried that tear. "Will you tell me more about Reagan?"

A sweep of ebony across her eyes. "He had to bend memories three more times before his death—the authorities used him until he couldn't stand it anymore." Her voice had become quieter and quieter, a bleak descent. "He broke when he was asked to bend the memory of a psychopath who happened to have murdered three young boys. The murderer was a Tk. Important. Worth, the order said, more than three innocent lives."

Flat words without anger or reproach, but her irises had vanished, her eyes obsidian. "He sent me a time-delayed message, a last note. Said he'd always been scared of death so he'd done what they'd asked, but now he knew there were things far worse than death. He told me not to mourn him, and that he was proud of me for living my life with honor."

No open grief in her voice, nothing but the track of that single tear, but Adam knew his J now, understood that this loss had devastated her. "I'm sorry you lost him," he said, and it was a truth.

She meant more to Adam than his rage.

"I wish he'd lived to this time." Eleri swallowed. "The Es say that Js with that facility might be able to help trauma victims by—with their permission—altering their *internal* memories so the horror doesn't haunt them night after night.

"It's not something anyone has ever done—we take memories and morph the imprint, not the actual internal memory—but there are young Js working with Es to figure out whether it might be viable. Wouldn't that be astonishing, Adam? To have this ability be a healing tool and not a leash used to manipulate?"

"Yes." He fought back his own tears at the dull wonder in her at the idea that *she* might've been a gift had she been born in this time. One day, she'd understand that she was a gift to him—the best gift of his life.

He didn't know how long they stood there swathed in the losses of the past, but when they moved it was as one, their hands linked. He plucked a wild berry for her, watched her taste it with a deep concentration.

"My mom taught me about the berries," he told her, "the other edible plants in the area. She was born to this land, my father the handsome stranger who won her heart."

"I was born as a result of a fertilization contract," Eleri said in turn. "I know who my father is—it's part of my medical history—but he had no hand or say in raising me."

Adam didn't wince at the cold-blooded nature of Psy procreation under Silence; that same system had created his mate. "You lived with your mom?"

"Until I was six. Then I was placed permanently in boarding school—a J, even a 9.2, wasn't much use to them in terms of the family's bottom line."

"So they just let you go?" Adam couldn't process the idea; he'd fight tooth and claw to keep Ollie and the other babies close, where he could protect and shield them. To just eject a child from the nest? *No.*

"I was scared at first," Eleri admitted. "But then I met Bram, Saffron, and Yúzé, and I understood happiness for the first time." Her words ended in a gasp, her eyes trained forward.

The Green Grotto opened out in front of them, a paradoxically secret space created by the way the canyon walls touched at the top high above, while allowing in spears of light that made the water below glow a luminous jewel green.

"Tell me what you feel," he said, because he knew she could feel to a certain extent. That single tear, the way she'd fought for Jacques, the way she'd stared at Ollie with such silent wonder.

His Eleri's heart was damaged but not destroyed.

She turned to him, her face pristine in its false peace. "It's as if I perceive emotion through a thick layer of smoky glass." Dropping his hand, she walked forward to the edge of the water and sat down.

When he came down next to her, the side of his body pressed to hers and she didn't pull away.

"Js feel too much," she said, the words sounding like a confession inside this place distant from everyone, a cocoon where they could pretend they were just another couple who wanted to steal a romantic moment. "That's always been the problem. We can't be Silent when our literal job is to walk in the minds of monsters.

"Each reconditioning attempted to re-create Silence by scraping away the weight of emotion, and if that didn't work, overwriting it," she explained. "But we also *can't* forget, so the technicians added what they call 'obstructions' in our neural pathways. Like a circuit that never quite closes, it was meant to allow us to remember without the emotional impact of remembering."

"It sounds like bullshit," Adam snarled. "A way to use you like machines."

"Yes." Eleri continued to stare at the water as green as glass. "I think sometimes, that if they'd let us read good memories in between, we might've done better, might have been balanced, but that was never on the table. Only the monsters. Only the evil. After a while, it seeps into you."

She shook her head when he would've spoken. "I don't regret the people I executed. Especially not the ones who beat the system and got out—had they remained alive, they would've destroyed countless lives. But the girl I once was would've felt regret, would've questioned who she was becoming. That's what I regret—losing her." Her next words were a whisper. "In losing her, I lost you, too."

"No." He took her jaw, made her look at him with those eyes become obsidian pools. "*You* are who I want. You as you are today. I'm not that boy anymore, either."

Eleri couldn't fight the compulsion any longer. "Can I touch you?" she said to the angry falcon in front of her, because she would allow herself to be selfish this day that would be the only one they'd ever share. "Even through the smoky glass, the fog, I've always reacted to your physical presence like I have a hunger within."

His pupils expanded, the yellow ring bright with grim satisfaction. "That's the call of the mating bond." Lifting her hand to his face, he said, "Do what you will. I'm yours, Eleri Dias."

His jaw was hard and solid under her touch, his skin lightly bristled. When it grazed her palm, she wondered what it would feel like on softer, more delicate parts of her.

Chapter 28

> Sexual contact *must* be verboten if Silence is to succeed. There is no other option—there's too much sensation in it, too much chance of emotional bonding.
>
> —Excerpted from draft discussion paper on the Silence Protocol
> (1 January 1973)

ELERI KNEW WHAT she was feeling was a dulled echo of what it should be, but this was her only chance and so she would take it. Moving her hands to the buttons of her shirt, she began to undo them.

Adam sucked in a breath. "Eleri, what—?"

"I want contact," she said, her shirt partially unbuttoned. "I want skin to skin, so much contact that I *feel*."

He stopped her hands, and for a moment she thought this was it, Adam ending the experience before it began. But then he nudged her hands aside and said, "Let me," and her pulse kicked up a notch.

Not enough, not anything like it had done during their first meeting so long ago, but for now, for who she was . . . she accepted it, embraced it. As she embraced the warm sensation that spread through her entire body when Adam ran his knuckles down the strip of skin he'd already exposed.

"You're not wearing a bra," he said, a slow smile on his lips. "Now, how are you getting away with that with a white shirt, hmm?"

"I don't have large breasts, and while the color is white, the material is thick."

Adam ran the back of his hand over her right breast without warning, and she felt her abdomen clench. He was watching her, gave a small nod. "You felt that, didn't you?"

"Yes." As a dull stab deep within her.

Adam did it again, before moving his hands to the buttons at her cuffs. He undid them with a slow deliberation that she knew she should savor, but—"I need things to be fast, Adam. Sensation layered atop sensation. No time for anything to fade."

A desperation of sensation.

The ring of yellow around his irises seemed to glow, become brighter. "Falcons are the fastest creatures on the planet, our diving velocity so ruthless that our prey never sees us coming."

Rising to his feet in a sharp movement, he hauled her upright, too, then tugged her with intent toward an opening that seemed to lead back into the lower part of the Canyon. "Caves," he threw back over his shoulder, an intensity to him that pushed against her. "Including one carpeted with the softest sand."

It took them only four minutes to reach it, and though it had been semi-dark to this point, the cave itself rippled with a glow of sunlight. It took her a second to see it—tiny holes in the rocks to one side that must be a hollow in the Canyon that permitted a dance of light inside.

She didn't have much time to take in the wonder of it, however, because Adam was suddenly in front of her, his hand sliding around the side of her neck to her nape to hold her close while he undid the rest of the buttons on her shirt with his other hand, tugging it out from her pants at the end to finish the job.

His hand on her skin, stroking up in a hard glide to close over one taut breast and squeeze. She sucked in air, the sensation strong enough that it wasn't a dull throb but a spear. "More. *More, Adam.*"

Making a deep rumble of a sound in his throat, he released her instead—but only to rip off his own top and throw it aside before moving his hands to the waistband of her pants. A glance at her through hooded lids. "How far?"

"All of it. Everything." She had no limit, no point of overload, wished she did.

Adam, her *mate*, took her at her word and dropped to his knees to undo her boots, get them off, along with her socks. "Cute feet." A wink as he looked up, his hand on the top of one foot.

And Eleri realized for the first time that sensation in such a context wasn't always tactile. Looking at him, at his smile, the way he was so big and beautiful and . . . happy to be with her. It intensified everything already building in her. She undid her own pants, worried her feelings would vanish behind the wall of numbness.

Adam groaned as her pants fell to her feet, but pulled them away when she lifted her feet one at a time. However, before she could push down the plain white cotton of her underwear, he leaned in and *bit* the inside of her thigh . . . as his stubbled jaw rubbed against her.

She'd been right.

She felt more.

So much more.

Her thigh was over his shoulder before she knew what she was doing, and from the way he kissed the little bite he'd just taken, he didn't mind. Instead he gripped her thigh to hold her closer, and then, without warning, her underwear was gone, cut neatly away from her body by talons she'd never seen emerge.

Eleri wasn't ready for the next sensation, that of his mouth on the most sensitive flesh on her body, the lick of his tongue deliberately rough as he gave her what she'd asked for: sensation atop sensation. Then he was kissing her with raw intensity, and her other leg would've buckled if he hadn't been holding her up.

The cool, calm, rational part of her created by the reconditionings knew she was still only catching the edge of what she should . . . but this was more than she'd felt for an eternity. And it was with him, with her beautiful boy. She let herself fall into it, fall into him, and when he rubbed his jaw deliberately against her inner thigh, she allowed the buzz of sensation to haze her mind.

He pulled her to the ground, using his strength to control the movement so she landed on the sand with the lightness of a feather. Rising above her, he spread her shirt apart and made a deep sound in his throat. "So damn beautiful." His hand on her breast again, his knee nudging her thighs apart so he could settle in between.

He had only the faintest line of dark hair low on his chest, a trail that led into his jeans, his abdomen hard and ridged. "I want to feel you crushing me," she said, still fighting to outrace the numbness.

Adam came down on her without warning, sliding his hand down to curve around and grip her buttock as he put his partial weight on her, keeping a large amount off by bracing himself on the forearm of his free hand.

She pulled at his shoulders. "All of it."

"I'm heavy, Eleri," he said, but gave her what she wanted.

She could barely breathe and it was wonderful, Adam rubbing up against so much of her exposed skin. "Jeans," she gasped out.

"Demanding." A kiss that tasted of her, and the unexpected intimacy of it added another layer of sensation to this interlude where Eleri was determined to drown in the tactile, in emotion . . . but mostly in Adam.

Cold rushed in where Adam had been the instant he left her, and the numbness, it began to eat away at the depth of sensation she'd hoarded . . . but Adam hadn't been lying about changeling speed. He was on her again almost before she'd processed that he was gone, and this time, he was naked.

The hairs on his thighs rubbed against hers, his chest crushing her breasts as he fisted a hand in hair she hadn't even realized he'd undone, and he dropped his head to kiss her with a deep, wet intensity. She surrendered, opened herself, gave him all of what she had left, and he gathered up the dregs and somehow saw beauty.

"You're driving me crazy," he said as he moved his hand to between them, his thumb pressing down on a body part she knew was called the clitoris but whose purpose she hadn't ever understood. At the same time, he speared his fingers through her labia to touch the highly sensitive entrance to her vagina . . . and Eleri got it.

She'd been taught the body parts in biology class but was never told that those parts weren't only about function. The clitoris's whole purpose, it appeared, was pleasure. Her body was *designed* for pleasure.

Her breath caught, her torso twisting as she reclaimed her right to feel. "More, Adam," she gasped, able to sense the looming wall of nothingness waiting to crash over her.

"I don't want to hurt you." His chest heaved, his hair falling around his face as he looked down at her.

She looked up at him and wanted him beyond bearing. "You could never hurt me."

His face twisted, a raw anguish in it. "Never." A rough promise. "On the honor of my clan, mate of mine."

Her eyes burned, and in that moment, she knew she could cry. She drew Adam down to her. "All of it, Adam. Please."

A shuddering breath before he kissed her even as he resettled his body so that the blunt hardness of his erection pushed against her. It should've felt like a violation, that penetration to a body that had never felt its like . . . but it felt the opposite. An embrace.

Adam inside her, around her, the smell of him, the weight of him, the wild honor of him.

For a pulse in time, she did drown, her body rippling in a faded echo of pleasure—but it was pleasure true and real—and her tears were of a woman who *felt*.

LATER, Adam held Eleri against him, spooning her too-slender body with his own as his falcon spread its wings over her spirit. "You cold?"

A shake of her head. "You burn like a fire." Cool words, but he'd tasted her tears at the end, felt her body shiver around his. He'd have thought he'd done it wrong, not given his mate what she needed, except that she'd kissed him in the aftermath and said, "I felt, Adam. All through me," as tears yet streamed down her face. "I *felt*."

He snuggled her closer, distraught in ways he fought to hide. Because he knew from her physical responses that she'd caught only the merest edge of sensation, the barest whisper of what could be between mates. Those fuckers had hurt her so much, her mind and spirit grievously wounded.

"This is just the start," he murmured, kissing her ear because it was close and he just wanted to adore her. "We're going to get stronger with every day that passes."

Eleri's body went motionless before she turned in his arms and shifted so they lay face-to-face, her head on his arm and her hair trailing over her body in smooth, dark strands as she pressed a hand to his heart. "I feel your frustration now at being unable to reach me. I don't want to feel it—or for you to feel it—for however long I make it before Exposure."

"I'll handle it," Adam said, aggravated with himself for allowing her to see it.

But she shook her head, her eyes lost in the mists inside her. "I would rather carry this one perfect day forever, than have you watch me degrade, watch me become less and less until I lose all of myself."

"You don't get to make that decision unilaterally." He leaned in until their breaths mingled, his hand over the side of her head, her hair so soft under his palm. "Not when this is about the two of us."

"Adam." His name said in a way that was . . . just her. Only her. "Attempt the mating bond."

Shocked, he said, "If you think I won't, Eleri, you're very wrong, so you'd better be ready."

"I am." Her fingers curled into his skin.

His falcon more than ready, Adam let go of the knot of energy he'd kept contained inside for ten long years, and it arrowed toward her. He waited for it to crash, bind, and return to him twofold. He waited to see her as she would see him.

He waited to become hers.

But . . . the energy recoiled back into him with the sense of hitting a huge block. Hard enough that he jerked, might have fallen had he been standing. As it was, it stole his breath.

"You think you're proving something by using shields to block me?" he said when he could speak again, curling his fingers around the side of her neck as he did so. "I'm a wing leader, Eleri. I don't give up just because I hit an obstacle."

"I can't block you." A quiet reminder. "I've flatlined my psychic abilities."

A shot of ice in his veins, his fingers tightening on her neck. "You're mine. I can feel it, never stopped feeling it."

"I could've once been yours." Broken words coated in numbness. "But I lost that ability with the repeated reconditionings. The mating bond can't reach me because the me it wants to reach is dead. Buried under so many memories of evil that she can never again exist."

Adam felt his talons release, his eyes change. "Mating doesn't work like that. It's forever." And he'd never, not once, stopped sensing her. Being aware of her existence somewhere out there in the world. Being angry with her.

Dreaming of her.

She just shook her head in a silent repudiation.

His falcon swooped in, tried to claim her again. Only to bounce off that hard wall . . . that smoky glass that the monsters in power had used to destroy her. "I won't give you up," he growled. "We can have a thousand fucking arguments, get through all the shit, but I'm not giving up. That's not what I do."

Eleri didn't want to argue with the man who had once been a dream and was now central to her very existence. But she knew that if he saw her once she hit Exposure, it'd destroy him. Adam Garrett was built to protect those who were his own, and for better or worse, she had always been meant to be his.

As he had been meant to be hers.

It would be so easy to give in, to just accept this life where she could be part of a winged clan, welcome at their table and in this man's arms. And she would . . . for a splinter in time. Because there was one thing she hadn't told Adam, one lie she'd told by omission despite all her promises.

But in her defense, she'd told the lie to herself, too, by refusing to look the truth in the face.

No more. She had to be honest with herself. Doing what she'd done with Jacques had eaten away the last of her reserves. She'd sensed the pressure of the world all around her right before she flamed out—and she'd been inside the Canyon at the time, with the majority of the people nearby having natural shields.

Exposure was no longer a future possibility but an unstoppable process that would begin in a matter of days.

If she stayed, her mate would see her bleed from her eyes and her ears as her overwhelmed brain began to shut down in explosive bursts. She would lose control of her limbs, other functions. She wouldn't know him, wouldn't know herself. And in the end, she'd drown to death in her own fluids.

No, she didn't want him to witness that, to bear the horror of it all his days.

As soon as she recovered from the flameout, and after she'd double-checked that the task force had full access to all her notes about the Sandman, with all data also backed up to the Quatro Cartel system, she'd set herself on a path out of town, find a remote place in the desert, dig a grave.

Then she'd lie down in it and pull the off switch in her brain.

She'd built it after finding Reagan. He'd used an old-fashioned gun. There'd been blood and brain matter everywhere.

Turned out that a Psy mind could figure out how to turn itself off permanently if that mind had enough impetus. Hers had begun with finding Reagan's brain matter on her clothing after she was sent home and his body taken away, but it had morphed over time to the firm decision that she didn't want her last living memory to be of pain and anguish and madness.

Eleri planned to go right before Exposure rather than while she was mired in it.

However, her desire to set Adam free of the bond between them, without leaving a scar on his psyche, had just eclipsed her initial motive. Her mate should never—would never—have to watch her fall into Exposure.

Chapter 29

Clan begins here, in our home, Ashkii Anádlohí. Always hold your sister close, even when you fly far from one another, because how can there be a clan when there are no bonds of family born or found?

—Taazbaa' Garrett to Adam Garrett (age 4) (17 September 2059)

"WILL YOU SHOW me more of your world?" she asked Adam, not too proud to gather a final few scraps of time with him, experiences with him, before it was too late.

He scowled. "What? You want me to ignore what just happened?"

"No, but today, you promised to be my beautiful boy." She wished she could smile at him, but the wall was thick and viscous again, only echoes of emotion getting through. "That boy would've taken me exploring in the caves, I think."

An even deeper scowl, followed by a kiss. "I know you're manipulating me, but you're doing it so obviously that I can't even be mad at you." Another kiss. "We *will* discuss this."

Eleri tucked her head against his chest, let her skin draw in his heat.

A sigh, a nuzzle of her head. "Stubborn wild bird." A kiss pressed to her hair. "Come on, then."

And despite the wall, the numbness, their intimacy had left a mark on Eleri. She felt every bit of her clothing as she pulled it on over her body, every tactile sensation multiplied a thousand times over. "I smell like you," she murmured as she buttoned up her shirt.

A raised eyebrow from where he crouched to pick up his shirt. "You complaining?"

"No." She drew in another breath. "I won't shower." She wanted to take him with her at the end, even if only on her skin.

Chuckling, he came over to kiss her lips with a familiarity that made her ache. "I plan to get my scent all over you on a regular basis, so don't worry about washing it off." A deep smile that lit up his entire face. "Let me finish buttoning you up."

He did so with playful care, and afterward, she buttoned his shirt in turn, and when her mind tried to go into the future, imagine a thousand mornings with him where they got dressed together, she wrenched it back.

Today, she would live in today.

He watched her as she reached back to reknot her hair. She couldn't anchor it using the pin because that pin was lost somewhere in the sand, so she slipped off the hair tie she'd returned automatically to her wrist and used that. She had no use for her private dissonance loop any longer, the most powerful memories in her mind those to do with Adam.

To be overwhelmed by them would be a dream, not a nightmare.

"Your hair was longer the first time we met," she said. "To your waist."

"You want me to grow it back?" he asked with a grin. "For you, I'll deal with the upkeep."

The idea that he'd just do that for her . . . The ache grew deeper into her bones. "I . . . love you exactly as you are, in all the seasons of your life." She knew that what she thought of as love was a pale imitation, but it was all she had to give.

Adam's eyes turned falcon. "I love you, too, Eleri. And me and you? We're forever, through hundreds of seasons to come."

. . .

ELERI said nothing in response to his declaration, but Adam had expected that. He hadn't fought for her once, but never again would he abandon her, even if she thought that the best option. "For today," he said, "I'm going to show you a secret place."

She came with him without questions, and the trust of this J who'd been betrayed over and over . . . it tore him up even as it shored up his determination. "I found it as a kid," he said. "Jacques is the only other person who knows about it as far as I'm aware—we were roaming the caves together at the time."

"You weren't afraid of getting lost?"

Adam shook his head. "I don't know if it's a falcon thing or just that this is our home, but we—all of the clan—have always been able to find our way back to the sky from anywhere in the Canyon."

Though he could navigate the labyrinth with ease, his night vision excellent, he was conscious that to Eleri, the deeper they went, the darker it would get. Taking out his phone, he used the flashlight function to create a glow around them.

He also made sure to keep a careful grip on her, and to assist her up the more jagged or slippery sections. "A lot of water goes through the Canyon," he said. "The arteries of the planet, my *shimásání*—my grandmother—used to say. WindHaven is lucky to have always had a fresh source of water so close yet hidden from enemies."

Eleri ran her fingers along a ridge of limestone, as stalactites began to appear in the ceilings above them. "Do you speak the language of your mother's family? I've heard it's a complex one."

"Yes. WindHaven was founded by a small group of Diné falcons, and though the composition of our population has changed over the years, we hold true to the ways of our ancestors." The outside world often referred to them as Navajo, but in their own tongue, they were the Diné, their lyrical—and yes, complex—language Diné Bizaad.

"It's part of our identity as a clan," he added. "Built into our very being, the language a living, breathing element of who we are as Wind-Haven. All the fledglings speak it because they hear it every day."

He squeezed her hand. "Don't worry, though, wild bird. We welcome our mates into the clan and embrace their own histories and languages. It is a thing of winged clans—we're used to distant travelers flying into our lives and our families.

"Amir, my brother-in-law, was born in the Persian Gulf, while Dahlia's mother flew in from Ecuador, though her own parents are based in Iran. Harper's parents were born in the Arctic, went adventuring as young adults, and ended up in another part of Arizona." Every winged clan had stories of distant origins among its population. "Pascal, who you haven't met yet, was born in Belize, joined the clan as a young man."

To date, he didn't know of any Psy who had mated into a winged clan—but that would change if he had anything to do with it. "Careful here," he said, "we have to go downhill a bit."

He used his thighs to stabilize them down the slope, Eleri held close to his side, until they emerged into a much wider and higher conduit where they could walk with ease again. "Let's see, exactly fifty steps." He counted them out. "Turn left."

And there was the entrance.

Smiling, he led Eleri to it after turning off the phone flashlight. "Look. I named it Mirage as a kid."

A small gasp of air. "What is it?" she asked, walking inside to run her fingers along the sparkling lines of minerals that held a bioluminescent glow that turned the huge cavern into a wonderland.

"I managed to get a sample to Bayani to test. He said it's bioluminescent moss that's growing over particular minerals." He leaned against the edge of the doorway as she walked deeper inside, toward the sound of rushing water from an underground river behind the back wall of the cave.

Eleri stopped in the very center of the cavern, her gaze tilted up. "It's so quiet here, Adam," she murmured . . . just as what felt like a thousand bats took flight from the ceiling and dived down to exit past Adam.

Laughing, he ran in to rescue Eleri, who'd ducked down with her arms over her head. "Sorry!" He put his arm around her. "They don't usually move at this time of day—we must've disturbed them."

They ran out and down the passageway, Eleri's breath fast and shallow when they stopped. "I've never seen bats before," she gasped out. "Much less in flight."

"Hang around the Canyon at sunset and you'll get quite the show." He began to walk them out, phone flashlight back on. "I still haven't figured out how these exit to the outside, but they're part of why I haven't brought others down here. It's their home."

Eleri leaned into him, her hand tight on his. "Thank you for showing me. It's been a day beyond anything I could've imagined."

Adam nuzzled her. "Do you have the energy for one more thing? I'd like to introduce you to my sister."

A long pause before Eleri said, "I would be so proud to meet her . . . though I will have to shower beforehand."

Throwing back his head, he laughed, because there she was. His girl. Locked behind the gray walls of reconditioning, but still fighting, still breaking out of her cell at unexpected times.

No matter what Eleri believed, she was far from done.

SINCE Saoirse was at work at the lab where they manufactured delicate and cutting-edge aeronautical parts, he messaged her to ask if she could take a break that afternoon. That wasn't always a given with Saoirse—if she got into a project, she'd work straight through for hours.

Her response was very Saoirse: You finally going to introduce me to the woman at whom you are making goo-goo eyes per my eldest and very smart child? I was about to disavow you as a sibling. Bring food with you—I forgot to eat lunch. I also want to interrogate her in private, so we're not going out.

"My sister's protective of me," he told Eleri as he drove them to the plant through Raintree, the requested food in the back of the car. "Can't quite stop seeing me as her little brother." She'd held him tight after their parents' deaths, the two of them locked in a grief only they could understand.

Because in that moment, they'd lost the twin anchors of their world.

"Even though you're her wing leader?"

"Context," he reminded her. "Family interactions are a different matter from clan interactions."

Eleri looked forward, at the low curving building toward which he'd just turned. "Underground?"

"Yeah, most of the facility is underground. Easier to maintain climate control." He took a minute to park the vehicle in the spot assigned to the CEO.

Eleri looked at the sign, then at him.

Adam didn't blame her for the reaction—most Psy had never been close enough to changelings to understand the working structure of their packs and clans. "The leader of a clan or pack is also always the CEO of our businesses. Being wing leader isn't only about dominance or strength—to be wing leader is to care and to protect and to tend."

Catching a movement out of the corner of his eye, he glanced over to see Saoirse striding over dressed in a white jumpsuit that she'd accessorized with a beaded belt that had once been their mother's. She always walked with intense purpose, his big sister. "There she is, right on time."

Falcon stirring within, he turned to Eleri. "I'm so fucking happy that I get to introduce you to my sister." The fury of his delight filled his heart. "Family is the foundation of a clan, the foundation of *me*. Let me show you a huge part of that foundation."

Chapter 30

To recap: no fingerprints, no DNA on the pages slipped under Eleri's door. Analysis still being done on the ink and printing itself, but the techs tell me it's unlikely to help unless we have a machine against which to compare the documents.

But I've received authorization to head to Raintree. We'll see you tomorrow afternoon, Eleri.

—Message from Senior Detective Tim Xiao
to the Sandman Task Force (today)

My dearest Eleri,

I've realized I'm disappointed at having you on my home turf. It means I have to stop our private game just when it was getting fun.

But don't worry—our last game together will be the best of them all. I've prepared everything just so for you, and I can't wait for it to begin. She's a pretty little thing, isn't she? Adam Garrett's niece. All hair and energy and bright colors.

And clever. So, so clever.

I like them clever.

I know, I know, I'm cheating since I won't send this letter to your task force until well after the game has ended, but it amuses me to write it nonetheless. Because here's the thing, Eleri, you'll never get to read this letter, never get to pore over its contents to try to figure me out.

Such a shame, but you really brought this on yourself—and on sweet Malia.

You should've never, ever set foot in my town.

The Sandman

Chapter 31

Forgive me, Adam, that I couldn't bear to allow you to stand witness to my descent. I couldn't stand for you to see me that way.

I want you to remember me as that girl in the hallway, as the woman you showed pleasure beyond pleasure under the Canyon, as the lover you fed little morsels in bed.

Sugared almonds and plum chocolates, popcorn coated in lemon meringue frosting and baked, tiny and sharply salty preserved prunes... I never knew such things existed.

I feel your grief at all whom you've lost, and I'm so sorry to add my name to that list—but don't mourn me, Adam. I'm free now. Your wild bird in flight, my mind whole and my spirit no longer locked in a cage of reconditioning.

At last, I'm Eleri again.

—From the mental draft of Eleri's farewell letter (5 a.m. today)

ELERI WOKE TO the knowledge that she'd lived a lifetime yesterday... and to the awareness of a strange buzz at the back of her once more psychically active brain. The thoughts of the clan, pouring through psychic barriers so thin that they would tear sooner rather than later.

It didn't matter that over three quarters of the population of the Canyon had natural shields—at this level of psychic sensitivity, the merest suggestion of a thought was enough to create pressure on the brain.

It would only get worse from here on out.

But she had enough time that she was able to have breakfast with Adam. He'd asked her to stay through the night with him, and she had. They'd shared their bodies again in that way that made her feel whole for a pulse in eternity, then lain on their sides facing each other, and he'd told her stories of his childhood, of how he'd learned to fly, and the pranks he'd pulled on the ferociously loving sister who'd grilled Eleri the day past.

Saoirse Garrett was strong, opinionated, and loyal in the fiercest way.

Eleri had expected the other woman to hate her, but Saoirse had frowned for a long time after they met, looked from her to Adam, then sucked in a gulp. "What are you playing at, Bear?" She'd slapped him on the arm, the action far too light to do any actual harm. "You just forget to tell me she's your *mate*? Did you think I wouldn't notice?"

Chuckling, Adam had squeezed his angry sister close even as his eyes met Eleri's over Saoirse's curls. *See*, those eyes seemed to say, *she senses it, too, the potential between us—it's worth it, Eleri. Take the chance. Jump into my arms, into my world.*

And despite knowing she literally couldn't open to the mating bond, Eleri had wanted to attempt it, wanted to jump into his arms and hold on, forget that her brain was in the process of its final evisceration—and that all that would remain of her in a few days was a screaming nothingness.

Today, as they ate in the privacy of his rooms inside the Canyon, she drank him in with an unquenchable thirst. She'd watched him deep in the dark hours, too, after she woke too soon. She'd been glad of her insomnia for the first time, because it gave her time to just look at Adam while he rested, his lashes dark shadows on his cheeks.

Who, she'd allowed herself to think, would they have been to each other had they come together the first time they met? They'd have grown together, become together. Would she have laughed with him as Saoirse had laughed after her initial shock? Would his niece have jumped into her arms in excited hello as she'd jumped into Adam's? Would she have become so familiar to the fledglings that they'd think nothing of landing on her arm or shoulder?

Then she'd let the dream float away, where it couldn't hurt her in the morning light.

Now, she tried every small bite Adam offered her but tasted little because her attention was on him, and she kept on lying that one lie that made her an oath breaker. Today, she'd go to the inn with the excuse of removing all her security devices, and use the time to make sure those who'd carry on her work would have all the data she'd collected.

It galled her that she hadn't finished her last case, but she couldn't be sorry for helping Jacques, or for the time she'd had with Adam. The task force would be in Raintree late this afternoon, so she'd done that at least, brought the team here, to the killer's home ground.

The team was excellent, and now that she'd led them here, she had every confidence that they'd find the Sandman. She knew Adam wouldn't let go even if, for some unknown reason, the task force failed.

This was his territory, his to protect, his to shield.

She planned to send him a time-delayed message with her Sandman files so he'd have every piece of knowledge at her disposal. That done... she'd drive out. It'd be hard to avoid falcon eyes en route, but she'd planned it down to the wire. She'd tell Adam she was going to meet an associate, would be back by darkfall.

All aboveboard.

She'd also write him the letter she'd already composed in her mind in the silent hours before dawn, telling him exactly why she'd made the choice she had. She'd add that letter to the time-delayed message. And she'd hope that one day, he'd find room in his wide-open heart to forgive her one final time.

"Come on, we'll go grab your security equipment," Adam said after breakfast. "You can work as well from up in the Canyon—your computer's still locked up in the car, safe and sound."

Eleri's mouth was dry but her resolve unshakable under the weight of the whispers at the back of her mind, the awareness of the bulging inward of her translucent telepathic shields. "I'm driving out to speak to a profiler associate of mine today."

Adam frowned. "You sure that's safe?"

"Adam." A soft rebuke, a reminder that she'd walked this road a long time.

He scowled but didn't argue. "When are you planning to leave? I'll join you on the wing after I clear up a little clan business."

"Probably in a couple of hours," she said, certain she could get far enough out and lost enough in that period to throw him off the trail.

Adam nodded. "I should be able to join you an hour after you start out."

Too soon, far too soon.

Eleri twisted and turned her plan in her head, knew she could still evade him if she went at speed. "Is it all right if I visit Jacques before I leave?"

"I was planning to drop by anyway." A deep smile. "I'm hoping I can harangue him into waking."

While that didn't work, Jacques did look far better than the last time Eleri had seen him. His skin glowed with health, and his physical readings were excellent. When she brushed his hand, she sensed only the same wildness as Adam. "His shields are fully operational."

"Good. Now, wake up, you asshole, so I can introduce you to my mate," Adam said before they left.

Eleri waited until Adam stepped out to chat with Naia for a moment to lean down and whisper, "Watch over him, Jacques. He's going to need you in the weeks and months to come, so wake soon, and watch over him." She wished she could stop her mate's pain, wished she could turn back the clock.

But those gifts she couldn't grasp from destiny's cold arms.

All she could do was hope that those who loved him would make sure he didn't fall in the aftermath of her death.

"Eleri?" Adam's body in the doorway, his hands on either doorjamb. "Ready to go?"

"Yes."

ADAM left her at the inn with a press of his lips to her temple that made her stone tears turn to stabbing shards. This man, good and kind and with a heart as huge as the sky that was his home, would forgive her anything. And she was about to brutalize that heart. Because if she didn't, she'd destroy it, destroy him, and devastate the clan that looked to him as their strong, loving center.

Acting on autopilot, she checked her files were updated and loaded to the correct systems. She didn't bother to remove her security devices after all, and in doing so was able to bring her departure time forward by at least forty-five minutes. She wrote her letter to Adam, set the time-delay email.

And was done.

You promised you'd never lie to me.

She rubbed a fisted hand over her heart at the words she knew he'd say to her if he knew her plans, the ache a dull throbbing. And she was glad she couldn't feel the full strength of it, because this, it was bad enough. "I'm sorry," she said aloud as she went to walk out the door.

Her phone buzzed.

Glancing down, she saw it was Adam. And the same instincts that had led her to this town turned her blood to ice. "What's happened?" she said as she answered, her nails cutting into her palm and her mind a glacial field.

"Malia's been taken." His voice was clipped, hard, determined. "Left the Canyon at eight to attend a breakfast picnic with her friends. An hour into it, they turned around and she was gone. We tracked her scent to the parking lot."

This is because of me.

If anything happened to Malia . . . "Send me the location. I'll meet you there." And hope she could hold back Exposure long enough to find the beautiful, bright girl raised in happiness who'd never touched darkness until Eleri led it straight to her.

"SHE'S on the way," Adam said to Dahlia, who stood at the top of the path that led to the grassy picnic area in Raintree. The best tracker in the clan due to her unique genetics, the wing-second had already flown a wide circuit and failed to pick up any trace of Adam's niece.

Rather than wearing her out by having her flying aimlessly, Adam had asked her to return in the hope that all of them working together could narrow down the search area.

Another member of his clan was keeping watch on the site from above.

Detective Beaufort and Deputy Whitten had been on shift at the time of the call and were already doing interviews with everyone who'd been in or around the park at the time, with Hendricks scheduled to join them after he'd caught a few more hours of sleep post his recent night shift.

Enforcement and WindHaven had already blasted Malia's name and likeness across the state. They all knew that no child of WindHaven would just take off, wings or not. It was one of the first things the clan taught their fledglings—to have wings is freedom, but with that comes responsibility, and of the latter, their Mali had an inordinate amount. She was the quintessential big sister, the organizer among her friends, the girl with a seven-year plan for college and beyond.

Never would she worry her family and clan this way.

Amir's wing swept by to the east. Adam's brother-in-law was terrified but determined, as was Saoirse; they'd both taken to the air the instant they'd heard that Malia had gone missing.

Following his gaze, Dahlia said, "All I need is a hint of a scent and I'll track down that murderous fucker."

Because everyone agreed this was the Sandman. Raintree hadn't had a kidnapping in decades upon decades, and for it to happen now, while Eleri was on the trail of a serial killer she believed resided in this town?

Not a coincidence.

Adam's mouth tightened. "We need to keep you fresh," he said. "Go to the Canyon, handle things there. I'll call you the instant we have a direction."

Everyone else who could search in the air was up there, including juveniles supervised by adults they'd promised to obey. Adam hadn't been about to force Malia's friends to sit on their wings when they were smart, strong young people who knew how important it was they do this right.

But there were others who couldn't fly, or who had to stay put to take care of their vulnerable. The flyers, too, would be returning to regroup and refuel. One of their senior team needed to be at home base. "Wake Pascal and Maraea if I call you." The two wing commanders had gone to sleep just thirty minutes earlier and didn't even know of the emergency.

"I'm going to call the wolves and leopards, see if they have anyone close enough to assist," Dahlia said. "They're excellent ground trackers."

Both packs knew to give Adam a heads-up if they were going to be close to Raintree, but otherwise, their alliance allowed them to roam at will across WindHaven lands, so Dahlia was smart to consider that they might be able to get terrestrial assistance. "Good. Let me know if you get a yes."

Not saying another word, his second stripped off and threw her clothes in the clan vehicle parked in the lot, then shifted. Her body broke apart into a million particles of light before re-forming into the biggest falcon in the clan—not a peregrine but a gyrfalcon.

She spread her wings and took off with a single powerful push.

The wind of her departure yet stirred the air when Eleri's vehicle turned into the small road that led to the four-car parking lot. "Where?" she said the instant she got out, a tightness around her eyes and mouth.

"This way." He began to move. "Park is only a ten-minute walk from town. The path's used regularly by everyone—Raintree and Wind-Haven." The area was forested but well-trafficked; how the killer had managed to abduct Malia without being seen had Adam certain the Sandman was someone they knew.

Someone Adam's niece had trusted.

"There," he said, his voice holding an edge that was the contained fury of his falcon.

No one hurt one of Adam's people and lived to tell the tale. And this was his little *Mali-bug*, whom he'd held in his arms when she was a squalling newborn, who called him her favorite uncle, and who came and camped on his couch when she was having a teenage fight with her parents.

Cold, thin fingers closing over his, Eleri sliding her other hand around to his nape to squeeze and hold. "We'll find her." An icy promise, her eyes obsidian with determination. "We will find her, and we'll end him."

Talons out, Adam took a shuddering breath, pressed his forehead to his mate's for a second, and found his feet again. "There's the pond where folks like to jump in to cool down in the heat," he told her after they separated, "and this side with all the trees is where everyone picnics."

It wasn't a huge green space by the standards of bigger cities, but it was plenty big enough for a town the size of Raintree, with patches of soft lawn and enough trees that people didn't have to battle over shady areas unless it was an exceptionally busy day. "And there"—he pointed in the opposite direction from the parking lot—"that's the pathway from the town."

"His compulsion is tied to time. We have seventy-two hours." Eleri tried not to think about what he might be doing to Malia in the interim, to that intelligent, sparkling ball of sunshine who was Saoirse's child.

Looking up when she felt a shadow fall over her face, she saw a falcon with dark wing markings doing slow circles over the area. "Show me what's been found so far."

Walking her to an evidence flag, Adam indicated a glitter of gold almost lost in the green of the grass. "Bracelet with preserved flowers in it that Amir and Saoirse gave her for her birthday last year. Broken clasp." His gut twisted at the memory of how her face had glowed at the gift, how she'd put it on at once. "She was careful with it, only wore it to special events."

"Why was this event special?" Eleri crouched down to look at the bracelet. "Could it have been a setup to lure her out?"

Adam came down beside her. "No. It was a double date with her best friend. Amir and Saoirse let her go because it was just going to be a hangout with the four of them—they don't want her dating seriously until she's sixteen, but she's a levelheaded kid, so they don't restrict her from more casual gatherings."

His sister and brother-in-law were walking the fine line all falcon parents did—to offer freedom within boundaries that ensured safety and strong growth. Adam wouldn't have raised an eyebrow at this breakfast "date" either, if the couple had come to him for advice in his role as wing leader.

Why reward Malia's honesty in admitting it was a date by forbidding her from it?

Eleri rose to her feet. "This place feels desolate now. Would it have been at the time she arrived?"

"No," he said from beside her. "She flew over to Raintree with Polly—her best friend. The two used the secure WindHaven locker room near the school to change, then walked to this spot. The boys who'd asked them out were already here. Both human, both out to impress, so they were early, said they didn't see anyone who worried them."

He looked up to the sky. "It's a touch cloudy, so the area wasn't as busy as it usually would be on a weekend morning, but there were still at least ten people scattered around. They tried to help look for Malia when her friends realized she was missing."

Sweet Polly had sobbed and sobbed in his arms while describing what seemed to have been on track to be a successful first date for all four teenagers. They'd already been discussing lunch ideas, with Malia and Polly having told the boys they'd have to call their parents for permission to extend the outing.

"The four were chatting while seated on that picnic blanket over there, getting up to play with a Frisbee, or just walking to the pond to skip stones." All of which had been witnessed by others in the park. "Not a single person noticed anyone who set off alarm bells."

Eleri stared at the tree line. "He blends in, doesn't look dangerous—perhaps even looks harmless. There's a reason he was able to get four smart young women close enough to abduct them."

Adam's gaze was falcon when it met hers. "Mali's clever, but she's still a fledgling. She wouldn't have thought twice about helping someone who asked for it, especially if she recognized them."

Eleri wished she could protect him, could've protected Malia, from this terrible realization, but there was no hiding from it. Malia was a raptor—for her to go without making a fuss that drew attention meant it was someone she knew. A rabid dog who had fooled the town and the clan into believing him sane.

Chapter 32

Suspect is in his mid- to late twenties, single, with a stable job and income. He is intelligent and likely to be charming and/or good-looking, the kind of man most women don't distrust on sight.

While he'll have superficial friendships and relationships, he'll permit no one close enough to see through his mask. He is, at heart, a loner who can pretend to be social to fly under the radar. He will also prove emotionally immature—his letters reveal an almost juvenile obsession with his image, a kind of sneering petulance.

—Working profile on the Sandman, prepared for the joint California-Arizona Sandman Task Force (10 December 2083)

"TALK ME THROUGH how she vanished."

"The boys decided to jump into the pond. They'd dared each other in front of the girls and so of course juvenile testosterone meant they had to do it—pond's fed by an underground spring; it's freezing no matter what time of year."

Just kids showing off, playing, doing what they should at that age. There should've been no worse outcome than freezing off their nuts and regretting their choices as they sat shivering in the sun. And maybe a sweet first kiss for their bravery. That's what the boys would've been hoping for, dreaming about.

"Malia and Polly were cheering them on when Malia said she was feeling a chill because of the clouds and would run back to their picnic blanket to get her date's sweatshirt to put over her clothes." Another part of the ritual of teenage courtship, another sign to the date that he was on the right track.

"Polly said she'd keep cheering on the boys as they swam to the other side of the pond and back. When she turned, she was yelling for Malia to hurry up because they were getting to the end of the race, and that's when she realized Malia had vanished."

Confused, the fledgling had run over at once to look for her friend, thinking that maybe she'd decided to duck into the public facilities—even though Malia was notoriously fastidious about never using those.

"I knew something was wrong. Because we're *best* friends," Polly had said through her tears. "We're going to grow up and find our mates at the same time and be each other's maids of honor because maybe we'll have human mates and they'll want the wedding ceremony, and then have babies at the same time and we planned it all but she wasn't there and I knew she wouldn't just shift and fly off and leave me alone!"

After he shared that with Eleri, she said, "An intense and immediate response, given that it was broad daylight in a public place."

"Girl friendships at that age? They bond on a level where they become each other's shadows." He'd seen it with countless other young clanmates. "Polly knew without a single doubt that Malia wouldn't ditch her, *and* that she'd never miss seeing the end of the boys' race."

Oddly enough, Eleri understood what he meant when it came to such deep friendships. The Quatro Cartel would have all reacted as fast. "Who found the bracelet?"

"One of the boys. I talked to the kid myself—he was afraid but only for Malia. I've talked to enough fledglings who've been up to mischief to know he had nothing to do with it." He shoved both hands through his hair. "It's the speed and the silence of the abduction that gets me—Malia was loud even when she was Ollie's size."

"We'll figure it out," Eleri said, her tone stripped bare of anything but pure concentration—but her hand came to his, her fingers weaving through his own in a promise before she let go and walked to the tree line.

"Someone could've waited here, watched, waved her over. Bracelet could've fallen off by accident and been unnoticed in the excitement of the day—how badly was the clasp broken?"

"Minor." Adam scanned the area, but there was nothing to see, his niece gone without a trace.

"I haven't received a message from the Sandman about Malia."

His gut twisted. "Could it be a copycat?"

"No—not Malia, and not at this time." Eleri's gaze still that endless black, she said, "Pulling me into his perversion is important to him, helps him achieve whatever it is he achieves with these acts."

Adam saw it, the road she was walking. "There's no need for a letter this time." Because the bastard was right in town, watching, listening, mocking them all with his mask of neighborly concern.

Adam's jaw worked. "Be careful, Eleri. I can't lose you again."

"Malia comes first."

He cupped her face, too thin, dark shadows below her eyes. "You were meant to be a wing leader's mate. You understand what it is to hold a clan inside the heart."

She spread her hand over the organ that beat in his chest. "I'll contact the task force, get them on this—they should already be en route, but they'll have their gear on them, can run computronic cross-checks as they move.

"I also saw traffic cameras on the way into Raintree. I can access them through the local Enforcement computers if Detective Beaufort will let me—the task force will have to clear it through various channels, but the locals should have the cameras set up as an auto feed into their systems."

"Wait." Adam pulled out his phone. "If you need more eyes to scan the footage, call Dahlia—I'll send you her number. We have people who can't assist in the physical search, but their eyes are plenty sharp, and I don't fucking care about toeing the judicial lines right now."

Eleri nodded. "I'll start it up, see how many feeds there are, then speak to her."

Beaufort answered the call Adam had put on speaker and offered no resistance to Eleri's request for access, even gave her the code to get into the locked Enforcement offices. "Our admin's still out sick, but call me or Whitten if you have any trouble accessing the feeds." Unspoken was that he understood the falcons would be helping review the footage—the detective knew their team was too small to move on this as fast as they needed to move.

Malia's life was what mattered, not protecting evidence for a future trial. Because once Adam knew who this was, the killer wouldn't be standing trial. Brutal justice. Wild justice.

"We need roadblocks," Eleri said to Beaufort. "It's already—"

"First thing I ordered when I heard Malia had been taken," Adam interrupted. "Main access road isn't changeling territory, but fuck that. I have wings stopping vehicles in both directions in and out of Raintree. You want to go after us for that once we have Malia, Beaufort, you go ahead. We'll accept the necessary consequences."

"No need, Adam. I'm the acting chief, and as far as I'm concerned, I deputized the lot of you when this began." The detective sounded on edge. "He doesn't get to get away with this just because we're a small force. We'll find our girl."

After thanking the other man and hanging up, Adam said, "You should only need to review the first half hour after her abduction," to Eleri. "That's how long it took for the news to get to me and my wings to get out onto the road." After checking his phone, he told her the exact time his falcons had reported in as having their roadblocks up and running.

Eleri nodded. "Once I've scanned that half hour, I'll go back, review movements at night—just in case I'm wrong and he isn't based in Raintree, but came into the town in preparation."

Adam saw the sense in that. "While you're at the station I'm going to check on the roadblocks, then fly a wider circle, look for and investigate any places where he could be keeping Malia."

"Don't disregard ordinary neighborhood garages, sheds, anyplace where only one person has relatively private access. I'll make a list of those with the assistance of the cops and Mi-ja. She'll know."

"I'll attach a small comm device to my leg in falcon form," Adam said. "It acts like a long-range beeper and will alert me to priority messages on my phone. Call me the instant you get anything."

She nodded again . . . then hugged him tight, her thin body tense with determination. "We'll bring Malia home. I promise."

I don't make promises I don't intend to keep.

Crushing her to him, Adam said, "I know," his faith in her absolute.

WHEN she called Tim, the task force lead said, "I really wish your instincts had been wrong, Eleri."

"Me, too."

"We'll run every search we can on the residents of Raintree, see if we can pinpoint anything that might give you a starting point. See you in a few hours."

Once at the Enforcement station, it took Eleri only five minutes to get the traffic surveillance up and running on the station's two large screens. Four feeds, two from either end of the main road in and out of Raintree, the others from the two major intersections in the town.

Seventy-two-hour memory capacity.

The latter pair of feeds would be unhelpful at this juncture—too much local traffic, no way to tell the origin or destination of the vehicles.

Calling Dahlia, she explained the situation. "If we can run and clear all the vehicles heading in or out of Raintree in that critical half-hour window, we might be able to confirm whether Malia is still in town."

"We have enough people to do all four at the same time," Dahlia said. "But we can run the data on the intersections after we've cleared the main route."

After a short discussion, they worked it out so the falcons would review the taped section of the feed, which Eleri was able to forward to them; the reviewers would in turn send Eleri the plate numbers as well as the makes and models of all the vehicles they spotted in the relevant window of time. Eleri would then use her J Corps credentials to log into Enforcement's ID database to run the vehicles.

"We begin from the time of Malia's abduction," she said. "We can always go backward later, check for vehicles coming in. Right now, we need to know if she's here or if we need to be looking for a vehicle on the road." The girl had been gone for over an hour now, the clock counting down at frightening speed.

The first plate numbers appeared on her phone screen within five minutes of her call to Dahlia, and she started doing her end of the job. Ten minutes. Fifteen. No suspicious hits. Every single one of the departing vehicles belonging to women, or to men at least two decades outside the profiled age range of the Sandman.

It was possible the profile was off or the Sandman had a female accomplice, but they had to start somewhere. As it was, she was sending the names back to Dahlia to see if any of them—all locals so far—threw up any red flags, but the second was also batting zero.

To ensure nothing fell through the cracks, Eleri also forwarded the names to the task force, to be run through every database the team could access. Could be a local had moved in fifteen years ago and kept their nose clean but had a record in another distant jurisdiction.

When her private line rang twenty minutes into the search, she picked it up without looking at the ID code onscreen. Not many people had her number—Adam, Dahlia, Sophie, the three local cops, the Quatro Cartel, the task force, and a very short list of other people with whom she worked regularly.

"Eleri Dias," she answered even as she ran the vehicle plate Dahlia had sent her just prior to the call.

"Eleri, it's Malia." The fledgling's voice was thick, sluggish, but recognizable.

"Malia, where are you?" Eleri was already at the station's comms desk, her fingers entering the passcode Beaufort had given her to access their systems.

"That's enough proof of life." A genderless computronic voice. "I assume you're about to contact someone. Don't. Or I'll slit her throat. Shame to finish the game so quickly, but oh well."

Eleri froze.

The game.

No more doubt. This was the Sandman.

"Don't try the PsyNet, either," he said. "Any hint of anyone other than you heading this way," he continued, "so much as a fucking feather in the air, and she dies."

Why was he using that redundant computronic voice? The task force might not have his DNA, but all circumstantial evidence said he was male. He'd confirmed it in his third letter to her, when he'd referred to a childhood version of himself as a "sad little boy." While continuing to doubt the veracity of his claims about himself, the task force profiler had been firm in the belief that the serial killer was too concerned with his image to refer to himself by the incorrect gender.

> *My mother used to call me her sad little boy because I'd just sit in corners staring off into space. She had me tested for neurodivergence, but the doctors said I was normal, probably only trying to act up for attention. But my mother kept asking why I was sad. I wish I could show her how happy I am now—all it took was a murder.*

He had to believe she'd recognize his voice.

Eleri tried to think who on the list of people she'd spoken to during her time in Raintree fit the profile—there were too many. She'd been active, had made it a point to talk to all Psy in their twenties that she could reach.

"And no trying to get cute with a teleporter just in case you know one," the Sandman continued. "I've rigged the little falcon's place of captivity to blow at any unauthorized movement—don't worry, I've already put her to sleep so she doesn't accidentally move and blow herself up.

"Honestly, she's nowhere near the perfect game piece for me—a bit too young, and—not to be a bigot—but I prefer my women without talons or claws. Still, I knew she'd bring you to me, so I suppose she was perfect for this special game."

He had to be lying about the explosives—that kind of rigging took time. But what if he'd prepared it much earlier? Eleri couldn't risk Malia's life on a hunch. And while she knew people who she could contact on the PsyNet who wouldn't put Malia's life at risk, would help get word to Adam, she couldn't do it fast enough. Her bruised brain needed too much prep time, might even overload and break if she attempted to enter the Net.

Her eye fell on a pen one of the officers had left lying around. She'd write a note, leave it here—

"Put down the pen." A computronic laugh. "I can seeeeeee you." Singsong, a taunt.

Eleri looked out through the large glass window in front of her, but it just faced the wall of the building next door. Which left a single possibility. "You hacked the station's systems." He'd also managed to get her private number, she thought with a frown. She was missing something. "What do you want?"

"You in exchange for her. You ruined the game by coming here, and now you have to pay the price." A hint of petulance, of the lack of emotional maturity their profiler had predicted.

He was mad at her for not acting as he'd planned for her to act, for not being the perfect game piece.

Eleri had no qualms about making the swap, her for Malia, but she knew it couldn't be that easy. "How do I know you'll keep your word?"

"You don't. But at least this way you tried." Another laugh. "She ends up dead and you could've helped her, how will you ever face Adam? You two seem cozy."

Eleri's mind raced. Not only did he have her number, he knew about her and Adam. Was it possible the Sandman was a falcon? They flew vast distances, and changelings were used to keeping caches of clothing in multiple locations. He could as easily keep caches of supplies he needed for his murder fantasies.

No, the report from the pathologist had been unequivocal:

Their brain injuries are inconsistent with any type of external trauma. Even a sound wave wouldn't do this. The only references I've discovered to similar trauma relate to those who've died as a result of a powerful telepathic assault.

A falcon couldn't kill that way. Neither could a human.

"After we end this call," the killer said while she was still calculating her options, "I want you to leave your phone under the desk, where it won't be seen, then walk to the back door of the station. There's a closed drink container sitting inside to the left of the door. Drink it and wait."

Inside?

Knowledge of her direct call code.

Access to the cameras at the station.

Able to take Malia, an intelligent young woman who wouldn't trust just anyone.

Beaufort, Whitten, Hendricks, were all human.

Who was she missing?

Her memory was her greatest asset, and today, it flashed with a snapshot of a little girl she'd met only for a minute, a girl who'd wanted to telepath to her to practice.

Sascha Duncan's child.

Half-Psy. Half-changeling. Not in the PsyNet but a telepath all the same.

A man who was half-falcon, half-Psy would be a predator more deadly than anything the world had ever imagined.

Chapter 33

You know why I'm so smart, Eleri? I know falcons don't have a great sense of smell, no better than humans. I don't have to waste time covering up a scent trail, because they can't track me or you that way—and this town doesn't have many surveillance cameras.

—Unsent message written by the Sandman

THE PROBLEM WITH her theory, Eleri thought, was that Psy had stopped procreating with changelings over a century ago, with Sascha's child one of the first—*the* first?—of the new generation.

Unless someone had defected before Sascha. Not just defected, but sired or borne a child? It still didn't make sense, not given what she'd seen of Adam's pack. They lived in and around each other on a daily basis. No one would miss a half-Psy child. And Adam had been clear that he had no Psy in his clan.

"Convince me you're who you're pretending to be," she said, fighting to buy time so she could figure this out. "I'm not moving for a copycat." Of course she would because losing Malia was not an option, but she had to play the game, get what she could.

So she used his need for validation, his focus on his image, against him. "I'm only interested in the Sandman."

"I'm glad you understand the importance of my work—I always knew you did, but it's good to have that confirmed." No laughter in his voice now. "I make them red dresses. Beautiful red dresses that turn them into goddesses in death."

That piece of information hadn't been released *anywhere*. Neither the fact that all three victims had been found dressed in red, nor that the dresses had obviously been made at speed, the seams ragged and the cut far from professional. He might believe them beautiful, but even Eleri knew no woman would choose to put those creations on her body.

"Now, move," he ordered. "You have thirty seconds to get that drink down you or she's dead." He hung up.

And Eleri was out of time.

Throwing her phone under the desk, she just managed to push the emergency assist button built into the back. Invisible unless you knew it was there, it would send up a red flag with the Quatro Cartel, along with a GPS location. She wished she'd reset it to Adam's phone, but they'd had no time . . . would've had even less if she'd left this morning.

Even if that failed, Dahlia would realize something was up when Eleri stopped forwarding her the IDs of the vehicle owners, would no doubt send a falcon to check. Eleri had to do whatever she could to give them a trail to follow in the few short seconds she had left.

Lifting her hand to her mouth as she ran, hoping the movement would be hidden in the motion of her flight—or that the Sandman was too distracted by excitement to notice, she bit down on the thin skin on the inside of her wrist hard enough to draw serious blood, then dropped her hand back by her side. Someone in WindHaven could track by scent—they'd traced Malia to the parking lot.

This was Eleri's chance to give them a stronger trail to follow.

The numbness inside her that had stopped her from feeling Adam's touch in all its primal intensity also insulated her from physical pain.

Her suit jacket slid neatly over the wound, covering it from view.

Whatever she was about to drink would no doubt affect her ability to make conscious decisions, but her blood would continue to drip. Whether in a vehicle or elsewhere, it'd leave a trace.

The silver flask was exactly where he'd said it'd be.

Silver flask.

She had it, his identity. But it made no sense. And she had no way to let anyone know because her brain was shutting down, whatever drug she'd just ingested acting fast.

Her knees went out from under her, her mind a blank.

ADAM zeroed in toward the purple signal flare that had just gone up.

That color was reserved for him and to be used only in emergencies. Landing on the Canyon plateau at rapid speed, he shifted—to find Kavi standing there with a comm in hand.

"Call from some guy named Bram," the nurse said. "Says Eleri sent out an SOS. Dahlia's already on her way to the station—I was helping scan the road surveillance footage and Eleri stopped responding to our messages right before this call came in."

Heart thundering, Adam grabbed the comm. "Bram, where's Eleri?"

"Her phone sent out the alert from the Enforcement station in Raintree. No response to PsyNet attempts at contact. Her shields look normal, but as a J, she has heavy-duty ones that won't show any external damage until it's too late." No attempt at calm in that voice. "Adam, she's never sent out an SOS in all the years I've known her."

"I'll call you from the station." A glance at the ID screen and he'd memorized Bram's call code before he shifted and took off at brutal speed.

Beaufort was just jogging into the station when he landed. The detective took Adam's shift in stride. "Adam, what—"

But Adam was already inside. Even as the senior detective threw him a pair of sweatpants from a gym bag, he'd already spotted Dahlia at the far end of the station, near the back door. "D!"

"Eleri bled here," she said, because unlike him, Dahlia had a dazzling sense of smell.

It wasn't because she was a gyrfalcon. Neither peregrines nor gyrfalcons had a great sense of smell, but while Dahlia's father was a gyrfalcon, her mother was a vulture. Most changelings with parents from different species shifted into one, with little to no crossover, but Dahlia had inherited her mother's acute sense of smell alongside her father's raptor form.

It made her one hell of an asset.

"He's got her." Teeth gritted, Adam pulled on the pants because he knew his nakedness would distract any humans or Psy in the vicinity. Beaufort was having difficulty even looking at Dahlia. "How far can you track her?"

The answer was—not far. "Droplet here," she said after taking a few steps outside. "Nothing else. He put her in a vehicle." She looked up.

"Go! Eleri and Malia, hunt for both their scents."

Shifting in front of him, Dahlia took off on a powerful gust of wind, a stunning bird of snowy white with gray and white top feathers who would be a ghost if she hunted in the snow. Her scent receptors were some of the best in the sky, but she had to have a pungent smell to track from above. The traces left by Jacques's shooter hadn't been enough, had dissipated on the wind by the time of her arrival.

But fresh blood that was dripping and falling to decay on the earth? That, Dahlia could track.

As she flew, he ran back inside the station. "Phone."

When Beaufort threw over his own, already unlocked, Adam called Bram. "Is Eleri still in the Net?"

"Yes. What—"

"Abduction." His eye caught on a glint below the desk.

Grabbing a disposable glove out of a box on the wall, he used it to crouch down and pick up Eleri's device. "Do you know how to get into her phone?"

"No. J devices are heavily secured—iris print, live voice code, all of it. No way to get into it even by the manufacturer."

Fuck. "Watch for her on the Net, contact me if anything changes."

"Adam, I've got it," Beaufort said at the same time that Adam hung up. "Outside camera feed."

Vaulting over the desk to the screen on the other man's desk, Adam watched as a black van he recognized as belonging to the local bakery stopped by the station's back door and a black-clad figure in a grotesque horror mask got out. The person went into the station, dragged a limp Eleri out, and bundled her into the van before driving off.

All in under a minute.

"Not one of the Thompsons," the detective said. "Definitely male." He was already programming an alert on the vehicle.

Falcons on the ground would hear it, too, signal wing mates to new data via screens mounted on their ground vehicles. This wasn't WindHaven's first search; they'd long ago learned to coordinate from ground to sky and back.

"You talk to the Thompsons," he said to the detective, aware that the elderly couple—both women—probably hadn't even noticed the van was missing. "I'm going up." The recording showed that Eleri was taken only eleven minutes ago.

Adam and his clan would find her and Malia both.

As it was, he saw Dahlia dive down in the distance as he took off. Arrowing toward her, Adam a far faster flyer than his gyrfalcon clanmate, he dived at the same spot thick with trees—to find her standing beside the open sliding door of the van.

She shook her head, her hair a tumbling darkness to her waist but for that streak of white. "Gone, but she bled in here."

The abductor had driven Eleri out of the central area and out of sight of any security cameras before moving her into his own vehicle and taking off. "Can you track on?"

Leaning close to the carpet, Dahlia took a long breath. "Fresh. Not coagulated." She shifted and was in the air a heartbeat later, Adam at her wing as they chased the scent of violence.

WindHaven didn't advertise Dahlia's ability, not even when they used that ability to help find the lost. No one outside the clan knew she could track over literal miles with the merest hint of a scent.

And today, she had a blood trail Adam's mate had left for them.

The murderer's first mistake had been to take one of their fledglings, his second to go after Adam's mate.

He wouldn't get the chance to make a third mistake.

Chapter 34

Js with weak shields are at catastrophic risk of a memory seizure, where the memories of another overwrite all of their own. There is no remedy for this because no J has ever survived a total overwrite.

—*J Corps Medical Handbook* (updated 2083)

ELERI WAS INSIDE a nightmare, her world shattered pieces of color painful and jagged. Everything hurt, but she couldn't pinpoint any of the pain. It was everywhere and nowhere.

Nausea churned in her gut.

Twisting instinctively to the side, she pressed her hands to a floor coated in straw and dust and retched. Nothing came out, her body refusing to release its pain. And all the while, the insanity inside her head wouldn't stop—erratic flashes of memory, a throat being slit, a falcon in flight, a glass shattering.

It cut her.

Except it couldn't. It was inside her head.

Then the falcon's talons clamped on her arm. She shoved it aside, but her fingers were weak, and oddly, the talons didn't feel like talons at all. They felt like fingers even though her... Her eyes jittered, snagged. She wasn't wearing her gloves. Why wasn't she wearing her gloves?

Because this was a nightmare.

And that hand that wasn't a talon had taken hers and soon she'd be awash in another person's memories and nightmares. She braced herself as much as she could, even as her mind spun and spun and spun.

The hand was solid. The mind was solid. Nothing to see.

Relief kicked her in the gut. Whoever this person was, they had an impenetrable shield. She tried to look at them, take them in, but her brain was so scrambled that her visual cortex couldn't process the information.

Her hand clenched on the straw on the hard floor.

Lifting it up, she stared and tried to see. She couldn't, but some small part of her brain wondered why she'd imagined straw. She'd never been in a farm-like environment in her life, and that was what her brain associated with straw. Yet the tactile sensations she was experiencing told her that she was holding straw.

The hand that wasn't a talon shifted back to her arm, shook her hard. She couldn't tell if it was causing her pain, but she felt the desperation in the other person, and that, she understood.

Turning again, she tried to focus on the person to whom the hand belonged, because surely it must belong to someone . . . unless this *was* a nightmare and she was lost in her own broken brain.

Exposure. Had she hit Exposure?

An echoey sound, as if someone was talking to her through a long tunnel.

Again and again.

A sob.

It was the sob that reached her in a pristine ball of clarity.

A child was crying.

She didn't know why, but she reached out her hand into the chaos of color and sharp edges that cut and made her bleed, telling that crying person to grab on to her. The fingers released her arm to grip her hand.

Solid, strong, shielded.

Feathers in her mind, against her hair.

"—please, please!"

The echoey words had taken shape, become a plea. She still couldn't make out the shape of the person who held her hand, and while her mind stretched and tried to reach the PsyNet, it couldn't.

It was too shredded, too twisted.

But this being was pleading with her, and the part of Eleri that had assisted survivors of abuse escape murder charges reacted out of primal instinct, hearing in the plea the cry of a being who was trapped with no way out.

Their leg in irons.

Their freedom shackled.

She squeezed the hand.

It squeezed back, and the echoes continued, as did the nausea and the lack of clarity.

"—drugs! He said—your gloves—removed—"

It took a very long time for Eleri to process those scattered words, to even begin to gain some comprehension of the shape of them. It was the part of her that she'd designed to flick the shutoff valve to her life that got it; she'd separated the valve controller from all the normal pathways of her mind so it could flip the off switch even if the rest of her was compromised.

It was small and restricted and had only one real goal, but right now, it was also the only part of her that had retained even basic function. Cut off as it was from all other pathways, it had been accidentally protected from both the drug that had sown chaos in her brain and the impact of any direct contact she might've had with the person who'd peeled off her gloves.

All these thoughts happened in that same secretive part. The rest of her was a puppet with its strings cut.

Whoever did this knows Psy react badly to most narcotics, murmured the tiny hidden part of her. *They overdosed you with something that ensures you can't reach for help on the PsyNet. I can't. I'm your secret. I'm not designed for communication, my only function to flip the switch.*

Something dripped from Eleri's nose. It smelled of iron.

That hand left hers and a soft sensation was dabbing at her lip . . . and that was when Eleri realized she was starting to regain a hint of clarity. Though the PsyNet remained out of reach, she'd been able to connect the sensation with the act, could now see the blurred outline of the person with her.

Young, so young. And such beautiful hair.

Malia.

Malia's head jerked, her hand dropping as her breath caught.

When she grabbed Eleri's hand again, the connection cleared up the chaos enough for her to comprehend the words the girl was speaking. "He's coming. He'll drug you again so you can't telepath for help."

Eleri wanted to tell the child that she couldn't telepath anyway. The drugs had broken something in her already wounded brain. Things were never going to sit quite right again; she felt that in the deepest fiber of her being. That same part keened with a sense of loss and grief, but uppermost was her determination to save this child who was Adam's.

Adam.

She couldn't speak, couldn't say anything, but she made her hands move and took the child's face in her hands, then jerked her head to the side, even as she pushed the child that way.

Malia's eyes were panicked, huge.

This time, Eleri pushed at her shoulder, shoving her toward the darkness in the corner.

"You want me to hide in the shadow? He'll still see."

Eleri shoved again, and this time, Malia, this child who was scared but trusted Eleri to help her, went where Eleri had thrust her.

A sound in the chaos, a creak. A door opening.

Eleri had already dropped her head to her chest as she slumped against the beam behind her. Drops of red in her vision as her nose bled onto the white of her shirt.

That was good. The more blood, the more . . . She couldn't follow that thread, but an instinctive part of her knew not to worry about the blood, that it was something that could help Malia.

Only one chance, whispered the fragment of her she'd saved so it could kill her, but that she would now use to save this child so loved and protected. *A second drug overdose and no part of you will come back.*

Eleri felt footsteps, felt thuds, the man's voice so loud it was shards inside her brain. But none of that mattered, because she really only had one final card to play.

"Fuck! The fuckers are on the horizon! What the hell did you do?"

As the ranting man came down on his knees next to her, she set that one functioning part of her free and let it take full control of whatever remained of her mind. Her vision cleared, she saw the pressure syringe, saw the distorted mask he wore to hide his face, and punched him hard in the throat with all her strength.

He flew back, gurgling and clutching at his throat.

Turning to Malia, Eleri waved her arm, telling the girl to run. But the man was scrabbling back at her, and the ounce of clarity she'd gained by sacrificing that one functional piece of her was already fading.

He slammed the pressure injector into her palm instead of her neck . . . and worse, grabbed hold of the bare skin of her wrist.

Evil poured into her brain in an unstoppable wave of filth and despair and horror, shattering things inside her as they pushed and shoved and violated. His memories. His fantasies. His . . . sadness.

He had been a sad little boy once, after all.

Screams, so many screams. Not his.

Vivian's.

Kriti's.

Sarah's.

Laughter. That was his.

He was spreading through her brain like a virus, an infection of cruelty and torture.

He would kill her long before the drug reached her brain, but in this moment, she somehow had enough of herself left to kick him hard in the same spot she'd punched. Blood flew out of his mouth to splatter on her as his head lolled onto the ground, and this time, the girl was moving.

But instead of running out, Malia came to Eleri, tried to get her upright. Eleri pushed her away. "Go." A garbled simulacrum of a word. "*Go!*" Her legs were paralyzed as her brain began to go haywire, her chest jerking.

Malia was sobbing, pleading with her.

Eleri found one last ounce of strength and shoved at her back. "*Run, Malia! Find Adam!*" At least that was what she thought she said.

Racing heart, skin so hot it burned, a blankness that wasn't peace.

She had just enough left in her to attempt to write the Sandman's name on the wooden floor in the blood that dripped down her wrist to her palm and her fingers.

Then it ended.

Chapter 35

The packs and clans in the Trinity Accord are willing to attempt to blood-bond Psy children into their networks. It may save those children's lives should the PsyNet collapse—and in that eventuality, the changelings will treat the children as their own.

They are aware of the scale of the potential loss of life, and the resultant lack of Psy adults who will be able to step in—however many children survive, the changelings (as well as the Human Alliance) have agreed to care for them.

All they have requested is that we make an emergency handbook on a Psy child's non-negotiable needs for healthy psychic and physical development.

—Aden Kai to the Ruling Coalition (28 October 2083)

ADAM'S PEREGRINE CALLED for his mate and for the child of the clan.

They'd be together. Because wherever Eleri had gone, whatever choice she'd made that had led to her abduction, it had to do with Malia. She'd willingly walked into a trap. Such a stupid choice for a smart J—only she wasn't smart when it came to things like this, was she? Eleri *cared*. That was her Achilles' heel, and someone not only knew that, they'd utilized it to get her alone.

The tug on his heart that was Malia felt stronger now, as if she was either conscious or physically closer. He tried to follow it, but that wasn't how changeling bonds worked, no matter if he wanted it to be different. He just knew she was alive, was breathing. That gave his wild heart hope even as another part of him whispered that if this had been about luring Eleri, then his niece was no longer useful.

Opening his beak in a cry of rage, he swept left over the sand and rock beyond Raintree, while keeping Dahlia in sight. She'd lost Eleri's scent trail at a certain point, likely after she was contained inside the other vehicle with the windows up, was attempting to pick it up again—but the area was vast, and they were relying on droplets of blood.

Other teams continued to search on the ground and in the air in different directions.

Nothing. Nothing. *Nothing.*

It was as if both Eleri and Malia had vanished off the face of the earth. How much longer would they both be safe?

The desert sands lifted at that instant, turbulent in winds that howled out of the canyons as the weather began to turn. Fuck. That would play havoc with Dahlia's scent tracking—and they were losing any physical tracks before they ever had the chance to spot them.

A panicked falcon's cry almost snatched away by the rising wind, but Adam's falcon heard it, *knew* it. Dahlia angled sharply toward a low valley in the desert at the same time that Adam responded to Malia, telling her she'd been heard and urging her to keep on calling to him.

Her call was even weaker the second time around, but he was closer and had no trouble catching it. It was clear that Dahlia had already caught her scent, too.

They wouldn't lose her, not now.

And this child of the clan was defiant and strong, because though her third cry was all but inaudible, she made it. And Adam heard it.

There she was, all wild hair and vivid turquoise jumpsuit as she looked skyward through the gritty dervish of the sudden sandstorm, one arm raised in a frantic wave.

He landed with speed.

"Uncle Adam!" A sobbing Malia ran toward him before he could shift, and he cradled her in his massive wings, knowing at once why she hadn't been able to fly out, and why her call had held none of the falcon's power.

Her left arm was broken.

Her wing would be broken in changeling form.

Though she was sobbing, she was trying to speak, too. "Eleri!" She rose on wobbly, weak legs. "He drugged her like he did me, but worse! I ran and ran like she told me to! But he's with her!"

Adam shifted, uncaring of his nakedness because they were changeling; their ways weren't human. Malia wouldn't even notice. "Hush, little wings."

He cupped her face in his hands and forced his voice to be calm. "I'll find her. What can you tell me about where you were held?" Dahlia hovered, on watch, both of them aware that Malia could have a deadly tail—and the killer had already proven he wasn't against using guns.

"A place under the desert." Malia wiped at her face with her good hand, leaving behind streaks of blood.

"Where are you bleeding?" he asked sharply, because while his niece's arm dangled in a viciously wrong way, he saw no blood on her jumpsuit.

"What?" She looked down at her hand when he pulled it up. "It's Eleri's. She was bleeding so much, Adam."

His chest squeezed. "Okay, baby girl," he said, keeping his tone composed because she would take her cue from him, "tell me where you were. I'll go get her."

"It had straw everywhere, open beams, and the floor was dirt, I think. It's not far and I only got out because Eleri did something to him!" She shouted to be heard over the winds. "I was scared to call you straightaway because I thought he'd hear me, but I had to do it. I couldn't wait anymore!" She pointed to the east. "I came from that way! There were rocks! Black rocks!"

Dahlia landed and shifted. "Clan incoming. I need a fresh scent—winds have messed up Malia's backtrail."

Malia thrust out her bloody hand. "Here, DeeDee. It's Eleri."

Shifting, Adam lifted off even as Dahlia inhaled the scent because more wings were coming down, more falcons landing—including Naia. Knowing Malia would be safe under their healer's protective wings, he headed off in the direction his niece had pointed.

It was a risk not to wait for Dahlia, but Malia couldn't have run far, even powered by adrenaline. She'd been weak, shivering from her unset broken arm. And Adam was faster than Dahlia, something that might make a critical difference if Eleri was badly injured.

The call of a gyrfalcon on the air, confirmation from Dahlia that he was on the right trajectory.

A tumble of black rocks.

He halted, his falcon's gaze spearing through the desert sands that swirled around the fall of stone.

There.

The hatch was small and colored to blend in with the desert.

Dahlia called to him as he landed.

She'd picked up some kind of scent, wanted to follow it.

He called back to tell her to go—on the slim chance the Sandman had carried Eleri out, he wanted Dahlia on their trail while he searched for his mate under the desert. Others of the clan were now also close enough that both of them would have backup. His people were trained, good at their jobs—they wouldn't need his order to split up, with half heading toward Dahlia, the others to him.

Shifting as she shot off, he hauled open the hatch, his skin so tight over his body that it hurt. "Be alive, Eleri. Just be alive." Logic told him her abductor had to have panicked when he realized Malia was gone, had perhaps even heard her call to clan.

If he was smart, he'd have run straightaway. No time to waste. No time to hurt Eleri even more than he already had. No time to take her with him.

The smell of blood, thick and rich and *fresh*, hit his nose the instant he threw open the hatch, the scent contained in the small space bursting out into the desert. Rage bubbling inside him, and conscious that the noise of the winds when he'd opened the hatch had blown any chance of stealth, he called Eleri's name as he jumped down into darkness now lit by the daylight from above, sand swirling inside with him as the winds continued to howl.

No reply from Eleri, but he didn't need it.

His mate lay slumped against a beam that held up the roof of this place designed for confinement. The prison was otherwise empty of life.

Falling on his knees beside her, he took her into his arms.

Dark red stained the front of her shirt, and when her head tipped back over his arm, he saw that her tears were blood. Darker than when she'd worked with Jacques. And it wasn't just her eyes.

Blood everywhere.

Eleri was bleeding out from her pores, as if her body was pumping the life-giving fluid outward as her brain misfired.

"No, you don't get to do this," he snarled and laid her flat on the straw-dusted dirt floor so he could better check her vitals.

Her skin was warm, but he could barely feel her breath even when he put his face only an inch away from her mouth. As for her pulse, to call it thready was an exaggeration. She was so close to death that she was standing on the precipice of the cliff into nothingness.

Then she stepped over.

Her heart stopped beating. Her chest fell and didn't rise again.

"*No.*" Adam didn't think about it; he semi-shifted to slice his palm with his talon, then did the same to her palm and clamped them together. "You fucking *stay.*" They weren't done by a long shot.

He didn't know if the attempt at a blood bond would work, but it was all he had. She wasn't falcon, but she was *his*, and if he could blood-bond Psy children to keep them safe in the event of a PsyNet collapse, why not his J?

The girl who'd wanted to give him a bandage, her eyes soft and vibrant with life. The fellow adventurer who, hand in hand with him, had run out of a cave with annoyed bats winging around them. The determined J who'd fought for the life of his best friend. The mate with wonder in her who'd held out an arm so a tired fledgling could land on it.

"Don't you do this to me." It came out a harsh repudiation because Adam wasn't going to feel grief, refused to feel grief. "You don't get to just *leave*!"

He knew the lack of a heartbeat meant she'd have lost her connection to the PsyNet. He also knew Psy could be pulled into changeling networks. So he *pulled*, using all the strength that made him wing leader, all the power that made him her mate.

"We haven't finished this fight," he snarled, and pressed his lips to hers, giving her his breath before he used his hands to pump at her chest, try to get her heart going.

Their blood mingled again, her shirt drenched with it.

He breathed for her again. "I won't let you do this," he said, so angry with her that it wasn't anything rational. "You fucking *breathe*."

Another hard pump of her heart.

A kick . . . *inside* him. A jolt as another mind appeared in the network his wing leader heart knew without ever seeing it. She was there, with WindHaven, but barely. A flickering light about to go out all over again.

The sandstorm halted at the same instant, as if wary of snuffing her out.

The sounds of wings closing outside, the silence of the shift, then two clanmates jumping inside.

Naia was the second.

"Malia wouldn't let me stay with her," the healer said. "She was panicked, says the man who held her gave Eleri narcotics—he managed to give her a second shot right before she helped Malia escape. From what I know of Psy physiology and drug reactions, her blood is now toxic and will be affecting her mind."

Adam's eyes fell on Eleri's bare hands. If the murderer had touched her, she might be in even worse trouble—but he would not go down that path. She could call him deluded and too hopeful for it when she woke, could even laugh at him. He didn't care.

"She died. For less than a minute." It was hard to speak, hard to not just hold her tight. "I've got her, but barely."

His eye caught on blood on the ground. Shapes. Letters.

Hen—

Movement, a bag being dropped inside. Naia's gear. Adam reached to pull it closer with his free hand while locking his sliced-open palm to Eleri's once more. *You stay. Don't you dare leave me. Not again, Eleri. Please, my wild bird. Stay.*

Chapter 36

Well, I'm resisting the urge to tear off his head and feed his balls to the wild vultures for the time being.

—Reply from Dahlia Dehlavi to Adam Garrett (today)

SOPHIA RUSSO—ALERTED by Bram—had a PsyMed air-evac team waiting for them by the time they got Eleri to the nearest major hospital—it happened to be the same place Chief Cross had been taken after his heart attack.

Naia had done all she could, but Eleri was in bad shape.

"She needs specialized care," Sophia had said over a comm call, the fine tracery of scars on her face melding with skin gone too pale. "With the drugs and possible unshielded contact with a psychopathic mind, she suffered a catastrophic overload that most likely led to a seizure. The risk is nowhere near past—this could still turn fatal for her."

Adam hadn't argued; Naia had been clear that she couldn't reach Eleri, not even through the blood bond Adam had forced into being. If Eleri didn't want it, she'd have to wake the hell up and tell him. She could reject it, reject *him*, rejoin the PsyNet. He didn't care. As long as she was alive.

"I'm going with her. She's one of mine now," he'd said, not about to tell this near-stranger that Eleri was his mate, that she'd always been his, would always be his even if she walked away.

Because he'd fight for her every second of every day.

As for WindHaven, Dahlia, Pascal, and Maraea would handle clan security—and the arrangements for the man who was now an involuntary guest of the clan—while Adam was gone.

Malia was safe with Saoirse and Amir, with Kavita having already set her arm. Naia would also double-check on his niece as soon as she landed at the Canyon.

Adam had also made it a point to talk to his niece over the phone and was proud of her stalwart heart. He'd make sure her emotional bruises had the care they needed, but for today, she wouldn't miss him—per Amir, all Malia wanted to do was snuggle on the sofa with her family and watch reruns of her favorite comm shows.

"Our girl is almost asleep already," Amir had shared, his relief intermingled with a taut anger. "Adrenaline crash mixed with the aftereffects of the drug the bastard gave her. Kavi says it should be out of her system in the next couple of hours."

Edward, the nurse who'd joined Naia in the underground bunker, had found the pressure injector the killer had used on Malia and Eleri, and the empty drug ampule inside had proved to be nothing that would cause Malia long-term harm; changelings used a smaller dose of the same drug as an over-the-counter pain reliever.

The same drug, in such a concentrated dose, was poison to Eleri's Psy mind.

He held her hand throughout the evac flight, while the medical team tried to stabilize her in ways Naia simply couldn't. "How bad is it?" he asked the short and trim fortysomething medic with a cap of dark-blond curls who appeared to be the lead.

Her name was embroidered above the pocket of her dark green scrubs: *Agata Czajka*.

"Bad," was the clipped response.

Czajka checked a handheld device as the heavily stabilized air-evac jet-chopper took them out toward the nearest hospital with the right facilities—thirty minutes by air. "Js of Eleri's generation," she said as she worked, "were reconditioned by having a thin layer of their personality scraped off. Eleri is listed as having undergone the procedure eight times."

Recalling the brutality of what had been done to Eleri made his falcon's talons push at his fingertips, his voice dropping. "You sound like you know what you're talking about."

"I'm a neurosurgeon, not one of those Council butchers they called reconditioning techs," Dr. Czajka said in the same clipped tone. "I was brought onboard by Sophia Russo to lead a team whose goal it is to try to fix the neural damage across the senior cabal of the Corps."

Though her expression didn't alter, she was gentle as she used a swab to clear a patch of blood from under Eleri's eye. "The task is complex and difficult even with Js who were only reconditioned once. Add severe drug toxicity to that . . . the fact she's alive is what the other races term a miracle."

"Eleri doesn't give up."

"No, clearly not," the doctor said. "I didn't even realize that they continued to recondition after the fifth pass—that's considered a hard line in Psy neuro-medicine." The clipped tone was a razor blade by now. "Eleri's sense of self would have been hanging on by a thread."

Dr. Czajka glanced at him, her eyes a hard blue. "I'm seeing evidence of a memory seizure—if she wakes up, you have to prepare yourself to meet an Eleri whose memories have been overwritten or corrupted. It usually causes the impacted Js to turn either violent and aggressive, act for short periods like the person whose memories they now carry, or to become catatonic."

Cold in Adam's veins as he remembered how Eleri had spoken about Exposure. She'd danced around the road she'd choose to take if she was on the verge of losing herself, but he wasn't an idiot—he'd seen the answer in the dull sorrow in her eyes, in her refusal to discuss their future.

If I'm that badly messed up, you make sure I get to fly.

Jacques's words, but that had been Eleri's wish, too. She hadn't wanted to live if she had to do it as a woman lost in screaming madness. "Can you tell before she wakes?" he forced himself to ask the doctor.

But she shook her head. "No." A pause. "Working with Js . . . it requires compassion of a kind that a percentage of my colleagues might find against medical ethics. I don't. If a J has made their wishes clear, then my team will execute that request in a way that ensures a painless peace."

Anguish rocked him, but he wasn't going to let Eleri down—not in joy . . . and not in the terrible darkness. "I know who to ask." Bram would categorically know Eleri's wishes on this point as no doubt Eleri knew those of the man who was her brother chosen. "Until we know, fight for her."

When the doctor moved to the back of the plane to consult with a colleague who was monitoring Eleri's neural readings, he leaned close to Eleri's ear. "You did it, wild bird. We've got Hendricks." The killer had run his car off the road and got himself stuck in the desert in his attempt to drive out of a dust storm. "No one will even find his bones by the time we get through with him."

They had, however, given Detective Beaufort and Eleri's task force colleagues the identity of the man known as the Sandman. "We told them it was his scent in the bunker, that he must've escaped into the desert. Beaufort has to know we have the fucker, but he's not going to spill."

And the task force could verify Hendricks's identity as the Sandman via the DNA in the little prison cell he'd created to feed his warped needs. "Your people are ripping apart his house right now," he told Eleri. "From the message I got before we took off, there's not going to be a problem with evidence to confirm his guilt."

Hendricks himself wasn't talking, was barely conscious. He'd made the bad mistake of attempting to take Dahlia on first with a gun and then a knife. She, a changeling who could read the desert storm—and who was forewarned—had easily avoided the attempted strikes, then come down on top of him. Needless to say, she'd shredded his back to ribbons, then broken his arm the same way he'd broken Malia's.

"The pathetic piece of shit tried to goad me to slit his throat with my talon." A snort from his wing-second. "As if I'd make it that easy for him. He'll be here when you get back."

Recalling everything Eleri had told him of the Sandman murders, Adam had said, "Keep the human population of the Canyon away from him, and check his genealogy. Eleri said all the victims showed signs of a telepathic assault. Whatever Hendricks is, he's not fully human."

Now, while his clan made sure a vicious murderer would never again claim a victim, Adam held Eleri's hand, skin to skin, blood to blood, in a silent reminder that he was here, that she was part of something bigger now . . . that she was his mate and he'd waited for her for a lifetime.

Oh, I'm so sorry. I should've been looking up instead of at my organizer.

. . . you've cut your knuckles. Let me get a bandage from the first aid—

No, stay, it will heal up real quick.

"Stay," he whispered as his heart threatened to break. "Please, Eleri, just stay."

"PREP for landing," came the pilot's instruction after too long.

"Stabilize her." Dr. Czajka indicated for Adam to hold on tight to the board on which the medics had strapped Eleri down. "We want as little movement to her brain as possible."

The doctor and two other medics took hold of other parts of the board, all four of them bracing themselves to take any impact. But the pilot managed to land with a skill that was a falcon gliding to home ground.

"I don't know much about changeling bonds," Czajka said to him as she ran down the hospital hallway beside the hover-propelled gurney a minute later. "But if you believe physical contact will help with her medical status, then scrub up and join us in the operating theatre."

Then she was gone, taking Eleri with her.

Adam turned to the nurse who'd been on the flight. "Show me how to scrub up."

It took far too long, even with the facility's high-tech sanitizer, but he was finally ready. He walked in to find Eleri in surgery, Dr. Czajka about to use a fine drill to make a hole in her skull. "Easiest, fastest way to relieve pressure on the brain," the surgeon said.

Adam realized Czajka was buying them time to think about what else they could do.

He took Eleri's bare hand in his, her flesh too cold, her bones so fragile.

"You really need to eat, mate of mine," he said to her in the language of his grandmother. "I feel like dropping a fresh kill in front of you." He could just imagine her reaction to that bloody show. "Trust me, to a falcon, that's a declaration of true love."

The drill shut off, the smell of bone in the air.

Then came the wet iron of blood. Too much blood. He jerked up his head. "She's bleeding inside her skull?"

"Yes." Czajka continued to work, her face set in grim lines behind the clear plas of her surgical mask. "But the pressure's going down. No way to check her psychic status at this point, especially since she's no longer in the PsyNet."

The operation ended far sooner than he'd thought it would. When he spoke to Dr. Czajka afterward, while Eleri was being hooked up to the systems in the surgical ICU, she took off the head cap she'd worn with her scrubs and threw it in the nearest biohazard bin. "The real damage with reconditioned Js isn't, despite the interference with their brains, physical.

"I know it's what many of them believe, but their physical brains are, for the most part, in good shape. The major damage is psychic—and while that might not sound bad to a human or changeling, Psy are who we are *because* of our psychic abilities. Damage to that element damages our entire self."

"No, I get it," Adam said, recalling when Eleri had flamed out. "She said she felt unmoored without her abilities, as if she'd lost a critical organ or a limb."

The doctor put her hands on her hips, her curls flat due to the surgical head cap. "Exactly. Unfortunately, with Js at the stage at which Eleri was prior to this incident, there's almost nothing that can be done except for intricate shield rebuilding by empaths.

"It's the shields that are the biggest problem because nothing else works without shields; their minds become open wounds. I've *proven* it can succeed with less reconditioned Psy—it's not a perfect solution, but it can add at least a few years to their lives."

A few years was nothing . . . and it was everything. "Why unfortunately?"

"Because Js at this stage won't cooperate with Es. We've had zero successes so far." The surgeon glanced through the glass wall of the ICU room. "I asked Bram why. He's—"

"I know him." The man would probably be in this hospital right now if he wasn't in Raintree helping tear Hendricks's place apart.

Per Dahlia, all three of Eleri's closest friends—her family—had shown up.

Now Dr. Czajka said, "Bram told me that it's because they can't protect the Es at this point—anyone who goes in will become trapped within the sheer weight of psychopathic memories they carry. Eidetic psychopathic memories."

She folded her arms. "The worst of it is that I can't argue with him. Working with the low-level reconditioned Js was tough enough for the empaths. I don't want to accept it, but I think he's right—trying the technique on Js like Bram and Eleri would kill our Es."

Walking closer to the large glass wall that fronted Eleri's ICU room in the secure ward, she said, "The only reason Eleri and the others at the same stage are still around is because Sophia's somehow managed to talk them into it—they want to die." Flat words.

"I know." Adam had been arguing with Eleri about the future all this time without ever listening to her—because he couldn't bear to listen to her, couldn't bear to imagine a future without her. But that time was over; Eleri needed him to face the truth, no matter if it broke his heart.

Stay, beloved mine. Stay just a little longer.

"This isn't how their lives should end," Dr. Czajka said. "Per Eleri's file, she's personally responsible for locating and stopping seven serial killers on her own, saving life after life. She's a hero. They all are."

"The shield is the most important thing?" Because while Adam would accept Eleri's choice, even fight for it if it came down to that, it didn't mean he was going to surrender to his J's belief that she was out of options.

"Yes. Nothing else can begin to heal without it—and I'm certain Eleri no longer has *any* telepathic shields. Her PsyNet shields fell right before she died." A glance at him. "Does it matter in your network?"

"No. She's the only Psy in WindHaven." No one could take advantage of his J while she was so exposed. "Can that help her in the long term?"

"No," was the curt response. "She *needs* her telepathic shields to protect her brain against the psychic noise of the world. Like we all need our skin to protect the structures beneath; it's non-negotiable."

Adam's fingers curled tight into his fist, his heart thudding hard and slow as his focus coalesced to a single point as he fought to think, find answers . . . while knowing the best minds among the Psy had already been at the problem since the fall of Silence and failed in their quest. "Can she wake up without a shield?"

"Yes. But she'll either have a seizure or fall unconscious again almost at once due to the overload." A penetrating glance. "Imagine walking into a room of a thousand people where *everyone* is screaming at you, then multiply that by the population of a city and you'll have some idea of what Eleri will experience if she wakes. There will never, *ever* be quiet in her mind—and each time she wakes, she'll bruise her brain anew, wound on top of wound."

Unspoken was that even if pieces of Adam's J had survived, the nightmare of waking would tear those pieces into so many tiny fragments that she'd be gone even if she breathed and her heart yet beat.

Chapter 37

"Saoirse, will you build me a rocket ship?"

"Sure, Bear. I just have to collect a bit more money. Rocket ships are expensive to construct. But here, let's plan it out, get the schematics ready for when we have the cash."

—Conversation between Adam and Saoirse Garrett (circa summer 2063)

SOMETHING FLASHED ON the large wall screen to the left of Eleri's room, with Dr. Czajka's name at the top of it. "I have to go look in on another patient," she said after glancing at it. "I'll be back to check hourly on Eleri, however."

Adam pressed his hand to the glass, as beyond, the three nurses in Eleri's room seemed to be going through a checklist to ensure they'd finished their tasks. Not interrupting them lest he break their concentration, he grabbed his phone and called Saoirse. "Malia?"

"She's doing so good," his sister said, her voice rough. "Hendricks drugged her before he broke her arm. She didn't see or feel him break it, was in pain and scared when she woke with him looming over her in that hideous mask, but then she got angry."

A sniffing laugh. "God, my baby is a tough cookie. She was planning how to semi-shift and use her talons on him, but then Eleri was there and—Adam, she saved our girl by letting Hendricks take her. We might not have found Malia in time without her. Please tell me she'll be all right."

"I need you to build her a shield, Saoirse."

"What?"

"Eleri's telepathic shields are gone. They were already failing before Hendricks attacked her and now she has nothing to protect her mind—she can't heal without a shield."

"Bear"—a careful, tender tone—"I'm a shield engineer, yes, but I engineer *heat and radiation shields for jetcraft*. I have zero idea about psychic shields."

"You're the smartest person I know, Chirp." He swallowed hard. "And I figure psychic powers are a kind of energy, a kind of signal. Sound is a signal, and you build internal sound shields, too. And heat is energy. If you can block heat, you should be able to block telepathy."

He talked over her when she tried to interrupt; he didn't know if he was getting the science right, but his desperate mind was seeing the blurred whisper of a truth he needed his sister's virtuoso engineering intellect to turn into reality. "Teleporters need a physical image lock—if anything changes in that image, they can't arrive at their destination. That means psychic abilities aren't divorced from the physical.

"And something in the Canyon stops them dead regardless. That means psychic energy can be stopped on a physical level. You just have to find the right element or the right frequency."

Saoirse no longer sounded distressed or gently careful when she responded. "You say the craziest shit, Bear, and why am I always letting my little brother talk me into bad ideas?"

But despite her big-sister muttering, he could tell she was already sketching something on one of the pads she always had at hand. "Let me work on it. I'll get Malia on it, too—it'll keep her mind off things, and she's always been one to come up with off-the-wall concepts. Gets that from her uncle."

When she hung up without saying good-bye, he knew she was caught up in the undertaking. He also knew it was a near-impossible task he'd given her, a request from the little boy he'd once been who'd believed his big sister could build him a rocket ship.

Lifting his phone again, he called one of the few people who might know the effect of the blood bond on Eleri's current status.

"Adam," Lucas Hunter said when he answered. "How's Jacques?"

"Naia says he's rising through the levels of a coma and is close to the point where he might regain consciousness on his own." The update he'd discovered on his phone after he came out of Eleri's surgery had been the one bright spark in this hellish day. "Luc, I need to ask you about your blood-bonded network."

The alpha of DarkRiver didn't react as an alpha might once have—as Adam probably would have even recently. Prior to the request to blood-bond Psy children into changeling clans and packs, Adam hadn't given any thought to the fact that he created a psychic network when he blood-bonded his seconds to him.

As a changeling, he couldn't see that network, just sense the bonds.

"Ask." Lucas's tone held the weight of experience. He'd been alpha of DarkRiver for close to fifteen years at this point, and mated to Sascha for over four years.

He understood both what it was to lead, and what it was to fall in love with a Psy.

Adam told him about Eleri's disintegrating shield, about how he'd blood-bonded her in a last-ditch attempt to keep her alive, and how Dr. Czajka had told him she'd probably not be able to successfully come to consciousness without a shield. "Is it possible the blood bond could protect her?"

A long pause. "That's one hell of a question, Adam," the DarkRiver alpha said at last. "I don't know anyone who's come into a pack with absolutely no shields. I didn't even know that was survivable. But we have a strong group of Psy between DarkRiver and SnowDancer. You okay for me to pull them in to answer the question?"

"Yes." They were allies, the trust between them a thing of unbreakable stone. Which is why he said, "She's my mate, Luc. But her mind refuses to permit the mating bond."

A hiss of air, the understanding silent. "I'll call you back the instant I have anything."

"Thank you." Hanging up, Adam slid away the phone as beyond the glass, Eleri lay motionless.

The minutes ticked by.

Turned into hours.

Until three hours had passed and he was seated in Eleri's room going through his messages and making short comm calls while talking to his mate—because a wing leader couldn't simply vanish from his people's lives.

"The fledglings especially," he told her, "and at this time—the older ones know what happened to Malia, while the younger ones have picked up on the tension in the clan. That call I just made to the littlest birds? It'll mean they sleep easy tonight." Adam had smiled and even chuckled in that call because the littles needed to see him as a pillar that would never fall, never break, their safe place to land.

A new message arrived just then.

He shoved a fisted hand against his mouth as he read the name of the sender: Eleri Dias.

He didn't want to open it, didn't even want to believe it existed, but at the same time, he was desperate to hear from his mate, even if it was through a message that could have no good tidings. She had to have sent it this morning—that was the last time she would've had a chance.

Right before she'd told him she was driving out to meet a colleague. Right before she'd planned to leave Raintree . . . perhaps leave him.

Adam touched the screen . . . and the pillar cracked, bled.

... but don't mourn me, Adam. I'm free now. Your wild bird in flight, my mind whole and my spirit no longer locked in a cage of reconditioning.

At last, I'm Eleri again.

ELERI screamed.

She knew she was locked inside her own mind. She also knew she was exhausted. Her personality, what remained of it, lay shredded in fine threads around her feet. At least it was *hers*, her thoughts still those of Eleri Dias thanks to the self-termination switch that she'd thrown at the end when she'd felt the virus of Hendricks's memories and thoughts attempt to take hold in her mind.

Had it succeeded, she'd have been either insane ... or an extension of him for however long it lasted before her mind collapsed.

Kill the virus. Die as Eleri. Adam. Child, the child—

The last garbled thoughts she remembered having.

It hadn't worked. She wasn't dead.

And through the shredded memories of her ran a line of vivid yellow.

It reminded her of Adam's eyes.

She focused on that because it was beautiful and it made her happy. A dazzling happiness far beyond the numb gray in which she'd existed for years. A gray that wasn't a product of Silence, but of being a J.

A nothingness where she should be.

But she existed now inside her mind and she *felt*. Oh, how she felt.

Something had happened to her, that much she knew, but what it was, she didn't remember. There'd been pain, bright edges, talons on her arm that had become a soft female hand, but they were nothing but flashes that soon faded.

Only the bright falcon line remained.

It was a barrier, she realized in slow fractures of knowledge. One that stopped her from stepping over into the quiet dark that beckoned. A place without pain, without loss, without grief. A place ... without Adam.

She stepped back even as the happiness faded.

Because emotion was a multifaceted jewel, and that jewel had just spun . . . but even as it did, her tired mind shut down again.

The falcon yellow blazed, the wildness of it the last thing she saw.
Adam.

Chapter 38

"Not many Js get a second chance."

—Sophia Russo (circa March 2081)

MAX DIDN'T BOTHER to tell Sophie to take it easy even though she got tired far faster these days, needed more rest. While she cleared her schedule and delegated tasks, he arranged transport to the facility that was looking after Eleri.

It was part of a network of hospitals that contained J-specific units Sophie had helped put in place. This one was one of the smallest, but had all the high-tech equipment it could need, thanks to the funds Sophie had managed to get out of their boss.

Nikita Duncan liked money, but she'd chosen a J with a conscience—a J who'd had a habit of eliminating very bad people—as an aide for a reason. Nikita also had a daughter who was an E, and plenty of things for which she needed to atone, whether she'd ever consciously admit it or not.

She'd stumped up the cash to fund the J units.

Sophia, in true Sophia form, had said, "This is just the start, Nikita. You don't get to forgive yourself so easily."

"Who spoke about forgiveness?" Nikita had responded. "We all make choices. I live with mine—and for many of them, I will never ask forgiveness."

Nikita Duncan was a complicated woman.

"How's the peanut?" Max asked as he walked his powerhouse of a wife into the hospital, one hand on her lower back, the fabric of her full-length dress of dark green jersey soft under his palm.

The early evening air was balmy yet, but he'd made sure Sophia had a thick shawl to put around her if the hospital environs proved cold. It sat inside the satchel he wore cross-body to keep his hands free.

"The peanut is so relaxed that he's clearly a clone of you," she muttered with a scowl, her hand on the belly that was compact for a woman in the second half of her seventh month of pregnancy.

But per their doctor—and more importantly, per Ma Larkspur, who'd adopted them into her brood—both Sophie and the baby were "fit and well." Sophie's body just happened to carry that way.

"Seriously, our baby is the definition of mellow. *I* keep getting anxiety and checking up on him because he's so undemanding even now that he's at a point in development that his brain should be reaching out for mine on a constant basis by instinct."

Chuckling, Max rubbed his knuckles over her cheeks. "He can't be my clone, then. I'm very demanding of your attention."

She made a face, but let him pet her. He knew she was in pain, hurting for her Js. He could've wished she'd never taken on this burden, but he also knew who his Sophie was—and she could no more walk away from her fractured brethren than she could stop checking up on their child.

Sophia Russo had a heart that didn't quit.

"Let's go see Eleri," she said with a deep breath. "Dr. Czajka says the prognosis is grim, but with Adam bonding her into WindHaven . . . I want to hope, Max. I want a miracle even when I know that's illogical and I'm setting myself up for heartbreak."

A shuddering breath. "Eleri thinks I don't know how close she was to Exposure prior to this. No J has ever survived that level of psychic damage—you can't develop shields when the foundation on which shields are built has been wiped out of existence."

He rubbed his hand on that spot on her back that always ached by the end of the day. "She's alive, breathing on her own. One step at a time."

They arrived outside Eleri's ICU room to find Adam Garrett pacing in front of it, phone to his ear and his hair roughly tousled as if he'd been thrusting his hand through it. "What?" he said into the line just as he spotted them.

He gave them a short nod as he spoke again into the phone. "You're sure? Fuck. Yeah, I'll deal with it." Ending the call, he said, "Sophia, Max."

While Max had never met the other man, Sophie had given him the heads-up on her own fleeting meeting with the WindHaven alpha. "Adam," he said in greeting.

The other man shook his proffered hand. "No change," he said, his jaw tight.

"Can I go in?" Sophia asked.

Adam nodded, and Max's wife slipped inside to see this wounded member of her J family. Max, meanwhile, stood with Adam, certain beyond any doubt that Adam wasn't here because of the assistance Eleri had provided to his clan. He was here because Eleri mattered to him the same way Sophie mattered to Max.

Max's own gut was tense, the scene reminding him too much of another J, another violent act, another monster.

No more. My Js deserve a better life than this!

Max agreed with everything his wife had said, everything she wanted for the J Corps. This kind of ending—violated at the hands of psychopaths, or dying because their shields just couldn't cope any longer and gave out? It was a too-common scenario, and it needed to fucking *stop*.

"You were a cop, right?" Adam said without warning.

Glad for the distraction, Max turned to look at the other man.

Adam's profile was sharp, his skin tense over his bones. "Yes. I run security for Nikita Duncan now." That turn in his life, he could've never foreseen. But like Sophie, he went toe-to-toe with his boss when required and never once had he deviated from his ethical principles.

Nikita knew she couldn't push him. She could fire him but she hadn't. Which also said something about her. Complicated. Definitely complicated. "Why?"

"You armed?"

"Always." He had the required permission to carry inside the hospital as the global head of security who oversaw the security setup of all the J units. Despite how he'd described what he did to Adam, his job had long ago altered from protecting Nikita to managing a vast network of security personnel under her banner.

"Look after her," Adam said, his eyes on Eleri. "That was her friend Bram on the phone—the team ripping apart Hendricks's home found a number of disturbing photos. It's possible everyone was wrong and he *did* have earlier victims who haven't been discovered—I need to go talk to the asshole."

Max didn't point out that Deputy John Hendricks had supposedly disappeared into the desert after having crashed his car into a ditch. One of Max's closest friends was a changeling—he knew how justice worked for the primal race and, having seen what he had during his years in Enforcement, he didn't blame the changelings for what some would call a brutal philosophy.

"I've been where you're standing, Adam," he said. "Complete with a bastard who was holding the locations of his victims' graves hostage. I had access to a powerful telepath. I asked him to strip the killer's mind."

He held the other man's gaze. "I know it isn't the changeling way—but I'll tell you that I've never regretted my decision. Fucker would've continued to manipulate and delay, continued to use every opportunity to cause harm."

It had broken his heart to talk to those who waited for their loved ones to come home, to tell them that they never would, but he also knew he'd given them a painful peace. No more wondering. No more questions.

The terrible gift of being able to give their lost a loving farewell.

Adam's eyes narrowed. "I wouldn't have thought of that as an option," he admitted. "But you're right. Eleri told me Hendricks likes to play games—he'll love it if we come to him with questions that give him the upper hand."

A curt nod, as if the falcon leader had come to a decision. "You'll watch over Eleri?"

"You have my word. Go find out what the bastard knows."

But Adam looked through the glass again. "Sophia."

"I'll have to wrangle her into resting at some point," Max acknowledged, "but she's not planning to go far. The staff's already told her she has a berth in the room they keep for staff. I'll keep watch over Eleri till you return."

Adam hesitated for a long second, touching his fingers to the glass of the window. Whatever he said to Eleri, it was silent, but Max felt the power of it all the same.

No, Adam Garrett and Eleri Dias weren't just acquaintances or even colleagues.

Max knew what hell it was to worry about the woman you loved, what it was to wait for her to wake up. He and Sophie, they'd gotten their miracle, but Eleri wasn't Sophie. Eleri's mind wasn't woven into the PsyNet like Sophia's.

Eleri wasn't even *in* the Net any longer.

And the twin neosentience that had saved Sophia's life was diminished and wounded, barely hanging on as the PsyNet continued its inexorable collapse. Max had stayed awake night after night tracking the collapses. Because the very thing that had saved Sophie's life could now end both her and their child.

Sophia could never leave the PsyNet, could never defect into a changeling network like Sascha Duncan or Faith NightStar. Sophia was *part of the Net* itself, her being anchored into its very fabric. If it crumbled, she would fall.

Max forced himself to breathe.

They had time. The blue spiderweb that had infiltrated every fracture and through line of the Net had bought them that time. Enough to figure out a long-term solution. Because being on Nikita's most trusted team meant he wasn't like the vast majority of the public: Max knew the blue spiderweb wasn't a fix but a patch.

The PsyNet was far from safe.

So yeah, Max Shannon understood Adam Garrett's fear all too well.

Chapter 39

I suppose I could tell someone . . . nah, why would I do that when I can use it? Now that I know what the whispers are, it's not annoying. No, now it's *interesting*.

—From the notebook of John Hendricks (age 12) (circa winter 2069)

BRAM WAS WAITING for Adam near the turnoff to the Canyon, his own dusty vehicle parked to one side of the night-draped road. Not wanting to be wiped out by the time of his arrival, Adam hadn't flown on the wing. Instead, he'd managed to get a commercial jet-chopper flight into Raintree, landing on the high school's sports field under the blaze of the football lights the school had switched on for him.

Pascal had been waiting with one of the clan's vehicles—after handing it over, the senior wing commander had flown back to the Canyon on the wing because he needed some time in the air.

Now Bram got into the passenger seat of Adam's vehicle and said, "You need John Hendricks's memories stripped?"

Adam had given Bram a call en route, told him only that he needed an assist. The other man had asked no further questions. That he'd figured out WindHaven had Hendricks wasn't the issue—the entire town probably knew the falcons had Hendricks. You didn't touch a Wind-Haven fledgling and live to tell the tale.

It was his assumption about memories that surprised Adam. "I thought I'd ask you in person, see if it bothered you. No foul if it does—I can—"

"Let's go." Bram had obviously started the day dressed in what seemed to be the J Corps uniform of black or gray suits with white shirts, but though he still wore the gray pants, his jacket was missing in action and his white shirt smudged with dust, the sleeves rolled up to the elbows in rough folds.

Adam drove on through the stillness of the night, taking the other man at his word. "We'll give him back if necessary." He'd made that call on the road. "We were in hell with Malia gone for such a short time—I'll never withhold him if seeing him face justice in a courtroom will bring peace to people who've been in the same hell a lot longer."

Bram tapped his finger on the window ledge. "You can't talk to them because they don't know you, but Tim Xiao—the head of the task force—can and did; he told them there was a strong possibility Hendricks had become lost in the desert while attempting to escape apprehension, and chances were that he was dead.

"All they wanted was proof of death. None mourned the loss of a trial—they already see how he has all the media coverage while their girls are relegated to being footnotes. Giving him a trial would be everything he ever wanted."

Adam's talons pushed out in a rage born of the grief of three families he'd never met. "We can make sure his remains are found in the desert." He picked up speed. "Xiao a J like you?"

Bram shook his head. "No, he's human and dangerously smart . . . but he's been half-in love with Eleri for years, so he's willing to swallow the report about Hendricks having stumbled off into the desert."

. . . half-in love.

All this time, Adam had just assumed Eleri was his because of the mating bond, that she'd never felt that kind of pull to any other man. That was one hell of an assumption.

"Eleri's not in love with him," Bram said, as if reading Adam's thoughts. "I don't think she even realizes."

Adam forced his talons back in, forced the subject away. If Eleri had felt the pull, she'd have acted on it. Adam's mate had a spine of titanium.

His phone rang on the car's system, Detective Beaufort's name flashing on the screen. "Beaufort," he said, answering the call. "You're on speaker. Bram's with me."

"The chief's woken up." Open relief in his deep voice. "Best piece of news I've had on this nightmare of a day."

"He remember anything about what happened to him?"

"Says he knows Hendricks came to his door, but that's it. Total blank from then on. Aside from that little bit of memory loss, he's his old self."

Adam frowned. "Why would Hendricks do anything to him? Just because he was the most experienced member of the Raintree Enforcement team?"

"No, Chief says he was probably worried about the vehicle Jacques found. Chief surprised Hendricks at his place about a year ago. He wanted to drop off a pie after Mrs. Cross made too many and didn't bother to call ahead. I remember him dropping off two pies at the station, too.

"Hendricks's back garage was open at the time, and the chief commented on the truck. Said Hendricks told him it was an uncle's and he was fixing it up so the uncle could sell it. You know Chief Cross has a steel-trap mind. He would've remembered the vehicle soon as he looked at Jacques's file that morning."

"Hendricks could've got out of it with a little fancy footwork with Jacques and anyone else," Bram said, entering the conversation for the first time. "Cop to hiding it in the desert because he didn't want to pay the registration and insurance on the vehicle—he'd have got a slap on the wrist at most. No reason for anyone to investigate further."

"I guess he panicked," Beaufort said. "Couldn't be sure there was no victim DNA in it—but instead of lying his way to a lesser offence and paying up what he owed, he shot Jacques and made sure the vehicle would be processed."

"He got away with murder because he had time to plan it," Adam said, "but he doesn't think fast on his feet."

He'd witnessed that himself while in the air one day.

A child had run across Main Street without looking, while Jocasta Whitten and Hendricks had both been nearby. It was Hendricks who'd been facing the child, but it was Whitten who'd sprung into action to grab the boy off the street—while Hendricks blinked indecisively.

Adam had seen that because he'd landed by then, having dived the instant he saw the child step onto the street.

"I think you're right," Beaufort said. "Man never did react well to unexpected changes. I should've known something was up when he was so calm and helpful after we found the chief. Even offering to go in and tidy up. Christ."

Bram spoke again. "It's not your fault. Psychopaths have the ability to wear a mask so well that no one sees beneath. Nice, quiet neighbor, would've never thought it was him. Sound familiar?"

"Yeah." But from the tone of the other man's voice, it'd take him time to get his head around the fact that one of his deputies had been murdering women while working under him.

Spying the entrance to the Canyon garage up ahead, Adam ended the call soon afterward. "You claustrophobic?"

"No. Why?"

"We're going to go deep," he said, and drove straight through the garage to a large roller door on the other side that stayed shut most of the time.

Today, it was up, with two falcon soldiers on guard outside it.

"Close it behind me," he told the women as he passed.

It was already being rolled down as they passed through.

"This was built as a winged escape tunnel during the Territorial

Wars," Adam told Bram, "but my grandmother had it enlarged to fit vehicles."

"Impressive."

"My wing-second, Dahlia, put Hendricks in the deepest part of the Canyon, the farthest possible spot from any unshielded human minds." She'd also offered to interrogate the male on the subject of the other possible victims, but Adam wasn't about to put that on her.

Some things, a wing leader had to shoulder.

He drove on through the unlit tunnel, his headlights making the minerals in the rock sparkle. "Until today, I never truly understood the vulnerability humans live with on a daily basis."

Unlike changelings, most humans had no natural shields, and thus just had to *trust* the Psy around them not to violate their minds. "That takes incredible strength."

Bram nodded. "Give them a shield and humans could rise to become the most powerful of the three races—they've been honed by centuries upon centuries of forced sheer, blind courage."

"My sister's trying to come up with a solution for Eleri's shields," Adam said as he navigated a tight corner with care. "If it works, it might work for humans, too."

"An artificial shield for Psy?" Bram sat up straighter. "Has she liaised with the people working on a human shield?"

Adam's hands clenched on the steering wheel. "Are they ahead of the curve? Will they help with Eleri?"

"No," Bram said after a pause. "No, I think it's better your sister works in isolation. All attempts at artificial shields so far have failed. Better she start from a clean slate."

All attempts at artificial shields so far have failed.

The headlights caught Dahlia waiting for them beside the small chamber where she'd stashed Hendricks. Leaving the rugged vehicle where it was, Adam turned off the lights and allowed their eyes to adjust to the more muted glow provided by the electric lantern in Dahlia's hand.

"What's he doing?" Adam asked after he and Bram joined her.

"I have two people inside with him at all times and they say he's basically either raving at them, threatening their lives, or trying to sweet-talk them into letting him go." Dahlia's upper lip curled. "Man is batshit, but he definitely understood what he was doing and that it was wrong. No fucking insanity plea for him if we decide to let him out to face the courts."

"Any luck tracing his bloodline?"

A hard shake of the head. "He was surrendered by his birth mother at a hospital—literally left in the bassinet they keep there for that purpose. No record of who she was, or his paternal line. Dead end.

"Don't feel too sorry for him, though—folks who fostered him that night ended up adopting him. They're genuinely nice people and you know I don't make that judgment lightly. They have two other adopted children who turned into caring adults. One teaches kindergarten; the other's a paramedic who volunteers at homeless shelters in his off time."

She paused, her expression torn. "No signs of abuse from external forces during his childhood, though I guess no one would know if he didn't talk. Not that it would excuse any of what he did, but at least it'd be a reason instead of Hendricks just being born wrong. I don't like saying that about any child."

BRAM had never met a woman as deadly as this one, of that he was certain—and he was in the Cartel with Saffron and Eleri. His J colleagues could kill, yes, but this woman, tall and with dangerous curves, she'd tear a man limb from limb and then mark her face with his blood. The energy coming off her was violent and primal, and Bram felt punched in the face by it.

Her eyes flicked to him, dark and angry. "You the Psy who's going to see what's going on in Hendricks's head?"

"Bram," he said, wanting her to know his name. "And yes. I can also find out if he was in fact abused as a child."

She jerked her head toward the door. "Well, go on in, Psy who looks like a linebacker and has a fancy-ass name like Bram."

Even his strange, startling reaction to this falcon didn't override his need to finish what Eleri had started, what she'd almost died trying to finish. He walked in behind Adam, aware of Dahlia remaining in the doorway after she hung the lantern on a wall hook.

Two other lanterns lit up the space, so they hadn't left Hendricks in the dark as Bram would've done—but then, Bram was a twisted fuck after years spent trawling through the minds of serial killers. Though Hendricks was tied to a chair, and wore purpling bruises on one side of his face from his apprehension, it was clear he'd been fed and watered.

His broken arm had also been set, then strapped to his chest and the chair. No doubt the falcons had made sure he wouldn't bleed out from any other wounds, either. Not until they'd finished with him.

"Surprise," the former deputy said, staring straight at Adam and ignoring Bram.

Adam Garrett didn't play the psychopath's game. "Bram."

Bram went for the other man's mind while Hendricks was still fixated on Adam. Hendricks realized what was happening at once, began to scream and attempt to "punch" Bram with his telepathy. But while he was strong enough to have killed unshielded human women, and caused a heart attack in a human man of some seven decades, he stood no chance against a trained Gradient 9.1 J whose shields—even at their current levels—were titanium against his low-level Tp.

Bram slipped through Hendricks's own shields—such as they were—with ruthless ease. And the mind he saw ... it was unlike any he'd ever before walked. He'd been trained to take specific memories, but with so many years of experience, he *could* totally strip a mind of what it held.

The load wouldn't overwrite his own memories, not if he was in conscious charge of the draw.

First, however, he said, "We found surveillance photos of a brunette teenager with a small upper arm tattoo in your apartment, alongside those of a Black girl around the same age with braids worn in pigtails. Who are they?"

Hendricks laughed. "Wouldn't you want to know?"

Bram already did, because Hendricks's disorganized mind had brought up the relevant memories on cue. "Roxanna Johnson and Imma Fehr. Stalked but not murdered per his memories."

Hendricks's eyes grew huge. "You're like her, like my Eleri."

Bram sensed Adam's rage, but the falcon wing leader kept his calm as he sent the names through to Beaufort, who'd run them to verify Hendricks's story.

Bram had already moved on, was asking about the other images they'd found. Hendricks was making attempts to evade him now, but only the rare psychopath had that facility—and those psychopaths were universally Psy.

Hendricks wasn't Psy. But he wasn't quite human, either.

By the time Bram finished, the other man's head had flopped forward, drool dripping out of his mouth. "He's exhausted himself fighting me," Bram told Adam. "I think I have all of it, but I want to do two more reads to make sure we're not leaving anything behind."

Adam gave a curt nod. "Dahlia, make sure Bram gets the access." He held up his phone. "Task force has already pinned down the locations of the first two girls you identified. They're older now—around Hendricks's age."

"It tracks with what I saw; he began with stalking girls his own age. As for his bloodline . . . he's got Psy in him, likely passed down through the generations. No way to know if he's descended from the Forgotten, or from human-Psy pairs pre-Silence. *Just* under 1 on the Gradient, so he would've never linked to a biofeedback network, but I think as an unshielded child, he picked up thoughts—whispers, he calls them."

Adam's mouth tightened. "Did it cause mental illness? Do we need to treat him as sick?"

"No. I'm getting the sense of a boy who began to understand his ability and who took sadistic pleasure in listening for people's secrets."

A boy who'd had two adoring parents who'd have taken him to every doctor on the planet had he asked, but Hendricks had enjoyed his secret power.

"He had a lucrative sideline in blackmail as a teenager—that's why he could kill with such weak telepathy. He honed it to its sharpest point. Fact is, he should've never been able to cause death; that he did speaks to how much effort he put into refining his ability until it became a scalpel."

Bram made sure Hendricks's memories were well compartmentalized from his own. Later, he'd tell Adam that the serial killer's DNA and memories should be analyzed and studied, because there might be other outwardly human or changeling children out there who were *just* Psy enough for it to be a problem, but not Psy enough that their minds would search for a biofeedback link.

Not every such child would be a Hendricks. Some *would* be driven mad by the whispers . . . and perhaps already had been over the centuries. How many of the people in the asylums of old had ever been tested for minor Psy abilities? Those in the Trinity Accord needed to be notified of the need for a new and wide-ranging testing regimen.

For now, he looked at the woman who'd taken his breath away. "I think in this case, you have to accept that he was a bad seed."

Chapter 40

Bayani: I think this one's a fail, Saoirse. I'm moving on to batch 14.

Saoirse: Damn. I was hopeful about 12. I'm just starting on 13. Let's meet after we finish to discuss our next steps before we all fly home to get a few hours' sleep. We don't want to mess up the tests due to lack of rest.

Malia: I'll prepare food for the entire team—Dad's already muttering about dropping meal packages on your heads, by the way. Tahir's gonna help because I'm making him and he's still being a weirdo and treating me super nice. (Don't worry, Mom, I won't stress my arm—Naia did another healing session on me and says the bone is knitting at an "excellent" pace.)

—Team El-Shield (now)

HIS PART OF the job done, Bram stepped out to take a breath away from the killer, while Adam stayed behind to say a few quiet words to the two guards who had to remain inside with Hendricks.

Dahlia walked over to him, her body and face shadowy in the faint light that fell from the room into the driving corridor. "You look like you could use a drink."

"Psy can't process alcohol. Else all Js would be raging alcoholics."

"What you did, it messes you up, doesn't it?" Dark, sharp eyes.

"I barely have my own memories anymore," Bram admitted. "The spaces are filled up with those of murderers and other violent offenders."

"You do touch?" A nod at his gloved hands. "Eleri was okay with changelings, though she didn't go overboard."

Bram's skin prickled. "Then likely I'll be fine. Changeling shields are all but impenetrable."

"Then instead of a drink, how about you work off your funk in my bed?" She leaned in close so the words were a hot breath against his ear, her height perfect for his own. "I mean, all that sexual tension simmering under your surface can't be good for you."

Bram wanted to haul her close, *bite* down into the curve of her neck. His cock throbbed. He was careening out of control. And he wanted more. "I have to return to Hendricks's house, meet with the task force." No one was sleeping this night, not with open questions on the table.

"The invitation doesn't currently have an expiration date, Mr. Bram." Her hand on his nape, a burn of heat. "Give me your phone."

He handed it over after unlocking it on autopilot.

"There," she said after a few taps. "Call me when you're done." She slipped his phone into his pocket, and though she'd barely made contact, he felt as if she'd taken him over.

Adam stepped out of the room. "D," he said, "lock it up and get Naia to give him a once-over. We want him functional for the rest of Bram's reads."

"Got it." Dahlia was back in full professional mode. "What are we doing with him after?"

"He's going to die in that hole after Bram's finished," Adam said flatly after pulling the door shut behind himself. "That's what he did to his victims—he left them alone in that lightless prison, and only came in to torture them. He's getting off easy since we won't torture him, but he doesn't deserve light or company."

Bram hadn't expected such a pitiless punishment. "Will it haunt you?" he asked Adam once they were in the car—after he'd forced himself to walk away from Dahlia. "You're not the kind of man who's built for that."

Adam shot him a smile that was almost amused. "My grandmother literally tore off the head of the man who murdered my parents. I would've done it if she hadn't. Never, ever think that the leader of a clan or pack isn't capable of darkness when it's necessary. We just never allow it to swallow us whole."

"How?" Bram asked, desperate for an answer. "How do you keep from being sucked into the abyss?"

"Clan," Adam said at once. "We're not in the fight alone. Neither are you." He stopped the vehicle so he could look at Bram. "You're Eleri's family, so you're mine, too. Which makes you part of WindHaven."

Bram didn't know how to take that, how to imagine being part of a family that wasn't formed on a foundation of pain and fissures of the soul.

"And I don't care what you and Dahlia get up to in your own time," Adam said, "but she's got wounds of her own. Don't hurt her."

Bram wondered what the wing leader would say if he told him that Bram wasn't the one in charge, not by a long shot. He felt winded, as if he'd taken a blow . . . and he wanted to go back for another one.

"I'M pretty sure Dahlia's about to take Bram's virginity," Adam told Eleri late the next night while the hospital lay cloaked in soft evening light around them.

He'd flown in to see her on the wing, after having spent the day being the leader his clan needed him to be—with Dr. Czajka as well as Max and Sophia sending him regular updates.

Those updates had all been the same: *No change.*

"Though," he added, "your friend looks like he might be the type to have broken that rule already."

Eleri's chest rose and fell in silence.

Picking up the lip balm Malia had given him, he slicked it with tender care over Eleri's lips so they wouldn't dry out. As he moved, the material of the scrubs one of Dr. Czajka's nurses had given him after he arrived in falcon form made a soft rustling noise.

"Malia told me this stuff is 'magic!' and gave me stern instructions to put it on you." Amir and Saoirse's fledgling was already determinedly bouncing back—and had thrown herself headfirst into Project El-Shield, the name for the project Malia's brainchild.

"All fledglings have a few falls when they first start learning to fly—we make sure it's from low heights. But where most sit in the dirt stunned and confused until a parent comes over to dust them off, I remember watching Malia bounce up, dust off her wings on her own, and run over to Amir on those tiny falcon feet to ask to go again."

He'd grinned that day, delighted by her and knowing he'd forever remember her aggravated little face as she dusted off her fluffy wings before she got excited again and ran over. "That doesn't mean she doesn't need softness."

Adam had taken her with him to his aerie this morning, and they'd sat with their legs dangling off the edge of the exit into the canyon, with him cuddling her to his side while she poured out everything in her head and in her heart as he fed her small bites of breakfast.

Tough as she was, Malia needed to be spoiled and coddled until the fright passed, to be the baby bird under her wing leader's care. As did Tahir, the younger brother who loved to irritate Malia but who'd die for her. He was shaken by the thought that he hadn't been able to protect her from a predator. Adam had taken the boy flying, and they'd spoken beside Tahir's favorite grotto. The changeling sense of hierarchy would help here—Tahir's falcon understood the weight of responsibility was Adam's.

He'd spent time with Polly, too, the sweet girl who was still distraught over her friend's abduction from only meters away. "All the affected fledglings are talking about what happened," he told Eleri. "That's a good sign. It means it won't turn into a slow-acting poison within. I also reached out to the families of their dates and arranged for the boys to come on up to the Canyon to see Malia and Polly."

Naia was monitoring the entire situation and would arrange for empathic counseling because she was adamant that now they had access to the Es again, the clan should make such counseling part of their medical arsenal—per WindHaven's own ancient records, which Naia had dug up, Es had performed that function for the clan before the Psy immured themselves in Silence.

He exhaled. "And yeah, I'm pissed with myself for not seeing the snake in our midst, but I'll deal with it."

Picking up Eleri's hand, he clasped his own around it. "As for Bram and Dahlia and his impending debauchment, *Wild Woman* magazine is a staple in the Canyon, and word is that there are a lot of very dangerous Psy walking around who are in fact novices in the sheets. I wonder if Dahlia realizes that."

He wondered if Eleri would've laughed at the idea of Dahlia seducing Bram, or if she'd have felt protective of her chosen brother. He wished he could ask her, wished she was awake to tell him, wished the two of them could lie tangled in bed as the sun rose and discuss the unexpected attraction between his wing-second and her friend.

"I want to nuzzle my face into your neck," he told his mate, "just breathe you in. Stroke my hand down the lean lines of your body while I feed you tidbits that delight you. Kiss you in the softest, most secret places of your body. Hold you. Play with you."

. . . but don't mourn me, Adam. I'm free now. Your wild bird in flight, my mind whole and my spirit no longer locked in a cage of reconditioning.

At last, I'm Eleri again.

His chest compressed, his tears caught deep within. He'd lost so many people, had so many markers of grief on his heart. "I don't want you to go. I want to hold you so tight that no one can part us . . . but I'll never clip your wings. So if you want to fly, Eleri, fly."

The tears broke free, streamed down his face as he pressed his lips gently to hers, for even a wing leader's huge heart could break. "I'll watch for you in the skies, mate of mine."

ELERI felt her lungs expand, felt air inflate then deflate them as she exhaled. She sensed her own breath against her skin, and she sensed the brush of cloth against her limbs. It felt soft, much softer than the usual fabric of her suits and shirts.

Warmth, heat, roughness.

Salt on her lips.

A jolt of sensation through her nerve endings.

A harder heat pressing into her knuckles . . . and then came the avalanche of *noise*. Voices and voices and voices! Screams and shouts and quiet dream murmurs, all tangled together in a chaotic overload that was a crushing blow.

She didn't know if she made a sound, but her back bowed off the bed.

"Eleri!" Hands cupping her face, eyes ringed by falcon yellow looking into hers. "Hold on, hold on, baby. I've got you."

Wings wrapping around her, shoving the voices away with sheer brute strength. Feathers so soft against her skin, a barrier so fine and so strong. And already bending. She opened her eyes and was astonished she was herself.

Battered and damaged, with gaps in her memory . . . but the gaps were where she'd stored the memories of monsters. Her brain had known to discard those before it came for her own. "Adam."

Her throat ached but she spoke all the same, even as she lifted her fingers to brush his jaw. "What are you doing?"

"Giving you us," he said, his voice rough. "I shoved clan energy down the blood bond toward you when I heard you wake." He turned to kiss her fingertips. "It's working, Eleri."

The hope in his voice broke her in ways she didn't know she could be broken; she'd thought she'd already lost herself long ago. "It can't last," she whispered, astonished at how delightfully prickly his shadowed jaw felt against her fingertips, how the heat and strength of him beat like a pulse against her.

Sensation, bright as a scalpel, dazzling and multihued.

"Your wings are already under enormous strain."

He stroked back her hair, his big body blotting out the ceiling and becoming her world. She wanted no other.

"I can feel you, Adam," she whispered even as anger and despair darkened those beautiful eyes. "With all of me. No wall of numbness, nothing muted."

A hunger dark and rich tore through her. "Kiss me." In this stolen time between life and death, this unexpected and beautiful intermezzo, she wanted to experience all the lush layers of sensation of being with her mate.

"*Eleri.*" A rebuke, but he lowered his head, his lips just brushing hers.

She shuddered, her breasts aching and her nipples going tight and hard in a way that made her want to press up against his chest. She knew it felt good, the slide of his skin on her taut flesh, had experienced it . . . but now, oh now, how much *better* would it feel?

Eleri didn't know if she'd be able to bear it, but she wanted to try.

Her feet curled inward, her thighs clenching as Adam closed one hand gently about her throat, his other in her hair, and kissed her with an open mouth. The wetness, the heat, the way his body felt leaning over hers. His hair was so soft in her fist, his bristled jaw abrading parts of her face until she wanted him to rub his roughness across her . . . kiss her between her legs as he'd done in the cave.

Her entire body quivered as the erotic memory melded with the sensations of today to give her a glimpse of ecstasy. It was too much and it wasn't enough and it was all she'd been craving. She licked him back, one of her legs bending at the knee as she fought to get closer to him.

!!#!*

One shielding wing collapsed, even the power of an entire clan not enough to create a shield out of nothing and air. Eleri had two choices—fight a losing battle and cause more damage to herself, or put herself back under using a technique all Psy were taught as part of their studies.

Because it turned out that she wasn't done. If all she could have from Adam were kisses stolen in a breath, then she would take every single kiss he'd give her. "I'm not ready to go yet, Adam."

She took herself back under before the voices could rip her apart.

Chapter 41

... there are millions of humans who ... wake up knowing that today might be the day an invisible hand reaches in and rapes their mind."

—Bowen Knight, security chief of the Human Alliance (circa January 2083)

ADAM FELT ELERI go limp under him; not wanting to break contact, wanting to just hold on, he nonetheless laid her gently back down on the bed. He'd lifted her off it at some stage without realizing, pressing her body to his own.

Your wings are already under enormous strain.

How extraordinary that she'd seen his attempt to protect as shielding her with his wings. And how devastating to know that she'd been right. Because he'd felt them break, too, felt the clan's energy pour back into him as either her mind repudiated it, or it reached a critical point where it had nowhere else to go.

A rustle at his back, a nurse walking in. "Her vitals spiked," she said.

"Eleri was awake for a minute or two," he said and made sure the blanket he'd brought her from his bed at the den was warm and cozy around her. The falcon sense of smell might not be their greatest asset, but like humans, they could tell when they were wrapped in the scent of a person they loved and were loved by in turn.

"Fully conscious and coherent," he told the nurse. "But she couldn't hold on to a shield."

The nurse's mouth tightened. "Did she exhibit signs of acute distress?"

His mind flashed back to Eleri's fingers clenching possessively in his hair, her lips parting with eagerness under his, her leg rising as if she wanted to make space for him between her thighs. "No," he said. "A hint right at the start before I threw clan energy at her."

The medical staff here knew that Eleri was blood-bonded to him, that changeling "psychic" ability no longer a secret after they'd blood-bonded so many Psy children into their packs and clans.

"How long was she able to maintain with your assistance?"

"A minute. Ninety seconds at most." *A lifetime.*

The nurse made a notation on the chart, and though her manner remained crisp, she had a softness to her eyes as she said, "It's more than anyone expected."

Adam barely heard her, his falcon clutching fiercely at the last words Eleri had said: *I'm not ready to go yet, Adam.*

As far as he was concerned, she'd just torn up her good-bye letter and given him permission to go full throttle on attempting to save her life. Because if she could wake once, then she could wake again. Next time around, they'd talk solutions. Because Adam wasn't done with kissing his mate.

LUCAS'S call came the next morning, an hour after Adam landed back at the Canyon.

For now, his nights were Eleri's, his days WindHaven's.

"I'm sorry, Adam," the leopard alpha said. "Consensus is that while you might be able to help Eleri maintain a shield for a short period, you can't project one over her mind, not even if she mates with you. The shield she's lost is a fundamentally Psy thing, to be created from the inside out."

"I know." Adam told the alpha about Eleri's short waking.

"Shit, I'm sorry."

"Don't be sorry." Adam paced the plateau, letting the sunlight fill him with energy. "Your group came up with the right answer, which means they must have other answers. How about an artificial shield?"

"We've never attempted to create one for a Psy," Lucas said, "but Ashaya's been involved in attempting to build a shield to protect human minds against Psy interference."

All attempts at artificial shields so far have failed.

Squeezing his eyes shut, Adam said, "I've heard those attempts have failed," and he wanted Lucas to tell him that his intel was wrong, that someone had succeeded.

When Lucas confirmed the bleak truth, he opened his eyes to the beauty of his clan, the sky awash in reds and yellows, three falcons circling lazily against the horizon as the hungry cries of the littlest birds woke their parents.

Eleri would love this.

"My sister's attempting a shield, too," he said, determined that he'd stand here with his mate one day soon. "Working in isolation from all other ideas. One of Eleri's colleagues suggested we leave it that way."

If Lucas was startled that an aeronautical engineer was leading this task, he didn't reveal it. "It's good advice," he said. "Ashaya's asking the same of any scientists who come onboard—her take is that if they feed off each other, they risk making the same errors, or risk becoming locked in a singular loop of thought. She's even scratched her own previous concept and started again from an entirely new angle."

"What's Ashaya's Psy ability?" Adam mostly dealt with Lucas or one of the sentinels, so hadn't had any reason to speak in depth with the scientist.

"M," Lucas said. "Specialization in DNA. She was one of the Council's top experimental medical scientists, remains the best of the best in her field now she's doing independent work."

They ended the call soon afterward, and Adam kept on pacing, kept on thinking. An M-Psy, one who worked on the DNA level, had failed to create a workable shield. Yet he'd demanded his sister do it. Saoirse was at a massive disadvantage.

... her take is that if they feed off each other, they ... risk becoming locked in a singular loop of thought.

Where would an M start? Inside the body. Inside the mind.

He rang Saoirse, not knowing if she was at the Canyon or at the facility. "Chirp," he said when she picked up. "I have an idea about your shield."

No jokes about him being an engineer all at once, no sisterly digs. Because Saoirse knew what Eleri was to him. "Hit me."

"Don't attempt to create anything for *inside* Eleri's brain."

"Are you a foreseer now?" she muttered. "One of the concepts I came up with last night while Amir glared at me anytime I stopped eating—as did our own daughter who I carried in my womb, I should add—is an embed. I planned to talk to the doctor treating Eleri about it."

"Malia and Amir both know you forget to eat when deep in work," Adam said with a brotherly scowl. "They need to glare. And I don't think you should put the embed on your list."

He told her about Eleri coming to consciousness. "I'm connected to her directly through the blood bond"—it wasn't a mating bond but it was powerful nonetheless—"and I couldn't make the shield hold beyond a minute. For that to work, Eleri needs the building blocks, and those building blocks are gone."

Dr. Czajka had been clear on that point when he'd spoken to her last night. "Focus on the outside. Like you do with jetcraft."

"Eleri isn't a machine." He could hear the scowl in her voice. "But your reasoning makes logical sense. I'm going to take this to my crew—wouldn't it be something if a bunch of jet nerds came up with an answer that's eluded the Psy race all this time?"

Adam didn't say it out loud, but he knew why it had—because the Council had just used up those like the Js, pushing them to the point that they eliminated themselves from the equation. Fixing the damage had never been on the agenda; "used-up" Js were of no value to the Council.

Adam's falcon stirred, its feathers a shadow skin beneath his human form.

No one was *ever* again going to use his J.

Chapter 42

We are the Quatro Cartel. Here for each other forever! No matter what, we promise to always answer when one of us needs help.

—Bram Priest (age 10) (circa 2065)

BRAM HAD DONE everything he could when it came to the Sandman case in Raintree. He'd spent much of the past day with Senior Detective Tim Xiao going over documents they'd found at Hendricks's place, and pulling information out of the memories he'd scraped from Hendricks in order to answer outstanding questions.

Many of his answers had led to physical or forensic finds that *could* become part of the investigative file, adding more weight to the case against Hendricks.

He'd worried it would push Xiao's boundaries when Bram told him he now had Hendricks's memories, but though the detective had obviously been torn, he was also an experienced officer who'd seen far too much grief caused by killers like Hendricks.

"Just make sure his remains are eventually discovered in a condition where they can be ID'd," he'd said to Bram. "I promised the families that closure."

"It'll be done," Bram had said, certain he could trust Adam's word on that.

Unofficially, the case was already over, all other loose ends tied up.

The falcon team on former Sandman suspect Dae Park had even answered the question of Dae's lies, nocturnal movements, and disturbing presence: Mi-ja's son owned a small house in an isolated corner of Raintree that he'd turned into a manufacturing lab for a potent illegal substance. He was too smart to sell in Raintree, but he had a regular rota of customers in the nearest big cities.

He had also, it became clear, been tasting his own merchandise. That particular drug was known to incite its users to bursts of brutal violence after long-term usage—and Dae's blood had shown high concentrations.

Needless to say, Dae Park was no longer a free man.

As for Yúzé and Saffron, they'd left the previous night to go visit Eleri.

Getting into his vehicle, Bram knew he should follow the two out of town, get back to his personal mission of gathering as much data as possible when it came to devolving Js. It was important, might help the Corps come up with a system for helping future Js who were facing the same end as the entirety of Bram's tiny family of four.

And yet . . . he stopped his vehicle at the side of an isolated section of the road surrounded by verdant green. He'd already passed the Canyon, passed the road that would've led him up to the falcons' home base and the woman named Dahlia who'd offered to work out his tension with sex.

Bram hadn't been Silent for one hell of a long time—like all senior Js, he'd found it impossible to maintain adherence to the Protocol after close contact with mind after degenerate mind. Which had led to multiple reconditionings. But where Eleri had gone numb as a result, he'd become haunted by wakefulness. He felt *everything* and could process none of it, and it was slowly driving him mad.

He didn't need to further strain his already overloaded brain by initiating physical contact with a woman who had made his cock hard with a single heated whisper.

Yet he started the car with the intent to turn it.

Eleri was dying, despite all of Adam Garrett's ferocious belief in her and in them. There would be no second chance for any of the Cartel. Why shouldn't he go down in a scorching torrent of sexual pleasure?

Wings gliding down in front of his windscreen before he could start the turn, a huge bird with a snowy underside flying over his vehicle to come to a graceful landing on the deserted road in front of his SUV.

Not a peregrine.

A *gyrfalcon*.

A fracture of light even as he got out of the vehicle, the falcon no longer there even as the aftershock from the burst of light sparked behind his eyelids. Instead, a tall and voluptuous woman with dark hair marked by a single streak of white, and dangerous eyes, was walking naked toward him.

He'd seen other changelings naked in situations where they'd had to shift without clothing nearby, and none of them had affected him like this. It wasn't just because it was Dahlia—it was because she was making it a point to walk slow and easy while she ran a finger between the heavy weight of her breasts.

Bram had never seen so many curves, never wanted to grip all of them tight, never wanted to bite.

Until her.

Sweat broke out along his neck, his white shirt suddenly too heavy, too tight.

"Looks like you were about to blow town without saying good-bye," she said on a purr of sound as she came to a halt in front of him. "That hurts my feelings, Mr. J."

Fuck it.

Thrusting both hands into her hair, he bent his lips to her own . . . and felt the prick of talons on his sides. "You need permission for that, gorgeous."

Bram didn't know how to play games. "You already gave it," he said bluntly.

Husky laughter. "So I did."

Her hand on the back of his head, hauling him close.

Unleashed from the last of his inhibitions, Bram did what he'd wanted to from the first—he ran his hand down the curve of her waist and, cupping her ass, hauled her up onto his hips. She was luxuriantly soft under his hands, but beneath that was a layer of taut muscle.

This woman was a raptor, was dangerous.

But today, she was aroused and, for whatever reason, had decided she wanted him. He wasn't going to question her decision.

She rubbed against him, her kiss as fierce as her hold in his hair. "You an exhibitionist, big guy?"

They were on a public road.

Bram had completely forgotten that. But he didn't want to stop. So he just walked with her around the car and into the trees until they were hidden from view. She laughed, her hair trailing down her back to brush against his hands as she threw back her head. "Eager, I like it."

There was a delight in her . . . and also an edge. A broken shard. Bram recognized it because he had more than a few shards of his own. He was fine with Dahlia using him for reasons of her own—after all, wasn't he doing the same? Whatever happened, he wouldn't be around to pick up the pieces.

He could already feel it, the beginnings of a critical sensory overload.

Pulling her further up his body, he leaned her back over his arm and bit at her breast. Not painfully, but so he could get the taste of her inside him.

"Damn, you're strong." Real surprise this time, her thighs going tight around him. "No desk Psy, huh?" Teasing words, but her tone was breathless and he could scent a musk in the air that his primitive hindbrain told him was good, very good.

He bent her even further back, so he could kiss more of her, and it wasn't enough. Making a deep sound in his throat that no one who'd seen him in court would ever believe he could make, he looked around.

The ground looked hard and rough everywhere, and he couldn't bear to subject her delicate skin to that even if he wanted to devour her. So he slid her back down his body and took her mouth—but he was more than willing to follow when she seized control, her hands on his face and her tongue lashing his.

Lights flickered behind his eyes, his cock an aching rod in his pants.

Squeezing her ass, he broke the kiss only so he could bend down and taste her nipples, after once more pulling her up his body. She made a rough sound in her throat, her talons raking lines up his back that he felt on his skin.

She'd sliced through his shirt.

He didn't care. Leaning down, he sucked her nipple into his mouth.

A short, sharp cry before she hauled him up with a hand in his hair and kissed him with a fury that made him stagger. His knees threatened to crumple.

Then she said, "Down," and he went to his knees.

She'd unbuttoned and pushed his shirt off his body before he was even aware of it. When she shoved at his bare chest, he fell onto his back on the forest debris, his legs stretched out in front while she straddled his waist. Her breasts were marked by his bites and kisses, the nipples wet and ripe.

"I want to taste you," he said, and hauled her up his body.

She slammed her palms flat on his chest to stop him, talons pricking. "Why the hell are you so strong?" Her eyes weren't human anymore, a ring of yellow glowing in the muted forest light.

"I don't sleep much," he said. "I had to expend my energy somehow." He ran, lifted weights, swam, did anything and everything to exhaust his body so his mind could rest.

None of it had worked, but today, he was glad for all of it.

Because the next time he pulled her, she came, and made sweet, wild sounds as he took her taste right from her core. He wanted to inhale her, absorb her, wear her in his skin.

Giving a sudden high shout, Dahlia arched her back.

He stopped, looked up, unsure if he'd hurt her in his madness.

She shoved his head back down.

Guess not.

A minute later, however, she'd had enough and pushed him off to shimmy down his body and stare at him with changeling eyes, her chest heaving and her hair sweat-damp at the temples. "Where the fuck did you learn to do that?"

Bram, desperate to taste all of her before it was too late, had no time for questions and answers. "You're the softest creature I've ever touched. I want to sink into you, devour you."

Her breath went even more rapid, and then before he knew it, she was sitting up and had her hands on his belt. He willed her to hurry, and it seemed she was over the playing, too, because she ripped off the belt, then began to pull down his pants. "Shit, your boots."

He toed them off. "Gone."

Dahlia had his pants and briefs off him in three seconds, her hand around the jutting thickness of his erection in the next. A single downward stroke and his back arched. "Not yet," she ordered. "Not until I have you inside me."

Bram felt as if his entire skin was about to explode off his body.

Grabbing her hips, he maneuvered her into position with her full cooperation. The second she let go of his erection, he pulled her onto him in a single hard push. Only when she released a grunt of air did his brain clear. "Did I hurt you?" If he'd hurt this soft, generous, astonishing woman—

"No, but I'm sure I can feel you in my throat," she said, scraping her talons down his chest. "Now it's my turn to run this show."

Wet, tight, and in control, Dahlia rode him with a primal confidence that hypnotized him even as his body broke into every component cell. As if he was changeling and could open his eyes and re-form into a body and mind that weren't in the process of a final disintegration.

He felt the foundations of his shields begin to crumble one by one and couldn't find it in himself to care even a tiny bit. He was a being of pure need and pleasure for the first time in his entire life, and he wanted to live in this moment forever. Holding on to Dahlia's hips, he moved with her even as his mind collapsed, the pleasure racing through his nerve endings a sweet, hot fire.

DAHLIA went off like a rocket, Bram's hands clenched so tight around her hips that he'd probably leave bruises. Fair enough as far as she was concerned—she'd certainly scratched up his chest and back.

Damn, but it had been a long time since she'd been with a man who'd not only handled her strength and desire to share control—but reveled in it. The back-and-forth, the demands on both sides, the erotic release that made her bones ache, she hadn't experienced that for years, perhaps not since she was a young falcon who played only among her own kind.

Certainly not with the Dickwad, as Maraea had named Dahlia's ex.

Her thighs quivered as the orgasm faded to a dull throbbing, her chest heaving. Her body wanted nothing more than to collapse onto Bram's chest and have him stroke her back and hair . . . but that was for lovers or friends who were offering each other the comfort of skin privileges.

Not for a random hookup with a man she barely knew.

Managing to extricate herself from him with some semblance of control even when her body was just going "wow" over and over again, she stood, uncaring of her nakedness . . . or perhaps not. Because even as he pulled on his pants, his eyes never left her face and body, and her body wasn't against the looking.

Neither was his, from what was going on in the pants he'd just zipped up.

"You planning to return to Raintree?" she said, because why not have a Psy playmate if he was amenable to the idea? "Or are you based within a gyrfalcon's flight range? My wings can carry me long distances."

When Bram didn't immediately reply, she narrowed her eyes. She wasn't into games when it came to communication. Never had been. And why would he start that shit now, when it was clear he couldn't keep his hands off her? About to blast him for suddenly acting coy, she snapped to attention when he stumbled over nothing.

The man hadn't stumbled even when he'd carried her across the forest floor. Her focus shifted with force. "Bram? What's wrong?"

He looked at her with the softest eyes she'd ever seen on a man—and would've never expected to see on *this* man. "Thank you." Hand braced on the nearest tree, he kind of just folded down into a seated stance against the tree with his legs out in front of him and his bare chest yet gleaming with sweat.

Heart kicking, and mind blaring a reminder of what was going on with Eleri, she crouched beside him. "Get up," she ordered. "You have to drive home."

That same oddly tender look. "You are the softest, most beautiful being I've ever met."

The stark sincerity of the words, the way he said them, it healed something broken inside her, but she didn't have time to think about that. Panic was starting to stutter inside her because obsidian had begun to crawl in from the corners of his eyes, a creeping tide across the pale ice blue. "Are you delirious? Do you need me to slap you?"

"My shields are in the process of a final disintegration." He looked away from her for a moment to take in the forest. "I never thought I'd end it in a place like this, after an experience like the one we just shared, but—"

"No, no, *no*." Dahlia got up and grabbed his shirt, tugging it on and buttoning it haphazardly in a couple of places.

Air whistled into her back through the slashes she'd made in the fine cotton.

"Get up. Get up right now!" She grabbed his shoulders, but the man was a boulder. "You get up, Bram! I am not living with a reputation as the woman who fucked a Psy to death!"

His lips curved, but his eyes were heavy-lidded.

"You aren't helping if you give up and die," she said, forcing aside her panic to make her tone harsh. "You promised her, didn't you? That you'd do everything possible!" She had no idea what he'd said to Eleri, but it seemed the kind of thing a man like Bram would say.

He struggled to open his eyes. "I'm so tired, Dahlia." The words were so stark, so stripped of any artifice, that they shook her. "I want to go."

"Tough luck," she managed to get out past the lump in her throat. "You don't get to give up while Eleri is still dying." This time when she hauled on his shoulders, he helped her and managed to get onto his knees.

So, guilt worked to motivate Bram. Good to know.

Because Dahlia wasn't about to let him die in the forest. The way he'd said it—*I'd end it*—meant he had a conscious way to end his life. A poison pill? Or since he was Psy, maybe it was a psychic poison pill?

Not that it mattered.

Pulling one of his arms around her shoulders, she set her legs and *hauled*. He was heavy, but not as heavy as a changeling—Psy bones were built different—and Dahlia had always been strong. Which meant that with his help, she got him up. It sounded an involuntary grunt from her, but she wasn't here to look like a princess.

Getting him to the car took far too long, but she finally managed to belt him up in the passenger seat. She didn't even notice the grit of the road under her bare feet as she ran around to the driver's side and jumped in. "Stay awake, big guy, and program me into your vehicle."

He did so with voice commands, his voice clearer than before. "If I'm big guy, are you little woman?"

Dahlia shot him a glance that should've incinerated him on the spot except he was looking at her with that softness again that was doing really weird things to her. "Don't even try it."

Then she started driving hell-for-leather.

Chapter 43

I thought we deserved a lighter column after the events of the past months, a chance for all of us to catch our breaths . . . so let us dig into the topic of sex.

Yes. S.E.X.

I know, you're all yelling that, "Jaya, I had basic sex education in elementary school!" But I'm here to tell you that sexual reproduction as taught in Psy education under Silence, and *sex* as it pertains to the messy entangling of emotions in the post-Silence world are two wholly different things.

—*PsyNet Beacon* column by Jaya Laila Storm (medical empath and Social Interaction columnist) (2 January 2084)

THE WINDHAVEN HEALER got fluids and nutrients into Bram while he sat shirtless and unconcerned in a large infirmary armchair. "I'm going to hook you up so we can monitor—"

"Don't bother," Bram said, his eyes still on Dahlia, who was standing there wearing his misbuttoned shirt. She was all tumbled hair she'd somehow managed to get into a knot with nothing, kiss-bruised lips, bare feet, and long legs, and he could look at her to his last breath. "There's no coming back from what's happening."

"Don't say that," Dahlia ordered, a hot red flush on her cheekbones. "Eleri is Adam's *mate*."

He hadn't known that; now, the knowledge crushed the part of him that was still the boy so determined to protect his friends. All this time, Eleri could've had a life happy and extraordinary with a man who said her name like a benediction. "If I could do something to help her, I would," he said. "I want Adam to pluck a miracle out of the air, but in strict Psy terms, Eleri no longer has anything on which to build a shield—and soon I won't, either."

He was so susceptible to Dahlia that he'd allowed her to talk him into the vehicle, then bring him here. But it had been a mistake. His mind clear, he saw no way out . . . and he didn't want to die in a cold hospital room, or even this infirmary.

"So that's it?" She put her hands on her waist, a Valkyrie whose eyes were of a falcon wild. "You're just going to give up?"

"There's nothing I can do," he argued back. "If I could have donated my shield to Eleri, I would have." He'd been fighting for Eleri, Saffron, and Yúzé since the day he'd met them, but he'd failed and he'd take that failure with him into death. "At this point in time, we—every J about to hit Exposure—are all alone."

Dahlia scowled, but before she could snap back a retort, the healer interrupted. "Actually, there might be something you can do."

Bram forced himself to look away from the woman who crazed him. "I'd be happy to, whatever it is. As long as you"—he turned to face Dahlia—"promise you'll take me outside when it's my time to go. I want to die with the outside air on my skin."

A wildness in her eyes, Dahlia said, "Did you not hear me? You are *not* going to die. I refuse to live with the jokes afterward." She pointed a finger at him before turning to the healer. "What do you need him to do, Naia?"

"Act as a test subject. Saoirse's trying to create an artificial shield for Eleri. Probably go faster if she has a Psy with a similar brain on whom to test her theories."

Bram didn't say anything, unwilling to snuff out the hope on their faces, but he'd used his contacts to stay abreast of the Human Alliance's attempts to engineer a shield for their people. They had been trying for a long time—but humanity was still out there unshielded.

This Saoirse the healer had mentioned wasn't going to succeed in a day . . . which was all Bram had left—at the most generous estimate. But if it would make Dahlia happy for him to try, then he'd try. He owed her for bringing pleasure and softness into his life right when he'd believed he'd fall into the abyss with nothing but memories of evil as his companions.

TWO hours later, a woman of medium height, with skin of a deep brown that held coppery undertones, her curly hair twisted into a knot at the back of her neck, walked in with a box of items. Bram wondered if she was planning to run the no-doubt-necessary litany of blood and DNA tests right here . . . then she pulled out a literal tinfoil helmet.

Bram stared at it. He understood jokes, but given the tension in the room, it was obvious this wasn't one. Which left only desperation. "I'm sorry," he said bluntly, his patience dead at the thought of spending his last hours on something this idiotic. "But if that worked, the human prophets on street corners would be the most protected people on the planet."

The woman—Saoirse—glanced over at Dahlia, who'd changed into jeans and a T-shirt, to Bram's great disappointment. "He always this much of a smartass?"

"How should I know?" Dahlia scowled.

Shrugging, Saoirse said, "I mean, I'm no vulture or bear, but even I can smell you on him. And those look like talon marks on his shoulders, and oh gee"—a tone dryer than the desert—"that's either a hickey on your neck or you need immediate medical attention."

Dahlia shot the other woman the finger.

Apparently unbothered, Saoirse held up the ridiculous tinfoil creation. "This is not what it looks like."

Bram rubbed his face, suddenly understanding what humans meant when they said it was their dicks that had led them astray. "What is it, then?"

"A new alloy we're testing for jet heat shields," she said. "Flexible and extremely strong. Protects against radiation, so I figure why not try to see if it protects against Psy energy?"

"An external shield?" Bram looked up, interested despite himself. He'd never even considered a prosthetic of sorts—everything about the Psy came from the inside.

Saoirse's expression was grim. "It has to be external. Even if I had the best idea on the planet for an internal shield, there's no time. Adam's just taken off for the hospital—Dr. Czajka says Eleri's declining."

Bram's shoulder muscles locked. "Go, do your test." Already, the pressure of the people nearby was beginning to impact him. He couldn't hear anyone, but the murmur in the background was a constant.

Sooner or later, the murmurs would break through, crush his mind.

He wanted to be gone before then, did not intend to leave this world a raving lunatic. "Wait—do you know if Saffron and Yúzé are still at the hospital?"

"No, the doctor mentioned her friends left an hour prior to help another J, but told her they'd return the instant they'd pulled their colleague out of a high-risk situation."

That was what the Cartel had vowed once they'd all slipped into Sensitivity: that if there was a way to help a young J, a J who might make it, they had to take action.

Now, Bram said, "Good." Better that the two most fractured members of the Cartel didn't see Eleri die; they were going to be messed up enough as it was losing both Eleri and Bram at once.

"Dahlia says your shields are thin?" Saoirse's direct tone was that of a scientist. "I need a baseline—or you do—to judge the functionality of my attempts."

"There's pressure on my mind," Bram admitted. "Hundreds of murmurs, from the Canyon and around Raintree. I can't hear anyone, but if you put an unshielded human in this room with me, it won't be murmurs, it'll be words breaking through."

Dahlia sucked in a breath. "I'll take you outside," she said, her voice rough. "If it comes to that, I'll put you in the car and drive you out into the middle of the desert where the only other mind is mine."

Bram held her gaze, so dark and lovely. "Thank you." Then he turned to Saoirse. "If the murmurs cut out or fade, it's a success. If not, a failure. Trust me, I'll notice any fluctuation."

Nodding, she took the ridiculous helmet and placed it on his head, doing something to seal it around his skull. "So?"

"No change."

"Damn." With that single word, she removed the helmet and put it to one side before pulling out a square of an unknown material from the box. "I only had time to make one actual helmet, chose the material that seemed most apt to work, but I have samples of other materials. If I hold them against your skull, will you be able to tell if one works as a blocker?"

"I don't know," Bram said honestly. "But we can attempt it."

Seven samples later and the entire room was dispirited . . . and Dahlia had come to stand by him and run her fingers gently along his scalp, through the hair he kept buzzed military short. It had gone gray when he was only twenty-five, after two brutal reads in a row that involved a total of seventeen murdered and dismembered victims.

"I look that bad?" he asked her, his eyes closing under the pleasure of her touch.

He didn't even care that the ripple of sensation was destroying even more of his shields.

"Be quiet," she said, but her voice was soft, and she leaned down to whisper in his ear. "If Saoirse figures out a solution, then I owe you another round."

His skin prickled, a pumping beat in his blood. "It's a deal," he said, though he was all but certain he'd never get to collect. Still, it was a nice dream to have for the last minutes and hours he'd spend on this planet.

While Saoirse and Naia were talking at the other end of the room, near the box of supplies, he cupped the back of Dahlia's thigh with his palm and just drank her in. Another moment of lush softness with a woman unlike any he'd met in his life. "I could touch you forever."

She gave him a lopsided smile. "You're really good for my ego."

"Thanks, sweetheart," Saoirse said just then, after accepting a second box a teenage girl with curls the same shade as her own had just pushed over on a cart using one hand; her other arm, Bram realized, was strapped up with a highly effective and fast-acting compound designed to help bones knit together.

"Gen-seal?" he asked the healer after the teenager departed. "I noticed the slight glow to the cast."

Naia nodded. "I've found that using Gen-seal in conjunction with my own abilities ramps up the healing in our children by a significant margin. Doesn't work as well with adults, but with how many broken wings we handle in the fledglings, I'll take it."

"These," Saoirse said, having opened the box, "are samples of materials we rejected because they seem to serve no shielding purpose—but who knows with psychic powers? Let's just try."

It was only once she was close to him—and Dahlia had moved away so he could focus—that he saw the grief in her eyes, the way lines had formed around her lips. "Why do you care so much about Eleri?" he asked, wanting to understand why this stranger to him was fighting so hard to save part of his family.

"She saved my baby girl by giving herself to a monster," was the soft answer. "And Adam? He's my younger brother."

Bram understood. Saoirse had to try everything, even when the chance of success was less than zero. Bram would try with her; perhaps between them, they could save their siblings.

Chapter 44

I'm sending you this message so it'll be waiting when you wake up. Because you have to wake up. You're my sister, the one who always knows what to do. I need you. Please wake up.

—Message from Saffron Bianca to Eleri Dias (7 p.m. today)

Bram, why aren't you responding to your messages? We've almost finished handling the situation with Shiloh, but the two of us... we're not... doing okay with both you and Eleri MIA. You told me to always talk, always share my feelings. Please respond.

—Message from Yúzé Kanagawa to Bram Priest (7:15 p.m. today)

ADAM THRUST BOTH hands through his hair as he stood against the wall beside Eleri's hospital bed. One of the nurses had started up a huge comm screen on the other side of the room that displayed a peaceful forest scene accompanied by the sounds of nature: birdcalls, leaves rustling, a soft wind.

"The empaths recommend gentle stimulation to help keep wounded brains active," Dr. Czajka had said. "We may as well try it, though I think Eleri's down too deep to perceive it even with her subconscious."

Ironically, the sights and sounds were helping *Adam* maintain his composure. Naia had been keeping him updated on Saoirse's experiments with Bram—the man had managed to hold on to this point, but he'd started bleeding from the nose with the last batch of tests.

"He's in pain," Naia had told Adam. "Dahlia's already yelled at him twice for wanting to continue, but man's stubborn. There's a point at which this will become torture, but he's told Saoirse to keep going until she has nothing left to test. She's desperate—even tried lead."

She'd also told him of Dahlia's promise to drive Bram out into the peace of the desert, so he could die without the pressure of hundreds of voices in his head. "If that's going to happen," the healer had said, "it'll have to be within the next two hours. He's admitted that the voices are getting louder by the minute."

"Saoirse even tried the stone of the Canyon," Adam told Eleri, his shoulders in knots and his spine rigid. "Bayani managed to slice it out and the two of them put it on some kind of frame that they could place around Bram's head to see if the minerals within would stop telepathic noise."

It hadn't worked.

Adam hadn't expected it to—because while it blocked teleporters from getting into the Canyon, he knew Sascha and Hanz had used telepathy to communicate during Hanz's attempt to help Jacques. They'd been inside the Canyon at the time, the stone of it all around them.

"I wanted it to work even knowing it wouldn't." He walked over to stand beside Eleri's bed, take her hand in his. It was cold, and even thinner than usual. Rubbing it between his hands to warm her up, he was piercingly aware of the fragility of the blood bond, the way it had lost cohesion even compared to yesterday.

"Fight a little longer," he said, lifting her hand to his lips. "Give Saoirse and Bayani and their team a bit more time. Help the jet and rock nerds make history." It was a rough attempt at a joke that fell flat, because Dr. Czajka had been clear: Eleri's readings had been on a steady downgrade since she'd woken for that precious minute.

As if she'd used herself up to kiss him one last time.

Chest burning, he said, "I love you, my wild bird."

That was when his phone buzzed. It was Saoirse. "We're out of options, Adam." Tears in his sister's normally warm and confident voice. "We just tried and failed with our last idea. And Bram's done, will be leaving the Canyon as soon as he regains consciousness. He lost it two minutes ago, but Naia says he's not down deep, should wake on his own."

Adam swallowed hard. "You did everything you could. And tell Bram . . ." What did he say to a man who had spent his last hours on the planet fighting for the life of Adam's mate? It was a debt he could never repay. "Get Dahlia to call me when Bram wakes," he said. "I'll talk to him as they drive out."

Eleri's chosen brother deserved to say good-bye to Eleri if he wished, even if only through a comm. "Hey, Chirp?" he said quietly to his crying sister. "I love you. Go hug your fledglings and your mate. And thank you for trying so hard."

After they ended the call, he stroked nonexistent strands of Eleri's hair off her face just to touch her. "We don't say good-bye in Diné Bizaad," he told her, his voice grit and stone. "We say *hágoónee*, and inherent in it is the promise of another meeting." Bending down, he touched his lips gently to hers. "So I will say *hágoónee*, Eleri. Only that. Never good-bye."

Ripples of white and blue light across her blanket.

When he looked up, he saw that the comm had switched over to an image of another part of the forest, this one centered around a tumbling stream, complete with the sound of water falling over rock.

It's so quiet here, Adam.

He exhaled at the kiss of memory connected to their one magical day together. The stories they'd shared, the love they'd—

It's so quiet here, Adam.

He frowned, because it *hadn't* been quiet in that cave. The sound of rushing water had been a deep thunder. Not a constant thunder, either, one that became white noise. No, it had altered in pitch and tone as the water made its way along its ancient channels and carved new ones.

He hadn't even noticed that day—not after the bats decided to swarm.

My father's father used to say that our clan lands were blessed with the quietest places, that we were renowned for it until many came here to bathe in the silence . . .

His heart raced at the echo of his grandmother's words, his mouth dry.

There were endless peaceful places on the planet, from the ice fields of Alaska to the beaches of isolated Pacific islands, to the jungles of the Amazon. Why would people travel specially to a striking but not in any way exotic location like Arizona to experience that?

But his grandmother hadn't said the most peaceful. She'd specifically said the *quietest*.

Eleri had used the same word.

Quiet.

Aria's grandfather had lived in a time before Silence, a time when the Psy had mingled with humans and changelings on an everyday basis. A time where a *quiet* location could mean two very different things.

Eleri's body jerked at that same instant, her eyes flying open. Blood bloomed across the whites of her eyes almost at once, her breath shallow and rapid and her pulse a race car under his grip.

"Go under!" he ordered. "Go under, Eleri, so you don't give yourself a stroke!"

But it was too late. Her body spasmed in an unstoppable seizure, the readings on the monitors going haywire before she went limp. And he knew. He'd felt the wrench on the blood bond, had barely managed to hold on to it.

There were no more weapons left in her arsenal—or his.

Dr. Czajka rushed in, deep bluish shadows under her eyes and her scrubs wrinkled. He stepped back to let her and her staff work, but the doctor dismissed everyone else after two minutes, then faced him. "If she wakes again, she'll die in excruciating pain. Her official next of kin is Bram Priest—he'll—"

"He's in the same state as Eleri," Adam said, his mind set. "He made it clear he didn't wish to die in our infirmary. I don't think Eleri would want to die in a hospital, either. Is she stable enough for me to take her home to the Canyon?"

"Yes," the doctor said, and began to unhook Eleri from the monitoring systems. "You'll need sign-off from Sophia Russo—she's the secondary next of kin for all Js. And you have to make sure Eleri doesn't wake again." A hard look. "Allow her to go in peace."

"Is there a risk she could wake on the way?" If there was, Adam couldn't do what he'd planned—because he would never, ever permit Eleri to die screaming in agony, her mind crushed under a million voices.

"No, that last waking knocked her out. You have at least two hours."

Adam made a call.

SOPHIA didn't argue with him. "Yes, take her to your Canyon," she said, her eyes hollow. "To the place where she found happiness."

Max offered to fly him, having become a fully qualified pilot after joining Nikita's team, but Adam saw the worry in his gaze. "No," he said quietly to the other man when Sophia went to say good-bye to Eleri. "The commercial pilot I used last time should be landing at the hospital within the next ten minutes. You don't want to leave Sophia and you shouldn't. She's too pregnant and under too much stress."

If the Js had an alpha, it was Sophia Russo, and she was bleeding inwardly at the pain of her people. "You'll need to tell her about Bram, too." He laid out the facts in a quick summary.

Max muttered a harsh expletive. "I wish I could protect her from this."

Understanding the other man far too well, Adam said, "Saffron and Yúzé, they're the other part of their quartet." The other part of Eleri's family.

"We'll locate them," Max promised before Adam could ask. "Make sure they get warning of Eleri and Bram's status."

Having done what he could for the two Js he'd never met but who were important to Eleri, Adam walked into the room after Sophia drew back, then just picked Eleri up in his arms. "Faster than a gurney," he told Sophia. "And she's so light . . . too light."

Face pinched, Sophia nodded and came over to tuck the blanket neatly around Eleri so it wouldn't trail on the floor as Adam carried her cradled against his chest.

I love how your chest feels against my chest. The heat and weight of you on me.

Words she'd spoken to him after they'd shared intimate skin privileges the night she'd spent in his bed, her fingers tracing the lines of his tattoo with tender grace. He'd told her about the meaning behind the tattoo, felt her breath on his skin. "That's so beautiful, Adam. You wear memory in your skin."

Later, she'd said, "All I feel with you . . . it's more than I could've ever dreamed."

Just wait, he wanted to tell her today. *Just wait until the next time we're together, now that your numbness is gone.*

He walked out to the image of Sophia pressing her lips together as she fought not to cry, her body leaning into Max's as the other man tucked her close to his side. He knew that despite their own pain, the couple would do what was necessary to protect the remaining two members of the small family Eleri had called her own.

And Adam . . . Adam was going to throw the dice one final time before he let his wild bird fly free.

The jet-chopper was ready and waiting, and he made sure Eleri was securely strapped into the seat in the back next to him before he made another call. "Dahlia, listen," he said when his wing-second answered.

BRAM woke to the sense of his mind buzzing, the pressure atop it a boulder. If he was going to get to the desert, it had to be now. But— "Is there anything else?" he asked Saoirse, who was yet in the room with him, must've waited for him to regain consciousness.

Face drawn, the scientist shook her head. "No, that's it. We're out of options."

It was a knife through his gut, but his guilt at his failure was mingled with a sense of peace. He'd done all he could, could let go now.

"Then tell Dahlia I'm ready." He could hear her nearby, her voice urgent as she had a conversation. He waited for her to walk in, tell him that Eleri was gone, one more J life snuffed out in an endless line of candles no one had ever bothered to cup their hands around, protect.

But when she walked inside, her face was ablaze. "We need to get him to the cave system below the Canyon," she said to Naia. "I need one of your hover wheelchairs."

"I can walk," Bram said, though he wasn't too sure. It wasn't that he'd lost his strength but that parts of his brain had started to malfunction. His fingers were spasming every so often, and he could feel his thigh tensing up even as he stood.

Dahlia hovered nearby, as if she'd catch him.

But Bram got upright without a problem, and when she thrust a bottle of nutrients at him, he drank it. "Why are we going to these caves? Do you park the vehicles there?"

"Adam said he'd meet us there with Eleri," was her nonanswer, but then she touched his cheek with her hand. "The stars are like diamonds outside. An endless sky."

He hadn't even known night had fallen, but to die under the banner of the open sky and be able to say good-bye to Eleri? It was a better outcome than he'd expected. "Good, that's good." Drink finished, he left the bottle on his abandoned seat, then began to walk with Dahlia at his side.

She slipped an arm around his waist within two steps, and he said to hell with it and put his own arm around her shoulders. He probably could've made it without her, but to have her softness so close one more time? No, he wouldn't reject that.

His pace was slow regardless, but she didn't rush him. Probably didn't need to—even in a jet-chopper, it'd take Adam time to get here. Time enough for him to take one last walk with Dahlia.

The heat from her arm burned through the navy sweatshirt she'd brought him from Adam's closet. "You two are about the same size," she'd said. "He won't mind."

Because changelings were all about the group, all about community. "I need to call Saffy and Yúzé before . . ." He couldn't just leave them without a word. "We aren't a clan, but we're family."

"You can call them as soon as we reach the entrance to the cave system," Dahlia promised. "I just don't want to be late. You're not exactly sprinting right now."

He felt his lips curve. "Nice bedside manner."

That got him a sniff of apparent annoyance but she still had her arm around him, and when his leg spasmed, she braced him against her side. "Good thing I'm a big woman," she muttered.

"You're the perfect size. Endless curves and valleys."

Her cheeks glowed, her arm squeezing him as they began to walk again. "The way you look at me, Mr. J, I could almost believe myself beautiful."

Bram didn't get it. "You are."

"I'm the first woman you've had sex with," she said, her tone dry as they exited out into the cool desert night. "Of course I'm beautiful."

He drew in the air like an elixir, the stars an endless horizon over the breathtaking ripples of the canyons and desert of this region—but not more enticing than her. "I wasn't a virgin when we had sex."

It was her turn to stumble, then stare at him. "What? I thought hanky-panky was illegal under Silence."

He shrugged. "I stopped caring about a lot of things during the last few years." Bram had known the Council didn't give a shit about them, so what the fuck did he care about following their rules? "I just made sure I wasn't caught."

"Oh." They began to descend the path lined with scrubby grass on either side where it wasn't bordered by large pieces of broken stone. "So, you've been with other women? No, forget I asked that. We're both grown people and it's none of my business."

"Five women," he said. "Per non-Psy media, sexual contact was meant to be incredibly pleasurable and I wanted to feel pleasure. I chose an accredited professional for the first time, with the view that one of us should know what we were doing. The other four, I walked into a bar and found a woman who wanted to participate in sex."

Dahlia snorted. "Not that you're bragging," she said, but he could hear a smile in her voice.

"I'm not. It's just what happened." He thought back. "The women all had a pleasing appearance per the norms of society, and seemed enthusiastic, but I felt . . . mechanical. There was release but no pleasure. I could find release myself should I have the need. I decided five was enough for the experiment."

Dahlia laughed. "Ah, oh to be me, lucky number six."

"You pleasure me simply by existing." Turning his face, he nuzzled her neck just because she was there and didn't seem to mind his touch. "I was drunk on you the first time we met. The sex . . . it was beyond pleasure."

"Skin privileges," she corrected huskily. "Not sex. Intimate skin privileges."

"Yes, touching you was the greatest privilege of my life."

Dahlia's breath caught. "You're one hell of a charmer, I'll give you that."

Bram had never been called charming in his life, but he'd take it from her. As he'd take this strange walk in the night, the stars a carpet out in front of them that vanished beneath the edge of the Canyon the lower they got.

He heard the sound of the jet-chopper before he saw it as a shadow against the night, its lights the only thing that delineated it against the black. The pilot brought it to a perfect landing down on a flat section Bram could just see. Someone got out, reached inside . . . emerged with another person in their arms.

Eleri.

His brain finally processed what Dahlia had said about the *entrance* to the cave system. "Dahlia, you promised me the desert."

She looked up, her eyes shining with what he could almost think were tears. "I'll take you. I had a clanmate park a vehicle next to where that chopper just landed. But please let us try this first. One last tinfoil hat?"

Bram realized then and there that he'd do anything for her. "If I get to spend my last minutes with you, then it's a fair bargain."

Rising on tiptoe, she pulled down his head and kissed him until he couldn't breathe. "Oh and, big guy—there are going to be bats. They're friendly."

Bram had never known how to laugh, but that moment, he felt his lips curve, the laugh form in his chest. And as the stars spun overhead, the Milky Way vivid against the desert sky, he laughed with the most beautiful woman in all the universe.

Chapter 45

The quiet places in the world are the rarest gems, to be treasured and well guarded. I have been most fortunate to have stumbled upon not one but two such gems in my lifetime—but alas, their direction I will not share here, for to do so would be to extinguish the quiet.

—Fragment from *Memoirs of a Life* by Arici Carvalli (1894)
(out of print and unavailable online)

ELERI'S BREATHING WAS getting shallower with each step Adam took, the blood bond feeling as if it was cutting in and out. He fought the urge to run. He was sure-footed, but a single stumble and he could send Eleri plummeting to the earth, wounding her already fragile body.

Instead, he tucked her even closer to his chest and walked with intent.

He saw Dahlia long before he reached her and saw, too, how Bram was leaning his body against hers. The man's eyes were bloodshot as fine blood vessels broke under the pressure on his brain. "Follow me," he said, and ducked into the entrance.

Then he let his instincts lead him, and though he could've outpaced Bram, he didn't. The other man had fought his need to die in peace to help Eleri, and Eleri wouldn't forgive Adam if he left her brother behind.

But his jawbones were grinding together from the strain of it as they walked through passageway after passageway.

Bram's breathing was becoming labored, Dahlia's murmurs of encouragement holding an edge of panic. "Adam, how much longer?"

"Less than five minutes."

They somehow managed to get down the final slope, with Adam having to place Eleri down at the other end, then come back up to help Dahlia navigate it with Bram. Picking Eleri up again the instant they were in the wider passageway, he rapidly counted off fifty steps. . . . and there it was, the breathtaking cave with a bioluminescent glow he'd named Mirage.

Walking inside with Eleri, he ignored the sound of the underground river, ignored the stirring of the bats who were annoyed by the intrusion, and watched Bram's face with agonizing focus as the other man walked in.

The J-Psy was murmuring to Dahlia as they came in and didn't stop, his expression unchanging as he walked further inside.

Adam's stomach dropped.

Just as Bram's head jerked up and he said, "Fuck, it's so *quiet* here."

ELERI woke to the awareness that she was in Adam's arms. There was no question about it. She knew these arms, knew the body that cradled hers against it . . . and knew the triangle of stone she could see with its moss that glowed a luminous unearthly green.

Stirring, she spread her hand over the beat of Adam's heart. "Adam." It came out husky, almost a non-sound, but he heard.

He crushed her close, buried his face in her hair, and cried. Silent sobs that shook his big frame and made her desperate to hold him. But she could barely move in his embrace, so she just kept murmuring his name, telling him she was all right, and stroking his chest where she could reach.

It *hurt* her to feel him cry.

No more numbness. No more walls. Every emotion as searing as lightning.

"Please, Adam." She managed to turn her head enough to brush her lips against his jaw.

And tasted salt.

"I thought I lost you." He pressed a kiss to her lips, his fingers gripping her jaw in that way he had that made her feel so anchored, so wanted. "You were almost gone."

This time when he buried his face in her hair, she was able to twist around and wrap her arms around him, and the two of them stayed that way for a long time before she became aware of deep breathing elsewhere in the cave. "Who's here with us?"

"Bram and Dahlia. He crashed soon after he got in here." Stroking her hair, he pressed a kiss to her temple. "Dahlia's tucked against him. He asked her not to go, and she just lay down on the mattress I had the clan bring down here. Never thought I'd see our Dahlia do anything for a lover again."

That was when Eleri became aware that they weren't on the ground, either. And she couldn't see much of the cave, just that small triangle . . . that was the opening of a tent, she realized.

They were inside it.

Adam was seated against a couple of large pillows braced against the canvas back wall of the tent—which seemed to have stone beyond it, their bodies on a thick mattress complete with a sheet. A plush blanket lay over her as another did no doubt over Bram and Dahlia.

Bram and Dahlia?

"When did that happen?" she whispered. "*How* did that happen?"

"She blames us," Adam said, a smile in his voice for the first time. "Says it's our fault she ended up meeting the big Psy lunk and now she has to act as his teddy bear so he can sleep."

Eleri couldn't imagine Bram needing anyone, but fascinated as she was at this most unexpected turn in her friend's life, she was more interested in why they were in a cave . . . that was home to bats.

Her brain came back online in full glory. "Are we in a tent in the cave with the bats?"

"Yep. I know how much you love bats."

"Adam, why—" Her eyes widened, her breath rushing out of her. "It's *quiet* here." So, so quiet. Not a single mind pressing down against her own. She couldn't even feel Adam's or Dahlia's psychic presence, as if the quietness had given her back her ability to ignore the shielded minds of changelings.

Adam shuddered as he exhaled. "I almost forgot what you said that day. I was almost too late."

Eleri shook her head even as she luxuriated in the quiet, in the absolute absence of mental pressure. "I didn't even really process it that day, not with how the bats chased us out right as I felt it—and I was focused on how I just wanted to be with you again."

She took a deep breath . . . and wrinkled her nose. "I'm glad neither of us has an intense sense of smell."

A chuckle. "Poor Dahlia does. Yet she's tucked up with Bram."

"And he's sleeping? Without medical assistance?"

"Far as I know. Out like a light—Naia confirmed he's asleep, not unconscious."

Heart beginning to kick as she realized what this could mean, she said, "Why is it quiet?"

"I don't know, but Saoirse and her crew, along with Naia, are running every test under the sun there is to run." Lifting his hand, he brushed his knuckles over her cheek.

Sensation rolled through her in an intoxicating wave.

She wanted to close her eyes, sink into the feeling, but the way Adam was looking at her, she knew he needed her to be present. "You've bought us endless time." While she didn't want to live like a mole, she could manage it for a period if it was the only option. "With me and Bram as test subjects, your sister has a real chance to figure out an answer."

Furrows between his eyebrows. "She's feeling out of her depth." Then, as she listened, he told her about a scientist named Ashaya Aleine and her failed quest to build an artificial shield for humans. "Humans and Psy aren't the same in psychic terms, but I figure the energy is the same—Psy emit it, humans are vulnerable to it."

No one had ever talked to Eleri of psychic energy in such terms, but she saw his logic. "Any shield technology should be cross-compatible."

"That's what I think," Adam said. "While Naia was checking you were okay physically, I stepped out to get a signal, made some calls. Friend of mine in SnowDancer says Kaleb Krychek's also sponsored a group of scientists to find a solution to the problem of human shields."

"Krychek?" Of all the people in the world who she might think of as choosing to do good for the sake of it, the former Councilor and current member of the Ruling Coalition wasn't one. Though . . . "He's stopped breach after breach in the PsyNet, literally kept it from collapsing. He doesn't have to do that, is powerful enough to protect his own section and leave the rest to rot."

"Judd—my SnowDancer contact—calls Krychek a friend, and Judd's got a moral compass I trust. And wasn't it Krychek who dismantled Silence?"

"Not on his own, but yes," Eleri acknowledged.

Adam ran his hand down her arm, over the top of the blanket, and the weight and warmth of it made her entire body glow. "I'm sure the Human Alliance is probably working on a shield project of their own."

Safe and content, her mind more at peace than it had been in years, Eleri struggled to follow the thread of the conversation instead of just cuddling up to Adam and sinking into him. "Are you considering whether to invite others in to help Saoirse?"

"Saoirse thinks we need a Psy medical specialist, but the general consensus seems to be that it's better if the various parties work alone, to stop them all ending up at the same dead end. But we have a unique starting point now, one to which no one else has access."

Eleri put her hand on his raised knee, frowned. "How about parallel tracks? Bring in an M you trust, give them access, then they work on a possible solution while Saoirse continues on her own path?"

"It has to be Ashaya. We have an alliance with DarkRiver, a friendship beyond that. She won't breathe a word of this discovery to anyone else." He squeezed her close. "I'll step out to make the call soon. I just need to hold you awhile longer."

Eleri snuggled in. "Adam, I can feel *everything*." Just like at the hospital, but without the anguish of a crushing mental pressure that made contact a grasping, rushed thing.

She pressed a kiss to his throat, shivered.

His nostrils flared, his pupils huge against his irises when their gazes met. "First," he said, "we need to get some energy into you."

Able to sense her own weakness, Eleri drank the concentrated nutrient drink he handed her, then washed it down with a few gulps of water. "No." She waved off the other items he was picking out from the cooler to one side of the tent. "I'm really full."

He put the food back without argument. "Naia told me to allow you to control your food intake, that it'll take you a while to get back to normal."

Eleri didn't want to tell him this *was* her normal, but she couldn't lie to him anymore, not even by omission. So she admitted how food had stopped holding any significance for her long ago, that she'd eaten only to function.

Adam pressed a kiss to her palm. "That just means I get to play bear with you and bring you treat after treat to see what you like best. Or I could drop them into your hands from the sky—that's more the falcon way."

That single kiss made her shiver.

Tugging her closer, then manhandling her—with her enthusiastic consent—until she sat on his thighs, her legs on either side of his body while he held her hips, he leaned in to press a kiss directly over the pulse in her neck.

Eleri sucked in a sharp breath, her thighs clenching around him.

"Shh." A nuzzle of her neck. "Dahlia and Bram are sleeping."

Sinking her teeth into her lower lip, Eleri whispered, "Can I touch you first? I don't know if I can manage silence if you touch me." The sensations were amplified a hundred times beyond anything she'd felt even when he'd been inside her, and her inner muscles spasmed with needy greed when she dared imagine what it might be like now.

Adam's lips curved, a laziness to it that was somehow sexual in a way she didn't understand. "I can't wait to make you scream." A rough whisper.

Lifting her hand to his chest, he placed it against a button in silent permission.

"I saw a woman screaming in orgasm in a memory once," she told him as she slipped the small disk out of its hole to reveal the barest sliver of skin. "It wasn't a bad read, that one. One of my starter reads—a case of a regular threesome where one of the two males got jealous and punched the other one in the testicles right after he brought the woman partner to orgasm."

Adam winced. "I didn't think Justice did reads for penny-ante stuff."

"It's just luck if your case hits when an apprentice-level J is doing reads as part of their studies." She hadn't known it then, but those had been the best days of her life when it came to her work as a J. "Because the supposed assault took place during sex, the read included the section with the orgasm."

Still young at the time, with her emotions locked down well enough to pass for Silent, she'd just filed it away. "After the numbness, I found myself wondering how she could feel such pleasure as to scream."

She ran her finger down the strip of skin she'd bared on Adam's chest. The contact made her stomach tumble, her thighs clench again. Pushing the sides of his shirt apart as her pulse speeded up, she said, "I don't wonder anymore."

Adam groaned and leaned up to speak against her ear. "How wet are you?"

Breath short and jagged, she squeezed inner muscles that quivered with need. "Drenched."

His hands clenched on her lower curves, his mouth at her throat again.

Barely holding back the whimpers that escaped her, she pushed him back. But he paused before his back met the canvas against the wall. "I want inside you." A raw statement. "It's fucking primitive, this need I have to claim you, mark you, but I don't care."

Eleri's mind hazed. "Adam, I won't be able to be quiet," she said, moving her body on his thighs because she couldn't stop herself.

"Scream into my mouth," he said, before tilting her gently onto her back on the mattress.

Coming over her in a prowl that made her feel deliciously overwhelmed, his hair falling around his face and those wild falcon eyes glinting at her, he said, "Can I put my cock inside you, Eleri?"

Eleri's entire body clenched. She hadn't known that *words* could pump pleasure through her. Reaching down between them, she began to push down the elasticized pants she was wearing.

She pushed her underwear down with the pants.

"I can't go further," she whispered when she reached the limit of how far her arms would reach.

That feral smile. "Let me help you." He moved with lazy grace to tug her pants and underwear off and put them to one side, then pushed her thighs apart and just looked at her.

She was already on the verge when he said, "My mouth is watering."

Whimpering, she shoved a fist into her mouth to stifle the sound as her body arched up. She shook her head violently at him when he glanced at her. If he did what he was craving, she'd scream down this entire cave. She was barely able to bear the level of sensation now, from the soft rasp of the cotton of her sweatshirt against her nipples to the heat of his body lapping against her.

"I'll save that treat for later," Adam said, and began to undo his jeans.

Eleri couldn't look, stared up at the canvas. But she heard it when he put his jeans aside. Glancing at him, she said, "Not the shirt," when he would've shrugged that off, too. "I can't handle that much contact all at once."

She wasn't even sure she was going to survive the intimacy of his body sheathed in hers. She'd felt it when she was numb. How much more would she feel now?

A whimper threatened to escape.

"We'll work up to it," Adam said with a slow smile as he came over her again and leaned down to brush his lips across hers. It was the merest hint of a kiss, yet it made her breasts ache and liquid pool in her core as need clawed at her.

"I'm ready," she gasped.

Gripping one hip, he settled between her thighs, his hair-roughened skin pushing against the delicate skin of her inner thighs.

Eleri's mind overloaded.

At any other time, she'd have struggled against it.

Not today.

She just went with the overload, letting it drown her in erotic heat. But there was no way she was going to hold her quiet, so she hauled him down and pressed her lips to his, sealing them together as he began to push the thickness of himself into her.

Eleri began orgasming at first contact, her body primed and oversensitized and oh so willing. He trapped her scream in his mouth, her body as trapped under his as he brought his weight down on her—as if he knew exactly what she needed, that this sense of confinement wasn't confinement at all but a weight that kept her in one piece when she would've flown apart.

Holding on to him as her mind hazed and blurred and breathing became difficult, Eleri transformed into a creature of pure pleasure.

Chapter 46

We've implemented your suggested solution and slowed the degradation—but we can't stop it.

—Human Alliance Medical Team to Amara and Ashaya Aleine
(12 December 2082)

ASHAYA HAD LIVED with a quiet guilt ever since the chip she'd helped develop in an effort to create shields for the human mind had failed. Bowen Knight, the security chief and effective leader of the Human Alliance, had told her it wasn't her fault, that they'd rushed the implantation—but tests afterward had proved the chip would've failed regardless.

Now, as she walked into the cool depths of the cave network underneath the home of the falcons, her mate an edgy presence behind her and Saoirse Garrett in front, she clung to hope. What Saoirse had told her thus far had blown all her previous ideas out of the water.

A solution from the *outside*?

Neither Ashaya nor her twin had ever considered that. She was an M, a DNA specialist. Of course her mind had jumped to an internal solution. That the falcons had thought to go outside was a spectacular case of unconventional thinking—in truth, she wasn't even sure she could assist them, but she was going to do everything in her power to try.

"Here," Saoirse said. "Only the four of them inside right now."

No matter her assurance, Dorian slipped around Ashaya and Saoirse to enter the cave first before poking his head out to nod that it was safe. "Bats hanging off the ceiling," he muttered, the luminescence from the walls turning his white-blond hair a pale green. "Great."

Her leopard mate was not doing well being confined underground, but she hadn't even questioned that he'd come with her. Dorian would never allow her to walk into what might be a dangerous situation alone.

"You're my Shaya," he'd murmured late the previous night, then nipped at her ear in feline affection as he grinned. "My dangerous, intelligent, hot scientist. I'd let you experiment on me anytime."

Buoyed by the memory of his laughter and her own, she entered the cave to find Adam and Dahlia, whom she'd met previously, standing in the center of the room talking quietly, while two tents sat on opposite sides of the huge cavern.

"Eleri and Bram fell back asleep," Adam said when she reached them. "Their minds are still recovering."

"I can't even imagine what they've been through." The idea of lowering her shields to test the cave's protective nature went against her instincts—and those two had been stripped of the choice.

She exhaled. "First, the test."

Dorian's presence against her back, his hand on her hip in a silent reminder that she was his mate, part of a pack that had her back. And there, in the corner of her mind, burned Amara's star.

Her twin. A genius intellect. Total lack of a moral compass.

Not quite so broken these days, but still . . . damaged enough that she would never be safe to walk the world alone.

It was just as well that she had no wish to be apart from Ashaya.

Clutching at the mate bond for comfort today, Ashaya dropped her telepathic shields in a way she couldn't ever remember doing consciously.

Her body tensed as she waited for the expected noise of the world to hit her.

Nothing. Quiet. No, wait, there, the vague awareness of two unshielded Psy minds . . . but no onrush of thoughts, no overwhelm.

Ashaya opened her eyes, her mouth dry and heart thudding. "An outside shield," she said in wonder, hope alive in her heart.

Chapter 47

Adam, we've got a severe problem.

—Sophia Russo to Adam Garrett (today)

THE NEXT TIME Eleri woke, she was alone in the tent but could hear low murmurs outside that told her there were others in the cave. As she rose, her eye caught on a piece of paper taped to the inside of one of the tent's "doors."

She smiled and reached out to grab it.

The note was in a strong, sure hand full of generous loops. As generous as Adam's heart.

2:30 p.m.: Jacques just woke up. Apparently in one hell of a bad mood and out for Hendricks's blood. Naia says he's definitely all there. I'm heading up to hug the shit out of him—I'll stay upside until I've cleared clan business that's built up, but there'll be a runner posted outside Mirage throughout to run messages back and forth.

Phone signal doesn't get through.

Eat the food I left you or I'll put you in my lap and feed you bites like I do Ollie. I'll see you as soon as I can. Gotta do a flight with the fledglings, too. They've been missing our usual sky runs. —Love, Adam

Eleri ran her fingers over his name, over the word "love". He had such a heart, Adam. And he wasn't scared to display it. Wasn't scared to say that he was planning to hug his friend, or that Eleri's health mattered to him.

"Love, Eleri," she said, sounding out how it would be if she signed off her notes the same.

Smiling at the thought of writing just that soon, she put the note aside and, after pulling on the sneakers someone had sourced for her foot size, decided to head out and see what the clan had done about sanitary facilities. There had to be something—they were too smart not to have thought of it.

Saoirse was crouched down, a handheld sensor pressed to the wall closest to the entrance, but turned at Eleri's exit. Waving, her smile huge, she pointed to the back of the cave and the tall black box that had appeared there.

The sound of rushing water got louder the closer she got to it.

When Eleri opened the door to the box, it proved deeper than it looked and contained a compact but complete self-contained sanitary unit, including a radiant "shower" that most people eschewed but that came in useful in exactly these types of conditions. She'd heard they were popular with archaeologists and others who went to remote areas.

Eleri decided to take advantage of it after she'd used the other facilities, and went back to the tent to grab a set of fresh clothes she'd seen inside. Once back in the unit, she stripped, then stood in the center of the narrow stall—it'd be a tight fit for Bram—and switched on the shower. Light scythed out, warm but not hot, and while she knew it was divesting her of dirt, she'd much rather have stood under falling water.

Even Psy had never managed to convert to these.

The cycle complete, she dressed, then took her dirty clothes back with her to place in a laundry bag that had been left with the clean clothes. Feeling more herself, despite the fact that she wasn't wearing a suit but stretchy pants of black and a soft gray sweatshirt, her hair loose around her shoulders, she drank a full bottle of nutrients before wandering over to Saoirse.

"It's good to see you up and awake." Adam's sister rose to her feet, her face aglow.

"Thank you for what you're doing." Eleri didn't know the purpose of the device in Saoirse's hand, but she could see the bags under the other woman's eyes, the tension in her jaw.

Saoirse shook her head. "We're family," she chided. "Speaking of which, go talk to our runner. She's been asking every five minutes if you're awake."

Heart aching in a way complex and new to her, Eleri walked toward the doorway—but Malia appeared there before she could reach it. "I knew I heard talking!" Her body hit Eleri's with force as she wrapped her good arm tight around Eleri, her other one trapped in between their bodies.

Her own throat thick with emotions she'd forgotten she'd once felt, Eleri held the girl as tightly. All she could remember of their time in Hendricks's bunker was pushing at a sobbing Malia to run.

"Uncle Adam let me see him, the man who hurt us," Malia said, speaking in the embrace, her head tucked against Eleri's shoulder in the way of a fledgling taking comfort. "Mom and Dad weren't sure I should, but I got Naia and Uncle Adam to back me up. I really, *really* liked seeing him locked up. Felt much better afterward."

As Malia drew back, Eleri had the thought that this child was very definitely a raptor. What worked to heal her might not work on a human or Psy, and that was fine, because Malia wasn't human or Psy. "I'm surprised you didn't offer to claw out his eyes," Eleri said. "I would turn his brains to liquid if I could." Exactly as he'd done to his victims.

Malia's hand flew to her mouth, but her eyes were sparkling. "I *did*," she whispered after lowering that hand. "Make the offer. Uncle Adam said no—he thinks I'd be traumatized by it, but nope." A scowl. "I don't know why the bigs worry so much."

Saoirse, who'd just walked over, hugged her daughter to her side. "Because you're a piece of all our hearts, little bird."

Malia dropped her head against her mother, a child again rather than a raptor bent on vengeance. "I guess it's allowed, then," she said in a begrudging fashion.

Saoirse kissed her daughter's temple. "Time for you to work. I need you to take this data chip up, and return with the team's analysis of the last set I sent."

Eleri watched as Malia tucked the chip securely inside the small bag slung sideways across her body. "Gotta fly," the teen said and was gone.

"Have you eaten?" Saoirse asked in the aftermath of her whirlwind of a child. "Adam left me with strict instructions—not that he needed to give them. I'm a big sister." A stern but loving tone unlike any Eleri had ever before had directed at her. "I'm fully capable of bullying you into good nourishment."

"I drank nutrients," Eleri said, a touch intimidated . . . but oddly happy about it.

Care.

This was care, was family in a way she, Bram, Saffron, and Yúzé had been before their work had eroded away their beings. She'd already asked Adam to bring the missing members of the Cartel here, conscious how much the two needed her and Bram, and her falcon had promised her he would.

"I promise I'll eat a bar in a short while," she told Saoirse. "I feel hungry, but I don't think my stomach's ready for a full load at once."

Saoirse jerked her head toward the other tent. "Do we need to bully him, too? He's big, but I have Dahlia on speed dial."

Intrigued all over again at Bram's apparent total susceptibility to Adam's wing-second, Eleri shook her head. "No, Bram's always on me to feed myself properly."

Bram believed that nourishment was strength—he'd had no way to understand how hard it was to drink and eat even plain nutrients when there was *no* feedback, not even the dulled one of the tasteless items. "Was it Malia you were talking to before? I heard conversation when I woke."

"No." Saoirse indicated for her to follow as she went back to take more readings. "That was Ashaya Aleine—she was just leaving to head back up. Adam placed markers along the best access route this morning, so we can move without guides." She unfolded a camping chair. "Sit and I'll tell you all the news."

"Actually, I think I'll stand for a while, stretch." Her body, for all its thinness, had always been fit and fast. She'd kept it in peak form for a hunter and she wanted to get back to that . . . but with a few more curves. She liked how Adam's hands felt on her, wanted more skin surface to experience it.

"I get you." Saoirse frowned and adjusted her scanner before taking another reading. "It's hard enough for me being down here—the bats might like it, but there's no real space for my falcon to stretch out her wings unless I want to go in circles."

A shake of the head. "Malia's annoyed at not being able to try it out, but talked one of the other runners into doing it—he didn't need much encouragement, to be fair. I thought he'd cause a bat stampede, but our upside-down friends seem to have decided to ignore all of us for the time being."

"Malia's not scared at being in an enclosed space?" Eleri asked, thinking of Hendricks's bunker.

"No, I was worried about that, but she seems to barely remember it. She was drugged most of the time so the memories are fuzzy, then you were there, so she didn't get scared alone." A teary smile. "Thank you for being there for my baby, Eleri. I'll never forget it."

"She helped me, too. I fought harder because of her—and she ran to get help with a broken arm while a predator was nearby. That took incredible courage."

"I'll tell her you said that. She'll be proud."

Then, while Eleri went through a slow routine designed to stretch stiff muscles, Saoirse brought her up to speed on the parallel scientific approaches being taken on Project El-Shield.

The two leads—Ashaya and Saoirse—were talking to each other about cave discoveries but were being scrupulous in not discussing what they believed each discovery to mean.

A stir in the other tent, Bram stepping out not long afterward. One side of his face bore deep sleep creases. After raising a hand in greeting, he stumbled off toward the black box.

"Bram woke before?" Eleri asked.

A nod. "He was in better shape than you—never got to total shield failure, though he was within a hairbreadth." A glance over at Bram's tent. "You should talk to him. Adam got some news this morning—you were still asleep, but Bram was up."

Eleri's stomach twisted at the innocuous statement. She knew something was wrong well before a freshly showered Bram nudged his head for her to join him in his tent.

"Which one?" she asked the instant she was seated. "Saffy or Yúzé? Are they alive?"

Bram rubbed both hands over his face as he sat with his knees raised, arms braced over them. "Yes—and on their way here, but in bad condition."

Cold in her veins. "How? Adam told me that Sophie and Max were going to handle that."

"They did, and brought in empathic help afterward. It wasn't enough. You were gone from the PsyNet and my mind went into lockdown. They're more fragile than even I realized. Saffy had a full-on psychotic break in the midst of working with an E, which triggered Yúzé."

Panic studded Eleri's chest; she'd known the two were the most vulnerable members of the Cartel but had hoped the safety net Adam had put in place would protect them. "Where were they taken?"

"Psych department of the same J unit you were in—Sophia made sure of that. But no one can get Saffron to calm down, while Yúzé's fallen into near-catatonia."

"We can get through to them," Eleri said, because she had to believe the breaks in their minds weren't final. "Soon as they arrive, we're all over them." Touch mattered. Hugs mattered. Smiles mattered.

Bram gave her an assessing look. "I didn't think Adam would want two psychotic Psy so close to his clan."

"You're my family. All of you. Family is everything to changelings." She'd never understood the depth of that until she'd lived inside Wind-Haven for a single unforgettable day, seen how they were with each other. "And Adam . . . Adam is mine." In a way no one else had ever been hers, his place in her life solid and rooted and forever, mating bond or no mating bond.

She didn't know if that would ever form, or if the damage done to her would forever block it, but that didn't matter. She'd known who Adam was to her from the first day they met—and he'd known the same. "So," she said in an effort to distract herself from her worry about Saffron and Yúzé, "you and Dahlia?"

Bram dropped his head, rubbed both hands over his skull. "I don't know what I'm doing, Eleri." The words were a rough confession. "When I thought I was dying, it was easy." Ice-blue eyes met her own. "I fell into Dahlia, and I don't want to climb back out."

Eleri tilted her head to the side. "You've always been in control, Bram. Always trying to look after us, make things better." She held out her hand. "It's okay to surrender when the person to whom you're surrendering is worthy of that trust."

Bram wove his fingers through hers. "She stayed with me." A deep breath in, a shaky exhale. "When I asked. She stayed. And before she left today, she promised she'd come back after she'd finished her duties."

Eleri thought of the woman she'd met, the fierceness and joy of her. "Dahlia isn't the kind of person who does things she doesn't want. And, Bram?"

She clenched her hand tighter on his. "You're a good man. You've been the best big brother I could ever have. You know how to take care of your people. You understand *family*. You're the perfect mate for a changeling."

Bram's eyes were shining.

He looked away, but he didn't break their handclasp, and there they sat, two dented and damaged Psy who'd somehow managed to find their people.

ADAM glanced at Dorian when the DarkRiver sentinel landed the leopard pack's jet-chopper at the hospital that had helped save Eleri's life, and where Saffron Bianca and Yúzé Kanagawa were being held. "Thanks for this."

Odd as it was, especially given WindHaven's business interests, not many winged changelings were pilots—they liked flying on the wing, not inside machines. Flight tests for the business were done near universally by human or non-winged pilots.

His eyes hidden behind aviators, Dorian said, "We're allies—we might even become friends, though I make no guarantees about my cat not swiping at your feathers every so often."

Adam grinned, caught off guard by the quip. While the two of them had met multiple times, this was the longest period they'd spent together at a stretch, and he was starting to realize that the cool-eyed sentinel happened to be a man he'd enjoy calling a friend. "Long as your cat remembers that this bird has serious talons."

Dorian's cheeks creased before he pulled off the aviators, his tone turning serious on his next words. "You thought about how we're going to take these two back? Bianca is violent, and we only have room for two in the back—I don't like the idea of you back there with her while I have Kanagawa in the front. He could snap without warning."

Adam had been considering that, too. "When I spoke to Sophia, she said they don't want to drug Saffron because in her state it could have a catastrophic cascading effect."

Dorian nodded. "I get that. Our little boy is Psy, so we have to protect him even from over-the-counter stuff changelings wouldn't think twice about." The affection of a father in his voice. "Sophie give you any other option?"

"One of the Es at the facility can nudge Saffron into unconsciousness—basically forcing what Psy do naturally when they go in for surgery." Per Sophia, the Es didn't like to do it because it fostered distrust in their already disturbed patients, but they were willing to make an exception this time because Saffron was locked in a fear-and-panic spiral that they couldn't break.

Anything that might help was better than that.

"Her unconscious state should last long enough for us to get her to Bram and Eleri. I've also got restraints as backup." He didn't like it, but the risk of Saffron causing a crash if she woke agitated was too high to chance leaving her free. "From the sounds of it, Yúzé is nonresponsive and probably won't even notice; hopefully he'll sleep through it."

The doors from the hospital to the rooftop landing space opened up, a man in a wheelchair being brought out. He was followed by staff shepherding a hover gurney. Adam and Dorian both jumped out to get their passengers inside and restrained. As advised, Yúzé was a doll who moved if given physical direction, while Saffron was unconscious.

The E who'd come with the team had a bruise blooming on the right side of her cheek. "It's not her fault," the middle-aged woman said. "She panicked when she realized what I was about to do, struck out." The E stroked her fingers over Saffron's red hair. "I hope you forgive me, sweet girl."

There wasn't time for further conversation, the clock on Saffron's consciousness already on a fast countdown. They took off the minute the staff were clear, and Adam was tense throughout the flight—especially when he heard Saffron make a sound about twenty minutes out from the Canyon.

"She's starting to come out of it."

"Fuck. I'm already pushing this thing as fast as I can. Let's hope we make it."

Chapter 48

I am distressed whenever I consider the shape of the world did the changelings not exist. Humans and Psy, we are equal in our arrogance that we understand the natural world—while the changelings, who are closer to it than we will ever be, are ever its guardians, and humble in their belief that it holds countless secrets.

—Foreword by Professor Sera Shi to *Of the Wild* by Professor J. Sidorov (BlackEdge wolves) (1964)

ELERI HEARD SAFFRON before she saw her friend and sister of the heart. The other woman was screaming obscenities and threats of violence, her rage amped up to the extreme.

Eleri waited right by the doorway, her entire soul hurting for Saffy. The other woman had been the brightest and sweetest of them, a little girl who rescued ladybugs and stepped around marching ants, until the reconditionings shattered things inside her.

Adam appeared out of the darkness of the cave tunnel with Saffron clamped in his arms, Saffy's own arms restrained to her sides. The restraints had no doubt added to Saffron's panic, but seeing her, Eleri understood it had been a necessity.

As it was, she was kicking her legs as hard as she could, though Adam's strength as he held her tight meant she couldn't do any damage.

"Saffy!" Eleri yelled out.

Saffron's head snapped toward her, her pale skin splotchy and sweaty. "Lies! You're not here! You're dead and they hid you!"

Bram looked out from behind Eleri. "No, Saff, we're both fine."

Saffron went silent at that, but the paranoid suspicion remained in her eyes. Until Adam crossed the doorway into Mirage. At which point she sucked in a gasp of air and said, "It's so *quiet* here," and Eleri belatedly recognized that the shock of their vanishing from Saffron's life had thinned out the other woman's shields until she'd begun to feel the same inexorable mental pressure as she and Bram had.

Yúzé walked in under his own steam with a blond leopard male Eleri recognized from Sascha Duncan's visit. He was dressed in black, had eyes that saw everything. She couldn't remember his name but knew he was like Jacques and Dahlia for the leopards. A second to his alpha.

As Bram went to Saffron—he'd always been able to calm her down—Eleri took Yúzé's hand and leaned her body against his. "Yúzé, it's Eleri."

No reaction.

It would take time. Yúzé always withdrew when he was hurt.

But she had that time now, thanks to the man who'd fought for her family when she couldn't.

Who'd *understood* that they were her family from the first.

Turning, she met Adam's gaze, her heart reaching out to him. Something reached back, a winged creature huge and extraordinary and powerful that swept into her in a storm of wings and passion and possessiveness.

Generous heart. Grieving boy. Loyal wing leader.

He was all of that, and he was so much more.

A brother who laughed. An uncle who cherished. A lover who adored.

Playful raptor. Deadly hunter.

Protector to the core.

She saw the love in his heart for all those who were his, and all those he had lost. Saw, too, glimpses of Cormac and Taazbaa' as they laughed with their boy, then his grandparents walking with him hand in hand as they spoke the language of the Diné, complex and lyrical.

Anger, too, he'd felt. Brutal and cold. But it wasn't his natural state.

He was warmth, humor, love, a heart that could embrace every member of his clan . . . but that had a hole she alone could fill.

He filled her in turn, and she felt as if her parched cells were opening up, becoming what they had always been meant to be.

His.

Her being overflowed with emotion, her legs staggering on the earth. Then he was there, inside her mind even as his hands helped her stay stable on this plane. "I love you," she said, and she knew what that *meant*, understood the glory of it. "I love you, Adam."

The falcon flew higher, deeper, until it was part of her, her arms feathered on the inside and her eyes those of a raptor. They were one so completely that when the forces of mating finally retreated, they took pieces of each other with them.

Dazed, she leaned into him for a heartbeat before her mind caught up to where they were and what they'd been doing before the most extraordinary moment of her life. "Where's Saffy? And Yúzé. I had his hand."

"Bram has her. I managed to hand her over before I lost myself in the mating. I think he's taken them both into the tent."

At ease now that she knew the two were safe, she just sank against Adam, her body boneless. "I know I should be sorry for trapping you with me when such a huge question hangs over my head, but I'm not. I feel like this is where I've been meant to be all my life."

"You have," Adam said in a stern tone. "And, my beautiful wild bird, there's never any trapping when it comes to mates. Don't think that if we didn't mate, I'd find someone else. I wouldn't. Not after I met you, knew you."

Everything in her was warm and deeply . . . happy. "I want to tug you into our tent so we can lie there together and just be, but I need to help Saffy and Yúzé." She tilted up her head.

Adam's kiss was open-mouthed, a sensual promise. "We'll make up for it later." He stepped back, said, "Whoa," then grinned. "Hello, mate."

Feeling silly and young, she said, "Hello, mate," in return, and they both stood there smiling foolishly at each other while the bats got bored of the sight and decided to take off en masse—but not leave.

Giving a loud "Eek!" Eleri ran off deeper into the cave, where the bats didn't like to circle as much, while Adam ducked and dived while trying to stop laughing. She threatened him from her hiding spot . . . and that was when Saffron looked out of the tent and said, "This is the weirdest reaction I've ever had to meds, and I've had some weird reactions."

SAFFRON snapped back faster than Yúzé.

None of them took that as a sign that she was "cured." The fractures in Saffy ran too deep for that, but it was a start. As for Yúzé, he began to emerge the fourth day after his arrival at the cave, and Eleri knew he was back with them when he looked around while they were pacing the cave like contained tigers and said, "This cannot be real."

The complicated answer was that it was, the kind of real that was a thing of resplendent hope—but also the kind of dark and enclosed real that couldn't sustain lives, especially mentally unstable lives. All four of them were beyond grateful for the peace offered by Mirage, but they were also conscious that it wasn't a long-term solution.

Bram and Eleri could bear the confinement a lot longer and better than Saffron or Yúzé, but even they might crack at some point.

"What if they don't find a solution?" Bram said to her a number of days later, while the two of them were alone in a corner, Saffron and Yúzé having been attracted to where Bayani was working with a vein of minerals on the other side. "Living here forever isn't tenable."

"No." Even with the clan making an effort to make it more comfortable, they'd effectively be confined to a small area for months, maybe much longer.

Both Ashaya and Saoirse had attempted multiple tests with jerry-rigged shield options, but none had blocked even a sliver of the mental noise that existed beyond this cave.

Regardless of all that . . . "I want to live, Bram." She'd made that call, wouldn't back away from it. "I want to breathe in life as I once breathed in death. Enough to grit my teeth and push through it no matter how long it takes."

She looked at him. "You?"

"Yeah, I'm no longer looking for an exit." Folding his arms, he exhaled as he looked over at Saffron and Yúzé. "They won't make it more than a few weeks at most." Anguish in his tone. "I can't bear to watch them go, Eleri."

"We won't have to. I have faith." It was as if Adam's belief had seeped into her, taken root when they mated, until now she could see only hope on the horizon.

Bram put his arm around her as she slipped her arm around his waist. He'd become comfortable with such touch once she began to initiate it. They'd been family for so long that it seemed foolish they'd ever stopped these small but important markers of affection.

Turning around, Saffron beamed at seeing them, then bounced over—and for that moment, she was the little girl with red hair who'd bounced over to Eleri in the schoolyard. "Am I welcome in this hug?"

Bram and Eleri both opened their arms.

Laughing, she dove in, while Yúzé walked over with a faint smile curving his lips. "It's tent time," he said when he arrived. "The falcons are transferring the bats soon."

Eleri shivered, remembering how Adam had cuddled her last night as he explained how they'd do it. She felt bad for the bats despite her tendency to run squealing when they swarmed—which amused absolutely *everyone*—but he'd assured her they'd found an equivalent cave.

"No luminescent mineral veins, but we've rigged up a system that offers the same type of a greenish glow—these bats seem to enjoy the light. And there's even water nearby."

The process would be as humane as they could make it, with the clan waiting until the bats' usual time of flight out from the cave that would get rid of a good percentage.

It was never all of them—they seemed to go in groups, then return. At which point, another group would go off. This time, however, once the first cohort had departed, one of the smaller falcons was going to chase out the others. A simple annoying interruption would get them going without causing too much fear—they were used to the runners flying about now and then when they got restless.

Malia had joined that number as of yesterday, which was when Eleri had learned that winged changeling bones tended to knit faster than those of other changelings—especially when supported by the Gen-seal compound that Naia and her team had put around the break from day one. A compound which, unbeknownst to Eleri and Bram, had been developed by a clan of eagles.

Eleri loved learning new facts about falcons, about changelings, about WindHaven.

Once the assigned bat-relocation team had cleared the cave, they'd block it off with an already-prepared door and be on standby to reroute confused returnees to the new cave—which was very close.

These particular bats also had excellent olfactory senses, so the clan was planning to lay scent traces for them to their new home, while simultaneously erasing all scent traces from this cave.

Eleri would've preferred to be outside for all of it, but there was no point in subjecting her already bruised brain to more damage just because she was skittish where bats were concerned. "Come on," she said, inviting the others to join her in her tent. "We can distract each other."

Adam, Dahlia, and Maraea would maintain a security watch outside.

With so many of the clan distracted by the goings-on here tonight, the clan would otherwise be dangerously vulnerable.

THE first flurry left in a mass of high-pitched vocalizations.

They made many more sounds Eleri knew were imperceptible to her. One of the things Ashaya and Saoirse had both discovered independently was that the Mirage bats talked to each other during the day, in a tone range none of the non-bats could hear—though Dorian had confirmed it hurt his ears to be in the cave too long.

"Imagine what they're saying about us," Saffron said as they sat inside attempting to play cards and failing. "I feel bad for invading their home, then driving them out. They're so *cute* with their hand-wings, and they just hang about being adorable."

"You sound like you want one as a pet," Bram drawled.

"No, they're wild. Let them be wild. I'll admire from afar."

"We're giving them another cave in return," Yúzé said, and put down a card. "I hear it's just as unique."

"I wouldn't be sold if I was a bat who grew up in a psychedelic glowing cave," Saffron muttered as more high-pitched sounds broke into the quiet left by the first flurry.

Malia was in the air.

Eleri didn't know if it was ten or twenty seconds later that it happened.

Her eyes went wide, her gaze snapping to Bram's. "Do you feel that?"

"What?" A frown.

Eleri was already outside the tent, screaming, "STOP!" at the top of her lungs while waving her arms. "Malia, STOP!"

Bram was beside her the next second, adding his own voice to the cry.

It still took Malia too long to notice them in the cacophony created by the bats who wanted to escape the irritating falcon in their midst. By the time the fledgling came in to land, most of the bats were gone, only the odd few hanging about here and there.

Saoirse and Ashaya, who'd been standing by in a back corner out of the way, ran over. "What's wrong?" Saoirse demanded, looking from Eleri to Bram.

Saffron uttered a pained cry inside the tent, and Yúzé erupted out. "The voices," he said, clutching at his head. "They're just beyond the rock."

Eleri nodded, her breath harsh in her chest after the shouting while jumping up and down to attract Malia's attention. "The quiet isn't gone, but it's . . . thinner." She grabbed Saoirse's hand. "It's the bats!"

Adam's sister's eyes went huge. She turned to Ashaya, and the two women said, "*Ultrasound!*" in unison before ordering poor Malia to go outside and get the adults in the air to help her chase back any bats that were nearby.

"We'll be okay," Eleri promised when Saoirse looked at her in question. "We're together, will help stabilize each other." She met Yúzé's eyes. "It has to be all of us." A request.

He took a careful breath, then held out a shaky hand. "Quatro Cartel in action."

Chapter 49

Saffron: I feel good about this.

Yúzé: Me, too.

Bram: We can't get too carried away. It's early days yet.

Eleri: I'm with them, Bram. Team Hope.

Bram: They're bad influences. But fine. Team Hope.

—Conversation between the Quatro Cartel (undertaken on a notepad left in a tent and added to by each of them, one by one, in lieu of any phones or organizers with a signal) (today)

ASHAYA AND SAOIRSE, working together from that point on, came up with a prototype three days after the aborted bat transfer.

The El-Shield team had already done less intensive tests using mock-ups, and it had quickly become clear that it wasn't simply the bats' ultrasonic communication that was the key, but the sound in concert with the overall mineral composition of Mirage.

This was to be the first serious test, and though Eleri knew it had a high likelihood of failure, none of them could stop themselves from hoping.

"It's not pretty," Saoirse said from the other side of the entrance into Mirage, "but we can make it prettier if it works." A glance at Bram. "At least it's not a tinfoil hat, right?"

Bram's face cracked into a slight smile. "Progress."

Saoirse laughed and turned to Eleri, who'd volunteered to be the test subject as she appeared the most sensitive to psychic noise.

Inside Mirage, Eleri leaned into Adam for a second. "Wouldn't it be incredible if we were saved by bats?" She couldn't keep from grinning, her face having learned the shape of happiness with such rapidity it was as if she'd been born for it. "I might found a bat religion, become the first convert."

"I can't believe you're joking at a time like this," he said in a stern tone, but spoiled the effect by leaning down to kiss her. "Let's do this, bat lady."

Laughing, she took a step beyond the entrance . . . and almost crumpled under the noise of the world. It took everything she had not to step back, and she could feel Adam fighting his urge to shield her even the fraction he could.

They'd decided to do it this way rather than putting the prototype on her in the cave because it'd be more difficult to calibrate it inside a space that echoed with the bats' ultrasonic chatter. It was noticeably less apparent in the passageway outside, and Eleri's brain had healed enough to handle the seconds-long exposure.

Saoirse rushed forward with a device that was nothing more than a glittery headband with a circular metal piece on one side and other metallic filaments curving out from the circle. "Had to borrow Malia's headband," she said, and slipped it on over Eleri's head, pushing back her hair as Ashaya came around to situate the circular bit against the bone behind Eleri's ear.

"Nothing," Eleri ground out, disappointment heavy in her gut. "I'll step back."

But Ashaya Aleine's blue-gray eyes, so striking against the rich brown of her skin, were focused on the piece behind her ear. "It's not switched on yet." She turned to Saoirse. "Position?"

Saoirse looked at her scanner. "Yes, I think so. Go."

A tap on the circle.

The pressure of the psychic noise grew heavier and heavier . . . and was just . . . gone right before Eleri's legs would've crumpled, Adam already preparing to catch her.

She snapped upright, touched the side of her head where the circle buzzed very, very quietly. Around her, everyone was holding their breath—everyone but Adam. Who gave a huge "Whoop!" and picked her up to spin her around.

He was her mate. He felt her pain. And he felt her lack of pain.

Ashaya and Saoirse stood side by side, both literally biting their lips as they read things on their organizer and frantically checked two different scanners. Bayani, who'd been standing around the corner with the rest of the El-Shield team so as not to crowd the area, now ran into view. "We heard the whoop!"

"It works," Eleri whispered to him, before turning to Bram and the others. "It works!"

"Holy fuck." Saffron's eyes were huge. "Are you serious?"

"Saoirse, can Saffy try this?"

"Wait. We have to calibrate." An absent statement. "How's that?"

The buzzing went quiet, became more a faint vibration against her skull. "Not irritating," she said. "It's almost comforting being able to sense it."

Neither engineer nor M-Psy smiled.

Not then.

It took testing the device on Saffy, then Bram, and finally a Yúzé who was amazed enough that his cool exterior actually cracked, for the two women to turn to each other in an enormous hug as they said things that were incomprehensible because both were also crying.

So was Eleri.

Adam's own tears were ashine in his eyes as he bent so their foreheads touched. "Do you have a fear of heights, mate?"

When she shook her head, he said, "I bought you a glider. So we can go flying together."

Bursting into sobs, Eleri threw her arms around his neck. "I'll fly with you into every sky."

He picked her up, held her tight, and it was perfect.

It was life.

And it was happiness.

ELERI asked the shield team to name the shield the Ultrasonic in honor of its chiropteran cocreators, to the team's enthusiastic agreement. Its final design involved no sparkly headbands—unless requested—to Bram's great relief.

The circle piece that tucked behind the ear, against the bone there, became sleeker while retaining its comforting hum that told the wearer it was active, while the arcs of metal across the skull were fine enough that they could be merged into the hair if desired.

Methods of retaining it on the head went from the initial sparkly headband—which Saffy had chosen—to a much finer band for Eleri, which she integrated into her hair. Yúzé had gone for the same with a playfulness that was startling but made Eleri happy to see.

"I can rock it," he'd said.

She knew better than to think he was all better, but it was a start. Because WindHaven had embraced all three other members of the Cartel as family, because they were her family. Yesterday, she'd found Yúzé in the children's play area, coloring with them with a patience unexpected.

She'd stepped in to join them, only to find herself drawn to a child-sized acrylic paint set—where little Ollie had also joined her. They'd painted together for an hour, and at the end of it, Ollie had put one tiny paint-covered hand on her shoulder as he stood beside her seated form and said, "Wow, Eri, you paint."

To the littles in the clan, she was just Eri, and it brought her infinite joy.

Feeling shy, she'd nonetheless shown the piece to Adam, who'd whistled. "Baby, you can *paint*. This is the Canyon looking up from Raintree." A glance up. "You have a talent."

It was a strange feeling to know that she could become a painter if she so wished, or a plumber, or a teacher, or anything else that she wanted. Yúzé could follow his passion for tech and lose himself in code, Saffy could design clothes, and Bram . . . Bram could discover who he wanted to be beyond the protector of their small family.

"I can sleep now, *think* now," he'd said, it having become clear while they were still in the cave that his issues with sleep could be ameliorated by a shield—no longer fighting to just survive, his brain was able to reroute the necessary messages through undamaged neurons.

Eleri, for her part, had realized that she wasn't in danger of drowning in the same kind of anger that had haunted her as a young J. The ugliness that had fueled her rage was no longer a part of her life. Instead, she was fueled by joy, wonder, and surprise at the kindness of those around her.

Saoirse had given her a box of clothes the other day. "I figured you never had a chance to find your style, so Malia and I ordered you a bunch of stuff to get you started. Keep what you like, and we'll stick the rest in one of the caches."

Eleri hadn't ever considered clothing as part of her identity . . . but that day, she'd been drawn to a floaty summer dress of white with little green leaves on it. It was air around her body, and she had the feeling that she might like airy, floaty dresses that were nothing at all like the suits she'd worn all her adult life.

As for Bram and the Ultrasonic, he'd scowled at the idea of a headband of any kind, so the team had created a version that involved him having two small magnets embedded into the very surface of his skull, with the device locking onto them.

Dahlia was not happy with him over his choice. "I can't believe you had brain surgery rather than wear a headband!" Eleri had heard her say while glaring.

"It wasn't brain surgery. The magnets are literally sitting on top of my skull, just under my scalp." Bram had been unmoved, but he'd also been holding Dahlia close at the time while looking at her in a way that said she was wonderful.

Eleri wondered if he had any idea what that did to Dahlia.

She didn't think so; Bram wasn't manipulative that way, never had been. He just thought Dahlia was wonderful.

As Eleri thought the same of Adam.

"I got a call from Tim just before," she told this man she loved with every cell in her body, as the two of them sat on the edge of his aerie exit. "He wanted to say thank you. It helped the families a great deal when Hendricks's remains were found and identified. They feel as if his slow death—in the desert as they see it—was wild justice."

"Do you think we made the right call?" her mate asked. "He needed to be stopped, but did his untrained telepathy make him insane? It's not our way to execute those who are sick in the mind, but we were so angry at the time."

"No, he was sane. I spoke to Bram about it—and Tim looked into his personnel files all the way back to his start in Enforcement. He passed all the psych tests with flying colors. If he was sick in the mind, it was the same kind of sickness as other serial killers—he knew that what he was doing was evil, but he continued to do it because it excited him."

She knew Bram hadn't told her the full extent of that excitement, but he hadn't had to, not after he'd said, "No different from Bonner or Clarke or Tissera. Psychopaths who found pleasure in perversion while wearing a mask to fool the world."

Because she understood Adam's heart, his sense of honor, she told him all of that, without any attempt to hide the cold truth, and saw the human side of him accept it. His falcon already had, its mores far more primal.

"Trinity is already discussing setting up tests to pick up children with minor Psy abilities," he told her afterward, leaning forward with his forearms braced on his thighs. "It wouldn't have helped Hendricks, given the path he chose, but it might help another kid."

A nod in the direction of the Raintree Inn. "Talking of kids going bad, Mi-ja's furious with Dae now that she's past her shock and pain. Her friend Mary's being good about visiting more, and clanmates of her generation are dropping in at least once a day, too. They say that right now, she's in the venting phase, but the sorrow will come."

And when it did, Eleri thought, WindHaven would be there for the woman who had called Adam's grandmother a friend. Because that was the falcon way. Adam's way.

Eleri stroked her fingers through his hair, saw his eyes close to half-mast as he surrendered to the sensation. So did she, preening her mate with lazy pleasure. When she spoke a long time later, she said, "Does Saoirse realize she's changed the world?"

"I knew she could do it," Adam said with a brother's pride. "And not that it's a surprise given who she and Ashaya are, but they're going to credit the whole team, get everyone in the history books. But none of them—Ashaya included—will budge on only Saoirse being listed as the team lead."

The light wind pushed the silky green material of the pretty top Eleri was wearing today against her skin, and it felt like a caress. "She deserves that spot," Eleri said, thinking of what Bram had shared about how hard Saoirse had worked, and how devastated she'd been when her attempts failed. "Without her taking your challenge and rolling with it, the team wouldn't exist."

"Chirp was muttering I should be listed as team lead, since it was my 'lunatic' idea to create an external shield." Adam laughed as he shifted to play with her hair in a show of falconish affection that made her feel utterly adored. "I pointed out that I was just expecting my big sister to save my ass."

Eleri knew Saoirse, Ashaya, and the team behind the earth-shattering development weren't happy with how far they'd come. Wearable tech would never be as secure as internal tech, but as Eleri saw it, this was a blindingly brilliant start.

The discovery that it was a combination of certain metals and minerals *and* ultrasonic sounds on a specific oscillating wavelength that created a shield around the mind opened up whole new avenues for internal tech.

"Does it bother you?" Adam began to weave her hair into an intricate braid. "Not being able to telepath?"

Because that was the other thing. The Ultrasonic blocked *everything* going in or out. "I thought it would," Eleri admitted, "but it's not like when I flamed out. I'm still a fully Psy creature—I feel whole, nothing missing. It's just a case of not flexing that muscle until the team figures out a solution—and I'm okay with that."

"The others?"

"No problem with a lack of telepathic communication." She loved him even more because he always thought about her strange little family, always included them.

"Since all four of us have relocated here, we can talk to each other anytime we choose." The entire Cartel was also in the process of flux when it came to their work—they might wish to pursue other directions, but they also had priceless information in their heads when it came to hunting evil.

"You've done enough, Eleri," Adam said, picking up on her thoughts in that instinctual way that seemed to have come as part of their particular mating bond. "All of you. You're allowed to live away from the horror and suffering."

"We feel so much guilt about all we know, the good we could do with it."

"You don't have to be in the field for that. You can consult. Hell, set up a company—Quatro Cartel Consultants—and hire your brains out to Enforcement and other security agencies around the world on a limited basis."

Eleri's eyes went wide. "You're very, very clever, Adam Garrett." Because she could sell that idea to the others, especially Bram with his heavy sense of responsibility. All she'd have to watch was the workload—and she could get Dahlia to make sure Bram didn't take on too much.

Her chosen brother would never hurt Dahlia, and losing him to the work would hurt her—ergo, Bram would not be working himself to the bone. None of them would. Not anymore.

"I know." A falcon smile as he tied off the braid. "Especially since today, I've managed to shove all of my responsibilities onto a hale and hearty Jacques so I can make you scream."

Eleri's skin flushed. "Not here," she whispered.

"Soundproofing," was his response. "All bedrooms. No clan would make it otherwise." A nuzzling kiss. "But I've scouted another spot. Ready?"

Eleri took a deep breath and flexed her tights-clad legs. "Ready."

The air was warm under the ultralight powered hang glider Adam had gifted her, the falcon beside her a magnificent presence as they flew over the Canyon, over Raintree, and beyond, the desert glittering under the light of the setting sun. Other falcons dipped their wings when they passed, but no one interrupted their flight.

Eleri gloried in the sense of freedom, shouting in delight when the glider dipped with the wind and rose the same way. The device was designed to use as little power as possible, with the person gliding also having to use their muscles to retain control. They'd practiced at much lower altitudes until by now, Eleri was a pro.

As she was a pro at being loved by and loving Adam Garrett.

She'd carry the scars of the life she'd lived forever, but that didn't scare her. She was Eleri, and she *had* lived that life. She was who she was . . . and she was beloved by her mate, cherished by her family and clan, and—what a thing of wonder—adored by the little birds in Wind-Haven.

Adam had made her a gauntlet to protect her shoulder and arm now that the tiniest fledglings had decided she was one of their favorite landing spots.

A falcon call from her mate as he dived toward a secluded little valley in a distant canyon.

She followed in a slower glide.

He'd already left a picnic blanket there earlier that day, and tucked a picnic cooler into the nearby spring so it'd remain chilled. Lying naked on the blanket soon after their arrival, Eleri's back arched under a sky painted in sunset as her lover tasted her with slow deliberation, her scream of pleasure a song of freedom.

Chapter 50

Full instructions enclosed. The team is available to you at any time if you have questions or wish to discuss modifications.

—Team Ultrasonic to the Human Alliance (April 2084)

BOWEN KNIGHT LOOKED at the device on his desk.

His lab people had manufactured it per the instructions sent through by the team behind the Ultrasonic.

"It's not as secure as an internal shield," Heenali said, a glimmer of light in her for the first time since the death of her lover. "Easy to pull off a target, to make them vulnerable again. But . . ."

"Yes, but," Bo said, the others of his senior team of much the same mind. "The person on the street, the human running a shop, the human who works as a teacher, none of them are at risk of a targeted attack. This would be—"

"—enough," his sister Lily completed, while Kaia squeezed Bo's shoulder.

His mate wasn't human, but she loved a human and so she understood the value of this literal gift the falcons and leopards had given the Human Alliance. No payment, no favors requested.

Bo had barely believed it when Lucas called to give him the heads-up on the info packet.

The Ultrasonic had been designed for Js with disintegrating shields, but the shield team had tested it on humans in WindHaven and DarkRiver both, with total success.

Now, so had the Human Alliance.

The Ultrasonic *worked*.

"People won't have to be scared anymore," Lily continued. "Just go about their day without ever worrying about intrusion."

"It'll change the face of the fucking world." Cassius's hand fisted on the table. "They really don't want anything for it?"

"Only thing they requested is that if we come up with an upgrade, we share it," Bo said. "They'll do the same, as will the J Corps—though it looks like the Corps is relying on WindHaven's new Ultrasonic arm to supply them."

"I got no issue with that," Ajax said, to a round of nods. "Hell, I'll personally carry upgrade reports to them if they want—because what they've given us, it's priceless."

"Yeah." Cassius agreed. "Still can't believe they just gave it to us."

Heenali released a long breath. "Gives me back a little of my faith in the world."

Ajax spoke up. "You gonna tell Krychek?"

"I already did," Bo said of the dangerous Psy who'd become a friend. "He turned over all research on his own team's shield project when they thought the PsyNet was on the brink of a final collapse, and he's willing to send us assistance if we need technical support—but man's got no time to focus on it.

"This is confidential in order to stop panic, so don't share it outside this room, but the PsyNet isn't fixed, just bought itself a bit of time." Bo understood the weight of what it meant to hold an entire people on your shoulders and didn't begrudge Kaleb his focus on the failing psychic network.

The cardinal had more than kept the bargain the two of them had struck.

"The raptors and the cats have bought us some, too," Heenali said. "Our scientists can work without fear of being mentally raped if they make new breakthroughs. We can provide security support where needed to make sure of that."

Bo nodded. Because while an external shield wasn't the most secure thing in the world . . . it was still going to change that world.

The human race was no longer in third place when it came to the reins of power.

Chapter 51

Dear Aunt Rita,

I know this update has been a long time coming.

First of all, I want to thank you from the bottom of my heart for answering my very confused query back in last year's February issue. I know you get thousands of letters, so I didn't even expect a reply, and never one so soon after I sent it.

But you did answer... and you changed the course of my life.

After I read your advice, I decided to invite my falcon friend over for dinner. By this time, she'd also dropped an entire cheese basket in my arms, so I decided to make cheese fondue. I know it's old-fashioned, but it always seemed fun to me—and I had a *LOT* of cheese.

When she came over, she seemed nervous—and she'd brought me a giant bag of fresh green apples. So after we watched a movie and had fondue, we decided to make midnight apple pie.

And then, well, it was too late for her to go home, and I had so much food to get through... and... we're getting married in six months' time and would be beyond honored to have you attend the ceremony.

We did already mate but I've always wanted a wedding, complete with a huge white dress and lots of flowers, the whole romantic thing, and my falcon mate is happy to be married as well as mated—she says it just makes her mine twice over.

She's my best friend in all this world, and she's even talked her older brothers into flying past before the reception to drop chocolates into the guests' hands as wedding favors.

We're enclosing the invitation in hope. But even if you decline, know that you are the reason for our happy ending.

With grateful thanks and all our love,
~Soccer Fiend & Falcon Foodie

Dear Soccer Fiend & Falcon Foodie,
My dears, you have made this crotchety old lady shed a tear. I shall be at your wedding in all my finery, never you fear.
I also expect cheese fondue.
With love,
~Aunt Rita

—From the March 2074 issue of *Wild Woman* magazine: "Skin Privileges, Style & Primal Sophistication"

ACKNOWLEDGMENTS

It was important to me to get my research about the Diné correct. Even though I write in a paranormal world, with artistic license taken due to the structure of that world—including, in this case, the unique realm of winged changelings—I still wanted to do everything I could to make sure I got things right.

Diné Bizaad (Navajo) is a beautiful and incredibly complex language. That's why I used it sparingly and only where I was certain I was using it the correct way.

I'd like to thank the Diné teachers who run YouTube channels to teach others their language and culture, in particular: @daybreakwarrior, @navajotraditionalteachings, and @navajograndma. Thanks to them, I not only learned the particular words used in this book, but also found inspiration for further research about the Diné.

As always, if I've made an error, it was done without intent.

Thank you for coming with me on this flight into the skies above the canyons and deserts of Arizona.

Hágoónee'.